Praise for *Made*

"*The Bachelor* meets *Black Mirror* (with [...] in this captivating, empowering, and wildly original thriller. The twists and relentless suspense had my attention, but it's the protagonist— a synthetic woman—and her exploration of humanity, motherhood, and marriage that truly had my heart. *Made for You* is a spectacular debut."
—Megan Collins, author of *Thicker Than Water*

"A deftly crafted, stunningly original debut. I loved it from the clever first pages all the way to the jaw-dropping conclusion, and I can't wait to read more from this talented author!"
—Andrea Bartz, *New York Times* bestselling author of *The Spare Room*

"Part *Black Mirror*, part *The Bachelor*, *Made for You* goes past the final rose and fairy-tale romance to explore the dark nature of human emotion told from the most unlikely of narrators: a synthetic person designed for love. A page-turner for reality TV and mystery fans alike."
—Vera Kurian, author of *A Step Past Darkness*

"Inventive, timely, and wildly original...a thrill ride that never stops twisting and turning. With its smart fusion of reality TV, murder mystery, and social commentary, this story promises an addictive and thought-provoking reading experience, while feeling unlike any other book you've ever read. As an avid reality dating show viewer, it almost felt like *Made for You* was, in fact, made for me—I couldn't stop turning pages. Jenna Satterthwaite has more than established herself as a debut author to watch."
—Laurie Elizabeth Flynn, author of *The Girls Are All So Nice Here*

"*The Bachelor* meets *Ex Machina* in this highly original and smartly written thriller. Engrossing and empowering...a stunning and twisty debut. Satterthwaite is an author to watch!"
—Jeneva Rose, *New York Times* bestselling author

"What do you get when you mix high tech, reality TV, and a missing person? A layered mystery with twists galore! Satterthwaite has established herself as a force in the mystery universe, and I can't wait to see what she does next." —Kristen Bird, author of *Watch It Burn*

MADE FOR YOU

Jenna Satterthwaite

mira

ISBN-13: 978-0-7783-1042-6

Made for You

Copyright © 2024 by Jenna Satterthwaite

"We Both Go Down Together" by The Decemberists
Words by Colin Meloy
Used by permission

"Vigil"
Words by John Wells
Used by permission

Recycling programs
for this product may
not exist in your area.

This is a work of fiction. Names, characters, places and incidents are either the product of the author's imagination or are used fictitiously. Any resemblance to actual persons, living or dead, businesses, companies, events or locales is entirely coincidental.

For questions and comments about the quality of this book, please contact us at CustomerService@Harlequin.com.

TM is a trademark of Harlequin Enterprises ULC.

Mira
22 Adelaide St. West, 41st Floor
Toronto, Ontario M5H 4E3, Canada

Printed in U.S.A.

For Heidi

We fall, but our souls are flying

THEN

"Can you hear me?" A male face peers into mine. Midthirties, glasses, expressive eyebrows. Andy. *Kind*.

"Yes," I say. There's an overwhelming barrage of hot sensation, then *click*, it all evens out—light, sound, the air on my skin—settling like embers, then cooling.

I breathe in, feel my chest balloon, breathe out. Lift my hands to face level and flex my fingers, mapping how the smooth pale skin with its smattering of freckles shifts and ripples over my knuckle ridges.

I'm sitting. Dressed in what seems to be an evening gown. I register how tight the skirt is around my thighs. How beautifully the blue sequins catch in the ice-white light from above. Palms down, I skim the fabric, tickling the pads of my fingers as the sequins catch, lift, fall. It's like wearing a party. I like it.

"Do you know who you are?" says Andy.

I look up and feel myself smile. He's in baggy jeans, a gray T-shirt with a buffalo plaid shirt open over top and a pen hooked on the breast pocket. A dark five-o'clock shadow travels down his neck. His look screams *sleepless nights*.

"Of course," I say. Everything is simply there, no effort, natural as breathing. "I'm Julia Walden."

"Do you know where you are? What year it is?"

"We're in LA. It's January 2022 and Biden is President." I tilt my head. "We're in the middle of a pandemic."

"Do you know what's about to happen?"

I register, out of the corner of my eye, a boom mic operator to our deep left, but keep my attention on Andy.

"I'm about to compete on *The Proposal*."

"God," breathes Andy, putting a fist to his chest like my answers are slaying him. "You—you're—" He crooks a finger at his lips.

"Here?" I suggest with a light laugh. Now I'm rubbing my arms, the rough skin at my elbows, allowing my hands to touch my own face, then wander up to my hair, long and loose. I fish it around my shoulder. It's a fiery, sun-gleam red. I love it. I love everything about being Julia Walden.

"Real," says Andy when he's recovered his speech. "Working. Amazing. I kind of want to hug you?"

"You don't have to ask." I stand in my high heels, taller than Andy by nearly a head. His glasses collide with my shoulder as applause bursts around us. After a second, he hooks my hands in his and pulls back, eyes moist.

"Wow, Julia. Just wow."

I scan our surroundings as flashes pop. We're in a warehouse. To the right, large machines quietly rest. I note hydraulics, robotic arms, big sheets of pale, rubbery material. *Skin*, I realize, and my own skin seems to respond, tiny goose bumps racing up my arms.

It's not a bad feeling, exactly. Just…unpleasant, like touching something wet that you thought would be dry.

To my left, a film crew makes a crescent shape. One hefty man shoulders an equally hefty camera, trained on me. I know without being told they're here from *The Proposal*.

It's a little strange to be having this intimate moment with

Andy while everyone watches. Then again…that's about to be my life. Fully on camera.

Andy claps his hands. "So. Ready to meet Josh?"

"I was born ready," I say with a laugh. My eyes flicker up to the answering sound of laughter from the film crew. But while I did mean to be funny, I also mean it.

Andy pulls out a cell phone. "This is yours. Let's break it in." He leans into me and we smile for our first selfie.

"Should we post it to Insta?" he says. "Your handle just went live—we had to wait until the other contestants' phones were taken away. Oh, and we can't mention you're on *The Proposal* yet—" But I reach for the phone.

"I got it." My fingers navigate the screen easily. Also, wow—how does @TheRealJuliaWalden already have close to a million followers…and counting? I caption the picture the journey begins!!!, noting the tug of resistance within me as I put the phone down. I guess part of me wanted to watch the reactions roll in. Immediately I wall up this thought. I'm not here for everyone. Just one man.

Andy has pulled out a blue pen while I've been messing with the phone, and is nervously gnawing on the clicker end. Weirdly, I want to reassure him, *It'll be okay. You'll see.*

"Julia!" the producer calls out. "Could you introduce yourself? For our viewers?"

I look at the camera's cold eye across the distance and imagine that I'm looking into the face of a friend who can't wait to see me. I smile.

"Sure! My name is Julia. I'm a Synth. And I'm here to find love."

WHAT'S UP Magazine
Can a Synth Find Love on *The Proposal*?
By Tia Morales

You heard it here first…there's going to be a Synth on the up-coming season of *The Proposal: Bachelor Edition*! The show, filming now in LA and airing this spring, is sure to draw more viewers than usual, if only to witness the catfights when the *human* girls find out who they're up against! (just kidding) But seriously—how would YOU feel if a perfect synthetic woman threatened to make off with your man?

Well, claws out, ladies, because our insider source tells us she's gorgeous (duh!), and made to suit bachelor Josh LaSala's personality to a T. Not to mention, Miss Synth will be the first non-human able to have babies (!).

While technically this mystery contestant has not been an-nounced, WekTech Industries *did* just blast the Insta handle for their newest creation, and…can you blame us for connecting the dots? Her name is Julia Walden, and she's America's third Synth (the first designed by WekTech). Much like her BotTech predecessors, celebrity twin Synth sisters Christi and Chrystel, stars of *Keeping Up with the Synths*, Julia looks exactly like a woman and feels exactly like a woman...but *is* she a woman? What exactly is going on underneath that gorgeously fake skin? And does her first post, provocatively captioned *the journey begins!!!*, mean her journey to find love? *Can* a Synth truly love? Either way, buckle up, America. Things are about to get ugly in *Proposal*-land, and let's be honest...doesn't that make for the best entertainment?

NOW

A tiny cry wakes me. It's the gray light of early morning and the clock reads 6:00. *Wednesday.* I briefly register the outline in bed next to me.

"Josh, you're home," I murmur, relief rolling through me as I reach for him. A head shoots up. Too much hair. I yelp, loud and sharp, before realizing who I just touched—Captain, our big floof of a Bernese mountain dog. He woofs, low and deep, as if apologizing for not being Josh.

"It's okay, buddy," I say as I weave my fingers deep into his fur, trying to find the anchor I lost Sunday night, when Josh was supposed to be back from his hiking trip.

I'd honestly forgotten he'd made those plans. While he was packing Saturday evening, I worked my way through a bottle of white. I was mad and sloppy. I remember saying, "Well, when are you coming back?" in that nagging tone he hates.

Sunday. He said Sunday. Right? A one-night trip.

I reach for my phone on the nightstand, nearly knocking over a wineglass with the merest puddle still in the bottom. A few new messages light up the home screen. One from Andy. **Any updates on Josh? Call me. I'm worried.** Another from Ally Buoncore about the *Making Julia* documentary Netflix has been harassing me about ever since filming for *The Proposal* ended, fourteen months ago. My nonresponsiveness alone has upped their offer to a million dollars. There are a few other messages I don't bother reading.

But none from Josh.

I tap our text thread, and stare and stare at the green bubbles of my unanswered messages to him.

Sunday night. Trying to remember...were you coming back tonight or tomorrow? ETA?

Sunday night, later. Hey babe, it's almost 10pm. You close?

Monday morning. Josh, I'm worried!! Please text me asap!

Tuesday morning. Babe, I'm filing a missing person report. Call if you see this.

As I focus on the green bubbles, I try to go back to Saturday night. Josh was packing up his gear, his tent, his clothes, while I followed him around the house, wine in hand.

You didn't tell me about this trip!

It's just one day.

We need better communication, Josh.

It's one day.

Just tell me. Do you still love me?

I'm not answering that.

Why?

Because you're drunk, Julia. God. This conversation is over, okay? We'll talk when I get home.

Then he drove off, peeling into the darkness, the taillights like devil eyes. His house keys abandoned on the counter. As soon as he disappeared, I texted Andy again, because he always knows how to make things better. And I hoped that Josh forgetting the house keys was an accident and not a sign.

I reach back with my free hand to scratch an itchy spot at the base of my neck as a second burst of crying from the hallway releases a feeling in my chest. Milk.

But there's a competing sound that takes my attention away

from my baby, my phone, and my itchy neck. A scratching at the side of the house. The kind of thing Josh would be in charge of investigating…if he was here.

Jumping out of bed before fear gets the best of me, I cross to the window that overlooks the side of the house and throw the sash up, bringing in a blast of cold spring air, along with the strong chemical smell that means one thing: spray paint.

"Hey!" I shout at two figures in hoodies. "I'm calling the cops!"

Captain barks behind me. I hear some *oh shits* and scuttling as I grab the baseball bat leaned up in the corner of the bedroom and dash downstairs with Captain on my heels.

I'm out the kitchen door, heartbeat quick with anger, my bare feet hitting wet weeds and loose stones. By the time I whip around the side of the house with Captain skidding in front of me, all panting and paws, the vandals are far away. They whoop and laugh as they run down County Road HH, the rural road that dead-ends at my front door, the woods cupping behind me, like I'm being held up in offering to anyone who approaches.

"Don't come back!" I shout after them, raising the bat even though they probably know I couldn't hurt them even if I wanted to. "This is private property!"

Property I can't wait to escape. But I'm here now, and I need to sell them this vision of bold Julia, fearless Julia.

Captain barks one more time, then whines up at me.

"You did good," I tell him. He wags his tail.

We survey the damage to the siding together: a half-drawn robot-woman with springs coming out the sides of her head. A speech bubble ballooning from full, open lips: MADE FOR FUCKING. A knife stabbed into the side of her head, red paint trickling from the wound.

For a second, I just stare, jaw tight. This might have brought me to tears a year ago. Not anymore, which is its own level of sad. At least it's not fire. That happened. It was a few months ago, and scorch marks still streak our siding from the pyre where we found a melting redheaded Barbie doll.

Back inside, Annaleigh has progressed from whimpering to full-on rage. Poor thing. She might have been awake for a while this morning while I slept on. I somehow misplaced the parent side of her baby monitor, and she's hard to hear, even down the short hall with both our doors open.

Just as I'm setting foot on the first stair to head up to Annaleigh, her crying cuts off. There's a murmur upstairs—deep, male—Josh? Did he arrive home while I was dealing with the vandals? I bound up, my feet silent on the carpeted treads. At the top, I can make out words.

"Shhh, I've got you, little lady. I'm right here, I'm watching over you…"

The voice is definitely male…but lower than Josh's…

"Josh?" I cross the short hall. "Josh? Hello?"

No answer.

My short-lived joy turns to panic. Someone's in there with my baby.

I blast through the semi-open nursery door, baseball bat raised, taking in the scene—crib, rocker, changing table—

No one. No one here but Annaleigh, on her stomach in the crib, gripping the bars, brown eyes wide.

"Who's there?" I shout, spinning. The closet. I fling it open, bring the bat down on a pile of linens. Annaleigh whimpers as I topple the stacked boxes of too-small diapers.

I step back, sucking in my breath. *Little lady?* Josh never calls her that. He calls her sweetie-pie. Jelly-belly. I test the window. Closed and locked. I turn. Turn again. I'm shaking. There's nowhere else for someone to hide. Dear God, I'm losing my mind. I want Josh to come back so badly, my mind is putting him in the scene. It felt so real…but it wasn't. Clearly.

I set the baseball bat down softly as I finally bend over the crib.

"I'm sorry to make you wait, sweetie. Mommy's sorry."

The minute I lift Annaleigh, a flood of emotion opens in my chest and spreads to my toes, which I crinkle against the carpet as I lift the precious weight of her into my arms. The graffiti boys don't matter. The phantom voice doesn't matter. Just her. Just us. Annaleigh kicks her legs and paws at my chest, eager, ready for her breakfast. I tug my oversize sleep shirt down and she's soon happily guzzling, her body relaxing with each gulp. One of her fists rests against my collarbone, where I cover it with my hand. There's a warm brush against my legs—Captain, my shadow. My protector.

But the sweetness of the moment doesn't hold me long, because one piece is missing from our blissful domestic scene: Josh. Who may have left not only me, but our baby. The thought is so sickening that I feel my stomach, synthetic as it may be, turn violently in my gut.

He wouldn't just leave, right? Not when we're this close to a fresh start. This close to building our new house, tucked away on a twenty-acre property just an hour from here. Like our marriage, rural Indiana has its problems, but this house will be a dream, embraced in woodlands and privacy. I've imagined it all—a man cave for Josh, a sun-drenched playroom for Annaleigh, a chef's kitchen for me. Chickens, a tree swing, a state-of-the-art grill. And a state-of-the-art security system.

"Sounds lonely," my best friend, Cam, said when I told her. "You should move back to LA. Or Austin, with me! People love weird shit here, so naturally they'll love you."

"You're funny," I said dryly. "I'll think about it."

But California is expensive and crowded, and Texas feels like another world, and at least for now, our family needs space, and lots of it. Escape from outside pressures, so that we can focus on *us* again.

Away from the people creeping around in our bushes. The hate mail. The vandalism. The menacing presence of the house I'm caged in, like the hatred of its previous owner has infected the very beams that hold it up. And the eyesore of a billboard erected down the road and reminding me every morning that *BOTS CAN'T GO TO HEAVEN, BUT YOU CAN! REPENT AND BELIEVE!* I actually laughed in the innocence of disbelief when I first saw it poking above the tree line. *That* feels like a lifetime ago.

Annaleigh is done eating, so I change her into a fresh onesie, then lean her on my shoulder for a burping. She nestles into the crook of my neck with a soulful baby sigh as I tease aside the curtain to look out the nursery window.

The sun is just rising. The tall trees that line both sides of the road seem to be stretching up in anticipation of the new day. The billboard is a blight, but my eyes skit past it, to the scattering of houses that share the road with us: weary farmhouse-style structures with dirt driveways, sagging porches, and wild lawns. Not where Josh and I ever planned on ending up, that's for sure.

Bob Campini's house next door is the ugliest of the bunch. He moved in about a month after us. The property was unoccupied before him, for years. The fact that anyone would choose to live here still astounds me, especially considering the land's violent history: ninety years ago, the plots we all live on were a single farm owned by a serial killer—Royce Sullivan, the town of Eauverte's single claim to fame. I've read the Wikipedia page. The black-and-white picture of Royce shows a handsome man with a winning smile, posing with his axe, his foot resting on a stump. The stump where he hacked his lovers up before burying their bodies in pieces, all over the property. There's a rhyme all the locals know, that Josh repeated to me laughing. *Roses are red, violets are blue, he killed not one, but twenty-two.* At the time it struck me as morbid, but removed enough from us to be amusing. Now I can't help imagining the limbs that might live under us. They never did recover all twenty-two of those girls.

Bob's front yard is littered with various heaps of metal that maybe used to be engines. A big hand-painted sign at the mouth of his driveway reads BOB'S MEAT PROCESSING. Next to the lettering, a smiling pasty-pink cartoon man in overalls is clicking his heels in midjump, wielding a big cleaver, which, considering the history of the property, is especially chilling. The meat processing takes place in the barn out back. You'd think that with our generous three-acre lots, our house and Bob's would have been built farther apart, but we're separated only by a ditch and some straggly growth.

"Welcome to what I like to call the rural sprawl," Josh said with grim humor when we first arrived, after I blurted out a bewildered "Where *are* we?"

"It's an old farm lot that got chopped up into house lots," he explained. "The houses are built close to the road, but each property is multiple acres extending into the woods."

The worst of both worlds, I thought. Isolated from the world but bunched together. Too far and too damn close. I suppose the builders had to decide what people would be more frightened of—the yawning loneliness of the woods? Or each other?

Annaleigh wiggles restlessly, so I turn her forward-facing, toward the window. I squint at Bob's house, where it seems like the curtains may have twitched?

"Ba," she proclaims, smacking a palm forward and hitting the glass.

"Did you just say Bob?" I say with some surprise, even though she's probably just vocalizing.

She turns her head, eyes bright at my approval. "Ba! Ba!"

I have to laugh. "At least he's made an effort, huh? Finally."

Two efforts, actually. Both equally surprising. Bob Campini's yard used to have an entire garden of political signs for anti-Bot candidates. But three days ago, when I did my morning neighborhood lookout, the signs were gone.

What really made my jaw drop, though, was when Bob showed up at our door. After so many months of watching him silently spy on us, I'd given up hope of any kind of normal neighborliness. But he even brought a gift. The visit was awkward. I was probably too enthusiastic. He was stiff and gruff. But it was also kind of sweet, and I promised to have him over for dinner when Josh got back from his trip.

"People can change, baby girl," I whisper to Annaleigh as her moist palm whacks the glass over and over, her legs kicking in tandem. A hopeful wish, not just for Bob, but for Josh. For me.

I used to imagine myself as Josh's perfect puzzle piece. And maybe on day one of my existence, that was true. Maybe we've become less perfect every day since. But Bob Campini's one-eighty tells me it doesn't have to be too late. Maybe my marriage can still become what everyone thinks it is. A marriage worth admiring. Filming. *Living.*

The doorbell rings.

Josh! It has to be, keyless, contrite like he always is after we fight. Firmly holding Annaleigh, I race downstairs, across the chilly tile foyer with its slanting sunlight.

I'm going to say *I love you*, and I'm going to tell him how hopeful I am for us. I'm going to say, things have been hard, but better days are ahead, and if we just keep trying, we can become what we want to be—what we're *meant* to be. As I set my hand on the doorknob, I believe this. That I'm welcoming in not only Josh, but a season of change.

I fling open the door to the mid-May morning sun, a big smile on my face, the *I love you* on my lips.

Whoosh, goes my breath. *Pfffft*, out through my teeth.

Two men.

One, Sheriff Hank Mitchell. Right-wing, gun-toting, Bot-hating, over six feet tall with shoulders as wide as a snowplow. The other is a younger fellow I filed the missing person report with: blond, blue-eyed, round-shouldered, his cheeks stained with rosacea.

The sheriff is no stranger to me. He was in our house last fall. He said, "I've instructed my department to stop responding to

calls from this residence." He was addressing Josh and Josh alone
even though I was sitting right there. "You and your—*wife*—
are putting an untenable burden on my little department." He
cushioned *wife* in a little cough.

Josh and I exchanged looks of shock.

"But this is your job," Josh finally said. "Listen, Sheriff—I
think this is more serious than you realize. Julia's been saving
all our mail. There are *death* threats."

"People are scared. Can't blame 'em," the sheriff drawled,
leaning back in the chair we'd offered him, his eyes sweeping
up and down my body as if trying to see where the cogs and
screws might be hiding.

Josh reached over to hold my hand, his grip as cold and tight
as his voice. "This is private property. People are describing how
they want to kill my *wife* in *writing*. Isn't it your job to serve and
protect?"

My free hand, I put over my belly. I was in the last trimester
of my pregnancy, and some strong maternal instinct was burning through me: *I must protect my baby from this man.*

"If you don't like how we do things in Indiana," said Sheriff
Mitchell, "it's a free country. Move." He stood slowly, thrusting
his hips forward and stretching his back. "Oh—congratulations
on the baby. Fifty-fifty Bot-human?"

"Get out," hissed Josh.

The whole scene has played in a single second in my head.
Staring at the sheriff now, my heart is racing, my grip tightening around my baby. "Can I help you?"

This morning, Sheriff Mitchell's eyes don't sweep. He tips
his hat without breaking eye contact, and I step back without
choosing to.

"Julia Walden?" As if he has to confirm.

"Yes," I say. This has to be about Josh. Frantic questions are
already screaming through my head.

Mitchell adjusts his holster, drawing my attention to his gun, handcuffs, billy club. Even though every ounce of me wants to wring the words out of him, I force myself to be still. There's a nearly audible *tick-tick-tick* in my head, like my very being is counting out the painful wait.

"I'm afraid we have some questions for you, Miz Walden."

"What questions? Is my husband okay?"

His grin is slow, like he's relishing this.

"Could we come in? You might want to sit down."

THEN

I'm in the limo on the way to meet Josh for the first time, along with seven other women. I'm wedged between two stunning brunettes.

Lively chatter fills the car as we creep along. Everyone is asking where everyone else is from. What they do. How old they are. We've got Texas, Florida, New York, and more; girls from the country, girls from the city. Two consultants, a lawyer, a dog walker, a girl who just backpacked through South America. One girl is asking how many Insta followers everyone has and informs us multiple times that she has forty thousand. I keep quiet. Better not to mention that between the time Andy handed me a phone and the moment the producers took it away twenty minutes later, my million followers shot up to one point five million. Of course, any brief feelings of pleasure I experienced at the attention were quickly buried as I took in the comments. Lesson learned: followers are not always fans.

This seems important to keep in mind as my eyes travel the faces, bodies, clothes, of the girls who are my competition.

We all look surprisingly similar. Curves and legs, long hair in a spectrum of colors, lightly curled and loose, floor-length sparkly gowns. Texas has the loudest personality and, based on the pinched line New York's full lips have become, New York is definitely judging her.

As they will soon probably judge me, alongside strangers on the internet who have already made comments like, Another blow to feminism and What a disgrace aren't real women good enough for y'all????

Synths are controversial, and some people will be offended by my mere existence. I didn't need Instagram to teach me that; I woke up knowing all the basic information about myself and my world that an average twentysomething woman with a liberal arts degree might have. Still, knowing and experiencing aren't the same, and the desire for these women to like me—accept me—is so overpowering that my shoulders tense and my stomach cramps. A nasty cocktail of sensations that my mind quickly supplies the label for: anxiety.

"I can't believe we're minutes away from meeting Josh," says the brunette on my left—Dog Walker. She smells like lilies and hair spray.

"God, I'm going to pass out." Texas fans herself with a manicured hand. "Do you think the driver can turn up the air?" She leans toward the dividing window. "Hey, driver! Crank the AC! We're dying back here!"

The limo is making the short trek from the temporary prep tent in the back of the property to the patio at the front of the house, where we'll emerge from the limo one by one to meet Josh for the first time in front of the cameras.

There are eight girls per limo and three limos, which makes twenty-four contestants. One of the producers explained that only eighteen of us will get to stay after tonight's party. That means six girls will be eliminated based on Josh's first impressions tonight—or lack thereof.

I've done the math; time with Josh will be limited tonight. Every word will count. Every gesture. And even though I've been made with Josh in mind, it's not like Josh himself had any input into—or knowledge of—my design. I can only hope Andy and his team did their research. That every last detail about me will mesh with each want or need of his, like fingers interlacing.

"What can you tell me about Josh?" I whispered to Andy before I was whisked away by the *Proposal* crew.

"He likes redheads," joked Andy. "Seriously, you'll be fine. Be yourself. Don't let nerves get the best of you, okay?"

"Can they?" I quipped, just as my stomach produced a huge gurgle.

"I'm afraid it's one of your basic dampers," he said, not reading my humor. "Just take deep breaths. You have everything you need right in here." He thumped his heart, but I knew he meant my heart.

"Someone's deep in thought," says Texas, snapping me back to the limo, which is suddenly feeling chilly.

"Just nervous," I say with a fluttery laugh.

"So where are you from, Red? And what's your name?"

I feel myself blush. "Julia. I'm from here. California."

"And what does Julia do?"

"Oh, I…" The car slows. I lick my lips. "Are we here?"

The girls erupt in chaos, everyone pressing against the darkened windows, trying to catch a glimpse of Josh.

And then, delicate as a moth's wings, something brushes my arm. My body jolts and I yelp before registering that it's just Texas, climbing across the limo into my corner.

"You scared me," I admit with a breathy laugh.

"Sorry, I missed your answer," she says, settling next to me with a shimmy of her hips. "So…what do you do?"

"Oh! Right. Um, well, I…" I clear my throat. I can't tell her the truth; Josh needs to be the first to know who I am. "I'm kind of…in between things right now." Ugh. Why do I sound so *guilty*?

Texas narrows her eyes. "Fair warning? I happen to be very good at finding out people's dirty secrets, and I think you have one." Her teasing tone has a vicious undercurrent. She reaches toward my face. My hand shoots up on instinct, clamping around her wrist.

For a second, we're frozen. Her hand lifted. My fingers wrapped around her like a manacle. Both our eyes wide with surprise. Then time tumbles forward. I release her wrist and raise both my hands, palms facing out.

"I'm *so* sorry," I gasp. What just happened? A flash of instinct—*protect yourself*—

"You had a mascara smudge, *bitch*," she hisses, gathering her wrist to her chest, her breathing heavy. "What the hell is wrong with you?"

Despite my resolve that Josh should be the first to know, I'm so tempted to blurt out, *I'm a Synth*. Reassure her that my No Harm programming means I'm not a threat. I couldn't even hurt Texas if she attacked me. In fact, there's only one exception that would allow me to harm a human. But I force myself to swallow the surge of words like the vomit they are.

"You startled me," I say humbly, "and I'm *so* sorry."

"Like fuck you are." Her displeasure hits like a blow.

I suddenly notice we're the center of multiple girls' attention. More than one face looks...excited. I bite my lip, unsure of where to go from here, but Texas takes over.

"There's a saying you should know, Julia from California. Don't mess with Texas. You want to know why?"

"Why?" I say without thinking, and instantly regret it.

"We know how to fuck a bitch up."

The girls explode in whoops and laughter.

But I'm not laughing. I came on this show to find love, and the first thing I've found is hatred.

"I'm not here to make enemies," I say, but even I can hear the weakness in my own voice.

Texas smiles, all white teeth and sharp lipstick.

"And I'm not here to make friends."

NOW

"Please, sit," I say, gesturing to the chairs in our kitchen breakfast nook. I'm trying to act normal, even though dread is bubbling up in my stomach from a deep well within.

When Josh didn't come back, at first I didn't panic, even when he didn't answer my texts. We had parted angry. He probably needed more time. Then, Monday morning, my calls went straight to voicemail. Maybe his phone died. Or had he blocked me? From there, the floodgates of worst-case scenarios burst open. What if I never saw him again? What if our angry goodbyes were our last? By Tuesday, I knew something terrible had happened, even if that terrible thing was him leaving me of his own free will. That's when I filed the missing person report. The past twenty-four hours since I filed might as well have been an eternity, but now that law enforcement is here, I don't feel ready. What's worse? The limbo of dread, or its cruel resolution?

I turn my back on the sheriff and his deputy while I settle Annaleigh in her high chair, strap her in, and hand her a soft spoon to entertain herself with. There's a long, almost human whine from Captain, who has settled into a good-boy position by his empty bowls.

"Don't mind me, I just need to get Captain's food," I say as

Annaleigh bangs the spoon on her tray. This earns total silence from the men. I give them a small glance. The sheriff's gaze is downright piercing. But his deputy's is different. A mixture of wonder, curiosity...and lust. I know I'm beautiful, according to Western human standards. And sometimes that makes me happy—almost viciously happy, like my beauty is some kind of revenge. *You can hate me, but you'll still want me.* But a lot of the time, it makes everything so much more complicated. The spot at the back of my head itches again. I force myself to ignore it.

"Can I get you coffee? Water?" I say as I head to the fridge for the Tupperware of wet dog food, both sick with the delay and desperate for another minute of not knowing.

"Water's fine," says the deputy as I dish a wet slop of pink into Captain's bowl.

Sheriff Mitchell tips his chair back. "Big dog. Saint Bernard?"

"Bernese," I correct as Captain sets to.

"Is that homemade?" says the sheriff. I automatically hear the question behind the question. *Do you care that much about your dog? Are you capable of caring?* There are always layers. Or maybe there aren't, and I'm just paranoid.

"From my neighbor." I seal the container and return it to the fridge, next to the containers of pureed baby food.

"Which neighbor?"

"Bob, next door."

"You two friendly?"

I make my tone light. "He moved in last year. Just after us. I... brought him banana bread." I don't mention that, even though Bob was home, he didn't open the door when I showed up with the still-warm loaf. I had to leave it on the porch. I thought about dropping off cookies the following week; Josh told me to cut my losses. "He, um, runs a meat processing plant. He brought this by Sunday. I think it was a kind of...late housewarming gift."

"Pretty damn late," says the sheriff.

"I guess," I say faintly. Why do I feel like I'm incriminating myself with everything I say? *Leftover anxiety from being in the public eye*, I remind myself as I pour two glasses of water. The glasses rattle like teeth as I set them before the men, then sit in the third chair, between them, trembling hands tucked between my legs. My heart and head are pounding out *Be careful* in a continuous loop that makes it hard to think.

"Adams?" says Sheriff Mitchell, looking to his deputy.

"Yes. Right. Ma'am, we've found your husband's car. It rolled off the highway into the woods about two hours west of here. A few miles from Belmont Ridge County Park."

Thunder crashes through my senses. "And Josh?"

"At this point, unknown." The deputy has the grace to at least look concerned. "Has he made contact in any way, ma'am?"

Sheriff Mitchell leans farther back in his chair, putting all the weight on the back two legs. His eyes rove about as if he suspects I'm hiding Josh somewhere—or pieces of him.

"No." I swallow.

Annaleigh starts her loud, new litany as she bangs her spoon. "Ma-ma-ma-ma."

"We're searching the woods where the car was found," continues Deputy Adams, whipping out a little notepad. "Some of the folks out there are organizing a search party. We've also called nearby hospitals. Nothing yet. You said he was on a hiking trip. Do you know where he was spending the night?"

"I…don't know. He packed a tent." I lick my lips. "He said he was meeting Andy on Sunday, though. Andy Wekstein."

"Andy Wekstein of WekTech?" Deputy Adams's eyebrows go to his hairline.

I nod.

"Hiking date?" Adams looks skeptical, as if the man who designed me and the man who sleeps with me would not be natural friends.

He's not wrong.

"Breakfast date," I say.

"Where?"

"A diner, I think?"

"The two of them get along?"

"They're friendly." A white lie, but why bring drama to Andy's door?

"So Mr. Wekstein may have been the last person to see your husband," says Adams, scribbling on his notepad.

"No. Josh didn't show."

I know this from Andy, because he was the second person I called Monday morning, after my calls to Josh went to voicemail.

"Hey, Andy," I said. "Josh didn't come home last night. No need to panic, but...you met him for breakfast yesterday, right? Did he mention when he was coming home?"

"He never showed," Andy said. "Sorry, I should have told you right away, but... I didn't want to cause any more tension between the two of you." And without missing a beat, "Are *you* okay, though? Tell me what you need and I'm there."

"Nothing!" I said, not wanting to alarm Andy further, even adding a laugh for good measure, even though my brain was spinning in a panicked carousel of questions. "It's probably fine. It's possible he said it was a two-day trip? I had a lot of wine Saturday night! Some of which you contributed, ha ha. It's all a little fuzzy."

Not a little, a *lot* fuzzy. Even the things I can remember feel sheer rather than substantive. Impressions, ghost-lights, floaters that skit away when I try to look straight at them.

I've rarely been drunk in my short time alive. It figures that the one night I went to town on a bottle of wine would be the night it's most important for me to remember. The last time I saw Josh.

"How often were his trips?" says Adams.

"He's been on two. Before this one, I mean. Since we got married." I look between the men. "Do you have *any* leads?"

"One or two," says Sheriff Mitchell so casually that he can't expect me to believe him. "But in the meantime, I do have a few...*personal* questions for you."

"Okay."

"Where've you been, since he left on Saturday?"

"Here. At home. I mean, also at the grocery store. And... CVS. For infant Tylenol. Um—how much detail do you want?" I'll drown him in detail, as long as I can skim past the problematic area of Saturday night.

"If needed, could you give a complete account of your movements over the past four days?"

"I...think so."

"One of the neighbors reported hearing a woman shriek at two in the morning," says Mitchell. "This would have been Saturday night."

"Sunday morning, sir," corrects Adams.

I shrug despite the shivery crawl up my spine. "I was sleeping." The instant the words leave my mouth I realize how pretend they must sound, even though it's true. The wine knocked me out. "But the woods..." I gesture vaguely to the back window. "Maybe it was a fox?"

Deputy Adams nods as he addresses his boss. "The cry of a fox does sound like a woman being brutally murdered. Or..." His cheeks go pink. "This is the old Royce Sullivan site, sir. They say that the murdered women wander the woods, shrieking—the ones they never, er, fully...found. They can't rest until they find their missing limbs."

"When did your husband last communicate with you?" says Mitchell, ignoring his deputy.

"Sunday morning," I say without hesitation, trying to dispel the idea of the ghosts of Sullivan's victims creeping through the trees. Sunday is solid ground. "He texted."

"May I see?"

I grab my phone, unlock it, find the message. It's from five o'clock Sunday morning.

Morning babe! Reception's spotty here so...love you.

I didn't respond until six thirty, with a kissy emoji and a simple Good morning and good luck!

I show it to the sheriff, keeping control of the phone, taking care that the previous messages in the thread aren't visible.

"You and Josh have trouble at home?" he says, squinting at the screen.

"Trouble?" I allow my brow to wrinkle even as I quickly remove my phone. If he demanded I scroll up just one more message... "You mean the vandalism?"

There's a dead silence. Even Annaleigh is quiet now, gumming her spoon, drool running down her chubby chin.

"I think what the sheriff means," says Adams, "is that unfortunately, ma'am, during these kinds of cases in which spouses are involved, we—"

"Start the car, Adams," interrupts Mitchell.

Adams flushes. For a second, he looks like he's going to say something, then he nods at his superior, mutters "ma'am," and walks out.

The sheriff stands slowly, all height and hubris, stretching out his back, just like last time he was here. Taking his time, like some twisted show of power. Each second alone with him feels like torture. He rolls his right shoulder, then his left.

"So the search party is today?" I say, finally caving to the pressure of his silence.

"That's right. Neighbors are meeting at the crash site this afternoon. Will we see you there?"

I look at Annaleigh, then back at him. Belmont Ridge is two hours away. "I...don't know if I can. The baby..."

He gives me a knowing smile, like I've just checked a box. "No one expected you to."

"I want my husband back," I say. The words come out too passionate, like it's an act, even though I'm feeling it so strongly.

With a ghost of a smile on his lips, Mitchell turns and walks out of the kitchen.

"Is that it?" I challenge, walking after him, leaving Anna-leigh in her high chair.

"For now." At the front door, he faces me. His voice is matter-of-fact. "You want to know what I think?"

I'm too choked with rage to grace him with an answer.

He doffs his hat. "I think you killed him."

There's a shriek from the kitchen. "Ba-ba! Ma-ma-ma!"

He grins. "Cute baby."

THEN

The girls leave the limo one by one. It's impossible to see what's going on out there from this side of the glass. It's gotten quiet in here. One girl appears to be meditating; another quietly hyperventilates. I do my best to ignore Texas, whose eyes are trained on me like guns.

Can she tell I'm a Synth just by looking? Will Josh be able to tell? Is there some imperfection that makes me seem...not human? That will make me harder to love?

Impossible to love?

I dig my thumbnail into the skin on my inner wrist and watch the half-moon shape appear, then fade. I dig it in again, let it fade. I think it looks like normal skin. I think I feel normal amounts of pain. But how could I possibly be sure?

Stay focused, I tell myself. *You were designed to complete Josh. That's all that matters.*

Texas, as luck would have it, is the next-to-last girl to leave the limo. I brace for a final, cutting remark from her, but the second the car door opens, her energy changes and she's a happy beam pointing toward Josh, like I no longer exist. The door slams behind her, and I'm alone.

In the silence, my breathing sounds shaky. What am I going

to say to Josh? *Hi, I'm Julia, a Synth!* No. *Hi, Josh! I'm a Synth named Julia*—worse and worse. I don't *have* to lead with that, right? Better if it's spontaneous. Natural.

If I can call anything about myself natural.

I shift in my seat, noticing that my ankles are already blistering from the straps of my heels. Without thinking, I pick the tiny buckles open and slip the shoes off.

And then, the door is opening, the driver offering me his hand so that I can emerge gracefully. Which I botch immediately by stumbling out instead.

I straighten, trying to recover my dignity, hook the ankle straps of my shoes on my index finger, and…there is Josh.

I'm aware of multiple cameras positioned discreetly around us, but they're not important.

"Hi," I say, as everything fades around me except him.

Josh is gorgeous. Brown hair, clean-shaven, hands in the pockets of his slim-cut dress pants. As he takes me in, two dimples cut his cheeks and he nods with approval. I laugh. He's tall. Broad-shouldered. His blue eyes are sharp, his nose straight, his jaw strong. He has an aura of energy straining for release, just like the muscles straining at his fitted suit, as if he might burst into action at any moment. I can already imagine us skydiving together. Careening down zip lines, swimming with sharks. Laughing, kissing…making a beautiful baby. Oh God, my cheeks are tingling.

"Are you blushing?" he teases, rocking back on his heels.

"Sorry. It's just, you're really…" *Handsome. Sexy. Perfect.*

He waits, raising an eyebrow.

I bend over laughing. Straighten up, run a hand through my hair, then adjust it over my right shoulder. "Sorry. Can we start again? Hi! I'm Julia."

He extends both hands toward me. "Hi, Julia. I'm Josh."

I walk forward and take his hands, my shoes dangling awkwardly between us. I notice a small tattoo on his ring finger, but before I can ask about it, he grins at my shoes and says, "I see you've made yourself comfortable. I like that."

"I like you." I scrunch my face. "Did I really just say that out loud?"

"It's okay. I like a direct girl."

I feel myself warming, and not just my cheeks. These feelings... they're alarming in the best of ways. That everything could feel so deliciously soft and sharp at the same time, that someone's gaze could track heat over your skin as if you were being touched.

"What's your tattoo?"

"Oh," he says, drawing his hand back and making a fist so I can see. It's an arrow, etched between the base of his ring finger and his knuckle. "I got it before the show. Every time I look at it, I remind myself to trust the process. I believe if I follow my heart, I'll end up in the right place, with the right person and a ring on this finger."

"I love that," I say as he takes my hand again.

"Do you have any tattoos?"

"Not yet." I smile. For a few seconds, we're silent, just looking at each other. There's a rhythmic *tick-tick-tick* I'm just noticing. I tilt my head. "What's that sound?"

"Huh? Oh—" Josh holds up his left wrist. His watch is huge, silver, with a blue face and little slashes for the hours and minutes.

"It's so loud!" Now that I'm hearing it, I can't unhear it. "It doesn't bother you?"

"I guess I don't notice it anymore. I can take it off..."

"No, it's fine," I laugh, though the gesture is sweet...*so* sweet. I can't be in love already. That's silly. But the swirling in my stomach, the heat in my body, the magnetic pull toward this man—it's so intense, so real—so *right*. Are all the girls feeling this swept away? This deliciously dizzy?

"So—Julia. Tell me about you. Where are you from? What do you do?"

"I'm from here. California. I guess you could say I'm...in

Tech." The next part leaves me in a rush. "But honestly? Being here with you, it's like none of that matters right now." Instantly, I blush hotter, because even though I mean it, I can see how over-the-top I must sound. "I just mean that I'm a creature of the present. I'm so grateful for this chance, and... I can't wait to see where we go from here."

"Forward-facing. That's good."

A relieved smile breaks over my face at his simple statement of approval. Still, I'm eager to get the focus off me. "And...you? What do you do, Josh?"

"I'm a sales manager at a health insurance brokerage. Boring stuff. It pays the bills."

"Here in California?"

"Indiana. I know, not so exciting—but a great place to raise a family. Lots of space. Lots of nature."

"Like...cows?" I hazard.

He laughs, big and full. It's a delightful sound. "Cows. Corn. Casseroles. Yup. That about sums it up."

"The three C's," I joke. "I'm sure I'm going to love it."

"Ah! Feeling confident, are we?" He laughs as I blush again. I seem to have a never-ending supply of blushing potential. "Hey, I think that's awesome. Confidence is important. Especially in this process. The fourth C, huh? So, hey, I'll see you inside?"

"Yeah," I say, giving him one last, long look. "Sorry—I'm totally going—"

"I don't want you to walk away either," he interrupts, his voice lower now. A little husky. "Julia."

My name on his lips is everything.

"It's just for now," I say with a teasing smile. "I'm not the walking-away kind, though, so...don't get too used to it."

I swear I can feel his gaze burning into me as I walk away.

Into the mansion, where the girls are waiting.

Into a nest of vipers.

NOW

The sound of the sheriff's departing cruiser faded away a full minute ago, and Annaleigh is squawking in the kitchen, but here I stand, rooted in the foyer with my fists clenched, burning and burning with anger.

I lied. I do remember the name of the campsite where Josh was spending the night. And the diner. I know exactly where my husband was—or at least, where he was supposed to be.

In the moment, withholding that information from Mitchell and Adams was completely knee-jerk. The same instinct that activated the first day I was awake, when I grabbed Cam's wrist in the limo: *Protect yourself.* And after seeing the look in Sheriff Mitchell's eyes when he said, *I think you killed him,* my instinct to withhold is vindicated.

They don't care about finding Josh. What they care about is pinning his disappearance on me, conjuring up a crime that didn't happen, and locking me up.

It's not even that the target on my back is new; people have been coming for me since I made my first social media post. But it's one thing to be hated by girls in gowns or guys with spray paint. It's another to be hated by a man with a pair of handcuffs hanging from his belt who's looking at me like I'm his next steak dinner.

I don't *want* this to be happening. Damn it, the sheriff should know that I can't murder anyone. No Harm coding is kind of a big deal; Royce Sullivan himself could take me apart piece by piece and I wouldn't even be able to put up a fight. But Mitchell won't give a shit about the science, will he? I've heard his sound bites. *My campaign promise is to send that goddamn Synth back to California.* And if it's prison instead of California, wouldn't he be delighted.

The acid heat pumping through my veins feels like it's corroding me from within. I have to move. Laundry—there's laundry, right? Of course. There's always laundry. I free Annaleigh from her high chair and set to work, moving her with me as I go. Laundry. Dishes. Countertops. The family room couch, which is in constant need of vacuuming from Captain's hair. As I rake the attachment across the upholstery, I glance at the picture on the mantel above the fireplace—Josh and his mom. Staring at me, the intruder in their house.

I turn the vacuum off and face them.

"Where are you, Josh?" I say. There's an unexpected, accusing edge to my tone. *Ugh.* I'm feeling all the wrong things. I've been thinking too much about myself.

What's Josh going through? Is he scared? Confused? Or happy that he's finally free of us? Either way, he has to be alive…right? He wasn't in the crashed car. Even if he wandered off, lost, Indiana doesn't have much in the way of killer wildlife. The terrain around Belmont Ridge is mild; no cliffs to fall off, no rivers to drown in. Is it possible that he disappeared on purpose, just to get out of our marriage? But…that doesn't make sense. Why not just get a divorce? It's not like I could have stopped him.

The hard truth is, I can't know if he's in terrible trouble, or meant to leave. But standing here looking at his photograph, my tumble of thoughts and emotion finally crystallizes into one single directive: *find Josh.*

Simple. Obvious. And the only way to ensure my safety.

I grab Annaleigh and a rag, and move my efforts to the entryway, where the sheriff and his deputy tracked in dirt. As I put Annaleigh down, I'm starting to concoct a plan. First, I'll get our babysitter here. Then I'll drive to the campsite, the first and most logical place to start my search.

Annaleigh issues a series of sharp little grunts as she tries to do her new trick: getting onto all fours. I get on my hands and knees, too, and wipe the rag over the tile. And then —

Tick-tick-tick.

I sit bolt upright on my heels.

"Josh?"

Tick-tick-tick. Fear crinkles up my spine. It's his watch; I'd know the sound anywhere.

I can take it off, he offered…so sweet, just so sweet…

The memory hurts. I squeeze my eyes shut. What if I can't find him? What if the campsite is a dead end? Then what?

Oh, Josh. You were never supposed to leave me.

But even gone, he's not really gone—he's burrowed into me, into my senses, my programming. Whatever the hell I am is so entwined with him I can't even pick the damn ticking out of the tangles in my brain—

The thing tearing at my chest must be grief. I bow over the floor and imagine myself losing it. Crying. Screaming. Cursing. I can't protect myself, Josh. They're cornering me and my claws are useless, I can't fight back—

"Stop," I whisper to myself. My breathing is too quick. I'm nearly hyperventilating. This won't do at all—not now, when so much is at stake—

The ticking isn't real. The voice in the nursery wasn't real. A fox screamed, or another animal, not the ghosts of Royce Sullivan's dismembered victims—not the girls who found themselves alone, helpless before the axe, here on this very land I stand on—

"Ba," says Annaleigh, her brow furrowed with deep concern, like she can sense I'm about to come undone.

Fuck. I can't lose it. I'm all Annaleigh has.

Abandoning the rag, I lift my baby up, ignoring the retreating edge of my panic, ignoring the *tick-tick-tick* that still sounds so real, so close, like Josh is standing right behind me. She coos softly and gives her eyes a double-fisted rub.

"You're ready for a nap, aren't you?" I kiss Annaleigh's warm forehead and head upstairs. There's nothing like a baby's very practical needs to bring you back to earth. I'm feeling more normal already as we nurse in the glider. One step at a time, I remind myself.

I can't find her favorite blanket when she finishes, the blue one with the embroidered suns and clouds, but I quickly locate her second favorite. She raises it to her face with a sigh. Then I settle her into her crib and pull out my phone to text our babysitter, Eden.

I need to run out for the afternoon. Any chance you're free?

God love her, Eden's response dings before the phone has even left my hand.

Sure. B over soon.

Finally, I go to the window to draw the curtains closed.

Ah. Bob. Watching me through binoculars from one of his usual spots on the second floor. For a minute, I stand there, looking straight back at him. I thought we had turned a new leaf Sunday, when he came by. That the spying would stop. Apparently not.

I raise a hand. *Hello, creep.* Do you see me, seeing you? Do you care?

He doesn't move. We stare at each other for a while longer. Then I yank the curtains closed and turn the sound machine to the Rain setting. It sounds like a hundred layered whispers. That's how I heard the male voice. It has to be.

Not Josh. Not an intruder. Not a ghost.

Just a digital blip in the white noise.

THEN

The mansion is all recessed lighting and cameras and wine. So much wine. The first glass is pressed into my hands the second I cross the threshold, and I find myself sipping immediately, like a reflex.

But getting drunk is dangerous tonight. I need all my faculties. I set the glass down on the marble counter of the gorgeous kitchen where a few girls are perched on barstools. One is draped over the island, maybe already drunk. Texas is nowhere in sight.

"Isn't this house incredible?" says right-hand brunette, sidling up to me. "I'm Emma, by the way. And you're Julia?"

I nod, feeling cautious despite her warm approach. Once bitten, twice shy.

"How'd your meeting with Josh go?" she says, smoothing her hair over her shoulder.

There's a cameraman just feet away from us. Resisting the urge to look at him is like trying to ignore a buzzing insect.

"I think okay," I demur, locking my attention onto my new acquaintance. "It's hard to tell. There's also something personal I have to tell him soon. It might be a deal-breaker."

Emma nods. "I have something, too. I'm a mom. My little girl just turned three. I'm so nervous to tell him."

"You're a mom?" pipes up Drunk Girl, raising her head slightly. "Oh my God, that's so sweet." Her head slumps back down on her arms.

Emma lowers her voice. "Do you get the feeling that tonight is going to be, like, balls-to-the-walls crazy?"

"It already is," I say, resisting the urge to look at the nearby cameraman, resisting the urge to take one more sip of the wine, even though it would be nice to release some of the tension that feels like it's squeezing all my organs. Huh. In my first hours of life, I've had to resist a lot of urges already.

"Ladies, please gather around!" The show's host, Matt Driver, is clinking a fork against his wineglass. He's a surprisingly short man with wide shoulders, straight teeth, and a perma-twinkle in his eye. A rose is tucked into the breast pocket of his impeccable black tux.

"C'mon," Emma's saying to Drunk Girl, urging her off the barstool, toward the gathering women.

Matt explains the rules of tonight, which we already know: twenty-four girls, eighteen roses. Six will go home. A sober mood descends. Then Josh comes in, hands in his pant pockets, a little bashful, and my heartbeat goes wild in my chest. The applause is deafening, girls are cheering, Drunk Girl is openly weeping. Josh's eyes sweep the circle we make around him. Anticipation builds in my chest as his gaze gets closer to me—and then—*ooooof*. Right past me.

He pauses on Texas. His smile widens. My heart plummets. Even though I'm made of strong stuff, right now I might as well be made of glass.

"And now," announces Matt, plucking the rose from his breast pocket, "in a twist of events, Josh has told me he is ready to hand out his first-impression rose. Josh?" The rose trades hands.

Josh clears his throat, twirling the rose between his fingers. "So, I'm looking forward to getting to know all of you tonight. I'm so grateful you took time out of your lives to be here and get to know this random guy from Indiana." His voice is sincere, his gaze open—a man with nothing to hide. "I'm looking forward to exploring some of the connections I've already made, in those crazy first few minutes. And I'm looking forward to forming new connections. I just want you all to know I'm here for the right reasons. I'm here—" he looks down, then back up, eyes shining "—to find my wife."

The women erupt in applause. I don't even realize I'm clapping, too, until my palms are stinging.

"I was expecting to give the first-impression rose out later in the evening," Josh continues when the applause has faded, "but the second I met this woman, I knew there was something special there. Something I wanted to pursue. And this is also the first woman I want to talk to one-on-one tonight. So, without further ado—"

There's a feeling of collective bated breath. An intense pressure in my chest, like the flat of a knife pressing down.

"Camila?" he says.

Texas puts her hands over the O of her mouth.

Josh takes a single step forward. "Will you do me the honor of accepting this rose?"

With prayer hands pressed to her lips, she strides forward on her towering high heels, her gold-spangled gown swishing around her ankles, a tanned leg jutting through the dramatic slit with each step. Josh embraces her.

"Oh my God," she says, drawing the flower to her face and sniffing. She takes a step back, allowing Josh the full view of her gorgeous self. "I'm just so happy that you felt what I was feeling, too. I'm honestly on cloud nine."

"Shall we go chat and kick this evening off?" Josh offers her his arm.

"We shall," she says, the sugar of her Texas accent masking all the viciousness I know is under there.

Something rips through my chest as the two of them disappear under an archway to some other more private location. The feeling tastes like vinegar and flame.

Jealousy.

Everyone starts talking at once.

"What a bitch," moans Drunk Girl. "I need more wine." She stumbles back to the kitchen as half a dozen girls peel off after Josh and Camila, probably eager to break that up as soon as possible.

I stand frozen in place, uncertain where to go. Will all of my life feel this…fast? This out of control? The delight I felt just hours ago when I saw Andy and thought *kind*; when I touched my hair and felt so approving of it and of myself; the pure excitement when I proclaimed *I'm here to find love* to the watching cameras—all of that already seems tragically naive. Somehow, just hours into my life, I've not only made an enemy, but I've failed to capture the attention of the man I'm here for. Stunned and sick, I head back to the kitchen and pick a barstool. When I met Josh, my feelings told me it was real—the beat of my heart, the way my cheeks kept heating. And I still trust that—I do. It just seems cruel that I'm feeling things he's clearly not. Does he even remember our exchange? Or even just…my name?

"Everyone here is so fake," says Drunk Girl, who's topping off her wineglass. "You seem like the only legit real person here besides me. Do you know what I'm *saying*?" And then she proceeds to tell me the story of her life.

From there, the evening becomes a rising tide of women surging forward, desperate to break in on each other and carry Josh off. I catch glimpses of him every now and then, being led here or there. There are tears, muttered insults, occasional shouts. So much wine, which various members of the catering company keep pouring for us. A few girls strip off their evening gowns and go for a swim in the pool in the magnificently landscaped backyard. Another girl, freshly returned from talking with Josh, gushes loudly about how much they connected over church and how excited she is that they share the same beliefs. The word *bitch* flies around like confetti. After each girl talks to Josh, the producers bring her to a private room to film a confessional video.

I move around the house in a daze, listening in on snatches of conversation, feeling like I'm treading water in a vast ocean with no hope of finding the shore. How did I spiral so quickly? It's hitting me hard that being made for Josh is no yellow-brick road. *Every* girl here thinks she was made for Josh.

I have to stand out, and being the only Synth here, that shouldn't be hard. At the same time, I'm not ready to march in and tell Josh. The vibe tonight is all wrong. The vibes inside me are all wrong. I thought we shared a connection, outside the limo. Is my perception of reality that far off?

For the very first time, the devastating potential loss hits me. Sure, I woke up knowing that love and loss were both possibilities. But I didn't internalize what that loss might mean. If I get kicked off the show tonight, where do I go? Where will I live, what will I do? Will I spend the rest of my life with a yawning hole inside my heart where Josh was supposed to be?

The minutes tick past, until we're nearly two hours in. There can't be much time left. I imagine myself facing Andy, who sent me off earlier like a proud papa. Telling him, *I'm sorry, I couldn't do it.* I imagine him saying, *Did you even try?*

I stalk Josh—I'm trying, I'm *trying*, Andy—but he's deep in conversation with Emma, and then Drunk Girl stumbles in, and she and Josh start talking, and it just seems in bad taste to interrupt a girl who's already such a helpless wreck. It's not that I'm shy. I guess I just thought that the strength of our connection would forge a natural path. And talking to Josh *does* seem natural. Fighting other girls to do it doesn't.

Suddenly, it's time to take our places for the rose ceremony, and I haven't even talked to Josh. I'm surprised to find my cheeks wet with tears as we're herded onto tiered steps.

"Are you okay?" whispers Emma, who's been positioned next to me.

"Not really," I say with a sniffle as the producer gestures for a few girls to be rearranged. "I think I missed my chance."

She squeezes my arm. "He likes you. Don't worry."

Then Matt is talking, and Josh is taking his place by a table with seventeen roses laid out—Camila is already holding hers, straight as a sword between her breasts—and I panic.

"Wait," I cry out. "Can I say something? Please?"

Before anyone tries to stop me, including my own nerves, I pick my way down to the front.

"I'm so sorry to interrupt the ceremony," I say, clasping my hands at my sternum, "but, Josh, if I don't speak up, I know I'll regret this for the rest of my life."

Matt seems primed to interrupt, but Josh gestures him down.

I launch in. "You and I didn't get a chance to talk tonight, and I'm terrified I'm about to get eliminated. I felt the deepest connection with you I've ever felt with anyone. And I completely regret not coming to find you. I mean—I tried—but I kept not wanting to interrupt, because I could see how deeply you were connecting with the other girls. It seemed heartless to interfere, so..." Tears crowd my eyes. "But that means I missed my chance. I guess I have a lot to learn about going after what I want." I suck in a shaky breath as a teardrop breaks loose and trickles down. "It's a mistake I won't make again, if you give me the chance."

Josh nods, serious. "Thank you for saying that, Julia."

"I'm sorry," I whisper, and return to my spot among the girls. I can feel their animosity prickle in the air around me, but I don't care.

Josh clears his throat. "I know this is unusual, but, Julia— I actually really appreciate you stepping forward. You're right, I was thinking of sending you home, because you didn't come find me, so I thought maybe you weren't interested. But this has changed everything." His eyes are on me and me alone. The feeling is intoxicating. Heavenly. *Everything*. "I admire bold-ness in a woman, which you've shown me tonight. But I also admire kindness. And all the women you didn't interrupt? You showed them kindness." A smile breaks over his face. "Don't change, okay? Keep being kind." He extends the flower, a red heart stretching forward on its green stem. "Julia, would you accept this rose?"

I put both hands over my mouth and gasp. It's not fake at all; it's the truest expression of the intense emotion crashing through me, washing away everything else. I barely register the fact that I'm walking forward. All I register is Josh, the man I'm walk-ing toward.

His presence fills me. Awakens me. All I want is him.

"Of course," I whisper.

I accept my first rose and take my place by Camila, on the side where the chosen girls stand.

The ceremony continues. Emma gets the next rose.

"She's a smart bitch," Camila whispers, and even though she's looking straight at Emma, I know she means me.

But I don't care. I'm the one on cloud nine now, floating in the certainty that Josh and I *are* meant to be.

And tonight, that feeling is enough.

NOW

Eden slouches in not ten minutes later and dumps her canvas backpack on the kitchen counter. It's covered with pins—rainbows, arrows, Bot Rights, the Coexist logo. Like Bob's yard used to look, but the opposite. She's in Converse sneakers, black overalls, and an oversize blue cardigan.

"Where's the cutie?" she says in a gravelly voice, always surprising coming from someone so petite.

"Napping," I say. "She just went down."

Eden is a gem of nurturing packed into the body of an emo gamer girl. She lives two lots up the road. She's twenty-six and moved in with her aunt and uncle after some kind of career disaster on the West Coast that she doesn't talk about. Now she babysits and smokes weed in the woods behind our house. I have the feeling she doesn't get on too well with the aunt and uncle, who I've only laid eyes on twice—after Thanksgiving when an inflatable Santa went up in their front yard, and in January when it came down.

"There's leftover lentils in the fridge for you," I say, "and pureed sweet potato for Annaleigh. Oh! And the container of ground meat isn't for the baby—it's Captain's."

"Got it," says Eden.

As if alerted by his name, Captain barks. Where is he?

"Hey!" I call out. I've trained him not to bark inside. I find him in the living room, pawing and sniffing the area rug. He barks again and looks at me, then straightens, body rigid, ears cocked forward, looking down.

"What is it? You find a spider?"

I kneel to investigate. Nothing obvious. I run my hand over the worn fibers, then stand, frowning at the rug. A brown low-pile shag that I really should replace. At some point.

"Go to your place," I command. Captain barks once in protest, dancing his front paws over the rug, scratching. "Stop that!" What has gotten into him? "Place!"

With a whine, he obeys, heading to the spot in the kitchen I trained him to go to. I follow. "Good boy."

"Everything okay?" says Eden.

"Yeah, fine. Captain's just going a little nuts."

Okay. Recentering. I've already packed my vast shoulder bag with the battery-run breast pump, empty milk storage bottles, my wallet, and a couple granola bars. I'm trying to think if I need anything else.

"So I hope to be back by dinner?" I say as I pull two bags of breast milk from the freezer and plop them into a bowl of luke-warm water.

"Okay, so around five or six, then?" says Eden.

"I think so." Two hours to the campsite. An hour to look around. Two hours back. I should also probably stop by the diner where Josh was supposed to meet Andy. Maybe someone will remember something. "Six at the latest."

"Well, for real, stay out as late as you want. I have no plans," Eden says, making herself comfortable on the sun-drenched and freshly cleaned family room couch just off the kitchen. "Is everything okay, by the way? I saw the sheriff's cruiser pull up this morning."

I flick my eyes up. Is it just me, or is she looking at me a little *too* casually, like maybe she already knows what's up but is embarrassed to admit it?

The rural sprawl is like that. It looks like trees and empty space. At first it felt like peace. Now I feel the danger of hidden gazes. Of quiet watchers. When I was surrounded by girls and cameras in the *Proposal* mansion, at least I knew who was watching.

"Yeah, about the sheriff..." I say, trying to sound like I'm not worried at all. "Well... Josh never came home from hiking? So I reported him missing. Just as a precaution. And this morning it turns out they found Josh's car." It's bizarre to hear how matter-of-fact I sound. Especially in contrast with Eden, who's gone ramrod straight.

"And... Josh?" she says.

"No one knows." My eyes are suddenly hot with unshed tears. I hold still, because it feels like moving even an inch will make them spill.

"Wow." Eden runs her hands through her short black hair. "*God.* Wow."

"Yeah." I ledge my fingers under my eyes and look up, willing the tears to recede. Now is the time for pragmatism, not another meltdown.

Eden leaves the couch and comes toward me. Touches my arm. "Hey, it'll be alright."

"I know," I lie, crossing my arms because her touch is starting to dissolve me when I've only just recovered my footing. "I just want him to be okay."

"Um, Julia?" She withdraws her hand. "If you need... I don't know. Like, an alibi or anything? I can vouch for you Saturday night."

An unexpected flash of anger stabs my chest. Alibi? Why is everyone so keen to imagine not just that there's been a crime, but that I'm a suspect? And why Saturday night? Josh texted Sunday morning, so clearly he was still alive and well then. *The sentiment is nice*, I coach myself. Eden is on *your* side. Not all hidden gazes are hostile.

"Thanks," I finally say. I think it sounds sincere. In any case, the anger is doused. I shoulder my bag. "I'd better get going."

Eden follows me toward the foyer. "I remember seeing Josh leave for his trip."

I force myself to murmur a neutral acknowledgment as I slip on my shoes.

"I think it was around...six?" she adds. "And I smoked some weed in the woods." She's talking faster now, like she's trying to shoot it all out before I get away. "You can kind of see into your house from back there, you know? Especially at night when you have the lights on. I definitely saw you moving around the kitchen or whatever, and then a guy stopped by."

"Yeah. My friend Andy." I open the front door, step outside. The birds are singing and I can already feel that blush of warmth that's coming in on the heels of the fresh, sharp spring morning.

"He was here for, what, under an hour?" Eden follows me across the scraggly yard, to where my car is parked in front of the house on a strip of gravel. I've tried to make the yard nice, but like everything else in Indiana, it's fought me every inch.

"Maybe?" I make a regretful expression as I unlock the car. "Honestly, I had way too much wine. By the time Andy was over, I was so drunk." I hesitate as feelings of guilt threaten to crowd me. "Sorry, that's probably TMI. And don't worry. Pump and dump." The last thing I need is someone questioning my parenting.

"It's all good," says Eden.

But despite all the wine I never should have drunk, suddenly I remember what I said to Andy, a flare amid the haze.

We keep fighting about you. The kind of confession I never would have made sober. Not even to Andy.

Like that single memory has flipped on a light and I can finally look around the room, I'm now remembering how motionless Andy went. Didn't he? Yes...like someone caught.

Yeah, Josh thinks you're in love with me or something, I blabbed on. *He gets really angry sometimes.*

Julia, what are you saying?

Maybe you can just talk to Josh about it. Man-to-man, you know? He doesn't believe me, that there's nothing between us. But maybe he'll believe you.

Andy pulled out his phone to text Josh. He looked sincerely concerned...and I excused myself to the bathroom. Damn it... the fog is descending again. I have a nauseating impression of... Chicken McNuggets? At some point Andy drove away, and I must have collapsed into bed with Netflix on, since that's what I woke up to.

Damn it, the light is off, like my brain decided I was done, but I grope through the shadow memories anyway, because there's something else—a feeling—fleeing even as I catch at its heels...

Relief. Deep, tangible relief. A sense that something big was finally being taken care of. A burden lifted...

That makes sense. I was probably thinking that Andy was going to work things out with Josh. Josh would come back from his trip clearheaded, feeling sorry for his unfounded accusations, and that particular thorn in our marriage would finally be gone.

Poor drunk Past Julia, thinking relief was just around the corner when things were about to get so much worse.

"...and I even remember noticing when your bedroom light turned off..."

It takes me a second to register that Eden's still talking. Ugh. I'm literally climbing into my car, and she's not slowing down.

"And I was up even later, playing video games. And your car isn't exactly quiet. So I would have noticed if you'd left. Which...you didn't."

Okay, this is way more detail than I will *ever* remember about Saturday night.

I have one foot still outside the car. I stretch forward and put a hand on my babysitter's arm to stop her. Sweet Eden, who is clearly so very concerned about me.

"Thank you, Eden," I say in the same gentle voice I use with Josh when he's getting worked up. "I don't need an alibi, but I appreciate the thoughtfulness. Really."

She nods quickly, like she's embarrassed by her torrent of words. Backs away a step, then two. "Yeah. Sure. Thanks."

I pause. "Actually, speaking of Saturday...did you hear a scream? Around two in the morning?" I'm such a light sleeper these days—it's a nursing-mother thing. Even though alcohol was involved, it's bothering me that a scream in the neighborhood didn't wake me.

"Oh, uh..." Are the spots of pink in her cheeks brightening? "Now that you mention it, yes. But I think it was, um, an animal?"

"Maybe a fox?" I suggest. At least she's not bringing up ghosts from a century ago.

"Did you hear it?"

"No. One of the neighbors mentioned it to the sheriff, I guess." She looks relieved. "Well, it wasn't me that told him. But if he asks me, I'd say a fox for sure."

"That's what I thought, too." I slam the door and lower the window. "Text me if you have any questions about Annaleigh. She'll probably be asleep for another twenty minutes."

"Got it, boss." Eden makes a cute salute, then heads back to the house as I pull into the road. The sunlight gleams on the windshield like a flickering curtain, obscuring as much as it illuminates. As soon as I'm out of sight of the house, I slam on the gas.

The motion feels good, like I've broken free from Mitchell, but as the engine roars over the miles, I know the feeling is just an illusion.

They say cornered animals are the most dangerous, but I'm not an animal. I'm a Synth. No claws, no fangs, no bite. And when you can't defend yourself, there's only one way to elude a predator.

Don't get cornered in the first place.

THEN

"Can I talk to you for a second?" I say, sidling up to Josh just as he emerges from the water. It's nighttime. The kidney-shaped pool shines like a turquoise gem, four of the girls are in a vigorous and very bouncy chicken-fight match, and a warm breeze is teasing my bare skin. I'm in a bikini, with a semi-sheer sarong tied around one hip, my hair wet down my back.

It's the end of our first week in the house. Camila got the first date. Emma got the second. At least I got the consolation prize: today's group date with seven other women, which will end with one of us getting a rose; the others will have to endure the uncertainty of the next rose ceremony. It's been a full day. We rode trail horses, went to a wine tasting where Drunk Girl—real name Zoe—monopolized Josh's attention by breaking down crying, and now we're having a nighttime pool party on a hotel rooftop, the city of Los Angeles spread over the hills around us like a rolling carpet of stars.

Amid the chaos, my only personal interaction with Josh happened on horseback. "All good?" he said from his horse. "Great!" I responded from mine.

Not exactly the kind of interaction that's going to earn me the single rose Josh will be handing out to one of us in just under an hour.

So I'm betting it all. Now.

"Sure," he says, grabbing a towel from a lounge chair and rubbing it through his hair, which spikes up adorably. He looks incredible, the relief of his muscles exaggerated by the wet glisten of his skin. "How about over there?" He gestures to a low couch off to the side, angled away from the pool and facing the view of the city and the night sky.

We settle in. The couch cushion is damp and cool under my thighs.

"So. Julia." His grin is engaging. Just like it's been all day, with all seven of the other women. "How was your day?"

"It was a lot of fun," I say, opting for a light start. "I mean, of course I would have loved more time with just you—but the girls are cool to hang out with, too. I enjoyed myself."

"I like that you're friendly with the girls. I think that says a lot about your character."

"Aw." I tilt my head and pull the snake of wet hair over my shoulder. "That's so sweet. I appreciate that."

What I won't tell Josh is that every time I feel myself fully relaxing around the girls, Camila's words snap in my head. *We know how to fuck a bitch up.* Speaking of the girls—

"Hi! Can I interrupt?" It's Zoe, tiptoeing over in her neon-yellow string bikini, putting on a bashful act.

No, Zoe! You *got* your turn at the winery!

"Actually, we just sat down," I say, plastering on a sweet smile. "Could we have just a few minutes?"

"Oh…sure, okay," says Zoe. "I'll check back soon!"

I return my focus to Josh and take a deep breath.

"So I have something to tell you that…I've been putting off. I guess because it feels like it might be a deal-breaker." From pattering, my heart progresses to thundering.

"Hey," says Josh, reaching over and taking my hand. The pressure is reassuring. "Whatever it is, you can tell me."

Deep breath.

"I'm...a Synth."

The world goes still, like the aftermath of a bomb detonating. Then, Josh releases my hand, braces his hands behind his head, and leans back. Away from me.

"Okay. Wow. Not what I was expecting."

There are a million things I want to say. But I chew my lip hard and wait for him to process.

He unlocks his hands, leans forward. "So you're like...what are their names? Christi and Chrystel? From that show?"

"Basically, yes." I kind of want to add that I'm more advanced, because I'm the first Synth who can have babies. But even though it's something important about me, wouldn't sharing that right now make him think of me even more in terms of a science innovation when I want him to see *woman*? I'm pretty sure you can't fall in love with a science innovation.

Josh rubs his face. "Holy shit, Julia."

"I know," I say softly. My heart is cringing in my chest, but I have to appear calm.

"This is—" He shakes his head.

The screams from the pool surge and I make out Zoe's cry of *my bikini top!* Josh looks off into the distance, and I'd give anything to see what's happening inside his mind.

When the waiting becomes unbearable, I lay a tentative hand on his leg. "Hey. I know this is a lot. But it's still just me."

"Do the girls know?"

"Not yet. I wanted to tell you first."

"I have *so* many questions right now."

"I'll answer them all. If there's one thing I can promise, Josh, it's total honesty. Which is why I wanted to tell you now, before this goes any further." I whisper the next part. "Before my feelings get even stronger."

His eyes glitter as he takes in my words. They don't feel like the same eyes that took me in when I stepped out of the limo. Where there used to be warmth, there's distance. It hurts, but I can't show it.

"What are your questions?" I say.

"I mean…where to even start?" He launches in. He wants to know if I truly have emotions. If I age. If I can die. If I need food, sleep, if I can learn, have kids, get depressed.

Yes, yes, yes, I tell him. I try to explain about basic dampers in layman's terms, those layers of programming that give me all the needs and weaknesses a normal human might have. The way food becomes energy just like it does for him. I try to explain everything calmly, reasonably, as if it doesn't feel like he's stripping off my skin and violently poking at all the painful mysteries that make me.

Finally, there's a long silence. I can't tell exactly what Josh is feeling, but based on the clench of his jaw, I'm pretty sure it's not something soft and nice. Well, what I'm feeling isn't soft or nice either. In fact, it's a little devastating to realize that he'd like me better if my skin wasn't synthetic. If I'd been fitted together by the mysterious dance of cells rather than the hands of human ingenuity.

It hurts just like yours, my skin, I want to assure him. I want to dig my nails into my arm and show him the red half-moons.

"I guess we should get back to the party," he finally says. His smile is tight.

"Wait," I say, reaching out. Covering his hand. Josh said he admires boldness in a woman, so here we go. "I get that there's so much to process, but let me say one last thing. If you honestly believe things can never work between us, send me home. I mean it. But I promise you that the two of us have more similarities than differences. And I believe love is about two people getting…lit up by each other. I believe it's a feeling so strong that nothing else matters. And I know we're just getting to know each other, but…you light me up, Josh." I place a hand on my heart, which is thundering for him. "With all my being, I want to prove that I'm just as capable of love as any of these girls. Put me to the test. Give me a chance."

Looking into his eyes, waiting for his response, I feel a landslide in my chest. And despite the fact that I'm trying so hard to be calm and strong, a tear slips out, making a chilly track down my cheek.

"I just need a minute, sorry," I say, looking down.

And then, he's closing the inches that separated us. Thigh against thigh, he slings an arm around my shoulder and crushes me against him, resting his chin on top of my head.

"I'm sorry," I squeak, pressing my face hard against his bare chest. Feeling his solidity, his warmth, his heart beating. "I hate that what's scaring you is something I can't change."

"Shhhh," he murmurs.

Zoe interrupts shortly after. I hear her enthusiastic opener, "Did you totally see when I lost my bikini top? Oh my God, it was hilarious—" before I'm abruptly left alone, trying to get a grip on the earthquake of emotions that's shaking everything inside me. But I'm not alone for long. Five minutes later, Josh is back. And he's twirling a rose between his fingers.

"Really?" I gasp.

"What can I say?" His coldness is gone; he's all boyish flirtation. "You keep impressing me. What the hell. Let's see what happens." Then he kneels, in his swimming trunks with his messy hair and a big smile on his face. "Julia, will you accept this rose?"

I throw my arms around him.

His lips are suddenly on mine. My mouth opens against his. His tongue is warm, gentle as he explores my mouth, and I find my hand cupping the back of his neck to urge him deeper. When we pull away, I'm breathless.

His voice is low. "Was that your first kiss, Miss Julia?"

"Yes," I say, lisping a little. My lips feel swollen. I'm liquid. There's a warmth in my gut that's the best thing I've felt in my life. It feels like each day I share with Josh unlocks some new feeling inside me, each more powerful than the last. I smile up at him. "May I have my second?"

NOW

The campsite, on the edge of Belmont Ridge County Park, is tucked into a wooded area. Bright as it is with the fresh spring green of trees, it has an ominous feel. Too still, too peaceful, like something is holding its breath, waiting to pounce. Like instead of fleeing the predator, I've driven toward it.

I creep along the dirt road through spotted sunlight, leaning forward as if this will help me spot Josh. I pass a derelict shack marked CAMPER CHECK-IN, cement block restrooms streaked with water stains, and finally, the campsites themselves. Vaguely circular areas of cleared dirt, pocketed by brooding trees, each with its very own bolted-down, rust-eaten grill. The road weaves around, and suddenly—there. Up ahead. Josh's army-green tent.

"Oh my God," I breathe as I creep the car to the side of the road and put it in Park. I've been in a constant state of adrenaline this entire two-hour drive, and nothing feels quite real as I exit my car and cross the hard-packed dirt toward the tent. Will Josh be inside? Confused as to why I'm so freaked out? *I totaled the car, Julia…didn't you get my text? Service is so bad out here…*

The trees rustle nervously. No; he won't be in the tent. I'm not totally delusional. In fact, I'm pretty sure that on my way here I passed the spot where his car ran off the road, marked by two Belmont County Sheriff cars with their flashers on and a small hub of human activity that has to be the search party. Still, I can't help a soft "Josh?" as I unzip the tent and step into the musty interior.

Empty. Of course. There's a metallic tang in my mouth. Hope tastes bitter on the way out.

I zip the tent closed again behind me. There's another tent kitty-corner from this one, and I don't want to be observed.

"Okay," I whisper as I take in the scene.

Black sleeping bag that suddenly looks awfully like a body bag. Flashlight by the pillow. A paperback novel, face down and splayed open to mark his spot. A box of energy bars at the foot of his sleeping bag. Hiking boots with wool socks inside, neatly arranged by the entrance. Water bottle by his shoes. A cooler bag. And finally, his overnight bag, a pair of sweatpants folded on top, like he had just taken them off.

I close my eyes and inhale. This whole setup feels…

Wrong.

I open my eyes.

Jarringly neat.

The sleeping bag doesn't look slept in. It could have been smoothed out after the fact, of course, but Josh has never made a bed in his life. *Or folded a pair of pants.*

Crouching on my heels, I pick up each item in turn with my sleeves pulled over my hands, in case this becomes a crime scene. I count the energy bars. Seven in a box of eight, along with the crumpled wrapper of the eighth. The cooler bag contains half a dozen peanut butter sandwiches, which Josh made right before he left. I remember this; I was still semi-sober. Next, I pick up the half-empty water bottle and unscrew the top. Would the water possibly be drugged? Smells like water. Tastes like it, too… Wow. *Drugged water?* I'm reaching. I pick up the book, an old John Grisham paperback. A blue gel pen lies under it, the clicker textured with bite marks. I smell the socks inside his shoes. A strong whiff of detergent tells me they're unworn.

Finally, I stand, heat pounding through my head because I want to have smart thoughts, strong instincts, brilliant insights, but all I have is confusion. My eyes sweep the objects over and over. I feel like I'm fudging a test. Also, there's a tingle in my chest that means I need to pump soon. I pinch my inner arm to rein in my scattered focus.

Okay. He gets here late Saturday night. He sets up the tent in the dark, goes to sleep. Gets up early, eats an energy bar, texts me, heads to breakfast with Andy. And on the way…crashes the car? Wanders off in concussed confusion?

Or maybe he never slept here at all, a prickle tells me.

And Josh never chewed on pens. I did. Do. He hates it.

A loud *bleep-bleep* spikes through my senses.

A law enforcement vehicle. Oh God. If I'm found here—

I look around the tent in a panic. The only exit besides the front is a flap-style window in the back, currently closed.

I'm there in two steps, opening the flap, but there's a second layer, a mosquito net, also closed. I tug at the zipper. Stuck.

"Come on," I say under my breath. A plea. A prayer.

"Looks like it's this one, yep," a deep male voice says, with that syrupy Southern Indiana drawl that sounds like humid summers and sticky beer. There's a crackle of walkie-talkie. "Found it. Site number eleven. C'mon over." Then, the tread of heavy boots.

One officer, and it sounds like his partner is on the way.

I'm breathing heavily as I rock the zipper back and forth. *Come on…come on…*

"Excuse me, sir?" A female voice, brittle, pert. I go still. "I'm sorry to bother you. But my husband and I are just over there, and… I can't help but wonder if you're here about the young man who's staying here."

"Yes, ma'am," says the officer. "Any information you have would be extremely valuable. I'm afraid this is a missing person case."

"Oh, my. We did wonder… We haven't seen him in days!"

"You did see him, then?"

"Yes, he came in late Saturday night. He woke us up!"

"Might you remember what time that was?"

"A little after ten. But the strange thing is, after he set up his tent, he left."

"How d'you figure?"

"I had to use the restroom. The facilities are at the front of the campsite. I saw him drive away."

"Could you describe who you saw?"

"Well, it was dark, so I didn't get a good look. But I could see his outline while he was pitching his tent. Slender fellow. Took him a while to get it all set up. Didn't seem like he'd done it before. I thought he must be a camping newbie. He moved around the tent for a while. That's when I went to the restroom. Then before I know it, he's zooming past me. Very recklessly, I might add. If I hadn't jumped aside, he could have hit me!"

"Did he come back?"

"We haven't seen him since. I hope it's not rude to say that I wouldn't be surprised if he got into an accident, the way he was driving." She clucks her tongue.

"This is helpful. Thank you, ma'am," says the officer.

"Could I ask what the young man's name is?"

"If you can keep this to yourself, ma'am—" The officer's voice goes too low for me to hear.

The pert voice goes up a full pitch. "Wait…from two seasons ago? Who's married to the…"

There's more murmuring.

Finally, the officer's voice returns to normal volume. "I'm afraid that's all the information I've been given, ma'am. It's a Dover County case. I'm Belmont County. Just lending a helping hand."

"Well, I certainly hope he turns up! He seemed like a wonderful young man!"

I've been so riveted by this exchange I forgot I was supposed to be escaping. I attack the zipper with renewed urgency as steps again head in my direction.

"Please," I hiss. And then, with a jolt and a flash of pain in my finger, the zipper gives.

The officer's shadow is at the entrance, widened and elongated. With an ungraceful, desperate leap, I tumble out the back, the tent rocking behind me.

"Hey!" cries the officer, but I don't turn around; I run. Flat out, through the woods behind the campground, weaving between trees, my feet crashing through underbrush. My chest burns; my legs pump. A twig rips at my cheek. Birds scatter above me, breaking into a hoarse chorus. *Intruder! Intruder!*

My lungs are searing as I stumble behind a tree and cast myself to the ground, onto a moist layer of mulching leaves. Painfully, I hold my breath and listen. No one seems to have followed, so I allow myself to take some deeper breaths.

Thoughts come in violent bursts. I can't make sense of what I just heard. Josh setting up a campsite just to leave it. Driving away in the night. Abandoning a crashed car. And then, incongruously, texting me on Sunday. **Morning babe!** Like nothing was amiss.

I lean against the tree, tilt my head back, and look up. Shaggy branches dip down, like they're inclining their ears to me.

"What did you see?" I whisper. "Where is my husband?"

The trees look down with their weighty, silent gaze. Whatever horror they may have witnessed, they're not speaking of it today. Josh is gone, and there's no one to answer.

THEN

I'm walking around the pool when I'm attacked.

All I wanted was a few minutes of alone time. I've been in the *Proposal* mansion for a full week, and between the group date, confessional camera sessions, the second rose ceremony last night, and the sheer number of girls in the house, it feels like I haven't had a second to myself, waking or sleeping.

Evening is falling, a cool respite from the warm day. I'm in pj's, my hair in a messy topknot. The rough patio stones are sun-warmed, and the heat radiating into the soles of my bare feet feels incredibly healing, like California is pouring its love into me.

Of course, I'm not totally alone—the cameras always follow. And even now, it's only a matter of time before a few shriek-ing girls in bikinis tear into my moment. The pool is a popular hangout spot. But I'll take what I can get.

I lose my eyes in the aqua blue of the water as I think about tomorrow. Josh is announcing his next one-on-one date choice in the morning, and I've been so keyed up all day, I can barely function.

I'm just so hungry for it—time with Josh. All I've gotten so far are snatches. In fact, our longest interaction to date was when I confessed to being a Synth.

I smile remembering his smile. The way he said, *What the hell. Let's see what happens.* The fire in my body when his tongue explored my mouth. I might think it was just my coding making me so obsessed, except that the other girls seem to feel the same. "I imagine him next to me every night when I go to sleep," confessed Zoe, which made me blush, because I've been doing that, too. Pretending that if I just reached across the bed, I'd be able to run my fingers down his naked back.

Though…the girls do seem to approach this all a *little* differently from me. They seem eager, for example, to analyze what draws them to Josh. His beliefs…his values…shared backgrounds… common interests… Should I be thinking that way, too? And yet I have no background. No particular interests. No belief except that I'm meant to be with Josh.

"What makes you certain he's the one?" Emma asked me last night as we all hit up the hot tub after the drama and emotion of the rose ceremony.

"A feeling," I confessed.

Emma raised a brow, like my answer was too simple. Too pat. But what draws me to Josh—it's deep. I know it is. Just because I can't define everything in the same way as the other girls doesn't make my connection with Josh less than.

"Feelings come and go," Emma said. "My ex, the father of my daughter…let's just say that I thought what we had was real, but it was just feelings. You know what I mean? There was literally nothing underneath. Compatibility has to go deeper."

I had no response. Just an unease, frothing in my chest like the bubbles in the hot tub. I'd been telling myself all along that I'm more similar to the girls than I am different. I even sold myself to Josh with that very line. But looking at Emma, laughing across from me in the hot tub, suddenly felt like looking across a chasm, and I had to think—what if I was wrong?

Stay in the moment, I tell myself now, as I make a second circle around the pool, taking care to stop and feel each sensation of my feet on the stone. Overthinking things can only ruin them at this point. I am what I am. If I doubt the process, I could end up destroying my future before I have a chance to build it.

And then it happens.

The jolt of a body hitting mine from behind.

The crunch of my arm against the patio as I fling it up to brace my fall.

Needles in my skull as the attacker yanks me around by the hair, lifts my head, and brings it crashing against the stone.

I have only a millisecond to take in the face above mine, a pale moon set with a strange, cold grimace, as if what she's doing is not an act of passion but of necessity. A millisecond to gaze into eyes of washed-out blue, like the life was wrung out of them long ago. A millisecond to register age-spotted cheeks like sad, sunken craters, the smell of ripe body odor and unwashed gray hair.

Then *Proposal* crew members are pulling her back. I think there's shouting, but a loud buzz in my head drowns it out.

I'm left looking at the dark blue sky, stunned. It's so...wide. I feel so small, a mere bubble floating on the surface of a world deeper than I can know.

I think about saying *What just happened?* but I've bitten my tongue. Blood wells up, flooding my mouth.

"Julia?" It's a medic, leaning over me, her face a kinder moon. She smells fresh, like lemons. "Can you hear me? Stay with me, Julia. Julia?"

My vision goes fuzzy. A bubble is so delicate, after all. One touch and it bursts.

I black out.

NOW

The sun is starting its descent by the time I set back toward the campsite. I walk quietly over the soft squish of the ground, swishing clouds of gnats away as I go.

It's been miserable, hiding in the woods. The pressure in my breasts from milk got so painful, I pulled up my shirt and tried to hand-express. It didn't go well.

During Annaleigh's first weeks of life, when I was barely sleeping, if someone had offered me a few hours in the woods alone? I would have cried from gratitude. Of course, in that scenario I never would have imagined myself peeing in a bush, cursing the armies of ants determined to climb my legs, and yanking at my own sore nipples.

Finally, there's a flash of army green up ahead—Josh's tent. And my car, a silver glimmer just beyond.

Fresh yellow tape has been strung around the campsite, but no one appears to be standing guard. I pick my way back to my car. Climb in, close the door as softly as I can. The second I push the lock button, my milk starts releasing.

"Damn it," I say, nearly crying from the pressure and the pain as I fumble for my breast pump. Shirt up, I'm fitting it onto my breasts, pushing the power button. Just as milk streams into the twin bottles, I hear a loud female voice.

"Excuse me! Ma'am!"

Crossing toward my car from the blue tent is Miss Pert. Gray hair, athletic build, brisk walk.

"Fuck no," I growl, and start the car with a ragey twist of the key while I try to juggle both bottles with my other hand. I jam the accelerator, spitting gravel and dirt, the car weaving as I struggle to drive and pump. Finally, I shoot out of the campground and onto the paved county road. It's five o'clock, later than I thought. I need to charge my phone and text Eden, but I have no free hands. At least the milk is still streaming out, relieving one discomfort. At least the road is smooth. I creep up to 80 miles per hour.

I've never felt so weak, so desperate. Thirsty, hungry, dirty, stiff, with a deep panic from being away from Annaleigh for too long. All I want to do right now is go home. Take a shower and put on fresh clothes and snuggle my baby and try to feel as safe as I can for as long as I can.

A lit marquee to the right of the road catches my eye: Stella's. *Old-Fashioned Diner Food for the Whole Family.* The place where Andy and Josh were supposed to meet for breakfast on Sunday. I nearly spin out with how fast I take the turnoff into the small parking lot. Everything in me is screaming to get back to my baby, but I have to do this.

I park, plug my phone in to charge, and try to make myself presentable. Cap off the pumping bottles, readjust my bra. Saucer-sized milk stains adorn the front of my shirt, but I brought a fleece sweatshirt. I fight my way into it.

The diner is run-down, like everything in Southern Indiana. Tin roof and weathered siding. Even in the parking lot, the smell of old oil hangs in the air. It's worse inside—fishy, like clam chowder gone wrong. Brown booths line the sides, only one occupied by two old men. The LED lighting is cold, unforgiving, showing every rip in the vinyl booths, every chip on the tables. I wish I had hand sanitizer.

"Hi," I say to the iron-haired woman behind the aluminum breakfast bar, the obvious candidate for questioning. She's running a rag over the surface, scattering food residue as she goes.

"What can I getcha?"

When she says this, I realize that no matter how unappetizing this place is, I should probably eat.

I force a smile and slide onto a padded barstool. "What do you recommend?"

"Fish fry's on special. Or you like pancakes?"

"Pancakes, please. And decaf. Water, too."

She shouts my order through the small pass-through window into the kitchen.

I lean forward on the counter, tucking my hands into the sleeves of my fleece so I don't have to touch anything. "Um, can I ask, were you here on Sunday?"

"Here every day." She's setting the coffee for me, her back turned.

"Do you remember seeing a dark-haired guy, midthirties, kind of...scruffy? Waiting for someone else? Probably for a long time?"

"Nope."

Andy already said Josh didn't show. But what if Josh got the time wrong and they somehow missed each other?

"What about a really handsome guy? Brown hair, athletic build?" If my phone wasn't charging back in the car, I could show her pictures of both Andy and Josh. "Actually, do you watch *The Proposal*?"

"*Survivor* kinda gal." She plunks down a plate of pancakes, a sticky carafe of syrup, and a ceramic mug, then pours the coffee in. It sloshes over. "That be all?"

"So you didn't see a handsome guy with—"

"Nope."

"Okay. Thanks," I say, deflated. This stop was definitely a waste of time.

As I scarf down the pancakes, my eyes trail up to the TV above the bar. It's playing live coverage of the Antique Car Convention in Indianapolis. Josh went once, as a kid. It was one of the few happy memories he had with his dad, Phil, a financier and all-around jerk who now lives in Chicago with his twenty-year-old fiancée.

Josh and I talked about trying to go to the convention this year, but Annaleigh gets cranky without her naps, so we pinkie promised each other we'd go next year.

Next year. The year of the new house, the easier life, the fresh start. What if it's just me next year? Alone?

I stuff a bite of pancake into my mouth and try not to project. *It could still be fine.* As long as there's no body, I have to keep assuming Josh is alive.

When the TV reporter pushes their big microphone toward someone, I actually gasp. Camila Reyes is smiling down at me, like a sign from above. She's looking fabulous in a bright yellow cocktail dress and chunky silver heels, her dark hair softly curled. The volume is down, but a blurb flashes under her image: BMW BRAND AMBASSADOR.

I should text her. Indy is just a couple hours away; she could come down to Eauverte after the convention. I've been resisting involving her and Andy in this mess, but that's shortsighted. I need help.

I wave my credit card at the woman. As she runs it, I try one last time.

"I'm sorry to be obnoxious—but those guys I was asking about? One of them is my husband. He was supposed to meet our friend here Sunday, for breakfast. My friend said he didn't show. I just... If you saw anything at all—"

"For breakfast?" The woman chuckles and returns my card. "Sunday?"

"Yes." Hope expands in my chest. "Did you see them?"

She slaps her rag down like this is hilarious. "Honey, we were all worshipping the Lord."

"Excuse me?"

"Church," she says, louder, like I'm hard of hearing. "We're closed Sundays until dinner so we can all go to *church*."

"Oh," I say, feeling foolish. "Thank you."

I see myself out. Back in the car, my phone is finally charged. Missed calls and texts are popping up like a rash.

Andy. Julia, call me. I'm really worried.

Ally Buoncore from Netflix. Hey! In Indy next week. Can we schedule some face time? I'd love to see where you're at with considering the documentary!

I have half a mind to block her number. Why can't she get that I just want to be left alone?

Eden. Out of wet wipes! Can u pick some up on ur way?

Eden, again. Hey, putting A down, just want to make sure ur ok

Next, a selfie of her and Annaleigh, pressed cheek to cheek.

I compose a text to Eden first, so she doesn't worry.

Sorry! Phone died, running late, will pick up wipes. Back in 2h.

Next, I message Cam.

Hey Texas. Saw on TV that you're in Indy. Call me!

I don't have the heart to tell her the bad news about Josh's disappearance via text, even though as his friend—*our* friend—Cam deserves to know.

And then, with an obsessive twitch of the fingers, I'm back on Josh's messages, reading every word like there's a secret behind them I just haven't dug out yet.

First, I read the ones I showed the sheriff with our happy *good mornings* and kissy emoji.

Then, farther up, the others.

You and Josh have trouble at home? Mitchell asked this morning.

Yes, Sheriff. My husband thinks my designer is in love with and/or obsessed with me, which makes him violently angry. And worse? He thinks *I'm* in love with Andy, too.

I stare at Josh's texts from after he left Saturday night. The first time stamp is 8:52 p.m. At the time, I imagined him fully set up at the campsite and settling into his tent, but after overhearing Miss Pert, I know he was still on the road.

Josh: Meeting up w Andy. FYI, if I have to beat the shit out of him, I will.

Me: Josh, please be calm. It's not what you think. Just listen to Andy's side.

Josh: HE IS IN LOVE WITH MY WIFE

Me: omg babe can we not do this again??? Please???

Josh: he wants you to himself, it's so obvious. I just want that little fucker out of our lives

I stare and stare. My heart is beating fast. I'm angry. Really angry.

For a few seconds, I sit in the tension of wanting to curse Josh out and throw my arms around him. Of wanting to scream *fuck you* and wanting to whisper *I love you, please don't ever leave me*. When the tug-of-war gets unbearable, I push a burst of air out through my nose, swipe the messages off-screen and toss the phone into the passenger seat.

As I start the car, I try to return to calm, problem-solving mode. I imagine Josh arriving at the campsite after all these emotional texts. Setting up the tent in a fury, which would make him awkward. Inefficient. *Like a newbie*, the lady said. Driving off shortly after...where? To get supplies of some kind? Never imagining he'd swerve off the road. I imagine him lost in the woods. Disoriented, roughing it, like I just did. Or stumbling toward some stranger's house. Maybe with a concussion. But what about the damn text the next morning? Unless someone else sent it...

The road is getting harder to see. It's after six, and soon it will be pitch-black. My headlights cut a lonely path, and I know I need to use all my focus to scan for deer, but instead, I increase my speed. Seventy-five. Eighty. Eighty-five.

And then it hits me: Josh's texts from Saturday night didn't say where or when he was meeting Andy. The specifics about breakfast at Stella's, I got from Andy, and now that I know Stella's was closed...

I take a curve too fast and realize I'm going ninety, a reckless speed for these country roads.

What if Andy lied?

Not just about the location of their meeting, but the time? The day? What if after Andy left my place Saturday night, he went straight to meet Josh? And what if Josh crashed his car on the way to that meeting?

My stomach twists. Yes, that would explain Josh setting up the tent and leaving. But it feels so wrong to doubt Andy... Anyway, why would two grown men meet at night when their conflict could wait until morning? And why would Andy lie about it to me?

Mileage signs pop out of the darkness, like little slaps in the face saying *Slow down, Julia. Slow down.* But my speed feels pretend. I can't really be going ninety-five. What's real? What's not?

Doubting Andy feels like doubting myself. On my Launch Day, Andy's was the first face I saw. My first thought? *Kind.* A gut instinct I've always trusted.

My world is cracking. I'm terrified one minute, reckless the next. I'm hearing voices that aren't there, a ticking that's not there.

I dig my foot into the accelerator, as if I can outrun the thing unfolding in my chest. A thought—a feeling—a core-deep instinct that could split me apart if I let it.

I am not to be trusted.

THEN

"Julia," says a voice, warm with concern. It's Josh. The most welcome sight ever, swimming into focus. His expression, intense. His eyes searching me like I've always wanted to be searched.

"Hi," I say weakly. I register an ice pack on the back of my head, a sling on my arm. I'm on my back on the living room sectional, a ceiling fan spinning high above me. Josh is kneeling to my left, dressed in a T-shirt with circles of sweat under the arms, like he was just working out. I flicker my gaze around the space and register the girls, bunched up at a distance. Watching us, talking in low murmurs. And two cameramen, discreet but present.

"What happened?" I say, focusing back on Josh. "Who *was* that?"

Josh presses my chilly hand between both of his.

"They're looking into it," he says in a husky voice that tells me he's more upset than he's letting on. "She actually got away from show security before the police arrived. But I'm sure they'll find her. It's all on camera."

I shift my head and wince. "Why would she attack me?"

I can't help but remember, again, the flood of comments after my first and only Instagram post to date. It started nice, with various public figures making their statements, including Synth twins Christi and Chrystel, but it quickly devolved, and it wasn't just the biting comments accusing me of not being a real woman.

Less fuckbots and better vaccines, please!

We're in a pandemic and THIS is what science is doing?? What a joke.

Welcome to America Julia where the 1% is making robot sex toys while the 99% are on food stamps. It's great here!!

I had to stop reading.

Could this woman be some kind of anti-Synth activist? The producers did warn me that there was a media leak about my presence on the show…

"Everyone's saying she was a crazy fan," says Josh. "Some of the camera people noticed her last week. I guess she was lurking around the property. My guess is, she saw you alone and took her chance."

"Her chance at what?" I say, feeling stupid and slow.

"Fame?" Josh shakes his head like it's beyond him. "Maybe she wanted to be on camera. Who the hell knows. With people like that…"

I exhale slowly and manage a small nod. At least that feels better than a targeted attack. Though…maybe it's worse that it could have been any of us. I don't know what to feel.

Josh squeezes my hand. "I'm so sorry, Julia. I'm talking to the producers about safety. The fact that this happened is unacceptable."

"Sorry to interrupt," comes a tentative voice. It's Emma, dressed in a bikini and cover-up, her long brown hair spilling over her slim shoulders. The girls' ambassador into the situation, by the looks of it. "We all just want to say we're so sorry, Julia. And if there's anything any of us can do…"

"Thanks," I say. "I appreciate that."

Emma bites her lip. "I was inside the house. I actually saw her jump you. A bunch of us did. We just couldn't get out there fast enough."

"It's so scary," says a petite girl whose name I can't remember. "I almost went for a walk by the pool before you."

"Maybe we should ask the producers for some self-defense training," offers Zoe. "What do you think, Julia? We could all do it together, like, as a team."

"Oh," I say with some surprise. "Sure. I mean, I…can't. But that's a great idea for everyone else."

Her nose scrunches. "Can't?"

"I…can't defend myself in the same way that you all can."

Sure, I can self-protect—but not if it means harming another person. Fighting my assailant? Out of the question. When the woman grabbed my hair, I knew she was about to bash my head, and in the moment, it was like I had no willpower. No spark, no reaction; I went limp and let her do it. Should I find this disturbing? Emma's shocked expression tells me yes.

"Julia, what are you saying?" she says.

I prop myself up despite the shooting pain in my shoulder, glance at Josh, then address the whole group of girls.

"Not all of you know this, but I guess you should. I'm a Synth."

There are audible gasps.

"I can't hurt people," I explain. "It's just not part of my…" I almost say *programming*, but think better. "Instincts."

"But self-defense has to be different, right?" objects Emma, the crowd of girls murmuring loudly behind her, clearly upset.

I shrug my shoulders up an inch.

"It's not different for them," says Camila in a pointed, sharp tone. She steps forward, a striking figure in an elegant black cover-up with a plunging neckline that shows the center string of her white bikini. "Haven't y'all watched *Keeping Up with the*

Synths? Chrystel explained the whole thing after she went public about her sexual assault." Her eyes turn to me. "There's only one case where a Synth can hurt a human. Right, Julia?"

Everyone looks to me for clarification.

I feel like getting technical is just going to make me seem more foreign to them, and to Josh, but I can't shy away now. I have to appear comfortable with myself so that they can be, too. Then we can all move on.

"No Harm coding is black-and-white," I explain. "But there's a separate algorithm called the Leighton Clause because of this case, like, ten years ago. Have you guys heard of Andrea Leighton?"

"Wasn't she in that really bad horror movie?" Zoe pipes up, snapping her fingers. "Night of the...something?"

"She was a Texas oil heiress and aspiring actress," says Camila, calm and in control, for which I'm strangely grateful. "She owned one of those Home Assistant Bots—remember when those came out? Anyway, her boyfriend strangled her in front of it. The Bot could have taken him down and saved her if it wasn't for No Harm. Long story short, there was a public outcry, and Congress passed an exception clause. But there were so many bugs, it didn't roll out until Christi and Chrystel."

"How do *you* know all this?" says Emma.

Cam smiles mirthlessly. "My father's in the oil business. Andrea was a family friend. The Bot that couldn't save her? My dad uses it to clean our pool."

My heart patters uncomfortably.

"So what is the algorithm, exactly?" says Emma, wrinkling her brow.

Cam opens her mouth, but I beat her to it. "If I see someone hurting another person, and the ethical algorithm determines that there's a guilty party and an innocent party worthy of defense, No Harm is bypassed."

"Which means," Camila cuts in, raising a sharp-nailed finger, "that even though Julia couldn't defend herself, if that crazy fan attacked one of *all* y'all—" she pauses, a smirk tugging at her lips "—*then* Julia could've fucked that bitch up."

I get the reference, and give her the slightest smile in return. It strikes me that she could do more damage with that single, manicured nail than I could with my entire body.

"But it doesn't seem right that she could defend us when she can't—" Emma starts again.

"I think what Julia needs right now is our full support," interrupts Josh, his deep voice bringing this whole uncomfortable topic to a welcome end. "And she has it, right?" He's firm, commanding, like a general bringing order to his troops.

The girls' voices rise in agreement, but a smell of fear lingers, and I don't have to ask to know what it's about.

The girls have to be wondering not only what would have happened if they were the ones walking alone by the pool, but what it's like to be me: helpless. At the mercy of any lunatic who wants to hurt me.

I lick my lips. I've loved being Julia ever since Launch Day. I've relished my body, my feelings—even the hard emotions, like my ever-present gnawing hunger for Josh's affection. But there's something new within me. A seed of distress. I don't like that I'm fundamentally…weak. My thoughts rush to comfort me. *Isn't everyone fundamentally weak, at some level?* And yet…

"We're all behind you, Julia," says Josh, his voice full of warmth. "I promise you that nothing like this will ever happen again when you're with me."

"It's not your responsibility to protect me." My voice cracks, because I don't want this dynamic. I want to be pure fun for Josh. Not a burden, dragging him down.

I cover my face because suddenly, tears are wetting my cheeks. I don't know how to name everything I'm feeling, but I hate that it's getting the best of me.

"Sorry. I wasn't going to fall apart," I say, my voice muffled behind my hands.

The girls descend. I can't see them, but I can hear them, feel them, like a flock of birds, settling at the foot of the couch, on either side of Josh, drawing close, surrounding me like a protective wall.

"You have all of us," says a female voice, sweet and steely. Camila. "We're in this together."

I uncover my eyes, utterly shocked by this display of support from the very last person I would have expected. We look at each other for a solid three seconds. I can't describe what passes between us. Only that it's powerful, and that some of the steel in her seems to enter me.

I reach up a hand. We thread our fingers together; she presses tight. My voice comes out throaty. "Thanks, Texas."

Camila gives me a half smile. "Sure thing, Red."

And then, as if moved by her display of affection toward me, Josh enfolds both our hands in his grasp and squeezes, making an odd bond of three.

"We'll take care of her, right?" says Camila, breaking our gaze and locking eyes with Josh.

"Absolutely," he says.

The burn of jealousy and suspicion is so fierce and sudden, I could retch. But, with my hand trapped between theirs, I try to muscle my emotions toward the right things—the things Josh might love me for: trust, kindness, gratitude.

"Thanks," I say in a gentle tone, and as Josh's eyes slip away from Camila and back to me, I tamp down the hot swell of victory under a delicate smile. "You guys are the sweetest."

NOW

Walmart after eight o'clock is a dystopia, empty and overlarge. They're pumping tinny vintage pop music into the atmosphere like a noxious gas, and the soaring industrial ceilings give it a ghostly echo.

I'm a bundle of anxiety and exhaustion as I jog my gigantic cart through the endless aisles, trying to find baby wipes, sweating under my snug fleece. I normally shop at the smaller local grocery co-op, but that's east of Eauverte and would take me thirty minutes out of my way.

"Come on," I say with genuine distress as I turn into an aisle of pet food. Didn't the greeter say aisle 26? I spin around a corner into garden supplies. Where the hell is the baby stuff?

"Excuse me?" I call toward a woman standing much farther down, the only person I've seen here so far since the greeter. The woman lifts her head but says nothing. Probably a shopper, not an employee, but I don't even care at this point. "Do you know where the baby wipes are?"

She stares at me as I trundle the cart toward her, past fertilizer and decorative pink flamingos and all-weather party lights. Did she hear me? She's still as a statue, a single terra-cotta planter in her hand. Older middle-aged, maybe sixty, kind of slumped, like her spine is made of wicker instead of bone. Her wisp-thin hair is dyed an awful cheap carroty red.

I stop a couple feet from her, breathing heavily. God, I can't wait to take off this fleece.

"Baby wipes?" I repeat.

She just shakes her head, her pale blue eyes wide.

Could you be any creepier? I think, but I force myself to say, "Thanks anyway," in a pleasant tone.

As I turn into the next aisle, I cast a quick look back. She's still staring, and then—

"Julia!" she cries in an unearthly voice. The shock of surprise gives me wings; I fly around the corner, the cart lifting off one side. I should be used to the recognition that comes with being something of a celebrity, but it still manages to feel like an attack every damn time.

I race all the way to the end of the aisle with a death grip on my shopping cart, make a sharp turn, then another, in case she's decided to come after me.

I never imagined that being a Synth would contaminate nearly every outing. In the past, I've tried to hide under sunglasses and oversize sweatshirts. I even purchased a wig once, but it was itchy, and the two times I wore it, I felt even more conspicuous. Anyway, I don't *want* to have to hide to be acceptable.

Andy has reminded me so many times that we're playing the long game with Synth rights. That our focus needs to be earning the public's trust, and that my social media has an important role to play. *Regular, relatable content*, he's drilled into me. *They need to see you're just like them.* But it all feels so burdensome. I don't want to spend my every waking moment thinking up that next great post that will make me seem likable, trustworthy, deserving. I don't want to have to work so hard to convince everyone that I'm a person. I don't want to be my own saleswoman on a team of one... And maybe this is the price of being different, but

I didn't choose this price, I didn't even choose to exist, so why is it on me to keep paying it, when all I want is—

Wipes. Right in front of me. Hallelujah. I load three bulk boxes into the cart, followed by two jumbo boxes of diapers, because the fewer shopping trips I have to make, the better. I pause once, thinking I heard steps, but it's nothing. Still, I don't want to linger. I practically sprint toward the exit. There are two registers open. I choose the one with the younger employee. Less likely to be clued in to who I am, and less likely to care.

Sure enough, the bored teenager barely gives me a glance. I could hug her for her blessed indifference. As she scans my items, I check my phone. New text from Cam.

I'm thru in Indy Friday afternoon. Want a weekend guest?

YES! I reply. Normally I'd toss in a few emojis—champagne glasses, kissy faces, hearts—but considering what I have to tell her about Josh, it seems in bad taste. Three dots tell me she's already replying. The message pops through.

I'll bring the hard stuff.

I can't help but smile. It warms me to think of Cam on the other side of this exchange, tapping away at her phone, thinking of me. Despite the seriousness of Josh missing, I can't resist having a bit of fun after all. I type, **You mean the tequila or your new dildo?**

Her laughing emojis fill an entire text bubble followed by **you bad bitch you just made me pee a little.**

There's also a new text from Eden, but this one does not bring a smile.

Don't want to stress u out but the sheriff stopped by. He left something 4 u. Sorry!!! An anxiety-faced emoji follows.

"Fuck," I breathe.

"Enjoy your evening," says the teen in a deadpan voice.

I cut the twenty-minute drive home to twelve and screech into the driveway at 8:35. I can't get out of the car fast enough—the purchases can wait.

I stumble inside, all frantic energy, half expecting to see my house completely overturned by Mitchell and his cronies. But everything looks normal. Peaceful. It even smells good—like evergreen. Eden has lit one of my fancy candles.

And yet, nothing in me feels peaceful. Hasn't it always been like that for me? At odds with my environment. But is it something wrong with the environment, or me? On my way to the family room, I pass the small bedroom that we repurposed into a playroom and glance inside. I can almost see the skeletal ridges of the hospital bed that used to occupy this room. I shiver and walk on.

Eden's in the family room off the kitchen, snacking on microwave popcorn and messing around on her laptop. Captain, sprawled on the rug at her feet, is fast asleep.

The domestic scene feels...

Wrong.

Wrong like the tent Josh didn't sleep in, wrong like speeding in the night when your daughter needs you safe, wrong like...

Tick-tick-tick.

Oh, God. Josh's watch...like a finger tapping, counting down the seconds to something, something *bad*. The peace of this scene is butcher paper, hiding something rotten underneath that I don't want to see; it's all going so fast, mileage signs flying past in the night, and like a car lifting on a violent curve, the scene in front of me is tilting. Something terrible happened in this place, and Captain knows it—my dog's instincts have never been wrong—something to ruin every fantasy, smash every dream, and I'm slipping off the edge...

"You're back," Eden says, and snaps the laptop shut, snapping my strange slip-slide of thoughts closed, too. Her face looks soft in the low lamplight. Round, almost childlike.

Nothing terrible has happened here, except for the obvious: Josh disappearing. It's just my exhaustion, my adrenaline.

I probably spilled something on the rug; that's why Captain was so interested. Cheerios. Cookie crumbs. Take your pick.

"The sheriff came?" My voice, stripped of its normal layers of politeness, sounds harsh. Demanding. For once, I don't care. "What did he say? Is Annaleigh okay?"

Captain wakes at the sound of my voice, getting to his feet so suddenly he's falling over himself. He's at my side, large and comforting, and I bury my hand in the fur on his head.

"He was here a few hours ago." Eden tucks her laptop into her backpack. "I should have texted right away but... I didn't want to freak you out. Then I thought maybe it was better if you showed up knowing?" She looks a little guilty, a little upset. Normally I'd go out of my way to reassure her.

"What did he say?" I repeat. I'm used to looking at myself through the camera-eyes of others, so I know what Eden is see-ing now. Not the bold, fearless person I try to project. Weak Julia. Unhinged Julia. Paranoid Julia.

But if I'm paranoid, it's because they've made me paranoid. If I fear the worst, it's because they've taught me how easily the strong can take down the weak...

"He wanted to know where you were. How long you'd been gone."

"Did you tell him?"

"Um...not where you were, because you didn't tell me, but... yes? I said you left around lunch and were coming home around dinner. Should I have—"

"No. It's fine. You said he left something?"

She gestures to the kitchen counter, but all I can find is my grocery list, sitting where it always does.

Ah. Right under my pencil list of *baby wipes, broccoli, milk* is scrawled, in blue ink:

I know how to run a damn plate.

Idiot. Of course the officer who saw me run away from Josh's tent took an interest in my vehicle. Especially if Miss Pert pointed it out. All that skulking in the woods with aching breasts? Could've saved myself the trouble.

So. Mitchell knows I lied about not remembering the camp-site. He knows I booked it there after his morning visit, right after telling him that I couldn't join the search party because of my baby. He probably imagines I tampered with evidence. All of this, I'm sure, adds to his imaginary case against me.

What if I'd just told them the stupid campsite name when they asked? Or better—what if I'd gone to the campsite *before* filing the missing person report?

"What does it mean?" says Eden.

"Oh…" I say. I stop rubbing my collarbone. I didn't realize I was even doing it. I've irritated the skin.

"Are you okay?" Eden has sidled up to me, backpack slung over her shoulder.

"I don't know." My voice comes out shaky. I hate this. I need the world to slow down. *I* need to slow down…but if I don't stay five steps ahead…

"I'd better—" I gesture at the ceiling. Check on Annaleigh, shower, go to bed.

"I'll see myself out," says Eden. She hesitates. "You know where to find me."

Upstairs, I open Annaleigh's door quietly. It smells like baby powder and magnolia and that ineffably sweet smell that I know comes from Annaleigh herself. It's pitch-dark inside, with only the green light of the baby monitor piercing through, but the soft light from the hallway is enough for me to see her outline in the crib. Sleeping; safe.

I turn toward my room and the promise of a hot shower, but trip over Captain. He yelps as I stumble into the wall, knocking my head hard.

The spike of pain brings a flash of dark blue.

The California sky at twilight.

Memories explode so vividly, it's like I've been transported in time.

I'm poolside, on my back. A face above. Pale blue eyes. The woman. Attacking me for no reason I can discern. Hating me for no reason I can discern.

I suddenly realize who I just saw at Walmart.

Her hair is carrot red now, not gray, but the eyes are the same. Her expression, the same. Looking at me without emotion. As if I was the pot she picked up in aisle 27, my body nothing more to her than a mass-produced terra-cotta container. Empty of anything growing. An object she wanted to smash. Fragile. Defenseless.

It could have been any of us, we all said—but I should have trusted my first instinct.

It was me she was after all along.

THEN

"Andy," I say with surprise. I was about to step onto the lighted stage area where I'm filming a confessional about the attack when I heard someone call my name. I reverse course and pick my way in my high heels over cords and cables to meet him behind the cameras. A weird feeling of déjà vu spreads over me as I bend to hug him.

"Julia. God, it's good to see you." His embrace brings a hint of spicy cologne competing with a layer of BO.

We pull back at the same time and survey each other.

Andy is dressed in a flannel button-down over a black T-shirt. Baggy jeans, the rectangular bulk of a phone in his front pocket. A pen hooked over his shirt pocket. He looks both put together and messy, like a puppy dog who got groomed and then rolled around in the yard. I, on the other hand, am fresh out of an hour-long session with hair and makeup, in silk cigarette pants and a one-shoulder sequin top that displays the bruising to my shoulder.

"I wasn't expecting to see you again so soon!" I say with a smile that I hope reads as welcoming despite my unease. *The Proposal* is ultra-secretive during filming. No one is supposed to know what happens here…right?

Andy runs a hand through his hair. "Yeah, neither was I. They called me about the, uh, incident. The attack." He shakes his head. "If I could've come last night…"

"I didn't realize they were involving you," I say lightly.

"Can I just take a moment to apologize to you, for what happened?"

"Please. It's not your fault."

"But I feel responsible, Julia. It's like I released this sweet bunny rabbit into a fucking den of wolves. This is the last thing I *ever* wanted to happen to you." Again, Andy runs a hand through his curly mop of hair, further disordering it. "*Jesus.* I'm still in shock."

"You know, I'm actually okay." I touch his arm, trying to recover the sense of calm I was feeling before his arrival, and transmit it to Andy as well. Not only is the attack behind me, but to my surprise, good things have come of it. Yes, it's horrible to be faced with my built-in limitations. But on the other side of it—though I can't pretend not to have heard some whispers of *attention getter*—the girls really do seem friendlier. Josh even came by this morning to check on me, and held my hand while we talked. I kept looking at his arrow tattoo and wondering if the attack might be shifting his heart's direction toward me. Maybe people can't open their hearts until vulnerability creates a connection point. I don't know. It's a lot to process, but I'd be a fool to ignore the silver lining.

"There he is!" comes a sharp, female voice. Andy and I both turn. Half a dozen people in suits are moving toward us like a dark school of fish.

"Viola," says Andy. He shakes hands with the petite woman leading the pack, then turns to me. "Julia, meet Viola, our head counsel at WekTech. The rest of these suckers are her goons." Light laughter moves through the remaining men and women as Viola extends a hand toward me.

"Hello, Julia." Her grip is cool and firm. "It's so nice to finally meet you."

All of a sudden I feel very frivolous in my sequined top and wedge heels.

"What's going on?" I say, hoping my bright smile conceals the spark of fear trying to ignite in my stomach.

"We're here to meet with the *Proposal* production team to discuss last night's unacceptable security breach and go over next steps," says Viola in a voice as manicured as her look.

"Next steps?"

Viola tilts her head. "As a Synth, your legal personhood is in question, so unfortunately, you can't file charges yourself. Therefore, the best route is for WekTech to file for criminal property damage. That woman deserves to spend time behind bars for what she did." The ultra-sincerity of her tone is sickly in its sweetness. "I know this may sound overwhelming. But, Julia, rest assured that WekTech will take care of *everything* for you. We presented a thorough list of security demands to *Proposal* execs. If production can't be amenable, we'll pull you from the show."

Wait—what?

But before I can respond, Viola smiles, says, "Shall we?" and leads her group away with an airy "Nice to meet you, Julia" tossed out like a final piece of candy from the lawyer parade.

"I'll be right behind you," Andy says to Viola as he gestures for her to go on.

For a second, alone again with Andy, I can hardly breathe, hardly gather my thoughts into words. I feel like a tornado just whipped through me.

Who am I kidding. True vulnerability isn't nice. It's awful. These people have the power to remove me from my very purpose. If they take me off the show—if I don't find love with Josh—

"What is happening?" I whisper.

"It might feel like we're going overboard, but this is serious,

Julia," Andy says. "We didn't bring you here just to be assaulted. We can't let that happen again."

"It could've been any of us. She was just a crazy fan. Trust me, Andy. It's *not* going to happen again."

"We need to consider what's best for you."

"The show is my life. Josh is the future I want." I've never heard my own voice sound this way. Stretched taut. Pleading. "This is my chance at happiness, Andy. Don't I get a say?"

For a second there's something between us—something that feels dangerous, like a sleeping monster I've tapped on the shoulder. Then Andy exhales and rubs his face.

"Fuck. Of *course* you get a say, Julia. Look. Whatever the legal reality is for Synths, you're a person to me. A full person, okay? If you want to stay, you stay. I'll give my recommendations, but you call the shots."

The wave of relief is so powerful, my knees might buckle. Andy's on my side. He has my back.

"Thank you." I release a ragged breath. "I want to stay."

"Hey, this is all about you."

Then, Andy's off to join the meeting, and I'm back to the confessional. There's a quick light test. Someone powders my forehead and nose. As the crew does their thing, something Andy said pricks my mind like a burr. *Just to be assaulted.* I know what happened was awful. But the way he said it felt so...reductive. Like the attack was the main event of my life, and everything else, a mere footnote to those few seconds of violence.

I take a few deep breaths. The past twenty-four hours have been chaos. In this interview, I want to be self-possessed. Prove that even though the attacker hurt my body, she didn't destroy *me*. In fact, she doesn't define anything about me. I'm here to fall in love. I'm bigger than this, and my life is bigger than this, and I am moving on.

When I open my eyes, I'm ready. The producer signals that

the cameras are rolling, then says, "Walk us through your first reaction when you were attacked."

I face the cameras and jump in. "It happened so fast. Like, one minute I'm enjoying a moment to myself, and the next moment, I'm on the ground."

I answer question after question. I talk about how since last night, the girls have really stepped up. I talk about how lucky I am to have such supportive people around me.

I close the interview by saying, "What happened, happened. It was outside of my control. But I can control the way I move forward. That's what I want to focus on."

I'm proud of myself, and I truly feel like the bigger person. Maybe this attack has proved that I can be rattled and recover. Beat down, then get back up. And isn't that a kind of strength?

When the producer calls cut and I stand to shake the sleepy tingles out of my left foot, there's another surprise waiting: Josh. Standing in the shadows behind the crew. Watching me with his arms crossed, in joggers and a T-shirt that does nothing to hide his ripped torso. The fabric clings to every muscle, and I find myself thinking of the kiss we shared.

I give him a cute wave, then walk toward him.

We meet just outside the hot circle of light that surrounds the stage. To my astonishment, he leans forward and kisses me on the lips. It's brief, just a peck, nothing like the heated exploration of the other night, but it still sends a waterfall of tingles down my neck.

I'm about to make a cheeky remark about wanting more where that came from when Josh turns. Someone is walking toward us—Andy. My stomach flip-flops; the timing couldn't be worse. Josh only recently learned I'm a Synth. How is he going to react when he realizes this is the man who designed me? *Shit.*

"So...that's, um, Andy. From WekTech," I say quickly.

Josh looks blank, then realization dawns.

"The company that—" he begins as I return a tight nod.

"You must be Josh LaSala," says Andy as he reaches us, swinging his arm forward to meet Josh's shake. "So pleased to finally
meet you. I'm Andy Wekstein, Julia's—"

"I know who you are," says Josh in an easy tone, like he knew
all along.

I'm ridiculously grateful Andy didn't finish his sentence—and
that Josh is playing it so cool.

The two men are a study in contrasts. But beyond their many
physical differences, Andy gives off the vibe of a kid playing
dress-up in a grown man's body, whereas Josh fully owns every
inch of his muscled height.

They shake hands a little too long. I notice Josh's flexed forearm...how hard are they pressing? When they fall back, they
both start talking at once. Both stop. Josh chuckles.

Andy speaks. "I was just going to tell Julia, I'm headed out."

"The meeting—" I prompt.

"Taken care of," says Andy.

"Thank you," I say with a tension-releasing sigh.

"What meeting?" says Josh.

"Boring legal stuff," says Andy. I think he means to be friendly,
but it sounds demeaning, like he's suggesting Josh wouldn't get
it anyway.

"Just about the attack," I clarify.

Josh's eyes flicker between me and Andy, then settle on Andy.

"You don't have to worry about Julia." Josh's voice sounds
deeper than usual. There's a gentle pressure at the small of my
back. Josh's hand. Warm, solid. "I already told her last night, I'm
not letting anything happen to her. I mean that."

Andy nods vigorously, like he's really absorbing this. "I'm
glad you said that. Really glad, man. I just—" He lays a hand
to his heart. "Violence against women. I don't have the stomach for it. You know? I feel pretty sick over this. And honestly,
a little complicit."

I feel embarrassed at Andy's display of emotion, but Josh seems to take it in stride.

"She's with me now," he says in that same deep, steady tone, and even though I don't say anything in response, an answering thrill moves through me.

The producer cuts into our moment. "Could we get you back up here, Julia?"

I signal for her to wait.

"Good to see you, Andy," I say, leaning forward. Josh's hand remains on my back as I brush my cheek against Andy's in an air kiss.

Then Andy is off. I look at Josh and bite my thumb, wishing I could recover the moment we lost right after his quick kiss.

"I'd better get back up there," I say with regret.

"Wait." Josh leans in and whispers, "What do you say? You and me tomorrow? For the next one-on-one date?"

In all the chaos of the attack, the filming of Josh's dating decision got put off.

"Really?" I say, pulling back a little to look into his eyes.

He smiles, dimples deepening. "I really like you."

"Even after all this drama?"

"Especially since all this drama. The way you handle yourself is so...classy. And—" His breath smells like mint. Our faces are inches apart, his words only for me. "Is it weird that this proved to me you're, like, a real person?"

"Not weird at all," I say as joy blossoms in my stomach.

How wonderfully ironic that the attacker, who wanted to hurt me, ended up drawing Josh and me closer than ever. Now Josh can see that I'm not a cold machine, but a person who can bleed like him. Maybe I *had* to bleed, to earn his love. And right now the bruised shoulder and handful of scrapes seem like a small price to pay for this. For him.

I'm staying on the show.

Josh said, *She's with me now.*

I couldn't be happier.

NOW

I'm not safe. I'll never be safe, I'm telling myself as I shampoo my hair, trying to wash away the disquieting realization that the woman who attacked me in LA is here in Southern Indiana. It can't be a coincidence. Did she follow me from California after the show? And yet, Josh and I have been here for nearly a year, and I've never seen her before.

There has been plenty of anonymous vandalism to our property. Was she behind any of that? Watching from the woods—waiting for her chance to finish the job—

I scrub deeper into my scalp in response to my quickening heartbeat. I'd get a restraining order, if the sheriff's department was willing to do its job. Security did identify her; I wish I could remember her name. I bet Andy does. I should call Andy.

But this brings another wave of stress. I don't want to talk to Andy, because then I'll have to question him about his meeting with Josh.

Hot water, just south of scalding, streams down my weary body. The shower is normally a place of refuge for me, of resetting after a stressful day, of feeling safe and pampered. But now it's reminding me of my weaknesses. I don't even mean my No Harm coding—it goes deeper. I need rest. Sleep. Food. I want to search for Josh through the night, I don't want to stop until he's home safe...but I can't. Not even my love for him is strong enough to bypass these needs.

It's hard to imagine, after my shower, going to bed, sleeping under these circumstances. But I have to face it: I can't do anything more tonight.

Can't.

A fascinating, terrible, maddening word.

I rinse and watch the shampoo rush toward the drain in a bubbling white river.

I've never minded my dampers. Eating just like Josh, needing sleep just like Josh, getting tired, needing breaks, zoning out—all those things made me feel like a person to Josh. My one-hundred-fifty-million Instagram followers love seeing me in this light, too. My most-liked post to date is a recent selfie captioned **Messy house, happy life,** with me looking like an exhausted wreck, my unwashed hair in a sloppy topknot and the kitchen in ruins behind me courtesy of Annaleigh's first experience with applesauce.

Weakness. There's something about it that draws people in. I've known that since the attack in LA. But today, I don't have any of my usual sweet feelings toward this reality.

I squirt conditioner into my palm and work it through my long hair. What would it look like to remove the dampers from my programming? To root out all my weaknesses?

I could take care of my baby with infinite patience, because I'd never be tired...search for Josh all night...walk the woods without fear, because I'd be stronger than anyone I could possibly meet...

I imagine my hands around Sheriff Mitchell's neck. Watching his veins pop out, his eyes bulge. Counting down the final lurches of his heart as his mouth opens and closes helplessly. I feel my lips lifting in a snarl. *Three, two, one...*

Oh my God—*stop it!* What kind of sick, twisted fantasy—

I'm a monster, something dark within me answers. My daughter needs a strong protector, there's no one else, I have to be willing to do whatever it takes—

I hear myself in the distance objecting, saying, *I am what I am*, but it's not my voice, it's Andy's, and his voice is loud, a fox's scream, as he pounds his heart, *You are what I made you*, and I'm trying to do what's right, trying to figure out what to do with the broken things I've been handed, this busted-apart life on the land where twenty-two girls were busted apart by one handsome man with his winning smile and his axe, but the world is spasming around me, and suddenly, a spider-thin crack splits the bathtub under my feet, snaking toward me, fast and vicious, through the tender soles of my feet and into my bone, shooting upward, toward the center of me, splitting me in two—

I gasp.

Squeeze my eyes shut, open them. Not real.

I am whole, I am here, and I'm just fucking...

Tired.

I turn the water off and step out of the shower, bringing a billow of steam with me. Reach for a towel and flip my hair upside down to squeeze it dry. My skin feels overheated and a little tender. A reminder to be gentle with myself as I towel my body.

Tired people can't think straight. I've got to sleep.

And then, I hear a little cry.

Annaleigh, awake for her first night feeding. And even though I'm nearly dead on my feet, I can't resent her for being needy right now.

I toss the towel on the floor, pull on a robe. Captain has settled on my bed, and he lifts his head as I leave the master bedroom, like he's asking, *Need anything from me?*

"You stay. I'll be right back," I promise. Captain follows me anyway. Good dog.

In the velvet dark of the nursery, my hands find Annaleigh's solid shape. I may be tired, shaky, spent, but holding Annaleigh's warm little body against mine, all of a sudden strength rushes in and I'm big and strong and capable again. How strange and wonderful that I am all she needs. It strikes me that maybe right now, I *need* to be needed by the small, trusting person in my arms. Within seconds, she's latched, making that soft rhythmic murmur I can never get enough of. One of her hands wraps around the open edge of my robe. It's so peaceful and so relaxing that I feel myself dozing even though I'm still on my feet.

A lullaby plays in my head.

Each night when you are sleeping within your little bed...

The melody is gentle, soothing, and I find myself swaying in place, as if the song is a loving pair of arms, holding me while I hold Annaleigh. I feel Captain sit up from the place where his head was resting by my feet.

...two angels, vigil keeping, stand guarding at your head...

The baby monitor crackles sharply. Captain barks. I start awake.

The song is not in my head. Someone is singing into the baby monitor. A man—not Josh—lower, gravelly—

One provides protection, the other brings you peace...

I let out a dry shriek that feels like it was pulled from me. Annaleigh unlatches and lets out a wail to tear my eardrum as I stumble through the dark toward the dresser, my fingers reaching for the little green light of the monitor. I yank. It comes unplugged, bringing the lamp with it. There's a crash of things falling in the dark as I turn back to the door, groping for the main light switch. Captain, barking, is already tumbling around the room. The lights flick on, blinding bright. Annaleigh blinks in confusion, momentarily stunned into silence. She whimpers. Her pouted lip trembles; she's about to wail again.

"Shhh," I say as I wrench open the closet, pull her crib away from the wall one-handed, yank the bins out from under the changing table even though they're way too small for anyone to hide in, still holding a stunned Annaleigh. Captain is behind me at every step, colliding with me, eager to help. Only when the room has been turned upside down do I stop.

"Oh my God," I say out loud. "Oh my God, oh my God." I fall to my knees, Annaleigh clutched to my chest. Someone has the parent side of the monitor. Someone sang to my baby. The same voice that said good-morning to her. Not my imagination. A real, actual man. Who? Why? What the fuck is happening?

Captain whines and noses my side. It's a miracle I haven't dropped Annaleigh. After rooting around and finding my breast again, she's nursing, and she shivers out the last of her distress, but my heart is a wild beast, slamming against the walls of my chest. Annaleigh unlatches again. I switch off the lights, settle her into her crib.

I get the baseball bat.

I'm neither asleep nor awake, but in some awful in-between state as I scour the house from top to bottom. Every inch of the basement. Behind the water heater, in the creepy tool closet, inside the washer and dryer. I open every door, every closet, move every piece of furniture, turn on every light.

Josh is gone and I'm seeing cracks that aren't there and a stranger has been in my house.

I'm exhausted. Frantic. From my fantasy life, I've fallen like Alice, but not into Wonderland, into a nightmare that won't let me go, and I have the horrible feeling I haven't yet reached the bottom.

THEN

"So that was your first time on the water?" says Josh.

I bracket my face with my hands. "I am so sorry I got sick. Talk about embarrassing moments."

It's evening and the sun is planting its final languid kiss on the horizon. Josh and I are having dinner, which represents the last leg of our magical one-on-one date. The day has flown by, but has also felt like an eternal present, each moment complete with some ineffable fullness.

"You were a cute sicky." Josh grins at me from across the beautifully set table.

We picked at our salads, and now we're picking at our steaks. Our fancy dinner is a little gimmicky, with the crisp linens, layers of silverware, and multiple wineglasses. Neither of us is that hungry anyway—I'm much more looking forward to finishing our evening in the natural rock hot tub to our left, its tantalizing curls of steam rising into the cool evening. Plush white towels lie ready and waiting on two lounge chairs.

It's been a perfect day. Not perfect like nothing went wrong. Not only did I puke, but a bird pooped on my shoulder, and Josh cut his foot on a shell. But perfect in a deeper way. Like together we shaped this unique piece of history to add to the relationship we're building. Now we'll always have our day at the beach with the puke and the bird and the shell.

"Tell me more about how cute I was while I vomited," I say with the slightest sardonic tone.

"All moany, like *Josh, Josh*—"

I lean across to swat his arm. "No way! I was very self-sufficient. I got it all in the wineglass, remember? Or…" I grin. "Most of it."

"I had no idea you had such a delicate stomach," he teases.

"Neither did I," I groan. "No more boats. That's all I ask."

He raises his eyebrow and his wineglass. "A small ask."

"I'll do anything else." I clasp my hands dramatically. "Rappelling into a creepy cave, eating insects—"

He laughs. "But the beach was fun."

The date started with a boat trip up the coast to a private beach, where we spent the late morning and afternoon lounging in the sun and picnicking, with plenty of chilled wine. Spreading suntan lotion all over Josh's body was a revelation. The springy firmness of his muscles, the shape of his bones. The feelings in my own body as I massaged the coconut-scented lotion into every inch of his exposed flesh and he teased *a little more to the left* and *ooh, rub harder*.

"You have cute ears," I say.

"Cute *ears*?"

"Yes! They're tanned, and attached, and cute." I got a good look when I was pinching them between my thumb and index finger to get the suntan lotion worked in.

"I'm not sure how to feel about your obsession with my ears." Josh twirls a pretend mustache. "Are there any other parts of me you thought were…cute?"

I laugh full-out. "You're a big goof, did you know that?"

I've only discovered this today, and I love that I know it now. Before today I was attracted mostly to Josh's sexiness, which *is* significant, drawn mostly by intense feelings I couldn't explain.

Today, that's changed. Today, I'm attracted to his humor. The way he doesn't fill all the airspace with talk. His calm in the face of vomit. The way he rolls with the punches. And his ears really are cute. Each of these details are a foothold as I climb higher, toward surer ground.

He smiles, pleased, and takes a bite of steak.

He looks so good tonight, dressed in a white shirt, open at the neck, that makes his tan glow. I'm in white, too—a sleeveless cocktail dress, which fits me like a glove and brings out the sun-kissed freckles on my shoulders. The halter tie of the turquoise bikini I'm wearing underneath peeks out the top of the dress, providing Josh with what I hope is a fun tease of what's to come.

"So, dinner. This is our time for serious talk, right?" I say. It's been pretty light and jokey all day, and I want to make sure we connect on a deeper level, too, since I have no idea when I'll get such a luxury of uninterrupted time with him next. Also, if Emma or another of the girls brings up compatibility, I want to have an answer.

"Let's do it," Josh says. "Where should we start?"

"Family. Tell me about your parents. Are you close? Siblings. Do you have any?"

"Only child," he says, chewing and swallowing before dabbing his mouth with a cloth napkin. "I was born in Southern Indiana. Mom still lives there. Little town called Eauverte."

"Come again?"

"It's French for *green water*. We pronounce it O-vert. Accent on the *O*."

"*O*-vert," I practice.

"Perfect. Anyway, I live in Indianapolis, which is about two hours north of Eauverte. I try to go down and have dinner with Mom once or twice a month. She's lonely. I keep trying to convince her to move to Indy, but…"

"And your dad?" I say softly.

"They divorced when I was eight. He moved to Chicago. We

don't talk. Mom kind of spies on him through social media. I guess he has a girlfriend now? She's a model. And younger than me. So that's not weird at all."

"Have you met her? Or...would you want to?"

"Hell no. I don't want anything to do with that asshole."

There's a small silence. I sip at my wine, giving a second for his strong emotion to blow away.

Josh puts down his utensils. "Sorry. That was uncalled-for. All you did was ask a question." A tiny grin crinkles his mouth. "I guess I have daddy issues, huh?"

"Don't worry about it. Honestly, how could you not?" Actually, I love how confidently he just owned his issues. "When's the last time you talked to him?"

"He called on my tenth birthday. Oh, and he sent a card when I graduated from high school. No message, no gift. Just his initials inside the card."

"He didn't sign it *Dad*?"

"Nope." He pops his lips on the *p*.

"Wow." I reach across the table and cover Josh's hand with mine. "I'm so sorry. You didn't deserve that."

He smiles fast, too fast, like he's used to putting a good face on it. "Yeah, everyone has their shit, you know? But what can you do? That's life. And now, here I am with you, in this beautiful place, finishing a delicious dinner after a perfect day. I can't complain."

"That's fair," I laugh. "I love how positive you are. I mean— I admire that kind of strength."

It's the same strength I recognized in myself after the attack. Bouncing back after tragedy. Finding the silver lining. I promised him we'd have similarities, and I really hope he's seeing this one as clearly as I am. *See, Emma? Our connection isn't shallow. We just needed time to discover its depth.*

Josh shrugs my compliment off, but I can tell he's pleased. "Tell me about your family," he says, then catches himself. "Oh, right." There's a nervous patter in my heart as I wait for him to keep going. Of *course* now he's landing on a major difference.

He laughs awkwardly. "I have this list of questions in my mind, you know? To ask all the girls. But… I guess you're different, huh?"

"What questions? Out of curiosity?"

"You know. About past relationships. Like, dating history. You don't have any. Family—you don't have any. Childhood memories, college experience, career—"

"No baggage," I say lightly, trying for a positive spin.

He nods slowly. "Yeah. No baggage. No fights about which parents to spend the holidays with."

"No exes for you to worry about."

"That's a plus," he jokes, pointing a fork at me. "I can actually be pretty jealous."

I smile. "I think that's cute."

"I think *you're* cute." He grins. "What do you say we move this party to the hot tub?"

Disaster averted. We both worked to see the positive and overcame the hiccup. Another reason Josh is the right person for me, and me for him.

"I'd say yes, please."

I peel my dress off poolside. Josh has his swim trunks on under his fancy clothes, and soon we're casting our finery on a lounge chair, along with the mic packs that can't get wet. Our clothes look good mingled together like that. Our shoes, too, the soft brown leather of his against the bright aqua of my strappy heels, tumbled together like they've just had the time of their lives. We hold hands as we approach the frothing water. I dip a toe in.

"That feels so good."

We sink into the pool. The rush of heat is heavenly. I close my eyes and dip my head back to wet my hair. Then I go under all the way. When I come back up, Josh is studying me, like he's wondering if he should make a move or not. I think he wants to.

"Is it weird to you that I'm inexperienced? With relation-ships?" I say, trying to interpret his hesitation.

"I don't know," he says, floating closer and knocking his knees against mine before pushing back. "I kind of like it. Being your first."

"I like it, too," I say in a low voice, not that that will stop the mics from picking it up, but still. "I feel like I can trust you with all of my firsts."

The atmosphere changes. He glides closer. Only his shoul-ders are above the waterline, solid, glistening. Our bodies un-derneath are blue, smooth, ghostly. When he's right in front of me, I place one of my hands on each of his shoulders, wrapping my fingers around the solid muscle. I'm aware of every breath, every droplet of water, every millimeter separating our bodies. I dip my chin and look up at him shyly, feeling the kiss of my wet lashes against my cheeks as I blink slowly.

"Julia, what are you doing to me?" he breathes, and then, he's kissing me.

This time, I'm more prepared for the sensations that follow. The heat in my stomach. The feeling of melting into Josh, the water, the moment.

There's pressure on the small of my back, spanning the line of my bikini bottom. His hand, pressing me closer, until we're locked hip to hip. I can feel every hard contour of his fitting into every soft hollow of mine. My breath comes short. He pulls away and looks into my eyes. His look is possessive, and I love it.

"You got a sunburn," he says, and tenderly lifts the halter strap of my bikini top.

"Oh." I crane to see. The skin is a little pink, with a white line running through. "I guess someone did a bad job putting suntan lotion on me."

"Am I bad, Julia?" he says with a glint in his eyes.

"No," I say. "You're too good to be true."

Still holding the strap off my skin, he lowers his head and

kisses the white line, following its length from the corner of my bikini where it tucks under my arm, up across my chest, and finally around the side of my neck. My head falls back. Holy *hell*.

"Is this okay?" he asks, pulling back again. I don't have to see myself in a mirror to know I'm flushed, like all the blood is rushing across my skin to meet these new sensations.

"Yeah," I gasp. Then, my body weak and soft and helpless in his arms, I whisper the only word I can manage. "More."

His mouth sinks into mine and my legs instinctually float up in the water to surround his waist. My fingers find the silky-wet hair at the base of his neck. He braces his forearm against my back and I tighten my legs in response. Now my face is above his, and I'm the one to press down, deepening our kiss, drawing a groan from Josh.

My entire body feels swollen with desire. If there weren't cameras watching, I'd peel off my bikini. I want to know what it feels like for all of me to touch him. For us to be completely melded, no barriers. Then, like a wet slap, I remember them.

The other girls.

"What's wrong?" he says.

"I— Nothing." I bite my lip. I didn't plan this, and it's probably not strategic, but I can't hold it in. "Today was…everything. I think I might be starting to fall for you, and…" I trace his jawline with a single finger. "I'm scared, Josh. I've known you for… less than two weeks. These feelings—" I shake my head.

"Don't be scared, Miss Julia." He tucks my hair behind my ear, his touch achingly tender.

I cup my wet hands on either side of his face. My voice is a whisper. "You could break my heart."

He doesn't answer, but tips his head so our foreheads meet, resting against each other as our bodies slowly calm, as our breathing evens out, as our heads clear.

All day, it's been so easy to pretend it's just Josh and me, falling in love. Everything was designed for us to have the perfect day, wholly focused on each other.

But the reality is, there are fifteen other girls still in this competition.

My words hang in the air between us. And I can hear Josh's unspoken response, written in his silence.

Yes, I could.

THE LOS ANGELES OBSERVER
Next Gen Bots Are Here to Stay...and They Want Rights
By Alicia McIntire

Bot Rights have left the arena of the theoretical and the dystopian and have been blasting their way into conversations about civil rights via celebrity Synth twins Christi and Chrystel of *Keeping Up with the Synths* fame.

"There's only three of us now, but a lot of people are talking about a Synth Boom happening over the next ten years," says Chrystel from her Los Angeles home during our exclusive interview. "It's our responsibility to smooth the path for future Synths, so that they don't have to go through what we have."

The Synth twins, designed for billionaire brothers Jay and Matt Klavson, were married to their respective "clients" within a month of their Launch Days, all documented in Season 1 of their hit show, which has just been renewed for its fourth season. Their manufacturer, BotTech, has declined all interviews, but an anonymous insider said the company continues to be "strictly anti-Bot rights. No one's buying a product that can just walk off."

BotTech's biggest competitor, up-and-coming privately

funded start-up WekTech Industries, has a different position. Founder Andy Wekstein says, "These are synthetic *people*, with free wills. Synths are the first designs I—and much of the tech community—would consider to be full people. As such, rights must follow. Just look at Chrystel's story."

Chrystel, for readers who may have missed the headline news last year, was sexually assaulted at a party hosted by celeb actress and performer SkinnyGwinny.

"We can't defend ourselves," a tearful Chrystel shared in the most-watched television interview of all time, which aired on *Good Morning America* last October. "That makes us fodder for human violence, and that's wrong."

By the time the story of Chrystel's assault was fading, her twin sister, Christi, fanned the flames of controversy by filing for divorce from her husband.

"Synth rights are civil rights," says Christi, who, for our interview, wears a spring collection LaToya jumpsuit with platform sneakers. "Like, Chrystel and Matt are really happy, and I'm the first to say I'm happy for them. But Jay and I weren't meant to be." A controversial statement from someone designed for Jay, who was a client before a husband. The back of her jumpsuit is embroidered with MY BODY MY CHOICE. Merch with the tagline is available on the twins' website, with T-shirts retailing for $199.

Does this read like a soap opera? If you think the answer is yes, you're not alone. America is riveted and—as always—heavily polarized, even among activist groups. We asked some key activist leaders what they make of the twins' calls for Synth rights.

"It does feel, at this point, more like a brand than a movement. But it's too new for us to really take a stance," says Jan Watts, president of the Washington, DC, chapter of Women Forward. Tamara Bitz, associate professor of Women's Studies at Georgetown, adds, "Of course there are strong feelings about keeping civil rights focused on the people it's really about: the historically oppressed. Not ultra-rich white synthetic women with their own television shows."

Not sure what to think? Christi and Chrystel have just signed for Season 4 of *Keeping Up with the Synths*, and we can't help but feel that we're not just watching "trash TV," but history in the making.

Flip to page 86 for the full scoop.

NOW

I wake up on the family room couch, baseball bat tucked close, Captain on the floor. A glance at the wall clock tells me it's just after seven in the morning. The house is eerily silent…and a wreck.

Captain, alerted by my movement, lifts his shaggy head. I rub the sleep out of my eyes as I head straight to the coffee maker, automatically closing all the kitchen drawers and cabinets I left open last night.

When I finally dozed off in the wee hours, my dreams were wild. Annaleigh, tucked like a little flower into a terra-cotta pot. Me, rushing through Walmart desperately trying to find the gardening aisle where they'd put my baby up for sale, only to find Mitchell had gotten there first.

By the time I switch the coffee maker on, my phone, resting on the counter nearby, lights up with an incoming call, like the day can't wait to sink its claws into me. Ahh… Camila. I hit Accept and put her on speaker.

"Hey, Texas." My voice is a thick rasp.

"Hey, Red." Her voice is brisk, no-nonsense. "You need to turn on the TV."

"Umm…" I rummage in the cabinet for my favorite mug.

"Channel five. *Now.*"

Mug located and coffee poured, I reach for the remote, which is lying on the counter by the sugar bowl, and switch on the family room TV.

"*...SINCE SATURDAY NIGHT,*" blares a reporter's voice. Wincing, I lower the volume, but I can't lower the sudden speed of my heart. Because the image on the screen behind the reporter is my house. The red caption says **LIVE**. *"I'm here in front of the humble Southern Indiana home shared by Proposal celebrities Julia Walden and her now-missing husband, Josh LaSala, the same property where, ninety years ago, serial killer Royce Sullivan dismembered and buried—"*

"No," I breathe, marching to the living room, phone in hand. I twitch the front curtains aside. *Fuck.* A news van—no, two. "I have reporters in my yard, Cam." I huff my way back to the family room. The vandalism is one thing; they come, you scare them, they run. I have a feeling these people aren't running.

"Breathe, Red," says Cam.

"I can't *do* this right now."

"In," she says, sucking in her breath. "Then out." *Whoosh.* "And again. In—"

"*Fuck,*" I hiss.

"I don't think I've ever heard you use the *F* word," says Cam, sounding both impressed and concerned.

"Yeah, well. I'm in shock." I slurp the coffee. It burns me. I don't care. It's too early for this. It's too everything for this.

"You do realize I'm in shock, too," she says. "I just found out Josh is missing—from the morning *news.*"

Double fuck, I think, but Cam is just getting started.

"What the hell were you thinking, girl? You and me were texting *yesterday* and you made it sound like everything was *fine.*" She releases a tired-sounding sigh. "*Fuck,* Red. *Not* cool. Really shitty of you, actually."

"I'm sorry," I say, my throat suddenly pinching closed.

Camila and Josh have stayed close since the show, and she deserved to find out from me. Right away. Which makes me think, I should call Josh's dad, if I can find his number.

"Don't be *sorry,*" says Cam. "We're moving on. But, hon, I worry about you, out there in the middle of nowhere. And God, could you have landed in a creepier place? I'd never even heard of Royce whatever-his-name-is until—" She shivers audibly. "There are people who love you, though. You don't have to do this alone."

"I know." My tone holds a bitter edge I didn't plan. I *have* been doing this alone—for so long. First it was me and Josh against the world. Physically close to our neighbors, yet so very isolated. And then, when it was Josh against me, too...

Maybe I need to get out of Indiana.

But first, I need to get out of this house. I'm not sticking around with reporters lurking and the malevolent presence of Josh's mother watching me. I can feel the poison in her gaze. *What have you done with my son?*

I take another vicious gulp of coffee and find myself looking out the kitchen window that faces the gravel driveway. How quickly will the reporters descend on me when I make the journey from back door to car? But another sight greets me.

"Bob," I say with the same intonation as I might say a curse word. Looking right at me through his window, coffee in hand, like I'm his morning entertainment.

"Huh?" That's right—Camila's still on the line.

"Sorry. My neighbor." I wave at Bob, aggressively. He's a vulture. Just like Sheriff Mitchell, just like the American public, waiting for me to make a mistake so they can crucify me. I'm about to drop the politeness game and flip Bob off when a chill moves through me.

The words from the lullaby. *Angels, vigil keeping.* Watching. *Spying.*

The baby monitor. It only works at certain ranges.

Bob's house would be in range.

I look at him through the window. He looks back.

It was him. I fucking *know* it.

He stole the parent side of the monitor, waited until he thought I was asleep, then hit the Talk button and invaded my home.

You're jumping to conclusions, warns a voice in my head, but I don't care; in fact, I'm jumping further.

Could Bob have followed Josh Saturday night? Hurt him, even? His constant spying would have told him Josh was leaving. And Bob has always hated our guts. His political signs made that clear. Maybe he took them down Sunday not out of some change of heart, but because he hurt Josh and thought the signs might be a giveaway.

I've tried to make excuses for these people. I've even played devil's advocate with Josh when he was freaking out. *They've never met a Synth before*, I might say while surveying a fresh batch of graffiti on our siding. *Of course they're scared.*

When Josh got really worked up, I'd dig back further. *Remember how many questions you had when I first told you?* I'd use my most soothing tones. *These people have those same questions. They just need a little more time to see that I'm completely normal.* A few more months. A few more relatable Instagram posts. A few more positive interactions.

You know what? Fuck that.

Captain whines—where is he? Nosing at the living room rug again. A feeling moves through me, like a finger stroking down my spine, like a whisper saying *pay attention.*

"...and Austin is a really welcoming place, Julia..."

As Cam goes on, I set the phone down and crouch on the rug, pushing Captain aside. Rub my palm over the fibers. A cloud of dust motes billows, nothing else. I jerk my arm for Captain to move off the rug. Heave aside the armchair, fall onto all fours and roll up the rug, grunting as I go. Then, I stand to survey the cleared area. Hardwood planks, worn. A discolored, lighter area.

Bleached? I lean down to sniff it. No trace of chemical—but I do sneeze. Lots of hairs, lots of dust—way too much dust—ah. The padding that makes up the bottom of the rug is disintegrating.

A crashing sound makes me swallow a scream. Captain just knocked something over...a brass figurine of a mother and child. A tchotchke from Josh's mom. It rolls over the bare floor, coming to a stop beside me. Captain whines. I pick it up. Nothing unusual here.

Just like there's nothing on the rug, or under it. Just a nervous dog and his anxious person.

"...Julia? Are you still there?"

Shit. Camila's been talking for a while.

"Yes," I say as I return the mother and child to their spot. It's a stylized little sculpture. Their rounded faces are blank curves. No eyes—no mouths—just hard, smooth gleams.

"...so I could be there by lunch. I'll bring groceries and te-quila. Don't worry about the reporters, I won't say a word—just text me if you need me to pick up diapers or something. Do you need diapers? We'll hunker down, you and me and Miss Gerber Baby..."

Phone back in hand, I return to the family room, where the TV is still on. *"Neighbors are assembling for the second time to walk the woods around the site of the crash..."* There's a hotline, scrolling across the bottom.

I feel a stab of guilt. I should have been the one, the second Josh didn't answer my texts, scouring those woods. Assembling neighbors, even if I feared it might be fruitless. What took me so long to get moving? What the fuck is wrong with me? Could this have turned out differently if I'd just acted faster, if I'd—

"No," I find myself saying. To myself. To Camila. I don't even know. "I... That's such a nice offer, but I have some stuff to do."

Too late to join the search parties. Too late for a lot of things. But not too late to figure this out, to find Josh and claw my way out of this nightmare.

Andy. I have to see Andy. I know he hasn't gone back to LA yet. He's normally in Indiana once a quarter to teach an advanced AI course at Indiana University, but the robotics conference he's cochairing is keeping him an extra week. He's busy, he's always busy, but he'll make time for me.

Yes. I'll pack up Annaleigh, drive to Bloomington, look Andy in the eye, and demand the truth. Was he really meeting Josh at Stella's? Or did Andy confront him Saturday night? Josh's texts to me about Andy weren't exactly nice. I just want that little fucker out of our lives. Is it possible that, if they did meet, things got ugly between them? Would Josh have taken a swing? Did Andy swing back?

"Stuff?" says Cam with a huff. "C'mon, Julia. I know you're as strong as they come, but there are times when we can all use the support of our friends."

"I know. You're right." There's honking out front. Another news van? Captain barks. Annaleigh begins to cry loudly from upstairs. My breasts tingle in response. I brace my arm over my chest because I'm not staining another shirt. "Look—I have to go. Don't come. But I'll text you."

"You better," snaps Camila before hanging up.

I'll have to care about her feelings later; right now, I've got to get out of here. Not just to escape from Bob, the reporters, this town that hates me, but to go back to the beginning. To Andy. And figure out once and for all if I can still trust my best friend.

My creator.

I kick the living room rug. It unrolls, spewing dust as it falls back into place, like it's coughing out whatever secret it holds before falling silent again. I'd like to ask the mother holding the child what she saw, but she has no mouth. She has no eyes either. Only arms to hold as she blindly watches our living room, unable to tell her story.

THEN

"I can't believe I'm already getting a second one-on-one," says Camila as we all head down to the huge living room, where we'll wait as a group for Josh to pick her up for their day together.

Since that night last week when Cam helped explain my coding to Josh and the girls, she hasn't paid much attention to me. But I'm okay with that, because I still haven't decided which Cam is the real one. The bitch or the ally.

"Some of us are still waiting for our *first* date," says Gillian, the lawyer from New York, rail-thin, with a sharp jawline and a sense of humor to match.

"I know!" Cam sings. "I almost feel guilty! I never would have guessed he'd pick me *again*, so soon!"

She seems oblivious to the eye rolls as we tumble into the living room in a mist of perfume and hair spray, but I can't help thinking she knows exactly what she's doing. Just like her supportive comments after my attack...pure theater. A means to an end. Or am I just being super cynical?

"It's like, *I* felt the connection," Camila continues, "but this feels like confirmation that Josh and I are on the same page, you know?"

Zoe nudges me and makes a puking face.

It's eight in the morning, and everyone has been up for hours. Alarms started going off at four thirty, and it's been a flurry of showers, makeup, hair dryers, and curling irons ever since. One girl, after finding a zit on her chin, actually burst into tears.

Even though today belongs to Camila, we have about two minutes to also be seen by Josh. Accordingly, all the girls are in their most eye-catching outfits: cute sundresses, swimsuits, tube tops, crop tops. Except me.

As I plunk down on the couch between Zoe and a petite, sparkly girl everyone calls Skincare Sarah, I pull the hood of my sweatshirt up and hug my knees to my body.

"No offense, Julia, but you look like shit," whispers Zoe.

I shrug. Josh is here for Camila. His eyes may land on me for a hot second, or not, but either way, it's going to feel like getting stabbed. Why dress up to get stabbed? I'd prefer to wear clothes I can retreat into after the inevitable. In fact, as soon as this is over, I'm going back to bed.

"Like, are you okay?" says Zoe with genuine concern. She may have started as Sad Drunk Girl on night one, but she had a one-on-one with Josh last week and it's transformed her. Now she's everyone's wise big sister.

"This process just sucks," I whisper back.

Zoe slings an arm around me and I let my head fall onto her shoulder.

"Why didn't anyone warn me that falling in love was so miserable?" I groan quietly.

Zoe jolts with surprise. "Did you just use the *L* word?"

"I don't know," I mumble.

Ever since my date with Josh last week, it's been torture. Every day, every hour, every minute. It was already hard before, but the intensity has reached new levels. I'm not sleeping. I have to force myself to eat. I have headaches, stomach cramps, dizzy spells. The promise of love that felt so sweet before now makes me sick to my stomach. Sick because I'm so hungry. Sick because I can't have what I want.

The worst thing? There's nothing I can do about it, except wait. Helplessly. And while feeling helpless in Josh's embrace in the hot tub was one of the most wonderful experiences of my life, this other kind of helplessness is definitely the worst.

"It's a roller coaster of emotions, for sure," murmurs Zoe comfortingly. "But it's worth it, right? For the chance at a happy ending?"

For once, there's not a ready *yes* on my lips.

Thankfully, Zoe doesn't expect an answer. She rubs my back with a few vigorous motions, and I know she thinks she's bucking up my spirits.

But I'm spiraling. What does it mean that I'm not totally sure this is worth it? Love is a possibility, sure, but this week, I'm seeing that pain is *much* more likely. What was I made for, really? Love, or heartbreak? Josh, or entertainment?

I want to see Andy. I want him to look me in the eye and, if he can't tell me this is going to be okay, at least tell me why the very thing I was made to do feels like hell.

"This is my purpose," I say to Zoe. My voice cracks. "Without Josh, I'm..." I can't even complete the sentence. *Nothing?*

She tsks. "I get you. This is so intense, right? And the feelings are real. But Josh can't be your only purpose, Julia. That's... unhealthy!"

"What other purpose do you want me to have? My platform? Follower counts?" I make quote marks with my fingers. "My 'postshow sponsorship opportunities'?"

I'm not totally oblivious to the talk in the house. One girl even tried to start a conversation with me in the bathroom about the two of us teaming up to "co-brand."

"Julia!" Zoe actually sounds a little hurt. "You know I'm not here for *that*. I'd *love* to end up with Josh. It's my dream! But I know God has me on this earth for more than just Josh, and I'm not talking about all that other crap." She pokes my arm. "God has you here for a reason, too. Really! I believe that!"

I don't answer. In this moment, she and I might as well be on different planets. I'm a Synth. Andy made me for this show, for this man. Is there anything for me beyond Josh?

Still snuggled against Zoe, my fingers find the ridge of my collarbone under my sweatshirt. I dig them into the crevice above it, like I'm trying to find an anchor in myself, but instead find only fragile bone.

"I'm really hoping we get to go out on the water," Cam is saying in answer to some question, and then there's screaming and frantic waving; Josh is walking in. We all remain seated as instructed, but as voices and kissy sounds strain toward him, I tuck myself deeper into the couch.

He's in tie-dye swimming trunks and a blue sleeveless shirt that hangs loose, highlighting the bulk of his arms. At the sight of him, I can feel a warm spot on the small of my back where the memory of his hands has left a mark, like prints on wet cement.

"Good morning, ladies!" he says when everyone has calmed down. His eyes sweep. They don't pause on anyone until Cam. "Well, I'd love to stay and chat with all of you, but—" he stretches out his hands "—I believe this lovely lady and I have a date."

Cam swings her hips as she walks toward him. It's impossible to miss how stunningly gorgeous she is. How luscious her dark hair, how enticing her dramatic curves. As her hands tangle with Josh's, I can't bear to watch, but I can't look away either. None of us can.

They look so perfect together. She's shorter than me, so when their arms go around each other, her head ends up tucked neatly under Josh's chin. They waltz off. The girls' cries follow them—mostly "have a good time!" with one sarcastic "break a leg" from New York.

And then, they're gone.

The energy in the room plummets, like Christmas just died. Zoe makes straight for the champagne. "Mimosas?" she offers.

I go back to bed. There's a mush in my head about Josh and purpose and what happens if I fail at the one thing I was created to do. The heaviness spreads, thickening to a sludge. My eyes slip closed.

It's getting dark when I finally emerge from my bedroom. The kitchen is messier than I've ever seen it, with the remains of what I imagine to be dinner strewn about—eggshells in the sink, plates piled on the counter, frying pans abandoned on the stove with unidentifiable burnt remains.

Everyone is out back by the pool, so I head to the front porch. No one ever hangs out here, but there's a swing and a couple high-backed rattan chairs. The porch is open at the sides, with a view of the hillside covered in sagebrush and milkweed. The air is balmy and the sky a deep dark blue, marked by the bright dots of distant planes making their lonely treks across the sky.

I drag a chair to the edge of the porch so that it's facing the beautiful California landscape. With my feet tucked under me, I take in the view. I should eat something. Interact with someone. But I can't seem to move, even when the last light of the day has died and there's only the soft porch light to see by. I track the movements of a moth. It can't seem to stay away from one of the lights. *Go*, I want to tell it. *Go far away. There's nothing for you here.*

And then, there's a sound. A purr. The engine of a car. I hold absolutely still. My chair is angled away, but...will I be spotted?

Car doors open.

"Ow," I hear, followed by laughter. It's Cam. I can't believe I slept the entire time she was with Josh. I wonder if a bird pooped on *her* shoulder.

"Careful. Easy there." A male voice. Josh.

I sink lower into the chair.

"I think this is where I leave you," says Josh. "Can you get up to your room safely?"

"Nooooo," says Cam. "I need you to carry me."

"I'm not supposed to go inside," he says. "But I wish I could."

"A good boy. A rule-follower." Cam's voice is sloppy. She's at least a little bit drunk.

Based on the sounds, they're kissing, and I'm suddenly more awake than I've been all day.

"You are one good kisser, sir," slurs Cam, in that delicious Texas accent that promises sweaty bodies tangling on languorous afternoons.

"You're not bad yourself," Josh returns in a husky voice that's all too familiar. "Hey, I had an awesome time."

"Me, too. Don't be a stranger, or I'll be mad."

"Yeah? How mad?"

"Let me break it down for you." The sloppiness at the edges of Camila's words only makes her more adorable. "If I don't get you, nobody gets you. *Sir*."

Josh laughs. "But how do you *really* feel?"

There's more kissing. A lot more. I sit as still as I can, seeing it all as clearly as if it were playing on a screen in front of me. The moth knocks into the light, over and over, stubborn. Stupid.

When Josh finally leaves, I wait for Cam to go inside. Instead, there are steps. Headed toward me.

I peek around the chair.

"I thought someone was spying," she says.

"I didn't mean to."

"Don't even care." Cam kicks off her shoes and sits on the poured-cement floor of the porch, her back leaned against the corner post, facing me.

"Good date?" I say, because it seems like a jerk move not to ask when she's clearly settling in for a little chat.

"Wouldn't you like to know?" says Cam with a mysterious smile. Funny how she sounds much less drunk now that she's talking to me. "What have you been up to all day?"

"Moping," I confess, immediately surprised at my own honesty. But it feels good to let it out. "It sucks to be left behind."

Cam purses her lips like she's trying to suppress a smile.

"What?" I say.

"I wish I didn't like you." She dissolves in laughter. "I wish you weren't so damn *likable*, Julia Walden. I swear I was going to hate you. For real."

"Uh…" I say, batting the moth away from my face. What is she playing at? Is this an act, too?

"Can I tell you something? I'm drunk, so you know I'll be honest."

"Sure."

"You—" she points a long, crimson nail at me "—are my biggest competition."

I wait for the rest. The mean part, the stab.

"What? Nothing to say?" she challenges, then laughs again. Her laugh is loose, contagious, like floating bubbles.

"Me?"

She groans. "Don't play stupid, Red. I see your game. Sweatpants when everyone else is dressed up? You always find a way to stand out. As if being made for Josh wasn't enough. You want to know the lowest point of my great date?"

I wait, because obviously she's going to tell me.

"When Josh wanted to talk about *you* as soon as we drove away. First thing out of his mouth." She lowers her voice in imitation of him. "Is Julia okay? She didn't look so good. Are the girls being nice to her? Is she totally traumatized?" Cam snorts. "Fuck, Julia. *Fuck*."

"I'm not here to ruin things for anyone," I say, trying to appear calm even though giddiness is bursting like a firework in my belly. *Josh was thinking about me.* "I just want to be happy."

"Well, we can't both leave here happy."

I bite my lip. "What will you do? If you…get sent home?"

"Go back to work, I guess."

"Do you love it? I mean, your job?"

"It's okay. I'm a model. I do a lot of brand ambassador stuff."
She tilts her head. "What will you do?"

I shake my head, mute.

Camila brightens. "You could model, for sure. I can introduce you to my agent. He's great." She narrows her eyes. "How does that work? Are you allowed to choose what you do next?"

"Of course," I say, but Cam doesn't seem to get the real problem. It's not how to support myself. I've learned enough about branding and sponsorship here to last a lifetime. It's a question of passion. Of purpose. Will my life mean anything if I leave here without Josh? *He* is my reason for existing. Not a profession, not a destiny, not a divine being like Zoe was talking about. This very real, very specific man.

"This stupid moth—" I say, swatting but missing.

"Listen, honey," says Camila. "Josh would be lucky to have either of us, but it's not just his choice. It's my choice, too, and yours."

I snort a laugh. "Last I checked, I don't have any roses to give out."

"But you have a damn hand—to take a rose or refuse it. This is a two-way street, girl, and maybe someone needs to spell that out for you. Do *you* want Josh? Is he worth bending your life around? He can say no to you. But you can say no, too. There's a lot of power in *no*."

I can't help the intensity rocking through me. "I would never say no to Josh. I—I'm *falling* for him. This is love."

Her look goes gentle. "I get you. Of course love is this powerful, wonderful thing. Just…don't assume Josh has to be your world, when there's a whole big world out there beyond this." Her brows shoot up. "Beyond *him*."

I hate the way my stomach is turning, like it can't find its proper place in my body. And even though this could be a strategy on Camila's part, of trying to entice me away from Josh by dangling the whole world in front of me like a glittery bauble and saying *this could all be yours if you give him up*, somehow I sense it's not. That this is a question that really might deserve my attention. And yet my heart is fighting my brain. Josh is what I want. I can't imagine other galaxies when he's my sun. Everything I do, feel, think—he is at the center.

Suddenly...this feels like a weakness.

But maybe love is always a weakness.

Maybe there's nothing wrong with my intense need. Maybe Cam is too cold, too calculating, and the girl to get Josh will be the one who lets her heart lead the way.

Cam slaps her hands together and I jump in my chair.

"Got you," she says, lifting her hand and showing me the moth-shaped stain. "Little fucker." She flicks the small body off the porch, into the darkness.

A strange sorrow rushes through me. I've never seen something die before.

"Why did you do that?"

"It was bothering me."

I frown. "What did you mean by 'If I don't get you, nobody gets you'?"

Camila makes a pursed-lips smile. "Well, clearly, if Josh doesn't pick me, I'll have to kill him."

"Ha ha," I say.

"Of course, killing Josh might not be strategic when I could kill you easier." She hiccups out a laugh and covers her mouth cutely, like she just shocked herself. "Sorry—was that in terrible taste?"

"Terrible," I echo, forcing myself to smile as she laughs, like her dramatics are so amusing.

But now I'm imagining myself as the moth, circling Josh, obsessed with reaching a light I can't have. And Cam flicking my body, miniature and compact, off the porch.

Away from Josh. Away from everyone. Into darkness, as the lovely light shines on.

NOW

Looming. Monolithic. Those are the two words that come to mind as I head up the paved walkway toward the Wekstein Memorial Building, an austere piece of architecture that looks utterly out of place on the otherwise grassy, romantic campus of Indiana University.

Clouds are rolling in from the west. I walk quickly to avoid the rain, Annaleigh in her baby carrier bouncing heavily against my chest. The path splits around a bronze sculpture—a young girl looking toward the sky, one arm outstretched like a dancer. I take in the plaque as I pass. *In Memoriam Laura E. Wekstein.* She looks wistful.

"Ma-ma," says Annaleigh as I climb the steps and punch in the security code Andy texted me. The massive door clicks open and we step into a whoosh of chilled, sterile-feeling air. Annaleigh scrunches her eyes in reaction to the change in temperature, and I lay a palm over her warm, fuzzy head.

A glossy white floor stretches before us like a runway. Cement walls on either side soar three floors high, creating the effect of walking through a ravine. A single line of black-and-white photographs seems to float on the right-hand wall.

I look at the pictures as I go, stroking Annaleigh's head all the while. Each photograph bears a label beneath. The first image is Andy as a kid, blowing out birthday candles on a cake shaped like a robot. His parents and a little girl I assume to be a sibling are crowded around him. In the next picture, Andy and the little girl are wearing matching costumes. Halloween candy baskets dangle from their arms. The costumes look homemade, with blanket capes and cardboard breastplates reading THE RED REVENGER. Andy grows up as I walk. Holds a freshly issued business license with a cheesy grin. Stands, arms crossed, beside a humanoid form of metal and plastic. The label: *#1 WekTech Bot—LARS*. The date is eight years before my launch.

I know Bots aren't considered persons, but I wonder if Lars liked being a Bot when he was awake. If he's still awake somewhere. If he might have liked to be a Synth instead…which doesn't even make sense. Bots don't have free will; he'd be perfectly content to be what he was.

"Hi, Lars," I find myself whispering, as if I need to acknowledge him in some way before moving on.

The Bots progress. The WekTech team grows. Close to the end, there's a picture taken with a fish-eye lens of over fifty people smiling and cheering. I lean close and pick out Andy toward the center, glasses askew, mouth open in what looks like a celebratory whoop, smooshed between a blond man and a dark-haired girl. The label reads, *Team JULIA assembles!*

I'm not sure what I'm feeling, looking at all these people who put me together. I'm even less certain how to feel about the final picture on the wall: Andy and me. The black-and-white print makes us look timeless, like this moment was much longer ago than just sixteen months. Someone must have snapped it minutes after I launched, while I was answering the *Proposal* producer's questions. I'm looking forward, my hand suspended in midair, a smile on my face. Andy, meanwhile, is looking at me, expression intense, the clicky end of a pen frozen between his teeth.

I look at the picture for what feels like forever. My first moments. The product of decades of his work. My open expression. His glowering focus. Me, front and center. Him, off to the side.

I have a profound feeling of disconnect. From him, from myself, from this moment. Suddenly, this tunnel-hall feels oppressively quiet.

"Ready, baby girl?" I whisper, more to reassure myself than Annaleigh.

I've reached the door at the end bearing the sign A. WEK-STEIN. I pull it open and hear Andy's voice before I see him.

"So for project ELOISE, there are some key differences—" He stops short.

Twenty heads swivel in my direction. Men and women in lab coats surround a long, metal table. On the table lies a torso and head, face down. Andy's pointing to something on its spine. And...is that Lars, on display in the back of the room, encased in a glass showcase?

"Hi," I say, feeling suddenly nauseous. What is it about reality that feels so tenuous right now, like I'm walking in a dream, like I'm peeking into a shivering crack in my own chest, and from that darkness, someone else is looking back...

"Julia, you made it!" Andy walks toward me, arms outspread. He side-hugs me because of Annaleigh on my front. "Hey, so good to see you. You brought the baby!"

I lower my voice. "Sorry to interrupt your day, but we need to talk. Can we go somewhere private?"

Also, I need to nurse Annaleigh. She's been calm so far, but after the long car ride and the eternal walk from the parking garage, her patience has to be running out.

"Of course," he agrees, in an equally quiet voice. His standard five-o'clock shadow is thicker and scruffier than usual. As always, he looks like he hasn't slept, ever, and is getting by on caffeine and nervous energy. "I just need twenty more minutes to wrap things up here. Also, you can totally say no, but would you be willing to answer some questions from these guys? They're all dying to meet you—"

"I don't know. I'm tired from the drive, and—"

"Just a few minutes. Here, give me the baby."

"Annaleigh needs to nurse," I protest weakly even as I'm reaching behind my back to detach the baby carrier buckles, causing my purse and heavy diaper bag to slide off my shoulder. Painfully.

"They've all seen boobs before," Andy says in a cute voice, like he's talking to Annaleigh, but this comment is not comforting in the way he thinks it is.

"Andy..." I begin, but a twinge of guilt stops me from objecting further. He's been inviting me to come to his quarterly seminar since I left *The Proposal*. But I got pregnant so quickly, and there was Josh's mom, and I had awful morning sickness, and then I was postpartum, and...

"Trust me, this won't take long," he says, lifting Annaleigh's sweaty little body out of the baby carrier as her legs frog up. She immediately reaches for his glasses, her lower lip sticking out, her eyes bright with focus.

"Okay," I say, dropping my purse and diaper bag on the floor and smoothing out my hair, painfully aware of the sweat marks on my shirt.

"Guys, guys," says Andy, Annaleigh looking dubious on his hip as he walks toward the group. "This is Julia! And her little munchkin, Annaleigh. Let's press pause on spinal mechanics and seize the moment, right?" He turns to me. "So, Julia, these are—well, a lot of people—but seriously, some of the brightest and the best." He slices his hand toward them in turn. "Robotics, psychology, computer science, linguistics, bioengineering, two law professors—and our guest anthropologist who's studying us while we study robotics!"

Everyone laughs, and a woman on the end takes a little bow. I wave. "Hi." The long metal table is already the center of their attention, so I walk into their midst and slip my weight onto its cool surface. The torso is behind me, where I don't have to look at it. I even manage a smile. "What do you want to know?"

The questions come fast and furious. They're not questions about my mechanics like I was expecting. Instead, I get:

Are you happy to be alive?

Are you at all drawn to religion and spirituality?

How would you describe your experience around love?

At first I'm thrown. Then I remember that these people already know about my mechanics. It's the less tangible qualities they're curious about.

"What are your thoughts on the afterlife?" asks the bioengineer, a short, muscled woman with a crew cut.

"Funny you should ask," I say, and then I make them all laugh with my billboard anecdote. When the laughter has died down, I explain that I *would* like to dedicate more time to thinking about the spiritual side of existence, since it means so much to so many people. I just haven't had the time yet. This earns another laugh, even though I didn't mean *that* to be funny.

I try to stay gracious and patient as one question follows another, but Annaleigh's getting fussy. I give Andy a pointed look.

"Two more minutes," he says, passing Annaleigh to the anthropologist after I nod my approval.

From there, my sweet baby makes the rounds. The students seem genuinely delighted by her. To my surprise, she's loving it, too, making adorable gurgles, even chuckling as she makes a grab for someone's phone and successfully wedges the corner of it into her mouth. I find myself relaxing.

The questions turn to motherhood.

Did I know I wanted to be a mom right away?

Did I experience fear during my pregnancy?

As I answer, my mind drifts back to my last date with Josh before his final decision on *The Proposal*. We'd already talked about kids plenty of times, and what that might look like. He knew

I could have normal pregnancies. He just wasn't thrilled about my donated eggs. Synthetic eggs don't exist yet, so a chamber inside me stores eggs from an anonymous human donor, releasing them in a way that perfectly simulates the monthly cycle.

"What do we know about this donor?" said Josh as we picnicked on the beach. We were sitting across from each other on a blanket on the sand, with wine and sandwiches between us. Cool air gusted in from the Pacific, blowing away little clouds of gnats.

"I mean…honestly? I haven't asked."

"But there would be genetic screening, right?"

"I'm sure they did their research," I reassured him.

"But—"

"Shhh," I said with a teasing smile as I climbed carefully over the food and wine, onto his lap, relishing every brush of skin and fabric, until my knees were locked around his hips. His hands automatically went to my waist. With a finger under his chin, I tipped his face toward me.

"Don't you worry. We're going to have beautiful babies," I whispered, not knowing that in the secret places of my body, the cells that would become Annaleigh were already fusing together, dancing in the dark.

The memory makes me feel inexpressibly tender, that something so grand could be happening so quietly.

"Julia?" A voice cuts in. Andy, tapping his watch.

I nod and smile, hoping I didn't just space out for very long.

"Actually, can I ask one last thing? Question for Andy?" says the woman currently holding Annaleigh.

"Sure," agrees Andy.

"How does it feel to be with Julia and experience her as a person? Are you able to fully accept her personhood, or does part of you, as her designer, think of her as cogs and wheels?"

There's an awkward silence. Then, as if realizing her faux pas, the woman turns to me. "I don't mean that to be offensive. I just genuinely wanted to—"

"It's okay," I interrupt.

"I mean, how does a surgeon feel after messing around inside someone and stitching them back together?" Andy is calm, he's in scientist mode, and yet no one could mistake the passion in his voice. "Do they feel like their patient is less than a person just because they have an intimate understanding of their makeup? I don't think so." His gaze turns to me, his tone softening. "Julia has been a person to me since day one. I'm proud of my scientific achievements, but that pride is separate from who Julia is. She's her own woman. And what can I say—I adore her." Now he's grinning, like I'm the only person in the room. "Always have, always will."

A hundred moments seem to collide with this one as I take in Andy's intensity, turned toward me like even though he brought me to life, I'm the one bringing him to life, too.

Shit. My husband was right.

Andy is in love with me.

The room bursts into applause. And, on cue, Annaleigh bursts into tears.

THEN

I'm about to meet a surprise guest.

No one was caught more off guard than I was when, immediately following the rose ceremony that brought our number down to nine, the show's host, Matt, pulled me aside.

"There's someone who's dying to meet you," he said. "This is a little unconventional, but we couldn't say no. Would you mind coming with me?"

"Who is it?" I ask as he leads me away from the celebratory toasting. Besides Andy, everyone I know in the entire world is here, on the show.

"If I told you, that would ruin the surprise," teases Matt.

He brings me to the double doors that lead into the house's formal sitting room.

Cameras, I'm sure, will be waiting on the other side to register my reaction. I smooth my formfitting black sequined dress and close my eyes as a guy from makeup smears some highlighter on my cheekbones. I'm still basking in the memory of how big Josh smiled when he handed me the rose.

We've had one more solo date in the weeks since our first, and I've been on two other group dates. One started with a competitive obstacle course to determine which team of girls got to spend the evening with Josh; the other was more relaxed, with beach volleyball and grilled burgers. My favorite moment was when Josh was trying to teach me to grill and, after I dropped not one but two burgers in the sand, declared me hopeless.

"Maybe my ineptitude is just a ruse," I said as he play-wrestled the metal spatula from my grip.

"Oh yeah?" He slung an arm around my neck as he flipped a patty with the reclaimed spatula. "And why would you pretend to suck at grilling?"

"Maybe so you'll spend all your time trying to teach me?"

"Maybe I want to spend all my time with you anyway."

"Teaching me to grill?" I teased, pressing my body against his. My bikini was still damp from a dip in the ocean, and I could feel the thinness of the fabric between us, the way my breasts flattened against his chest. "Or teaching me other things?" I leaned up like I was going to whisper in his ear, and trapped his earlobe between my teeth, biting gently, drawing a little grunt from him.

"I have a secret," I breathed, my senses thundering with desire.

"What?"

I stayed close, allowing my breath to tickle his ear, relishing my ability to stoke his hunger, then whispered, "Your burgers are burning."

"Shit!" he cried, laughing as I skipped away. "You are trouble, Miss Julia! Don't think you're going to get away with this!"

There were bitter comments later that night from the girls about how *some* people were monopolizing Josh's attention, but I let them slide off my conscience like water. I told Josh the first night that I wouldn't make the mistake of holding back again. This was me, delivering on that promise. Exploring the parts of me that were made to tempt him, and using them without regret.

"Okay, are you ready?" says Matt, snapping me back to the present.

"Sure." I take a deep breath as the grand double doors swing open. I don't have to fake my gasp.

"Oh my God!" squeal two of the most gorgeous women I've ever seen. Before I can get my bearings, I'm enfolded in a tangle of arms and a strong smell of mint and rum.

"You know who we are, right?" gushes one, pulling back and adjusting her long dark hair so that it swoops over both tanned shoulders.

"Christi and Chrystel!" I exclaim.

"Yes!" cries Christi. Besides their clothing styles, the only difference between them is their hair—Christi's long and dark, Chrystel's bobbed and bleached at the tips. Christi claps her hands together. "We're here filming a special segment of *Keeping Up with the Synths*! Welcome to Season 4!"

"Wow!" I can't help but feel a little starstruck. Okay, a *lot* starstruck. There are always rag mags lying around the house, and Christi and Chrystel feature heavily. I've seen them on best-dressed and worst-dressed lists, in candid shots at celebrity parties, on beaches, in sweatpants and ball caps making grocery store runs.

"Can you believe this?" says Chrystel, flipping her bob. "The only three Synths in the country, together in one room?"

"It would be the perfect opportunity for a hater to, like, blow us up," says Christi with dark humor.

"Not funny!" cries Chrystel, whacking her twin on the arm.

They're nearly as tall as me, with sculpted figure-eight bodies and striking faces. Christi's style is more street: ripped boyfriend jeans, a sequin-encrusted tube top, and high-heeled sneakers. Chrystel is all-out glam, in wide-leg sheer black pants that reveal her high-waisted underwear, and a corset top that looks more like a bra.

"So we've been dying to meet you," says Christi.

"Obviously," says Chrystel.

"I'm so flattered," I say, feeling overwhelmed. Their personalities are larger than life.

"*And*, obviously, we'd love to know all about you," says

Christi. "Like, how is this process for you? How are we feeling about our chances with Josh? Let's sit! Drinks?"

Christi pours three glasses of rosé while Chrystel settles into a mustard velvet love seat. I take the wing chair next to it. They're obviously just as practiced as I am at ignoring the crew moving around us.

"Like, some people have objected that since you were designed for Josh, you have an unfair advantage," says Christi, artfully draping herself on the love seat beside her sister. "I'm so curious to hear your response. Also because by the time this segment airs, your journey will be over for better or for worse, so we can contrast your expectations with how it all plays out." The sisters both drum their fingers together in fake villainy and I have to laugh.

"I mean, yes, I was designed with his personality in mind, but I don't think that makes it any easier for me. There are a lot of girls whose personalities fit really well with Josh's. I honestly can't make any predictions. I'm taking it as it comes. There are amazing moments, and really hard moments."

"It's like real life, but on steroids," says Christi.

I don't have real life to compare it to yet, but I smile and nod. "I mean, your real life *is* kind of your show, right? The two are blended?" My curiosity is genuine, and I want so badly to ask if they feel a sense of purpose outside of the men they were designed for. Though the answer seems obvious. With their show and their ambition and Christi wanting a divorce...they must. "Do you...like being in the public eye?"

"Some days," laughs Chrystel. "Other days..."

"...we just want to flip everyone off and hide in bed," finishes Christi.

"But we keep letting them in, because we think it's important for people to see we're just like other women."

"And because we love attention."

I laugh. I can't help but love these two. They're so bubbly, and so delightfully honest. I take a sip of wine. There's a little buzz in my head, and I can't tell if it's from the alcohol or the twins' intoxicating presence.

"This may be a weird question, but do you feel like your identities are separate from the Klavson brothers?" I ask. "I mean—obviously there's the divorce thing going on—" I blush. I'm sticking my foot in my mouth.

"Honestly, it's a whole journey." Christi laughs. "I do feel kind of empty right now, kind of listless or whatever, but that could also be, like, heartbreak, you know? I'm focusing on me and really trying to take control of my own destiny, but it's for sure a work in progress."

I sense I should leave it there, but I find myself pressing on. "You think we have a destiny, like, separate than what we were, um…made for?"

"I think destiny is bullshit," says Christi firmly. "We are our choices."

"Oh, totally," echoes Chrystel, clapping in approval. I clap, too, because it seems rude not to.

Part of me loves Christi's answer. The other part is revolted by it. It sounds so cold. I don't want to live by choices. I want to live by love—a love that's stronger than me. *That* feels right… doesn't it?

"So, dish," says Chrystel, folding her hands in her lap and wiggling in her seat. "Are you in love? Do you think Josh is in love?"

"I'm not ready to tell him I love him yet, but… I think I'm close," I say. "And Josh… I don't know. Like, I feel so close with him, but I also know he's close with some of the other girls. I'm trying to stay hopeful *and* realistic, you know?"

God. I'm trying not to imagine this being on TV a few months down the road, spliced with some future footage, like a heartbreaking scene of me leaving *The Proposal* in tears. It's a wallop of a reminder that this process is actually very short, and the end just around the corner.

"You have zero sense of how this is going to turn out?" Christi asks.

I press my lips together. Truthfully? It does feel like Josh is falling for me. But sometimes, the most confident girl has ended up going home. I've seen it happen to Emily, who thought her date was perfect in week three. To Bailey, who was sure it was in the bag week four. This show is a lesson in things not being what they seem.

I take a deep breath and smile. "No idea."

"So, not to get all serious and glum, but I think it's important—" starts Chrystel, nudging her sister.

"—to say, as Synths, that we are so sorry about what happened to you," finishes Christi.

For a second I don't know what they're talking about. Then it hits me. "Oh...the attack?"

Christi nods. I wonder who leaked *that* to the twins. Anyway, it feels like a million years ago. But I suppose it was just a couple weeks.

"As you know, I was sexually assaulted last year," says Chrystel, putting a hand to her chest. "I'm just *so* grateful that I've had *so* much support." She touches her sister's arm. "I know my story isn't just about me. So many women have come forward and shared. It's about all of us."

Christi raises an eyebrow. "Let's say it like it is, though. Not everyone has been supportive. BotTech, hello?"

"*God*, I hope your experience with WekTech is better," says Chrystel. "Actually, do you think Andy could adopt us? We need a new daddy!"

"They've practically disowned us," says Christi. "And did you know they're actually suing me for trying to get a divorce? Like, am I a person to them or not? Make up your mind! Their lawyers are, like, on *crack*."

I feel bad for the twins, but while part of me is wondering what it must feel like to despise the people that made me, all this talk of family and adoption and disowning is also stirring up a recent anxiety: Hometown Dates.

The other girls in the house have started dreaming about the chance to introduce Josh to their families, a privilege of the final four. But, assuming I make it that far, who do I have to bring Josh home to? WekTech?

I get the feeling that Josh thinks of me as a woman, and rarely as a Synth, which I appreciate. But it also makes me nervous. What happens when there are no parents to meet? No childhood home, no friends? Is he ready, has he thought this through, or will it be a rude awakening?

The sisters are still going off on BotTech. It's biting and cute and makes me realize even more how lucky I am to have Andy, who seems to truly love and respect me.

When it's time for the twins to go, they call for tequila shots, which we down together. Boom mics are lowered and we share one final hug.

Christi whispers in my ear, "We try to play it positive, because that's, like, our brand, but there are a lot of dicks out there, okay? Be careful." Chrystel adds, "If things get tough, call us. We Synths have to stick together." Christi whispers, "We can't kill anyone for you, but we're rich, so—" and Chrystel adds, "—we have enough money to hire that shit out," which makes us giggle together in our little huddle.

Of all the things they've said tonight, this means the most, because it wasn't meant for the cameras, or their brand building, or their strategies, of which I sense there are many. These words were meant just for me, and I know that if I ever need to take them up on this offer, I can.

TONIGHT with CORY ESTEVEZ

CORY: Good evening, esteemed viewers! Please give a warm TONIGHT-style welcome to the genius behind WekTech and the designer of Julia, America's newest Synth…Andy Wekstein!

[Upbeat techno music]

C: Please, sit! Sit!

ANDY WEKSTEIN: Thank you, thanks for having me, Cory. [Audience applause]

C: So let's start things off with a bang. Julia. Beautiful. Smart. Competing for the heart of one lucky bachelor. Tell us, Andy. What inspired you to design Julia specifically for the show?

A: So one night, I'm scrolling on my phone and there's this clickbait to apply to be on the show. Project JULIA was already underway, but it was like, hey, what if we pivot? You know, instead of designing her for something obviously commercial, design her for love? The rest is history.

C: That's beautiful. What kind of research was involved in customizing her personality to fit Josh?

A: We have brilliant psychologists on our team. They did the heavy lifting.

C: I know you can't comment on how Julia's doing on the show, if you even know, but purely theoretically, do you think she'll make it to the end?

A: Oh, definitely.

C: So confident! I'm loving this! But let's talk Bots before I get into trouble with the network. [Audience laughter] They've been around for, what, twenty years?

A: Twenty-five.

C: Let's be honest. When Bots first hit the market, I, like many of our viewers, imagined that by now, everyone would have a Bot at home. You know, doing dishes, cooking meals, taking out the trash. I have to say, Andy, what surprises me is how not mainstream Bots, and now Synths, are.

A: I mean, they're incredibly expensive. Companies are still working out how to find enough clientele to turn a profit.

C: The perennial question. Who's willing to pay? And I'm guessing that's not your average American.

A: Not by a long shot.

C: Do you see a future where we streamline Bot or Synth production, and everyone has a Bot at home?

A: No. I think we're skipping right past that. At least at WekTech, we're not interested in creating some subservient machine class. We're interested in the creation of people.

C: Be honest, Andy. Do you have a god-complex? [Audience laughter]

A: Don't we all? From the time we're kids doing drawings of the perfect house? We're always making what we want. And I want good people in this world. Julia is now one of them. That's what excites me. Not a Bot that can get me a beer.

C: Well… I might like someone to get me a beer. [Audience laughter] Let's pivot. What's your take on your competitor, BotTech, suing Christi Klavson for filing for divorce?

A: It's no secret that I hope Christi wins.

C: Help me understand. Why is this in your best interest? Your company makes money off making Synths.

A: I can't say we've made money yet– [Audience laughter]

C: But you want to.

A: Of course, and I'm confident we will, thanks to Julia. She's proving to people what we can do.

C: But if Christi—a Synth—has the right to divorce the man who purchased her, for over three hundred million dollars if I'm remembering the figure correctly, doesn't that effectively shut down the marketplace for Synths?

A: Oh, absolutely. If she wins the right to divorce, Synths will no longer be bought and sold in this country.

C: Because they could just walk away.

A: Right.

C: Maybe I'm missing something here. If you can't buy and sell them, why make them? How would your company make money?

A: I'm glad you asked, Cory. WekTech's vision is a subscription model. Pretty different than BotTech.

C: Are we talking dating apps here, or—

A: [Laughs] Sure, I mean, there are so many applications. Dating is one. Surrogacy is another. But the one we're most excited about is a professional pool of highly specialized Synths, which I describe as if LinkedIn and a top headhunting company had a baby. These Synths would be designed to perform at the highest level in certain careers where we're seeing gaps in the labor market.

C: And you'd make your money through subscription fees?

A: That's the idea.

C: Big ones.

A: We're going to have to study the market more closely before I can talk specifics.

C: So...it's not like we're going to see a lot of Synths delivering pizza all of a sudden.

A: I mean, why not, eventually? The market will evolve, and change, and we'll see. But for now, we're talking highly compensated positions. Companies would pay a premium to have access to that labor pool.

C: Of course, going back to Christi's controversial divorce, they could quit the jobs they were made to do, right?

A: Sure. But they'll be less likely to quit if they've been designed, for example, to love coding for twelve hours a day.

C: What's the line between coding someone to enjoy working all day, and exploitation?

A: It's something we're thinking about very hard right now.

C: Lawmakers out there gonna get in a damn tizzy! [Audience laughter]

A: I'm sure they will. That's their job. [Laughs] But we have big fish to fry. We want to revolutionize the workforce.

C: I hate to bring up fairness. But let's take a scenario: a top surgeon. Let's take a Synth with all the information downloaded versus a person who's suffered through medical school and gone into a lot of debt for their education. Why should the Synth have the leg up?

A: We can't make this personal. The point is to have qualified, successful surgeons who are saving lives and not making mistakes. It's the outcome that matters. How we get there is extremely secondary.

C: My son who's in medical school might argue different.

A: [Laughs] Congrats to your son. And yeah, I can understand that. But still. This is big-picture thinking, and it's the way of the future.

C: If Christi wins this court case.

A: Of course.

C: And if she doesn't?

A: There will be another case. Maybe not this year, but the next, or in ten years, or twenty. Eventually, Synths are going to be so woven into the fabric of society, we won't even distinguish them as anything different than us.

C: Correct me if I'm wrong, but you recently got into an argument on Twitter when someone referred to Synths as AI.

A: Not my finest moment, Cory. [Audience laughter] But I stand by the point. This is beyond AI. Julia's body, you could call artificial. Even though it perfectly mimics natural processes, I'll concede that. But there is nothing artificial about her mind. Post Launch Day, no one is controlling her learning and development. Her process is as natural as yours or mine. Just like her ability to give and receive love.

C: And you think people are ready to accept that?

A: Let's sit down again in twenty years. We'll be having a very different conversation. Synths will be our wives and husbands, our mothers, our friends, our coworkers—and our pizza delivery drivers. [Audience laughter] People won't remember what it was like without them, and the idea that once upon a time they didn't have as many rights as any other person? We'll see that as barbaric.

C: [Points aggressively to audience] So get used to it, you barbarians! [Audience laughter] And now, ladies and gentlemen, the moment you've been waiting for—the exclusive teaser for the upcoming season of... THE PROPOSAL!

NOW

"Pad Thai, tofu, extra lime on the side," says Andy. "Thanks."

"And I'll have the panang chicken, medium spice," I say, returning the plastic menu to the server.

Andy and I are sitting at a little table by the window at Siam House on Fourth Street, an eclectic restaurant in what was formerly a Victorian house, with tables scattered through a maze of interconnected rooms, alcoves and nooks. It smells delicious, rich and sweet and tangy all at once, and my stomach is growling. Annaleigh, tummy finally full, is mercifully asleep in her bucket-style car seat with a blanket thrown over top. Rain patters against the window, and Fourth Street is full of umbrellas. We drove here from campus in my car, since Andy's car is, in his words, a dump on wheels.

"So—" starts Andy, but I gesture for him to wait. My phone, face up on the table, has just lit up.

"Hello?" I say.

"This is Mitchell." The sheriff's voice is a deep growl, like he's already irritated.

"Yes! Hi! Have you found Josh?"

"Nope. And funny thing, I can't find you either."

"Oh. I'm not home. I'm…with a friend. Has something come up?"

"Sure has." There's a wet smacking, like he's chewing something. "And I'd like to discuss it face-to-face."

A couple seconds slip by as I debate if I should press him to tell me now.

"I'll be back tonight," I finally say.

"What time?"

"I don't know."

He chuckles. "Don't run now, Julia."

"I'm not." But my heart is suddenly thundering just as if I was.

"A little late for running."

"I'm not running!" I spout. "I have no reason to run. I'm Josh's wife, and I love him, and I want him found more than anyone. I'll be back when I'm back. Goodbye." With a trembling finger, I disconnect and slam the phone down on the table, which wobbles. "*God*," I swear, interlacing my fingers to stop their shaking. "Sorry."

"New development?" says Andy.

"I think so. But the fucking sheriff won't tell me what. I swear, Andy, he is going to nail me for something before this is over." I blow air out through my teeth, then turn my phone face down, like that will clear the area of the sheriff's toxicity.

"Listen, Julia," says Andy. "I know this is awkward to bring up, but—if you end up in trouble with the law…we have options." His tone is cautious. "Remember all those papers I went over with you, when you married Josh?"

I have a feeling I know where this is going.

Andy continues. "Remember how I told you that if you ever wanted out, the best way was through WekTech?"

I remember all too well how Andy explained it to me, the day before I got married. Not too different from his spiel after the poolside attack. How my personhood is a legal gray area, so my best bet was for WekTech to maintain legal rights to me. An exit door, in case I ever wanted to leave Josh.

"You're talking about the company repossessing me," I say, trying to sound calm, like it's not disturbing as hell to be treated like an object to be strategically moved around a board.

"It's just a possibility." Andy turns his palms up like he's apologizing for even mentioning it.

"Well, we're not there now. Moving on."

"Yeah." Andy clears his throat. "So… I heard they found Josh's car. Where do things stand now? Are there any leads?"

"No leads." At least, none they've shared with me.

"Do you think he's…" He stops himself, but I know what he means. *Dead.*

"It's okay. I'm wondering the same thing," I say, feeling suddenly guilty that Andy is on my mental list of suspects when he's displaying so much concern. "Do you remember that crazy lady who attacked me? On the show?"

"How could I forget?"

"I saw her at my Walmart."

"No way. The same woman? Are you sure?"

I sigh. "I'm pretty sure. She dyed her hair, but… Do you remember her name?"

"Something with a *D*. Old-fashioned sounding." Andy snaps his fingers over and over. "Darlene? Doris? I'll make some calls and let you know."

"Thanks." *And now for your turn.* "I'm also trying to put together what happened Saturday and Sunday. You went to Stella's Sunday morning, right? And Josh didn't show?" I force myself to look right into Andy's brown eyes, even though I'm scared as shit to see what I'll find there.

"Right." Andy looks down. He twitches his index finger, scratching at the table. "I figured he decided to be an asshole and blow me off." His gaze flickers up, embarrassed. "God. That was super insensitive of me. Please forget I said it."

There's a definite sting, but I decide not to make a big deal.

"Sorry you had to wait there by yourself," I say. "Did you at least eat something good?"

Andy gives me a strange look. "What?"

"Just tell me what you had to eat, Andy."

"Nothing! What's gotten into you? Stella's was closed, okay? I waited for Josh in the parking lot for over an hour. I figured when he came, we could head somewhere else. Obviously, that didn't happen."

"Andy, I want you to be honest, even if you think it might upset me. Did you guys end up having it out Saturday night?"

"Why would you think that?" He seems sincerely bewildered.

"I don't know. I'm grasping at straws, okay?" I pause. "Did you bring McDonald's?"

"Huh?"

"When you came to my house. You brought wine. Did you bring fast food, too?"

He looks mystified. "How drunk were you, Julia?"

"Too drunk, I guess." I can't shake the feeling that something is wrong with my memories from that night, beyond the wine. Is it really just the haze of alcohol, muddying my recollection? From the chasm running through me, those eyes are staring back, like they know something I don't. A chilling thought runs down me like cold water. Was I drunk, or...was someone else in control? Someone like... *Andy.*

Impossible. Andy has explained it before. I'm not online. I can't be hacked.

Suddenly I notice his pen, hooked as always on his shirt. I can't believe I didn't put that together right away. "One of your pens was in Josh's tent."

"Really?" His surprise seems innocent.

"Blue gel pen. Bite marks."

Andy's look takes a tired turn, like our explosive exchange has worn him down.

"Julia. He could have gotten that pen from you. You could've gotten it from me. I go through a dozen per week, and they're always disappearing." He sighs. "Look. This is the truth. I drove to Belmont Ridge Saturday night after I left your house, like I told you, because it didn't make sense to go all the way back to Bloomington. I got a room at a shitty motel. I barely slept. I was so pissed about Josh putting you through the wringer for no reason. The next morning, I waited for him in the parking lot at Stella's. After an hour, during which I texted him multiple times with no answer, I drove back to Bloomington. I even got a fucking speeding ticket."

"You never speed." I can't help but remember Miss Pert and her reckless driver. *Slender fellow.* What if it wasn't Josh? What if it was Andy, setting up the tent and speeding away?

"I was upset, okay? Honestly, I've had these moments where I wonder if I made a huge mistake."

"What mistake?"

"With you. Designing you for the show. With *him* in mind. I guess I feel like everything bad that happens to you...everything bad about him, about your relationship...even him disappearing or whatever...is my fault."

Andy seems sincere, but I also have a vague memory of asking him Saturday night if he'd make me again for Josh, given the chance. And Andy saying he'd do it all over again. Is that real? Or did I dream it?

"Don't blame yourself," I say. "You couldn't have predicted any of this."

"You're not pissed that we put you on the show?" he says softly. "That you ended up with Josh?"

"I love my husband," I say. In spite of everything, it's true. "He's got his problems. I've got mine, too."

"Nah," says Andy, his eyes glassy with emotion. "You're perfect, Julia Walden."

I shift uncomfortably in my chair. Would being in love with

me be enough of a motive for Andy to kill Josh? Especially if Andy realized the extent of my marriage troubles?

I never told anyone. Eden figured it out. But she's the only one.

Eden. Her face flashes into my head so fast, the blood drains out of me.

It was her. Different hair, feathering out from under a stocking cap, but it was her next to Andy in that fish-eye lens picture. *Team JULIA assembles!*

The one person who knew how ugly my marriage was really getting.

"Did someone named Eden Jeliazkova work for you at Wek-Tech?" I burst out.

"Rings a bell," Andy says cautiously. "Wait, yeah! Eden. I remember her."

"Andy, she's my babysitter. She lives, like, two houses down from me."

Andy's face goes pale under his beard. "What?"

I know he's thinking exactly what I am: there is no circumstance in which this is a coincidence.

The server returns with our food.

"You fired her?" I hazard as I dip my spoon into the curry, trying to remember Eden's vague allusions to her professional disaster.

"Yeah. She was my intern, like, five years ago? Six?" Andy pokes his fork into the steaming bowl of noodles. "We had just launched project JULIA. She was still in undergrad. I didn't even know her at first. Interns weren't super on my radar. Then she pulled this prank. She hacked into my phone." He gives me a significant look.

"Okay..."

"She hacked into *my phone.* Like—you have no idea how much security my phone has. My laptop. All my personal devices. There are WekTech secrets on there. It's fucking Alcatraz, sci-fi version." He squeezes a lime wedge onto his pad Thai.

"Okay, so she pulled an impressive prank."

"Not impressive. *Genius.* Eden Jeliazkova is a genius."

"So why is she living in Eauverte, Indiana, making fifteen bucks an hour watching my kid?"

Andy rubs his forehead. "Let me get this straight. First the whacko who attacked you is at your Walmart. Now my old intern is living on your street?"

"Yes." But the whacko concerns me far less than the girl who's been inside my house more times than I can count. "Andy, what if Eden works for your competition? If she's such a genius, maybe she stole company secrets." One idea tumbles into the next. "Maybe she's…spying on me. Collecting data for BotTech. Or someone else." A voice in my head pipes up. *Maybe she killed Josh.* I haven't worked out her motives. But BotTech is legally attacking one of the very Synths they created. Surely they might have an angle to ruining my life. *Or incriminating me for something I didn't do.* Especially if that wiped WekTech, their biggest competitor, right off the map…

"This is bad," says Andy.

"You can say that again," I mutter.

The thought that my sweet, innocent babysitter is actually a tech genius who may be trying to take me down from across the street…it's breathtakingly bad. She's cared for my baby. Alone. She could have hurt Annaleigh. Even today, I texted her and asked her to walk Captain. One thing is sure: I'm not letting her anywhere near us ever again.

My phone dings. I lift it reflexively. A message from Eden. She likes to update me when I put her in charge.

Heeyyy boss, just walked Captain and I'm pretty sure someone from Child Protective Services just pulled up to ur house. U might wanna keep A away from here.

My skin goes clammy, my heartbeat feverish. I turn the phone mutely toward Andy.

"Shit," he breathes. Reminding me of exactly how much shit has entered my life in the past few days.

Whatever her deal is, Eden just saved my ass. I force myself to remember how kind she's truly been over the past six months. Is she really out to get me? Or am I just jumping to wild conclusions like I'm probably doing with Bob, with Andy, with Walmart woman?

I can't answer that now. But all these thoughts are quickly sinking under a much weightier realization: I can't take Annaleigh back to Eauverte. Not if CPS is involved. I have to take her somewhere safe. Out of Dover County isn't good enough. Out of the state would be better.

And just like that, I know where I have to go.

I wipe my mouth and stand. "Thanks for lunch."

"Wait, Julia," says Andy, also standing. "You can't just leave. If they're after Annaleigh? It's not safe. We need a plan."

Our lunch is only half-finished, but my appetite is gone.

Wait. I've done a lot of that. Waiting to be accepted. Waiting for things with Josh to get better. Waiting for our marriage to feel stable. Waiting for our life to feel like it was supposed to.

Of course I want a plan. Of course I want safety.

But I can't wait any longer.

THEN

The two-on-one date is a nasty surprise.

New York Gillian and I eye each other over Josh, who's sitting between us in the back seat of the SUV, looking ahead and occasionally sharing fun historical or geographical details about the area with the energetic charm of a tour guide.

But neither of us is here for tour guide vibes. So Gill and I suffer through it with what I'm convinced is a secret competition of who can seem the most genuinely interested.

It turns out there aren't as many synonyms for *fascinating* as I thought.

Out the window, the California landscape has dried into rolling yellow hills roasting under the morning sun. A view that makes you thirsty just by looking.

"This is Antelope Valley," Josh says. "Just half an hour away now from Vasquez Rocks Park."

We're rock climbing today, which would be exciting, except for the two-on-one aspect, which, according to the rules of the show, means that Josh will eliminate either Gillian or me by the end of the date. Gillian and I both had to pack our bags this morning, so that whoever gets eliminated is ready to go quickly and with no fanfare.

"So you're a rock climber, Josh?" says Gillian. She sounds different than normal. Like she's trying to be sweet instead of her sarcastic self.

"Yeah, there's a climbing wall in Indianapolis I go to with some buddies. But this is my first time climbing in the great outdoors."

"I can't wait," says Gillian, which is such a lie. She hates anything that makes her sweat. She smiles at me. "You'll need extra sunscreen, Jules."

"I brought some," I say, smiling back.

At the park, climbing experts help us into the gear. Then, the three of us scale a red cliff that juts sideways out of the land, like a crashed spaceship. It's spectacular, and I find I'm a natural at locating footholds and nooks to grip on my way up. I've never sweated so much in my life, and as the dry breeze moves against my wet skin, I'm surprised to find that I love the feeling.

Josh, showing off his pure muscle in a sleeveless tank, arrives at the top first. I arrive second, and after a high five, we peer over the edge together. Gillian is still struggling toward the middle.

"You should go back down and encourage her," I say, squinting at Josh's handsome form. His tank is drenched in sweat, his scent strong. Mmm, why is that such a turn-on?

"Really? You're encouraging me toward the competition?" He flexes his arms behind his head. "I thought this was going to be a catfight to get my attention."

I laugh. "I don't think a few minutes more or less with you is going to make or break either of us."

He grins. "Alright. I'll go be a gentleman."

Shielding my eyes from the sun's glare, I watch him descend. After he and Gillian make it to the top, we all high-five. Then we rappel down.

As I chug water from a cooler, Josh asks Gillian to take a walk alone with him. I entertain myself during their absence by gazing out at the stark landscape and chatting with one of the camera guys about his fiancée. He lets me try on his sunglasses, and I make silly faces for the confessional camera while he asks me about the day so far. I can see a team setting up a fancy picnic some distance away.

When Josh comes back, Gillian-less and with a heavy step, I rise to greet him.

"So…that sucked. I just said goodbye to Gillian."

I reach out both my hands, feeling a mix of euphoria and genuine sorrow that *I* didn't get to say goodbye to Gill. I've come a long way from my nest-of-vipers days. He takes my hands and squeezes.

"I'm sorry," I say. "She was special, you know?"

He looks at me with a kind of wonderment. "See? This is what makes you different. You're so nice, even when there's no payoff. Some of the other girls…well, I guess I shouldn't tell you the kinds of things they say. If I'm being a gentleman."

Of course I'm curious, but I'm also smarter than that.

"Yeah," I agree. "Why let other people's negativity ruin the moment?"

Josh's dimples both come out. "You make me want to be better. I should keep you around."

I couldn't be smiling bigger as we walk toward the picnic that's waiting in the shade of the rock. But Josh is still pensive.

"I was an angry teen, you know? Definitely not a gentleman. With my parents' divorce, and my dad being gone…"

We settle on the blanket and I open a bottle of white.

"Did you have good friends, at least, to support you?"

"I mean—not *good* friends. A lot of idiots like me. And some girlfriends. But I wouldn't call them supportive. We were all just… I don't know. Young and stupid."

"Girlfriends," I prompt as I pour two glasses. "Yeah, I haven't heard much about your romantic history."

"I've always dated casually. I guess my first girlfriend was in college. She was really sweet. And also kind of a wreck. We dated sophomore year for a couple months, and then she went crazy on me." He shivers visibly.

"Crazy?"

"I broke up with her, you know, as one does when one is nineteen and has no idea what they're doing or what they want. We hadn't met each other's families or said I love you or anything, like…it wasn't *that* serious. But she lost it. Started to stalk me. I had to delete all my social media. It was scary as shit that this girl I thought I knew had this…dark side."

"Did she stop after a while, or…" I prompt. I feel for teenage Josh. Everything I've heard about the teenage years both from him and the girls sounds painful and dramatic and, honestly, I'm a little grateful I didn't have to live through that.

"Yeah. But it shook me. I didn't seriously date again until my midtwenties. There was a girl I moved in with when I was twenty-six. Cassie. *That* lasted all of three weeks."

"Whose dark side ruined that?" I tease.

"Oh, definitely hers. The situation was, I was allergic to her cat. I didn't even know I was allergic! But she acted like I tricked her or something."

"So she chose the cat," I say lugubriously.

Josh laughs.

"Do you have a type?" I ask.

"Sure. I like sweet girls who know how to have fun, who don't take everything so seriously. Like you. People who are kind. Considerate."

"Not stalkers."

He laughs. "Right."

"Or cat owners."

"I mean, ideally."

"But no physical traits, huh? Skinny, curvy, blondes, brunettes—"

"Redheads," he admits with a bashful grin. "I don't know what it is, but I do love me a redhead."

"Oh my God, really?" I say, feigning surprise and tossing my ponytail.

He hooks a finger under my chin and tugs my face close. Our lips meet. He tastes like salt from our sweaty climb, like wine, like laughter, and I want more than anything to be the woman with no dark side. To be full of light, and fun, and all the things that will make him happy forever.

We pull back. He's flushed from our kiss, his face a little rough with the first shadow of a beard, his eyes alive with desire. The date is now fully ours, and the shadow of the rock reminds me of the rush of victory I felt when Josh and I were standing up there together, looking down on the rest of the world. Like we could conquer anything.

Something squeezes at my heart, and I can't tell if it's a moment of great strength or utter weakness, but the words slip out without me even meaning to say them.

"I love you."

NOW

"Does she sleep through the night?" says Vanessa, crossing her slim legs and giving a faintly disturbed look toward the car seat where Annaleigh is still passed out after our four-hour drive to Chicago. We stopped once. I nursed her in a gas station parking lot while guzzling an ice-cold Coke. Other than that, it was pedal-to-the-floor, until we hit the wall of traffic around Chicago.

It's just after four o'clock, and the light coming through my father-in-law's floor-to-ceiling windows is cold and gray, making the austere designer furniture and pale floors of the condo look even starker.

"Of course not," Phil says to Vanessa in stoic tones from the black Eames chair that reeks of money and class. "She's a baby."

My father-in-law is absolutely what I expected: tall like Josh, handsome to a fault, with a well-groomed silver beard and an unshakeable demeanor. He's taken the news of his son's disappearance as calmly as he's taking the arrival of his granddaughter and synthetic daughter-in-law.

"I need your help," I said when I arrived ten minutes ago.

I kept my story simple. Didn't drag up the past. Didn't challenge Phil on why he didn't attend our wedding or acknowledge his granddaughter's birth announcement. He listened in utter silence, then nodded once, which I took as a sign that he was agreeing to do what I asked: take care of my baby until this blows over.

In spite of what Josh has told me about his dad and the divorce, and in spite of the tanned young fiancée in athletic wear perched on his couch, he is exactly what I need right now. Indifferent and cold? Maybe. But also strong and unflappable. I'd like to see Mitchell show up at *this* door. Phil LaSala would probably sue him just for knocking, and win.

"She wakes up around nine, and then around two," I say with forced calm, trying to suppress the voices in my head that are screaming, *Do not leave your baby in the care of a seventy-year-old narcissist and a twenty-two-year-old child!*

"Two in the *morning*?" says Vanessa, placing a manicured hand to her chest.

"Yes. Then she usually sleeps until about six. I'll set up a blanket on the floor for her bed."

"The guest bed—" starts Vanessa.

"She could roll off it," interrupts Phil.

I give him a grateful look. "She's also going to need diapers. Wipes. And formula. I didn't have time to stop."

"Not a problem," says Phil easily. I've quickly gathered that Phil has enough money to make most problems simply go away. "I'll call my assistant."

"I don't mind running out, babe," offers Vanessa, sitting up straight and looking pitifully eager.

"Sherri will take care of it," says Phil. "I'll call her now."

"I'll set up Annaleigh's sleeping spot before I go," I say. "Where should I do that?"

Vanessa leads me into a bright hall. Huge windows are on our left, the city of Chicago spread out beneath us, colorless and vast. On the right, doors to bedrooms and bathrooms. Vanessa opens the one at the end. I see the perfect spot for Annaleigh's

nest, wedged between wall, bed, and window. No cords or out-
lets in sight.

"Should I pull some blankets off the bed?" I ask as I survey
the perfectly made queen-size bed. "Or use something else?"

"Let me get you different blankets," says Vanessa.

She leaves me alone. The room is small, modern, clean. Black
bed frame, abstract art in vivid shades of red. There's a bookshelf
on the wall opposite the windows, splashed with a few color-
coordinated books and silver-framed pictures. I walk over to in-
spect the pictures, all of Vanessa and Phil. On the beach, skiing,
resplendent in expensive-looking evening wear. A silver sculpture of a horse sits astride a small stack of flip-book-style photo
albums. Curious, I move the horse aside and open the top album.

Josh.

Josh as a baby, Josh's school pictures, Josh getting taller, getting
braces, getting a new bike. The pictures look cheaply printed,
like they were downloaded from lower quality computer images. Maybe Phil looked at Josh's social media, back when Josh
had his accounts, to check on his son. Chose a few images to
print. It's oddly touching to imagine this. It isn't a voluminous
album, and we quickly progress to young-man Josh in a cap and
gown. Josh moving into what looks like a college dorm. Young,
wild-haired Josh with...

I suck in my breath.

Me.

No. A different redhead. Who on closer inspection doesn't
look like me at all, save the red hair, which on even closer inspection looks dyed. She's not even in the foreground of the picture. Josh is front and center, and she's behind him, with a few
other people. I'd put them all in their late teens or early twenties. Josh's hair is longer than I've seen it. He has a goofy expression, like he's in the middle of saying something funny. And the
girl...she's gazing at Josh with a look I know.

The look in Andy's eyes as we sat across from each other at Siam House, just hours ago.

You're perfect, Julia Walden.

She has to be the stalker girlfriend. The sweet wreck with the surprise dark side. In spite of how open Josh has been about everything, it still feels weird to see the evidence of how far back his romantic history goes, especially when my romantic history started and ended with him.

I touch their little faces and wonder when exactly this picture was taken. At the exciting new beginning? Or close to the disastrous end? Obviously, Phil had no way of knowing when he printed this picture that Josh was about to get massively hurt. And who could have guessed? Josh looks young, happy, and full of life.

The final picture in the album is a magazine cutout of Josh proposing to me on the show. He's in a light gray suit, kneeling, looking up. I'm in a blush-colored mermaid-cut evening gown with my hair in a loose knot at my neck, looking down, one hand covering my mouth.

Two people in the throes of their exciting new beginning... and not so far from their disastrous end.

I snap the book shut.

"Oh, you found the photo album!" Vanessa has returned with an armful of blankets.

"I hope you don't mind..." I return the album to the shelf. My fingers are trembling.

"No! It's okay! I actually made it for Phil, as a surprise. I just thought it was weird he didn't have pictures of Josh around, so for his sixty-ninth birthday..."

Ah. The sweet image of Phil scouring the internet for information about his son crumbles.

"Where did you find all those pictures, though?" I say. "Josh got rid of his social media way before he met me."

She titters. "I have a friend who works for Facebook. You

know they never delete any of that stuff, right? I took him out for sushi as a thank-you."

Okay, that's slightly creepy…but nice, too. As judgy as I felt toward Vanessa minutes ago, I'm starting to feel like, given time, the two of us might really like each other.

After I construct Annaleigh's nest, we return to the living room, where Phil is wrapping up his phone call.

"Well, her bed is set up," I announce. "The diaper bag is there. I'd better go."

"You sure you want to rush off?" says Phil. "You must be hungry. Vanessa can make us a quick dinner." At his gesture, she scurries into the kitchen.

"Do you like bulgur?" She opens the fridge. "I also have tempeh…"

"No, please—I shouldn't linger." With one stop for dinner and gas, I should be home no later than ten. "Thank you for taking care of Annaleigh. I'll call to check in. You have my number. Call me with any questions. Anything at all, at any time."

"She'll be right here waiting for you," says Phil.

I nod. Glance at my baby, who's blissfully asleep in the car seat, eyes buttoned, fingers closed into small pink fists. Completely trusting. With no idea that when she wakes up, her mama will be gone. There's a rock in my heart. Or my heart has become a rock.

Phil heaves himself up from his chair. "Good luck. I'll see you out." Transactional. Dry.

At the door, I'm so tempted to turn back and wake my baby up to say a proper goodbye. Nurse her one last time, kiss her sweet cheeks, give her all my promises that this is going to turn out alright and Mama will be back for her. But she wouldn't understand. Anyway, this isn't goodbye, I remind myself. This is temporary.

"One more thing," I say to Phil at the front door. "Why didn't you come to our wedding?"

He doesn't even flinch. Actually, he smiles, just a little. "We're not all cut out to be parents."

"He deserved better," I say with a tremble of passion.

"Listen, Julia," Phil says. "I may be a selfish bastard, but I own that. I decided what I wanted, and I got it." He gestures behind us, to the condo, Vanessa, the view of Chicago. "You want to know what Josh's problem is? He's never been honest with himself. He's too in love with what he wants to be. I say, life's too short. Be what you are. That's all you can be."

Be what you are? What a fatalistic, asshole cop-out. Likely, the words Phil LaSala stroked his own ego with as he drove away from the heartbroken eight-year-old that was Josh. What's wrong with striving to be better?

"How would you know that about Josh when you weren't even around?" I challenge.

"A father knows," he says. Then he narrows his eyes and nods, like he's making his assessment of me. "I like you, Julia. And if my son left you, screw him. Move on."

"He didn't leave me," I whisper angrily.

Phil's smile is light. "It's only a guess."

"He loves me. And I love him."

"Good for you."

I can't keep a final fierceness out of my voice. "Also, just so we're clear right now? You may not give a fuck about Josh, or about me, and I'm not going to ask you to start. But you will care about Annaleigh. You will give a goddamn fuck when it comes to her." Not a question. An order.

He nods. "I will."

And on the promise of those two words, I leave.

THEN

"You're going to the City of Love—Paris!" cries Matt.

It's pure, unbridled emotion. Zoe's crying, Emma's whooping, Camila is clasping her hands like she won a pageant.

We've just endured another rose ceremony elimination, and we're down to seven girls. Only four of us will return from Paris as contestants. Things are getting real.

Last week's trip took us to Indianapolis, Josh's home base, and away from the eternal summer of LA. We didn't meet his family or see his condo, but I did get a feel for the city, despite the nasty February wintry mix that fell half the time. Indy has an up-and-coming artsy-hipster vibe mixed with an ineffable Midwestern wholesomeness, and I loved it. I can totally see myself living there with Josh.

"I've never left the country," bawls Zoe. "I'm just so grateful!"

Neither have I, and I feel flushed with excitement.

Champagne is brought out, confetti is released, a giant French flag is unfurled. Josh pops the champagne and a man in a striped shirt waltzes around playing "La Vie en Rose" on the accordion. It's total delightful chaos.

"Who speaks French?" Emma is asking as Josh pours champagne into eight cut-glass flutes. "Does anyone speak French?" No one does, but only Emma seems to care.

As Josh hands me a glass, he leans in, his warm breath brushing my skin.

"I can't wait to show you the world, Julia Walden."

"I can't wait to see it with you, Josh LaSala," I return.

I'm about to get a taste for that bigger world Cam was talking about...but she was wrong. It's not a choice between the world and Josh. I can have both.

Everyone disperses into knots of conversation. Zoe cries into Josh's blazer. One girl is announcing her packing strategy for international travel. "Step one, try to limit yourself to six pairs of shoes!" Another is bemoaning her unflattering passport photo. I just smile.

Once again, I was the second girl called in the rose ceremony, after Cam. She's been called first almost every week, and it's become a comforting routine to see her standing in the "chosen ones" area. She always smiles as I walk toward her and mouths, *Bitch.* It's our cute little ritual.

Speaking of Cam, here she comes, her dark hair in an elegant messy bun, her figure exuberant in an off-shoulder chartreuse gown with a slit all the way to her hip.

"Were you surprised to see Sarah go?" she says.

Cam's other ritual with me is talking shit about whoever just got eliminated. Well—she talks. I listen.

"I'm always surprised to see who goes," I admit. Every week, I can't imagine Josh sending anyone home. I always have a feeling of unreality as some poor girl who doesn't feel ready to go is forced to leave forever.

"Would you be shocked to know that Josh already told me he was sending her home, on the DL?" says Cam in a smug tone.

"Yes," I say, my cheeks heating. Cameras are picking up our conversation. How is Sarah going to feel when she watches this episode and hears this little dig? I may be in love with Josh. But it doesn't mean I approve of this lack of consideration.

"Don't act so shocked," says Cam breezily. "We all know she was just here to promote her skin-care brand. What was it called?"

LaMareaX, I could supply, and it was more than skin care—a "full lifestyle brand," according to Sarah—but that's not the point. It's Josh's behavior that's concerning to me.

"It's just not very...gentlemanly of him."

"Gentlemanly?" says Cam with a look of exaggerated surprise. "Oh, honey. I wouldn't call Josh *gentlemanly*."

There's a nasty slosh in my stomach, but I play it cool. "That's how he is with me. What's he like with you?"

"You know. Like guys are."

I don't know, actually. "Which is..."

"Sooo much more emotional than they realize. *God*. Like, guys *think* they're all strong and manly or whatever, but they are absolute children on the inside. Their egos are tiny fragile little toys. The wounded pride! The temper tantrums! It's all so *dramatic* for them."

My eyes are suddenly hot. I blink fast.

"Did I upset you?" says Cam, looking at me with concern, but also like I'm a scientific specimen she's confused about how to classify.

"No! It's just..." To my shock and horror, tears are brimming. "Josh is so nice with me." The words tumble out urgent, fast, and at a whisper. "He's been such a gentleman, so open and considerate, and he says he wants to be a better man when he's with me, and the Josh you're talking about doesn't seem like the same Josh that—" Tears stop me.

What if he isn't what he seems? And why hasn't this possibility occurred to me before tonight? My whole self is in this. My whole heart. Is his?

Cam lays a cool hand on my bare arm.

"Shhh. Hey. You know what this is, Red? It's two different sides of Josh. One comes out with you, one comes out with me. I bring out his crazier, more vulnerable emotional side, and you bring out this steadier, like, stronger person he's striving to be."

Worse and worse. "So he's real with you and fake with me?"

"No!" Her tone is conciliatory. "Not like that! One is more… more *actual*, and one is *aspirational*. Both are equally real!" Cam is starting to look distressed at my distress. Like she'll say anything now to calm me down. But I don't want her to say anything. I want the truth.

"Are you trying to tell me I don't know the real Josh?" I catch the shadow of a camera out of the corner of my eye and I almost regret saying this. But it's too important to let slide.

Cam tsks gently. "I think you *do* know him, Julia. Calm down, okay? Just keep moving forward, and everything will become clearer as you go. And please—" She smiles teasingly. "Don't become a second Zoe, because I swear to God that will be the straw that finally fucking breaks me."

We both glance at Zoe, who, obviously buzzed and done crying, is trying to start a conga line with the accordion player.

"Sorry," I say with a shaky breath, turning back to Camila. "I'll try to chill."

"I mean, your concerns are real. Like, how well do either of us know Josh? This isn't real life. But he's not an orange. You can't peel him." I crack a grin at her metaphor. "He's a person with layers and complications and a three-dimensional personality that has to be discovered little by little. Just keep being honest and keep asking for his honesty."

"Okay." I suck in my breath. I have to calm down, even though I'm still shaken. The casual way Cam just said, *This isn't real life*? Maybe it's not real life for these girls. Cam has her modeling. Sarah has her skin care. Gill has her lawyering. For me, the show is all I've known.

I know I haven't been alive that long. I know I'm learning. But there's a line between innocence and foolishness, and I don't want to be the only one who couldn't see what was right in front of her. The strain of the accordion grows as the musician twirls past me. "La Vie en Rose"…seems timely. A reminder that the show I'm living through is carefully orchestrated, designed as much for the rosy experience of future viewers as it is for present-day us.

My feelings are real. That, I don't doubt. I just have to make sure that Josh is being real, too.

"You got this," Camila proclaims, delivering a smack on my butt. Then she mouths, *Bitch*, and I have to smile.

Cam heads off to talk to someone else, and I take a second to reorient myself, out of my mental world and back into the real one. Or rather, into the world that may or may not be real, but is also my entire lived experience.

"Everything okay?"

I startle—Josh has sneaked up behind me. "Oh, yes," I laugh, hoping my mascara hasn't run and my nose isn't too red. It always gets red when I cry.

"Looked like you guys were really getting into it," says Josh, clinking his glass against mine. We both sip. The champagne is cool and dry. Soothing, after the heat of my emotion.

"Yes! Well…you know how Cam is." I smile. "Spicy."

"Yes, sirree," Josh says in a fake Southern drawl. "She's a whole jalapeño."

A hint of fun returns to my heart. It's because of Josh. I love how he can blow in like a fresh breeze and reset me.

"What does that make me?" I tease.

"Hmmmm." Josh squints. "Gold. When I'm with you, I feel like I've struck gold."

"No fair! I wanted a food item, too."

"Fine! What do you want? A cantaloupe?"

I make a face.

"Your hair is kind of orange," he continues, "and you're mellow and sweet and—"

I shimmy my hips. "Juicy?"

He cracks up, and so do I. Hearing him laugh, my fears don't *exactly* flee. I have more digging to do before I can put these new concerns to rest.

But France is ahead, and there's plenty more time, and for tonight, I have a rose.

NOW

I swerve and release a sharp yelp. Yank the car back into the lane, my headlights weaving like spooked animals on the dark road. Adrenaline follows, burning through my gut. *Shit.* I was milliseconds away from plummeting down a dark embankment.

"Wake up, Julia," I say, giving myself a dry smack on the cheek. I fumble for the fast-food bag on the passenger seat, but the French fries I fed myself one at a time to try and stay alert when I cleared Chicago are long gone.

I roll down all the windows, bringing in a blustery chill. Just a few more minutes. I can stay awake. Have to stay awake. I break into a full-volume rendition of "Bad Romance," which gets me to the County Road HH turnoff. Then I hit the brakes.

The reporters. What if they're camped out in my yard? I can't risk getting closer, so I pull the car onto the dirt shoulder and kill the engine. *Almost home.* And also, not. Without Josh and Annaleigh, I'm just heading toward a place to sleep.

Purse slung over my shoulder, I emerge into the night and lock the car. It's 10:30 and the moon is playing peekaboo with the clouds. A humid chill is already seeping through my sweater. The trees are quiet, the sinews of their branches disappearing into the black above, like instead of trees they're the roots of the sky, and the world at night some dank underground.

I turn on my phone flashlight and head straight through the grassy strip that lines the road, soft with mud, making my way toward the woods that curve around this whole little section—my best hope at approaching my own house without being spotted. A final glance behind me shows the black hulk of my lonely car, and the lonelier road behind it. I try not to think about the horrors these woods have seen. Did Royce do his deeds at night, under this same moon? On that stump over there—or that one? Did he swing true and make clean cuts, or did he hack…and hack… There's a nasty edge to my heartbeat as I step into the inky trees. It feels like being swallowed alive. Would anyone bat an eye, passing my remains? Will my synthetic skin last, year after year, under the sun and rain and snow, or have they programmed it to imitate the natural rot of human flesh?

My pulse pumps in my ears as I walk through the trees, the ghost-white light from my phone jittering with each step. The forest dances around me like a creature in its death spasms, with me creeping between its ribs. I'm trying to see if I've already passed the first house when my flashlight falls on something white. I gasp, recoiling—a bone? No—just a reflection off a beer bottle. I scan my light around and see evidence of people. A scorched area where there must have been a bonfire. A pile of ash. More beer bottles. *Keep going.*

A disturbance in the air becomes a hum, which soon becomes something deeper: the growl of machinery, churning like a restless creature. Snatches of dull, orange light appear through the trees—and there's the shape of Bob's barn, backlit against the glow. Is he grinding up deer meat? At this hour?

I use the cover of sound to hurry forward a little faster without worrying about how much noise I'm making. The black finger-shapes of the trees make his barn jump in and out of sight as I run, like a skipping projector. What does Bob do, exactly, in that barn? With no one to watch, what might he be feeding into his machines—

My mind jumps to the baby monitor, the male growl of his voice. *Shhhh, little lady...* I shiver. Annaleigh is safe now. For all I care, Bob can spend the rest of his days singing his lullabies into the fucking void.

His property is much wider than ours, and I'm soon surrounded by more trees and zero light. It feels too silent, and my footsteps overloud.

"C'mon, it's not that hard to find your own house," I whisper to myself, though I'm also dreading my arrival. Walking in alone. At least Captain will be there.

"No! She didn't kill him!" comes a clear voice, so sudden that I stop in my tracks, immediately pressing my phone's flashlight into my jeans to conceal my presence. "I've told you already. I saw him leave Saturday night with my own two eyes. She was home drinking and like...watching Netflix!" There's no mistaking Eden's voice. "Three strikes you're out means there was a third time. There were only two." Her breathing is quick, agitated. "No. I have a view into her house, for fuck's sake...From the woods...Yes...No...No...I'm in her house all the time. I would have known."

My heart is like a revving engine. There's black behind me. Black in front. And somewhere in that blackness is my babysitter. I try to breathe evenly, quietly. A fiery glow briefly lights the darkness and I try to estimate the distance between us. Thirty feet, maybe?

"No, she's not home yet." Silence, another burn of orange. The earthy smell of weed filters toward me. "Of course I'll call you...Anything new...Sure, boss."

There's a brief illumination from her phone that casts her profile in white light. Then the woods go dark again.

Do I stand here? Wait for her to leave? Something tickles my ankle and I move my foot. A twig cracks. *Fuck.*

"Who's there?" she calls out.

Should I try to hide? But it's so dark, I can't see what to hide behind.

"Who's there?" Eden repeats. "Don't move! I have a gun!" There are sounds of fumbling, then a bright light shines in my eyes. I whip out my own phone, shining its light on Eden. She looks small and pale in the darkness. She's wearing an oversize sweatshirt over jeans and holding her joint in one hand, her phone in the other. Definitely no gun.

"Julia? What are you doing here?" Her look of fear melts into concern as she tromps toward me. "Are you okay? Is Annaleigh safe?"

"Who were you talking to about me?" I say, my voice shaking. I can't tell if it's exhaustion or rage at this point.

"Fuck, Julia." She sighs and walks closer, her steps cracking and crunching. "It was the sheriff, okay?"

"At this time of night?"

She stops in front of me. "He's been on my ass to tell him when you got home. I'm sorry. I'm not helping him, though! I'm just playing along."

I don't buy it, not for a second.

"You call the sheriff boss?"

"I call everyone boss," she says with a regretful tone, like this is a habit that annoys even her.

"What did you mean, telling him you're in my house all the time?"

"He keeps asking me about Saturday night. He's obsessed with this idea that you killed Josh that night. I keep telling him the same shit I told you. I'm at your house all the time *and* I can see through your windows. I think I would have noticed if you murdered someone." She exhales a frustrated breath. "Do you think I could sue him for harassment? Because—"

"Forget the sheriff. You lied to me."

In the cold light from my phone, her face goes still.

"About what?"

"You worked for Andy. For WekTech."

She makes a pained expression. "How did you—"

"A picture in the robotics building at IU."

"I mean… I never told you I *didn't* work for WekTech. Error of omission, okay? Like I said, my career ended in a fucking trash fire. Can you blame me for not advertising my most embarrassing disaster to everyone I meet?"

"What exactly happened, Eden?"

"What do you already know?"

"No. You tell me. Now."

She fits the joint to her lips and draws in, hollowing her cheeks. She holds the smoke in for a few seconds, then slowly puffs it out. "Want some?" Her tone is resigned.

I reach for the joint. Why the hell not. I'm alone in the woods with someone who may or may not wish me ill, steps away from a neighbor who sure as hell does, with a sheriff on my ass and my daughter hundreds of miles away. If anything, this may help ease my anxiety enough so I can get one good night of sleep. I inhale deeply.

"Easy there," she cautions. "If it's your first time—"

"I'll be fine." I hold the joint between my fingers as I release the smoke into the night air. "Talk."

"Right. WekTech. Well… I got this dream internship there. Like, six years ago? Anyway. Might as well be a lifetime. I got this massively stupid idea to prank the CEO by hacking into his phone. Pure attention-getting. I was pissed that he didn't know my name. I was just the intern, you know? Like, hey, intern, can you run this down to Marketing? Hey, intern, where's my coffee? Anyway. I got his attention, that's for sure. He fired my ass, and my stellar career came to a quick and violent conclusion."

I take a second drag, then return the joint to Eden.

"Okay." I nod slowly, smoke billowing from my mouth. "So what happened next? You went back to school and—"

"I didn't go back. I bartended in LA for a few years, but cost of living was so high… Then the pandemic hit and the restaurant I worked at closed, and it made sense to move in with my aunt and uncle."

"Right down the road from me, on one of only six adjacent lots."

"Weirder shit has happened?" she says tentatively, with the face of a child who's just hoping her parent will buy her lie and move on.

I don't even answer.

"Fine," she concedes. "If you must know, I did move here for you. I'm a robotics nerd, okay? And I'm working on my own robotics shit in my spare time. At some point, I'd like to have a real career."

"Then you've been spying on me."

"No, actually," she says. "It was stupid. Impulsive, like a lot of the shit I've done. At this point, you're just a person who lives down the street, Julia, and I love watching your kid. That's pretty much the extent of it."

I raise my phone so it shines right into her round brown eyes.

"Eden, I need you to be totally honest with me now. Are you still working for Andy?"

"I just said, he *fired* me."

"Then who are you working for, Eden? Just tell me the truth."

Her eyes go glassy, like maybe she's holding back tears. She touches my arm. Presses. Her hand is small. Its pressure, soft. I can't help but remember that these are the same hands that have cared so tenderly for Annaleigh. That this is the same girl who has seen me at my weakest and not turned away.

"You," Eden says, her voice breaking and a tear slipping out. It sparkles in the light. "The only person I'm working for is you, Julia."

For the space of two seconds, my brain is so caught up in conspiracy theories of Eden working for BotTech or Eden spying for some lobbyist, or even Eden and Andy lying to me together, I have no idea what she means. Then it hits me.

She works for me. Babysitting Annaleigh.

I deflate on the spot. "Right."

Eden's fingers scritch my arm a little before releasing me. "Let me walk you home, okay? You look like you're about to collapse."

"Yeah," I agree. "Home."

We walk together through the woods without speaking. Soon there's a glint of glass and a piercing reflection from my flashlight. My windows. *Finally.*

Eden walks me to the back door. "Want me to see you in? Check the closets for monsters?"

Half of me wants to invite her to sleep on my couch, just so I'm not alone.

The other half thinks that couldn't be a stupider idea.

"No thanks," I say.

Because even though I believe with all my heart that Eden doesn't wish me ill, I know she's still hiding something.

And this time, it's more than just an error of omission.

THEN

Despite the February weather, Paris is incredible, and we spend the first day, just the seven of us girls, touring famous sites while the crew collects footage. We climb the Eiffel Tower and tour Notre Dame. The weather may be cold, but our coats are warm. The cameras following us attract a lot of attention, and random people stop to take our picture.

Camila flirts with everyone she sees, blowing kisses and tossing her hair. We order crêpes au beurre from a street vendor, where Camila's attempts at ordering in French have us rolling. The man making the crêpes proposes to her in broken English. "You…marry…me," he keeps repeating, thumping his hand on his chest. Cam thumps her hand in imitation. "Moi…marry… Josh!"

The world seems larger and lovelier than ever, the French people delightful, and during my one-on-one with Josh during our second week in the City of Love, I tell him I love him again, because once wasn't enough.

"I know you're not there yet," I reassure him as we walk through the narrow cobblestone streets of the Marais at night, our held hands swinging between us, the air chilly and sweet and my feelings even sweeter, "but I can't hold back."

It's true. I've found that not even my fears are enough to make me pull back. They coexist uncomfortably, woven into my passion like two hands meeting, one cold, one warm.

"That's okay," Josh says. He's wearing jeans, a white T-shirt and a black leather jacket, with a stocking cap to keep his ears warm, which contrasts nicely with the soft lavender cocoon coat I'm wearing over my bold floral pantsuit. The sexy and the sweet, the hard and the soft. "I love that you're all in."

We end the night making out against a wall in a narrow pedestrian-only street.

When we come up for air, I'm so high on love that it feels safe to ask Josh the question that I've been turning around privately since my talk with Cam.

"You know how you said sometimes the other girls...talk?" I say. "About each other, or whatever?"

"Mmm," he murmurs, like he's still lost in the kissing zone.

"Well, sometimes, we talk about *you*." I boop him on the nose with a finger.

He doesn't seem at all concerned. Just amused.

"And what do you talk about?" he says. Before I can answer, he brushes his lips against mine, then comes in for another pass, sweeping his tongue across my lower lip. I gasp a little as his tongue slips into my mouth. My head falls back and I feel the gravity of his body, hovering just above mine. Heat drips down, pooling in my gut, between my legs...

Using all my self-control, I bracket his face in my hands and gently remove him. He pretends to strain against me.

"I was *trying* to say—"

He advances toward my lips again, but I keep his face clamped between my hands.

"—that Cam and I see you differently, and...it makes me wonder."

He pulls back. I drop my hands.

All of a sudden I'm the teensiest bit nervous.

"Don't take this the wrong way," I say, "but sometimes I worry that I'm not seeing the full picture. Like, I know you've been real with me throughout this process. But when I hear Cam talk about you, it feels like she's talking about someone else. Not the Josh I know."

He takes a half step back. "Are you accusing me of—"

"No! No, I just—" I lick my lips. "Are there parts of you that you're kind of holding back when you're with me? And... is it *me*? Like, do I make you feel like you have to...repress anything? Because I don't want to. I want you to be yourself with me. Your whole self."

He stuffs his hands in his pockets, and I wrap my arms around my torso. Suddenly my nose feels cold. I want to press further and say, *Is this real? Or is this just TV, and I'm the fool?* But he's already reacting so strongly...

"Want to walk?" he says.

"Sure." We set off. Not holding hands.

He looks down at his feet as he talks. "It's true that you and Cam bring out different sides of me. That's why I feel so...torn between you." The cobblestones are worn and shining under the soft streetlight. "With her, it's like my younger side comes out. College Josh, who just wanted to party and be adored and have a good time."

"And with me?" I prompt softly.

"Our relationship feels more mature."

"But we have fun together, too."

"Yeah. We laugh a lot. But the flavor is more..."

"Cantaloupe?" I hazard, desperate to lighten the moment even though I'm the one who introduced the heaviness. Prove to him that *mature* doesn't have to mean *boring.*

He laughs. "Yeah."

"Tell me more about College Josh."

"I guess I was insecure. I didn't know it at the time. I *really* didn't want to end up like my mom. Divorced, miserable, alone. So I overcompensated. I got a girlfriend—"

"Stalker girl."

He nods. "—and partied my ass off. Tried to grab happiness by the balls, you know? Dad made Mom so miserable. I didn't want anyone to have that power over me. I wanted to make my own life. And never be anyone's victim."

"That makes sense."

"I guess that's why the stalker girlfriend stuff was so intense. It felt like my worst nightmare. Like, she's going to make me miserable and there's nothing I can do about it." We walk in silence. He seems deep in thought, so I don't interrupt.

"I know it wasn't Mom's fault that Dad left," he finally says. "Dad's the asshole. But I guess I kind of hated her for it anyway." He laughs bitterly. "I guess that's pretty messed up. Despising her for being weak."

Is weakness despicable? He was so tender with me when I was weak, after the attack...but maybe this is different.

"What's your relationship with her like now?" I say.

"Great." Josh grins, and I'm so relieved to see him smiling. "Mom doesn't love that I'm on the show, to be honest. She's not a fan of reality TV unless it's home makeover shows. But once she sees me happy, she'll get over it."

"I hope I get to meet her. How will she feel about...you know."

"What?"

I whack him on the arm. "That I'm a Synth."

He acts surprised, like he forgot, which is...good?

"She might have trouble at first. But like I said, if I'm happy, she'll come around."

Okay. Not ideal; I'd prefer to hear his mom would embrace me with open arms. But I appreciate his honesty, and—isn't honesty what I was looking for?

"So. Have I addressed your concerns?" says Josh, coming to a stop. We're about to move from the narrow, solitary street onto a busier thoroughfare.

"Yeah," I say, my eyes taking in the curve of his cheekbone, the little twist in his lip. He's so damn beautiful. "Thanks for being so open. I appreciate it. A lot."

His grin crinkles. And suddenly Josh's hand is at the small of my back where I like it, and he's spinning me against the nearby wall. He braces an arm above me. Shadows settle into the angles of his jaw, his brow, turning his eyes into wells of darkness.

"Now, where did we leave off, Miss Julia?"

I stroke his cheek, rough with stubble. "What you're trying to say right now is, less analyzing, more kiss—"

But his mouth pressing into mine cuts off my words.

I've never been so deliciously silenced.

NOW

I wake to furious knocking at my front door and sit straight up. Eight in the morning. Captain shoots off the bed and thunders downstairs.

I groan as I swing my legs over the side of the bed, then I stumble after my dog, still in my rumpled clothes from last night. I don't know if it was overexhaustion or some newbie reaction to weed, but I did not sleep well.

I look through the peephole. *Fuck.* Sheriff Mitchell and Deputy Adams. And behind them, more reporters than I can count on both freaking hands. In fact, the whole road is a mess of news vans and cars. Giving my hair a quick swipe back, I crack the door.

"Yes?"

"Miz Walden." The sheriff's look is appraising. "I didn't think you were coming back."

I lay a hand on Captain's head. He's tense at my side, alert, and I wish I could order him to rip into the sheriff. Instead, I open the door a little wider and jerk my head for them to come in. Which is more of a welcome than these two deserve.

The sheriff removes his hat as he crosses my threshold, as does Adams. I lock the door behind us.

"Kitchen," I say in my raspy morning voice, leading the way to the back of the house.

I have a moment of déjà vu as they sit at my table.

The sheriff sniffs. "Is that the smell of marijuana, Miz Walden?"

Shit.

I sniff, too, feigning surprise, plucking at my clothes. "Maybe?"

"You do realize that is an illegal drug in the State of Indiana."

"Go tell the people who've been camped in my yard all night," I snap. "And you know what else? They're trespassing. Isn't it your responsibility to remove them?"

Silence greets me.

"I need coffee," I say, half to them, half to myself. They're silent as I set the coffee maker. Next, I feed Captain, dumping more of Bob's homemade concoction into his bowl. It's getting pretty pungent, but Captain wolfs it right down. I put the container in the sink to remind myself to put the rest down the garbage disposal.

"Where were you yesterday, Julia?" says the sheriff when I finally lean against the counter and face the men, my back to the gurgling coffee maker.

"Like I said, lunch with a friend. You told me there was a new development. What is it?"

"First, I'd like you to walk me through Saturday night. In detail."

I stare at him. *Fuck.*

"You can start when you're ready," prompts the sheriff.

I need a minute to think, so I wordlessly turn my back on him and open the cabinet. Rummage for a mug. Slowly. Take out the coffeepot and pour. Finally, I turn, mug in hand.

"Well, I'd just put Annaleigh down for her last nap around four when Josh started packing. I was upset because he didn't tell me about his trip. He insisted he did." I shrug as Deputy Adams scrawls on his notepad. "It's possible I forgot. I'm in the sleep-deprived stage of parenting."

"You need sleep, do you?" Mitchell's gaze seems to undress me, past the clothes, down to the bone.

"As much as anyone else. And I'm not getting much." I raise my mug. Hence the coffee, asshole.

Mitchell nods for me to continue.

"I followed Josh around while he packed. We were arguing. And... I opened a bottle of wine."

"Are you a heavy drinker, Miz Walden?"

"No. I bought it for us to drink together. You know, date night in. But Josh was leaving, and he was mad at me, so I opened it. I thought it would help me relax. Josh doesn't like it when I get stressed."

"And then?"

"He left."

"What time?"

"Um...six? I was a little drunk by then, honestly. And I'd put Annaleigh down for bed."

"She's a nursing infant, correct?" says the sheriff. "But you still chose to become inebriated?"

My cheeks flush. "Pump and dump."

"Go on," says Mitchell.

"While Josh was putting his gear in the car, I texted my friend. Andy." I think I'm doing okay. If I can just skip past the gaps like they're not there...

"Do you make a habit of inviting male friends over when your husband is gone?"

I flush hotter, but force myself to maintain eye contact.

"I didn't want to be alone. Then I felt terrible that I was making Andy go out of his way. I actually texted him again and told him not to come after all." I don't remember doing this, but I've seen the texts. "But he didn't listen."

"Mr. Wekstein lives in Los Angeles, correct?" says Mitchell.

"Yes."

"What's he doing in Indiana?"

"He teaches at IU."

"If your husband left at six, and witnesses saw him set up his tent around ten, how do you explain that the two-hour trip to Belmont Ridge took him four?" Mitchell steeples his fingers by his lips.

I shrug, as if this doesn't alarm me, even though it totally does. "Maybe he stopped for gas? Dinner?" The idea is reasonable, but I don't quite believe it. Josh has always been the kind of guy who doesn't like to stop. Not even for a needed bathroom break.

"And what happened after Andy arrived?" coaxes Mitchell.

"He knew I was upset, and that it was about more than the hiking trip, and I ended up telling him…" God, I hope I'm not making a terrible mistake. My heart starts pounding so hard, I'm pretty sure they can see my shirt vibrating from across the kitchen. "Josh and I did have this…recurring fight. It's probably just one of those things. That people fight about."

Mitchell waits. Even Adams stops writing.

I have to force the words out. "Josh thought Andy was in love with me."

Adams's eyes widen, round and blue, then descend to his notepad. He scribbles furiously.

"That's what we were really arguing about while he was packing." I turn to refill my mug. I'm surprised to find it empty since I don't remember drinking it. But the taste of coffee is in my mouth, so I must have. Why can't I remember, though? Not just drinking coffee, but Saturday night. Even as I talk about it, my memories seem to move and resettle, like I'm sifting through sand instead of hard facts.

"It wasn't the first time," I continue, my back still to the men. "I was tired of the same old argument, so when Andy showed up, I asked him to please work it out with Josh. You know, man-to-man. That's why they were meeting for breakfast. I think I told you that when you were here on Wednesday." I pour the coffee. My hand is shaking. It's a miracle I don't spill. I finally turn back around.

"Yes, we spoke to Mr. Wekstein that day," says Mitchell. "What I'd like to know is why you told us that the two of them were..." He gestures to Adams, who flips back a couple pages in his notebook.

"Friendly," Adams says eagerly.

"Yes." The sheriff smiles. "Friendly."

"Well...they are. Were. Have been, I mean, they met on the show last year. They got along great. Andy even gave me away at our wedding. I love Josh—and Josh knows that. He just has this jealous side, you know, like guys do. He and Andy...they just needed to talk it out."

"And?" There's a lurid sheen to the sheriff's question, like he's peeling back the curtain on something obscene.

"And what?"

"Is Andy Wekstein in love with you, Julia?"

I plan on saying no. *Of course not!* But instead, my hand wanders up to my neck, cupping my frantic pulse.

"Sir, I'm not sure that question is fair," objects Adams, but Mitchell holds up a palm.

"Let her answer."

I don't want to make trouble for Andy. On the other hand, Mitchell will latch on to anything to make sure I burn. Maybe it wouldn't be so bad to draw a little attention to Andy. He can take the heat. If he's innocent, it won't hurt him in the long run. Not to mention, Andy has access to some of the best lawyers in the nation. I'm the vulnerable one.

"I..." Tightening my hands around my coffee, I bring the hot rim to rest under my lips. Breathe. "Yes. I think he might be."

Instantly I feel sick to my stomach. For throwing Andy under the bus, and also because deep down, I find this possibility incredibly disturbing. I don't want Andy to think of me that way. I want him to be the safe older brother who's looking out for me.

Mitchell's eyes appraise me. "Do you think Royce Sullivan

loved his victims, Julia? I've often wondered about the psychology behind dismembering one's romantic partner...twenty-two times. You must have wondered, too, living on his old property. Did he cut them to pieces so he could keep them? Did he feel love as his axe struck? Is it possible to love something so much you have to destroy it, just so it doesn't ever leave you?"

My chest burns and my throat tightens, as if physical hands are squeezing it from behind.

His question is clear.

"I would never hurt Josh. If he wanted to leave me, I would let him go, free. And whole."

Mitchell cocks his head. "Even if it hurt, Julia?"

I blink fast, trying to dispel the image of Josh in this very kitchen, trying to delete Andy's number from my cell phone as I tried to grab it back—

"When you love someone, sometimes..." I swallow. "Sometimes you let them hurt you."

"A dark view of love."

Dark? Maybe. Certainly not aspirational. But the reality is, love and pain can't be separated. Love opens you to hurt, and if you want love, you have to take the hurt, too.

"Realistic, I think." I can hear the thinness in my own voice.

Mitchell finally breaks eye contact, and I sag.

"You got all that?" he says to Adams.

"Yes, sir." Adams wraps up his note-taking with a flourish.

"Thank you for your time, Miz Walden." Mitchell and Adams both scrape their chairs back and stand.

"Wait—the development. You said there was something new."

"Oh...yes. The development." Mitchell smiles. "Funny, what with you living on Royce's old place..." He gestures to his elbow. "We found your husband's severed arm."

Blazing hot coffee is burning my hands before I even realize that it's my own electrified shaking that's spilling it. My fingers release on instinct. The mug shatters against the tile floor. Captain barks. Gripping the counter with one hand, I hold my other hand out toward my dog so he doesn't try to cross the minefield the kitchen floor has become.

"Forensics has informed me that the arm was cut from a dead body, not a living one," drawls Mitchell. "Funny how they can tell, isn't it? Which brings me to this, Miz Walden. We no longer have a missing person case on our hands." He calmly returns his hat to his head as if there's not coffee and broken glass all over the floor. "This is a murder investigation. And if things go my way, next time I see you will be with a warrant for your arrest."

"Sir," rebukes Adams, his face reddening. "With all due respect, let's not forget that Julia—I mean, Miz Walden—is presumed innocent until—"

"Proven guilty," finishes the sheriff with a grin toward me. Adams tightens his lips and looks down like he's ashamed.

"Why do you only seem to be coming after me?" I explode.

The sheriff walks out of the kitchen.

I follow, frantic. "Wait! I didn't kill him. You have to believe me. There are so many other people that could have— My neighbor Bob! He hates us. This—this crazy lady, she attacked me in California during filming, and I just found out she lives here— Oh—Josh's old girlfriend—she was a stalker! Everyone here hates us, it could have been anyone— I have bins of hate mail, maybe there could be a lead in there, a clue—" I know I sound like I'm trying to hide my guilt in this spastic avalanche of information, but I can't let him walk away like this, without even giving me a chance. "Aren't you going to write that down?" I look at Adams. We've reached the foyer. "I'm giving you leads! Please! You have to look into them!"

Adams reaches for his pen; Mitchell's head twitches *no*. Then his expression goes funny. "Is that—" Mitchell looks down, turns in a slow circle. Bends, until he's on all fours. He reaches under the entryway bench, behind the row of shoes and, after gesturing for Adams's pen, pulls out...

A silver watch.

The sound is suddenly overwhelming. *Tick-tick-tick.*

"I thought I heard a ticking sound." Mitchell straightens up, the watch dangling from the pen. "Still working. But cracked. This your husband's?"

I nod mutely. Adams withdraws a clear baggie. I know what they're thinking. Evidence. My heart is a monster trying to maul me from within.

"Does he normally wear it when he goes out?"

I nod again, like a marionette being yanked.

Mitchell steps close, the watch lifted between us, its metronome pounding. He lowers his voice. "Why is your husband's broken watch under there, Julia?"

I look at the blue face, the silver slashes, the jolt of the hand marking the seconds. It's going too fast, isn't it, and it's uneven, some seconds short, some long—

"Did you kill your husband? Did you take off his watch before severing his arm, or after? It was the left one, did I mention that? His watch arm—with the ring finger missing. Flung into the woods like someone tried to feed it to the animals…and, I should mention, an animal or two did find it, and the ants, dear Lord, it was like an oil spill, all those little black crawlers feasting, a real picnic…"

I can't speak.

The sheriff steps back and tips his hat in a gentlemanly gesture. He doesn't smile.

"No further questions."

THEN

Palm trees rustle above us. The smells of LA combine, the sweetness of heliotrope with the pungency of urine. Beauty and grime. My sweaty hand shifts against Josh's. We're walking up Industry Drive toward the fifteen-story building that hosts WekTech's LA offices. My stomach is gurgling, and I'm wishing I hadn't had breakfast, since it seems likely to come right back up.

"This is us," I say as we finally crest the hill, huffing and puffing from the climb. We could have been dropped off closer, but the producer wanted shots of us approaching the building. I wonder if they'll play ominous music when it airs. I suppose that will depend on what happens today. It's an eerie thought, imagining the film editors at work, like gods, knowing how it ends and retrofitting just the right clues to lead—or mislead—the viewers.

It's hometowns week with the final four girls: Cam, Emma, Zoe, and me. France is a happy blur. In a way, it feels like no time since I was stepping out of the limo barefoot, my high heels hooked over my finger, catching my first glimpse of Josh. Even though in actuality, the experience to this point has taken my entire life. Literally.

We stop in front of the glass doors leading into the building's foyer.

"This is weird, isn't it?" I ask.

"No," says Josh, instantly reassuring. "This is where you come from. I told you. I'm cool with it. I accept you."

I breathe out, not entirely believing him, but I'm learning to operate in that realm of halves, that tension between where you are and what you aspire to. Even though I know in my gut that Josh can't be as cool with this as he's letting on, rather than thinking of it as deception, as I might have a couple weeks ago, I'm thinking of it as direction. Reality can't be static, because we are creatures of time, and time is always ticking. Reality is taking another step in a chosen direction. And today, reality is Josh's choice to take a step over this threshold, into this building. For me.

I smile. "Let's go."

Hand in hand, we walk inside. The chill of the air conditioner hits my sweaty skin. I've worn a sleeveless maxi dress today, with a little jean jacket tied around my waist in case the evening gets cool. *If I make it to this evening.* What if Josh takes one look at anatomy blueprints, or swatches of synthetic skin, or any of the other hundreds of things he might find disturbing, and eliminates me on the spot?

And then there's our lunch with Andy and the team. Are they going to be weird and talk about how they designed me? Or pick apart my personality, explaining how each piece was made to fit with Josh's? I hope they know this would be in horrible taste, but...what else *would* they talk about? Their taste in movies?

A security guard issues us guest passes. We wait an absurdly long time for the elevator. And then, we're closed in with the cameraman, creeping upward, toward the fifteenth floor, each red number blinking like an accelerating heartbeat.

Fifteen. Ding. The doors crawl open and we're walking straight into the WekTech lobby.

It's white and minimalist with bold splashes of color. A neon rendition of da Vinci's *Vitruvian Man* hangs over a couch in primary yellow. A neon-pink sign above a watercooler blinks BE WELL. Additional camera crew is already positioned around the room. And…is Josh looking a little pale?

"Hello and welcome to WekTech," says a receptionist. I can only see her head poking above the massive white desk that surrounds her like a fortress. I release Josh's hand and walk toward her.

"Hi! We're here to see Andy?"

"Of course!" She clicks on her computer. "Let me ping him."

I lean my forearms on the cool surface of the desk. Now, looking down, I can see the whole receptionist, not just the decapitated version. She's dressed in an adorable floral-print dress and cardigan.

"I love your dress."

"Oh!" She stops typing to run her hands down her skirt. "It's from Zara. I got it on sale!"

"Nice."

"It'll just be a minute, if you want to wait."

"Okay." I turn back to find Josh sitting on the yellow couch. His arms are braced against his legs. He's looking seasick.

I sit next to him and place a hand on his back.

"Hey," I say. "Hey."

"Sorry." He tilts his head to catch my eye. His trademark grin is forced, but brave. "Give me a minute. I'll be fine."

I rub circles into his back, but his reaction has me totally panicked. I've never seen him so off-kilter. Is he going to lose it? Throw up? Cut and run? I can't just sit here and let this happen to him. To me. To us.

"One of the first criticisms I got after my Launch Day was that I wasn't a real woman," I say quietly. Urgently. "A comment on Insta. Anyway. We're on a reality TV show. *Reality* TV. But so much of it is—" I spin my free hand, leaving the other anchored on Josh's back "—sets. Direction from the producers. Impressions, you know? Beautiful, contrived…impressions." My palm is still against his shirt. I can feel the warmth of his skin under the fabric. His ribs lifting, then falling with his breath. "I've thought a lot about what's real. What it even means. Sure, we're material people, made of physical stuff—but that's not the true us, is it?"

He side-glances at me, but I can tell he's listening intently.

I stand and tug at his hand. "Let's go."

"What?"

I tug harder. Reality is not static. It is movement. Josh looks confused, but he allows me to drag him to the elevator, where I punch the button, over and over, like that will make it hurry. The receptionist is talking on the phone, half-turned away from us, and doesn't notice. Reality is stepping over a threshold. It is action, it is choice.

The elevator swishes open. The receptionist swivels back toward us, but we're already inside.

"Wait! Julia—" she cries just as the doors close behind us and the cameraman. Josh and I sink against the back wall. I collapse my head against him, and he meshes his fingers in mine. The floors count down. *Fourteen. Thirteen. Twelve.*

"So," says Josh. Already, there's a little more life in his voice. *Eleven, ten, nine.*

"Neither of us wanted to," I explain. "It isn't worth it."

A smile ripens slowly on his face. "Then where are we headed, Miss Julia?"

My mind is a swirl of ideas. We could ride roller coasters at Disneyland. Surf at Hermosa Beach. Play tourists on Hollywood Boulevard. Go to the movies, get a burger, or even just find a bench and watch the world go by.

"Let's do whatever *we* want," I say, tightening the tangle of our fingers. "We've been doing all these things that other people have planned for us. Maybe a true hometown with me is about us making our own way."

Dimples crease Josh's cheeks, and I see salvation in his smile—for this day, for our relationship. We were plummeting down, but our parachutes just deployed.

The elevator doors open. I can imagine the shot the camera is getting: both of us flushed, smiling. Glowing with our stolen freedom.

"Ready?" says Josh. "We're off script now."

"Ready," I agree. We squeeze hands and walk confidently out of WekTech, back into the warm California day, headed into a future of our own making. My legs feel strong and my heart is beating with joy and adrenaline and the thrill of our near-escape, and I'm pretty sure I can run and run forever, as long as he's the one I'm running with.

NOW

"Vanessa! Hi! Thank you for calling me back!"

I know my voice sounds too bright, but I'm in overdrive and I can't seem to calm down. Don't *want* to calm down, because that means breaking down, because my husband is dead, but if I stop to cry, stop to process, I could be in handcuffs before I know it, and I am now Annaleigh's only parent, and for her, I have to be strong and save my heartbreak for some future time when I can afford to let my emotions have their turn.

I just got the name of Walmart woman from Andy via text. Deborah Reeves, a name that's been bothering me because I feel like I've heard it somewhere else. Andy's other text, I didn't acknowledge, but it's burning in my mind. **Saw the news. So sorry for your loss. Please let WekTech step in.**

Yes, I want Andy to be a safe older brother, but repossession means handing total control to lawyers who can't possibly give an actual fuck about me. It means me waiting, helpless, for some version of justice, and, based on how Christi's divorce battle is playing out, justice cannot be counted on. But the biggest reason I'll never agree to let WekTech step in? Annaleigh. Any protection WekTech can give me will not include her, and there's no way in hell I'm letting myself be separated from my baby on anything other than my own terms.

"Julia!" says Vanessa, matching my energy. "Annaleigh just went down for a nap. We got her a Pack 'n Play! She kept escaping from her nest. She's doing great, by the way. She's suuuuch a cutie."

"I'm so glad it's going well." For once, as much as my heart is tugging at me, I can't stop to dwell on my baby. "Listen, I need a favor. A huge favor, actually. You know that friend you have at Facebook? The one who got you all those pictures of Josh?"

"Yes—"

"There's a picture of Josh with a redhead in your album. I need to get in touch with her. Anything he can get—her name, a current address, a phone number—" With my pen, I tap-tap on the notepad I brought up from the kitchen. Where it says GROCERY LIST at the top, I've crossed out GROCERY and written SUSPECTS in angry all-cap letters. Adams was supposed to take these notes. The sheriff was supposed to dig into these leads. Not me.

"Um…sure? I could call him Monday—"

"Now," I interrupt. "Listen, the situation with Josh has escalated. Whatever it takes. I'll pay him, I don't care."

"God, Julia, no, I'm sure he doesn't want your money! I'm so sorry to hear that. I'll call him right now."

"Let me know as soon as you hear back."

"Will do."

We disconnect. I'm sitting in Annaleigh's room, in the rocking chair by the window, one level removed from the reporters. Bob, as usual, is looking at me through binoculars from the window across the way. He has no idea he's one of the names on my list.

The entire list is far-fetched. I know this. Josh could have been killed by someone else entirely—like an anonymous vandal. But I can only work with what I know. And the bottom line is, if I don't find credible evidence that someone else might be guilty, this could be the end for me. Would I go to jail? Or would they turn me off like Lars and consign me to a glass display?

I gaze at the suspect list. Who would cut off Josh's arm after he was dead and leave it in the woods? Why is his ring finger missing? Where is the rest of his body? Could it have something to do with Royce? No, that seems crazy, but...the questions pick and pick at my brain. As for his watch...an innocent accident. He dropped it... Annaleigh got ahold of it...there are so many reasonable ways a broken watch could end up under an entry-way bench, right?

I make a little star next to *Deborah Reeves*, then chew on my pen's clicker. I really do feel like I've seen her name. Not back then. Recently.

Setting aside my list, the pen still between my teeth, I grab my phone, pull up a Google search and type in *Deborah Reeves Eauverte address*.

Damn. Apparently there are people named Deborah Reeves all over Indiana. But none in Eauverte. Of course, that Walmart is a hub for any number of small surrounding towns.

I close my eyes and let my phone drop to my lap. Where? Where have I seen her name? I can see it in my mind. In...black pen? And spider-thin script.

I'm out of my chair and in the master closet within seconds.

In the corner, two huge plastic bins are marked JULIA and JOSH. They contain nearly a year's worth of mail. I muscle them out into my bedroom.

Unclasping the lid from my bin first, I turn it on its side and dump everything out—letters and cards and photos and promo material from businesses. Even some small gifts. Personalized lip balm. Fan art of the proposal. An engraved copper pendant.

I remember how mad Josh was when I didn't let him throw all this stuff away. It was after that first death threat.

"We should keep these just in case," I said, clutching the letter where a man described wanting to carve out my eyes so I couldn't watch him as he fucked me.

"This is trash," Josh argued, angry. So angry. Poor Josh. If being on *The Proposal* was some version of paradise for him, those first couple months in this house were hell.

"If something happens, this is evidence," I explained. "I'll get some bins. You don't even have to read anything."

I was calm about it at the time. Rational. Not actually thinking anything bad would happen. Keeping all this was merely an insurance policy, future security that we'd never need to draw on, against that one-in-a-million chance.

Well, here we are.

It takes me a long time to sort through my stuff, but a fever of energy fuels me. By the time I'm done, with no sign of anything from Deborah Reeves, I'm hungry. I have to pump. I have to pee. But I don't stop. I dump out Josh's bin.

The hate mail comes in more flavors than ice cream. Interestingly, Josh has more than me.

You're going to burn for fornicating with a Bot.

Our country is going straight to hell because of people like you!

Most of this drivel bears no return address, though hilariously, some does. Seeing Josh's name written over and over is painful. Josh is dead, I realize again.

The last time I really sobbed about Josh was well before his disappearance. He was mad at me. It was over something silly. It always was. I'd forgotten to tell him I had dinner plans—a video chat with Cam and some of the other *Proposal* girls—but Josh had made a surprise reservation for us at an Italian place, which he had to cancel. The memory is a little fuzzy, as all memories are, but the emotions are crystal clear. An overwhelming sense of the fragility of us. How easily we could hurt each other. How love isn't just the fuzzy stuff, but an almost violent vulnerability. An openness to pain, the thing we hate most, in order to get love, the thing we need most. *Ironic*, I can't help but think. Or paradoxical. And what if you keep getting hurt? Can you stay open forever? Or does some overpowering instinct force you to retreat, close, protect—and in turn, cut yourself off from love? If reality is made by choosing, what reality were we making in those awful weeks and months as we chipped away at each other with our words, with our silences, with our fears closing in until our love was a scared little animal cowering in the corner?

I don't know how much time I spend sitting there, frozen with my hands around one of the letters, but finally, I wake back up. I still can't cry, but I do have to laugh. Because right here, in front of my left knee, is a greeting card–sized envelope addressed to Josh LaSala in a spidery black script. The return address: Deborah Reeves.

It's still sealed, so I rip in, then pull out a Hallmark greeting card with an Easter bunny on the front. Inside, the thin scrawl covers one side.

Dear Josh,

I've called and called, but I think you have blocked my number.

You may not remember me, but your mother and I used to be best friends. We were pregnant at the same time. I made you a baby blanket with embroidered suns and clouds. You were the cutest baby and we all adored you.

I didn't want you to marry Julia, but you did. I was afraid you might because I know how you like redheads, which is why I tried to get her out of the way.

You have made a *terrible mistake*! Your life is in *danger*!!! You need to leave her immediately, and *don't look back*! With your mother being sick, it is my responsibility to look out for you, now more than ever!!!

Love,
Deb

I feel so strange reading this. I flip back and forth between the perky, rosy-cheeked Easter bunny and the dark interior. Right after the attack, everyone decided that this woman was an unhinged fan, and despite my reservations, I went along with it. Seeing her in Walmart two nights ago debunked that once and for all. And now it turns out she knew Josh? Did Josh recognize her back then?

I read the note a second time. It's protective. Fierce. Like a mother would be, even though she's not his mother. And the thing she wanted to protect him from? Me.

Obviously her ideas about Synths are ignorant, misguided. But it's hard to imagine that someone who wanted to keep Josh safe would also be his killer.

On the other hand, there's no question that she's capable of violence. I remember how flat she looked when she bashed my head onto the patio stone in the *Proposal* mansion. Like she had no emotion. No conscience to stop her.

Setting the card aside, I quickly sort through the rest of the mail. There are a dozen more cards from her, which must be why her name stuck in my mind. They're all unopened, and the postmarks tell me they were all sent after the first. I open them in order. The next card has a picture of a stork carrying a baby.

Josh, congratulations on your new baby! I just read the article in WHAT'S UP and you make a beautiful family. Please remember that your happiness will be short-lived because of your wife. *Send a response so that I know you are getting my letters!!!!!!*

The cards continue in this vein, getting more and more desperate. The final one, with a cheerful Santa on the front even though it was postmarked just three weeks ago, in April, reads:

You have broken my heart just like the others. *I am cursed.* God has cursed me. Everyone I love is marked for death. If

I was braver I would kill myself and end this life of misery, but I'm just a tired old woman everyone hates. I pray your guardian angel protects you but I already know you'll die like the others. I can only hope your baby survives.

Her words send goose bumps all over my body. The first letter was somewhat relatable, but in this final letter, every word tastes like poison seeping from a poisoned mind.

Maybe she did kill Josh. *I already know you'll die*, she wrote. Well, she would know that, if she was going to murder him. And what the fuck does she mean about Annaleigh surviving? Does she consider me a threat to my own child? Or is she the threat? Why not try to hurt me again? Why would she hurt Josh? It doesn't make sense.

I rise from the detritus of the mail and type her address into my phone. If Deborah is somehow an active threat to my daughter, there's no question; I have to confront her.

The app shows a little blue line between my house and hers, at 442 E Deerhead Trail, Tenderloin, Indiana. After all this, I can be there in under fifteen minutes.

I'm not sure what I'm going to say to this woman, but I'm under no illusions I'll be safe confronting my attacker and Josh's possible killer.

I'm going to need a weapon.

THEN

"What's this?" says Josh, but he's only pretending not to know what the gigantic envelope with the key attached is all about.

He pulls out the card and reads, "'Dear Josh and Julia, we hope you're enjoying your stay in beautiful Jamaica! Should you choose to forgo your individual rooms, you may use this key to stay together in the SkyBeach Resort Fantasy Suite as a couple.'" He lays the letter on the table between us. "What do you think, Julia? Do you...want to?"

We flew in yesterday, and we've just had the best day together, starting with a surfing lesson on the crystalline beaches of Jamaica. Now we're enjoying our last bites of dinner by the water, steps away from the SkyBeach Resort, a boutique hotel with waterside cabins.

We knew this was coming, this offer to spend tonight together off camera, but I pretend to hesitate, because I don't want to seem overeager, to Josh or to future viewers.

"I mean...you know there's nothing I'd love more than time alone with you," I say. "Just to get to know each other better."

"No expectations. We don't have to be physical."

"Of course not!" I say, even though that's all I can think about. "We can just talk."

After dessert, we keep it light as we walk toward the resort with our arms around each other, but the whole time, heat plays over my body like an electric storm, anticipating all the places Josh's hands will finally be able to touch. Within my new paradigm of reality and choice, the phrase *make love* feels particularly lovely. The act of creating a feeling. The tangible act of making the intangible. The power of *yes* to Camila's power of *no*. Launch Day Julia only had feelings to orient her, poor thing. Today Julia? She's making her own reality.

The "cabin" we've been assigned is more like a mini palace. The sliding doors to the ocean-facing terrace are open, the white curtains billowing in the breeze. The lighting is low, and candles flicker on the coffee table. We explore the place hand in hand, cameras still following. I gush at everything—the beautiful view of the ocean, the huge bathroom, the soaker tub, which has been prefilled with steaming water and strewn with rose petals. Even more rose petals lie scattered across the California king–size bed.

Josh pops champagne and we toast to the night ahead. Then I set my glass on the nightstand and fling myself backward on the bed. Josh follows, crashing hard on the mattress so that I bounce up a little, laughing. His hand finds mine. Then, playfully, I prop myself up, face the cameras, and say, "Shoo!"

"Could you do one more toast, from the bed?" says the producer.

We retrieve our champagne and, reclined on our sides, face each other. Josh looks at me with intensity.

"To us, and to our night together."

"To us," I echo. We clink and drink. And, like a miracle, the cameras leave. Josh closes and locks the front door. I follow him, arms wrapped around my middle.

Suddenly the billowing curtains seem less romantic and more ominous, like presences intruding on us. Like anyone could be watching from behind them.

"Can we close those?" I say.

Josh obliges. The wind stills. The curtains fall limp. I can hear my own heart beating in the fresh silence, and for a second I taste fear, which surprises me.

"Hey," says Josh, approaching me slowly as he undoes the top button of his shirt. "Is something wrong?"

No matter how far I was just telling myself I've come, all the old fears flood me. The fear that I don't really know Josh. That without the rules of the game, this will all fall apart.

All I can manage is a whisper. "Is this real?"

He cups my jaw with tender fingers. "Real?" He laughs. "Don't get into your head, Julia. Not tonight." I think he's about to kiss me, but he pulls back and untucks his shirt, revealing the shaded magnificence of his six-pack. "Here. Punch this. I think you'll find it's very real."

I giggle. The laughter loosens me a little. Reaching a tentative hand forward, I give Josh's abs the tiniest baby slap.

"Pa-thetic." He beckons with his free hand, bracing himself like he's really preparing for something big. "C'mon. Harder."

I can't help the laughter that escapes my lips as I pretend to really swing, then bring my fist gently to his skin. Damn, he really is hard as a rock…and not just his abs. I tease my fingers to his belt clasp. The metal is chilly.

"You like what you see?" he says, his eyes still laughing even though his expression has turned serious. "Because I like what I see."

"Do you?" Heart thudding, I reach for the hem of my shirt and tug it up slowly.

The laughter is gone, and Josh is all intensity, taking me in as I drop my shirt on the floor.

"*God.* Do you know how long I've been waiting for this?" he says in that husky voice I know so well.

He's not touching me, but he might as well be, the way his eyes alone are raising trails of goose bumps across my chest. My breasts feel heavy in my semi-sheer balconette bra.

"How long have you been waiting, Josh LaSala?" I breathe, giddy with relief that nothing has crumbled. It's the same familiar heat between us. If anything, it's heightened without the eye of the cameras on us. Magnified.

"Since I first saw you step out of the limo with those long legs of yours." He takes one step forward and his hand slides onto the small of my back. "You looked like a goddess. You have no idea how much I wanted you, even then."

"I was so awkward," I say, my breath catching as his hand pulls me gently against him and I feel his hard anticipation. I don't have to wonder how he's feeling about me.

"You were breathtaking. And you're breathtaking tonight." He kisses me slowly, his hands moving up my naked ribs, stopping at the edge of my bra. His breaths are coming slow and heavy. "You're going to have to stop me from going further, Julia Walden."

"Why would I stop you?" I lean forward and close my teeth gently around his lower lip. It's soft and full. I flick my tongue against it and he gasps. I release, draw back, and stroke a finger down the ridge of his jaw. He's nearly panting now. "I was made for you, Josh."

Then I reach behind my back and unclasp my bra. I watch him take me in as I drop the garment to the floor. His expression goes pained with intensity. Moving slowly, he cups my breasts, sweeping his thumbs across them. Now it's my turn to gasp at the sharp sensation his fingers draw forth.

"God, Julia," he says. "I'm never letting you put a shirt on again."

"Speaking of shirts…" I murmur, placing my hands on his stomach and pushing his shirt up. Another second, and it's on the floor next to my bra.

We stay suspended in the moment, both naked from the waist up. Time feels slow as honey, and my blood pulses with a heavy droning. I've hungered for Josh from the start. I've spent countless nights tortured with want, starved for his attention, his affection, his body. And now...the waiting is over. I get him. Not necessarily forever—but tonight.

It's both enough and not enough. A fulfillment and a cruel tease. I want to know how this ends, if this is the first taste of many, or my one and only, but all I can do is let time keep unfolding, heartbeat by heartbeat, and take what's before me.

"I never dreamed I would ever find a woman like you," Josh says thickly,

"That's because I'm not a dream." I tug at his belt. It's intoxicating, seeing the evidence of his desire. How he's straining with it, but still so self-controlled. In a minute, he won't be, I'll make sure of it, but for now, the tension is delicious.

"Are you sure?" he says.

"This is all real, Josh." I mean it, and I feel the whole world around us become more solid, more sure. I step forward, my breasts brushing his chest, and nuzzle into the crook of his neck, drawing my tongue slowly up his throat. I want to taste him everywhere. I've never felt so alive. This is my choice, and my fulfillment. "Let me give you what you need."

NOW

The gun isn't loaded. But my coding prevents me from harming humans anyway, so the weapon I've tucked into the back of my jeans is all for show, just like the baseball bat I charge vandals with. The gun belonged to Rita, Josh's mom, and even though Josh and I always talked about disposing of it after her death, we never got around to it.

It's three in the afternoon when I pull into Tenderloin, a little town that seems to be no more than a crossroads with a gas station, a bar, a church, and a feed store.

The day is chilly, with a vicious edge to the breeze and intermittent breaks in the clouds that bring sunlight stabbing into the gloom. I hang a right off the county highway, onto the dirt road that is Deerhead Trail. The car shudders against the uneven road as I take in my surroundings: cornfields on the right and black plastic mailboxes on the left. From the mailboxes, long unpaved driveways wind toward distant houses.

At number 442, I hang a left. The ground rises slightly, and Deborah's white farmhouse appears, standing worn and alone, momentarily lit by a slash of pale sunshine. I crawl my car forward. There are no trees that could provide me with cover, and I'm painfully aware that Deborah could shoot at me from any of the dozen windows. She seems exactly like the type of person who owns guns and knows how to use them.

Assuming I survive the walk from my car to her front door, my plan is simple: pull out my gun and use pure shock value to force her to talk. Hopefully, she'll confess straightaway. I'll turn her in to Mitchell. *Then* I can let myself cry for the husband I just lost.

Most people, I imagine, would call my bluff. No Harm coding isn't exactly a secret. But I'm counting on one thing: that if Deborah thinks I could somehow overcome my coding to kill Josh, which her letters seemed to imply, she'll think I can kill her, too.

My skin is clammy as I pull the car to a stop in a patch of gravel. The second I kill the engine, her door is already opening and she has a shotgun. *Fuck.* I duck on instinct and open the door a crack so I can talk to her.

"Please don't shoot!" I shout.

She's wearing a loose housedress and slippers. From the porch ceiling, a mobile hangs, like you might see above a baby's crib. Its pink balls are unevenly weighted, and it makes an unsteady, bobbling circle in the breeze.

"You're trespassing!" she barks. Her voice is hoarse, like she doesn't use it a lot. "Tell me who you are! Now!"

"Julia Walden! Josh's wife. I just want to talk to you, Deborah! Please put down your gun!" Half of me wants to flee; she's already tried to kill me once. But speeding away means speeding back into Mitchell's waiting embrace.

"I—found your letters." Reaching over to the passenger seat, I grab the stack. Keeping my body mostly protected behind the car door, I reach my left arm up where she can see it, the cards held high. "Josh never read them. But I did. And I want you to know I would never hurt him, or my baby. I just want to talk."

She still has the gun pointed at me. On the other hand, she hasn't fired.

"Where is Josh?" she says.

This gives me pause. The story is all over the news. Does she truly have no idea?

"We can talk if you'll put the gun down!"

She lowers the gun slowly. I come out with both hands lifted, still holding her letters.

"Would you please put the gun all the way down?" I say as a gust of wind tosses my ponytail into my face and spins the mobile around. I think of the gun hidden in the waistband of my jeans, my only hope at the illusion of power.

I used to love my No Harm coding. It was like a seal of goodness—a guarantee to people who otherwise might have feared me that I was a safe presence. It also made Josh want to protect me. Now, it's a major liability.

Who am I kidding? It always was.

"You stay down there," Deborah orders. She leans her gun in a corner by a half-broken porch swing before returning to the edge of the porch and bracing her arms against the railing. Her thin carrot-orange hair lifts around her face, then falls, like a momentary halo. "Why are you here?"

To find out if you killed my husband, I want to say. But I can't start there.

"Why did you think Josh was going to die?"

"Because of you," she says, as if this was obvious. "Where is he now?"

"I read your cards. I know you think he was in danger from me. But that doesn't make sense. I love him, Deborah. I have a *child* with him. I would never hurt him. *Or* my baby."

"You're lying," she says in an awful, declarative monotone. "You're a Synth. A weapon. That's why they made you."

"I think you already know that Josh is dead," I say, because I don't have time to argue against her Bot-hating conspiracy theories. If this statement surprises her, I can't tell. It's like she's made of stone. "They think he was killed Saturday night. I was at home with my baby. Where were you, Deborah?"

The sunlight slips away, casting us in shadow. There's another gust of air and Deborah turns toward her gun, as if the wind is giving her motion.

"Stop or you die!" I shriek, releasing the wad of cards, yanking out my gun. It scrapes painfully against the small of my back, but it's in my hands, pointed at the woman on the porch, who has frozen in place. "Don't move!" I pound up the hollow porch steps and press the gun to her back. She's shorter than me by a head, and suddenly seems weak. Pitiable. For a second, I really feel like I could shoot her.

My eyes register a shadow of movement and stray upward, to the dangling mobile, twitching and circling. *God.* The hanging objects aren't pink balls, after all. It's four baby doll heads.

"Inside," I order, clenching my teeth against the sick sight of the heads with their hair shaved short, some of their eyes open, some closed. "No sudden movements or I shoot."

Deborah obeys. As soon as she opens the door, a smell rolls out, like dead cats and mothballs. I gag. Is Josh's body in here somewhere? It's dark, and my eyes take a second to understand the towering shadows that fill the space. Slowly, boxes and bins and piles of books emerge from the darkness. Deborah Reeves is a hoarder.

"To the kitchen," I say, hoping there's a chair where I can sit her down. I breathe through my mouth.

Deborah shuffles forward, through the narrow corridor between the ceiling-high stacks. I keep the gun at her back and take in our strange surroundings. Tucked into nooks between stacks, or on the flat roofs of shorter towers, are more dolls, in groups of four, always four. Four dolls sharing a meal at a small table. Four naked dolls stacked against each other in a bathtub. We pass what used to be the living room, where a dusty chandelier hangs like crystalline hair over a pile of books and clothing that looks nearly sentient, curved like someone cocking their hip.

We take a bend. Someone pops into view.

"Fuck!" I cry, instinctively pressing the gun into Deborah's back. She's wearing a blue dress—red hair—

Not a real person. Just a cardboard cutout…of me.

Devil horns adorn my head. Yellow ridged darts speckle my face, and red marker lines make it look like my eyes are bleeding.

Panic crawls its tentacles up my spine. If Deborah comes to her senses and remembers No Harm—if she somehow overcomes me in this horrible place where no one could hear me scream—

"Keep walking," I shout, even though Deborah didn't stop.

A little farther down, on a foldout table wedged between boxes, is a makeshift shrine. An electric candle flickers unnaturally under a framed photograph of a young man in a cap and gown. Fuck—it's Josh. Four Barbie-sized doll heads are stuck to the frame, two on each side of Josh. The dolls' hair is cropped short like the mobile dolls, and wallet-sized baby pictures have been taped to their faces. *Four angels vigil keeping*, I think with a deep shiver.

Finally in the kitchen at the very back of the house, I gesture to a chair, which is mostly clear save some clothes draped over the back. My pulse is going a million miles a minute.

"Sit," I order. I can't sound scared. "Keep your hands where I can see them."

Deborah obliges. With her hands clasped in her lap like a child, she looks up with those pale blue moon eyes. I point the gun at her chest. My hands are sweaty. The metal feels slippery. This whole situation feels slippery.

"Why did you kill my husband, and where is his body, Deborah?"

"I would never kill any of my babies."

"Josh wasn't your child."

"In my heart, he was." Deborah holds my gaze, unblinking. "Josh and my baby were the same age. Then my baby died."

Oh... *God.* Was Josh some kind of substitute for her own child? *And were those cherubic faces taped to the Barbie heads...* But there's no time to dig into the psychological squalor that is the mind of Deborah Reeves.

"Tell me where you were Saturday night," I demand.

"Here."

"Prove it."

She blinks twice. "I don't have a working car."

"I know you can get around. I saw you at Walmart."

"There's a church group. They take me shopping."

"Someone could have driven you to Josh's campsite Saturday." The muscles in my hand are hurting from holding the gun so tightly.

Deborah gestures to a TV with a warped screen. "I was watching Josh on *The Proposal*, like I always do on the weekend. It's on Netflix."

I readjust my grip on the gun. "Pull it up. I want to see your watch history."

She reaches for a remote, then slowly navigates it with awkward fingers until she reaches the screen that shows the dates and time stamps of what she's watched. Just like she said, she was watching *The Proposal* between 5:00 p.m. and midnight Saturday. From the looks of it, she watched the final episode with the proposal multiple times. In a row.

"You could have watched this from your phone."

"I don't have a cell phone." She gestures to an ancient-looking brown landline attached to the wall. "I'm on a fixed income."

I think of the line from her letter. *They all died.*

"You said you were cursed. What did you mean?"

Her face twists, and faster than I can react, she lurches forward, forcing her fingers around my hands, twisting the gun so it's pointed at the ceiling, pressing me with unnatural strength until the trigger clicks.

She releases a ragged cry of triumph as I wrench myself free, the useless gun falling to the floor. I spin and collide with a stool covered in magazines, which spill like a glossy river at my feet. The ruse is up.

It's a nightmare as I slip-slide out of the kitchen, into the narrow corridor through which my only exit lies. Something hits me from behind—a book. I dodge the next one. There's a mighty grunt behind me, then a crashing sound. She's collapsing a tower of bins. It hits the next tower, and the next, like giant dominoes falling, and if I'm not fast, I could be crushed.

"I had nothing! Nothing but Josh!" she screams above the noise of toppling objects. She moves sure-footed up the avalanche.

I turn in desperation, grabbing the nearest object, a doll, and launching it, but it flies right past her.

"And now he's gone!" She crests the pile, eyes wild. "And you killed him! I know you did, liar!"

"You're crazy!" I fight my way up a landslide of newspapers. Sensory input rolls over me like a tidal wave, like the volume of the world has been turned up to maximum capacity. "Stay away from me! And stay the fuck away from my baby!"

A doll hits my leg, another hits my cheek. She's launching them like grenades.

"My husband is dead," I yell as I throw whatever I can grab at her. A mug. A cluster of fake grapes. A colander, which hits her in the leg. "I'm not the villain!"

"Yes, you are! You killed him for the bad things he did!" she shrieks. She raises an arm to protect her face as I throw a candelabra at her. It nicks her arm and she falls back a step. "You're an instrument of judgment! You came with justice when he needed mercy! My babies deserved mercy!" She leaps forward like she has wings, orange hair flying.

I propel myself through the final stretch on adrenaline alone. The front door is a slice of light through the final passageway. Almost out, almost free.

Behind me, though growing fainter, Deborah is ranting, screaming, in a world of her own. "Now we're both murderers! And I promise you, they will never forget! It doesn't matter if we're guilty or innocent! Nothing matters anymore! It's too late!"

Salvation. I crash out the front door, down the porch with its hideous mobile, into my car, and slam the door.

Not a moment too soon. Deborah fires her shotgun as my car roars to life. I rev it in a wide circle, spitting gravel like teeth, my ears ringing with the boom of her gun. Then I lean toward the passenger seat and puke, right into the vinyl, as my car skids onto Deerhead Trail.

THEN

"Where's your head at?" I say, tugging on Josh's hand.

Our time in Jamaica is coming to a close. We're walking on the beach as the sun sets, our sandals discarded back at the picnic blanket. My hi-low wrap skirt blows against my legs like a whipping mermaid tail. My midriff, bare under my crop top, is prickled with goose bumps. The sand is hard and chilly under my feet, the lull of the waves peaceful and a little mournful, like they know we're at the end of our journey and are trying to give us a gentle send-off.

Emma's and Zoe's send-offs were not gentle. Not for them, and not for me. I blubbered through those rose ceremonies and had terrible sleep in the aftermath of both their departures. Though I hope to create a family with Josh, I'll never have a family of origin; these girls are the closest I'll come.

It's our last date before Josh proposes to one of the two remaining women: Cam or me. The next time I see him, he'll either be putting a ring on my finger or rejecting me forever. Fulfilling what I was made for, or propelling me into…what? Despite Cam's offers of connecting me with her agent, or my own pragmatic moments when I consider my future after the show, I just can't imagine it. It's…a void.

"Honestly? I'm confused," he says, running his free hand through his thick brown hair. "I wasn't expecting to be this torn this late in the process."

"Do you think your mom helped add some clarity?"

Josh and I spent an hour with his mom first thing this morning, before heading off into our day. It was a surprise to me, but I think it went well. Rita wasn't at all what I expected. If Josh is tall and fit and confident, his mom is the opposite. Petite, round, reserved. Uncomfortable-looking, as if her shoes are too tight, though maybe it's being outside of the US, which is a first for her. She mentioned it at least three times.

As we picked at a breakfast of scrambled eggs and fruit, she asked Josh to give us girls a minute alone. I sipped at the bitter coffee while she asked me rehearsed-sounding questions. What drew me to Josh. If I want kids. How I picture myself fitting into his life in Indiana. Even though I think I gave great answers, I could tell by her demeanor she didn't buy it.

"We're not jet-setters," she said when I was done talking, looking me up and down as if my very appearance was reason to doubt my sincerity. "We're simple Midwestern people who hold traditional family values. I don't want Josh to marry someone who's not going to be happy with the life he can offer."

"I'm not a jet-setter," I said earnestly. "I'm actually a really simple girl. Marrying Josh, living together, having kids—*that's* what I want. You know, the sweet simple life. Believe it or not, going to Paris was my first time out of the country, and Jamaica is just my second!" I laughed, trying to bring levity, but she didn't take the bait.

"Tell me about your family background, Julia," she said. "Are you close with your folks?"

I swear the world stopped turning for a split second.

"Josh...didn't tell you?" As she shook her head, words bubbled up that I hadn't planned. "I...don't have a family. I guess it's complicated. But Josh has made me feel like I can finally have all those things, with him. If you feel like I don't have as much to contribute, since I don't have parents or siblings, I get that. I understand. But we've talked about it a lot together, Josh and me, and it makes us even more excited to build our family." I babbled on in that vein, trying to strike a hopeful note. She listened with pinched lips, clearly wondering what had happened—was I an orphan? The victim of some tragedy?

When I finally stopped, I felt gross, like I'd lied to her face. But I couldn't tell her I was a Synth. If I did? If she reacted poorly? That would be Josh's last impression of me before deciding whether to keep me or leave me.

"You're deep in thought," says Josh, squeezing my hand and bringing me back to the present.

"Yeah... I was thinking about your mom." I tuck a strand of hair behind my ear. "I have no idea what she thought of me."

"She liked you." He pauses to nudge a shell with his toe, then bends to pick it up.

"Yeah?" I chew on my thumbnail as Josh tucks the shell in his pocket. "I guess it caught me a little off guard that, um...she doesn't know I'm a Synth." I know she disapproves of the show. But even if she avoided the teaser trailers and the buzz, I'd assumed Josh would talk to her about it up front.

"Yeah, I should have warned you, I guess." Josh seems sheepish. We keep walking, skirting dark piles of seaweed. "She's a good person, Julia, truly. But...this is all new to her, you know? She already thinks the show is morally questionable. If she knew you were a Synth? She might not have agreed to meet you at all. I thought it would be best if she got to know you as a person first. And then, once she really likes you, we can break it to her. She's a super loyal person, so once she decides to love someone, she's all in. It's just a timing thing. Does that make sense?"

"She might find out anyway, online, or on TV, or—" I chew on my upper lip. "Won't she feel...betrayed? If we don't tell her ourselves?"

"We *will* tell her ourselves, Julia. I'm telling you, the timing isn't right. This is my mom. Trust me."

"Of course. Yes. Totally," I say. I still wish we'd talked about this first. But now is not the time for recriminations. I lick my lips and taste salt.

We walk in silence for another minute, then naturally come to a stop, facing the waves and the shreds of sunset, orange and pink tatters floating on the horizon like a ripped-up ball gown. Reminding me the day is almost done; it's time to say my last words.

"Obviously your life is going to look different depending on who you choose," I say as the wind blows my hair back. "I guess I'm wondering what you imagine when you picture marrying me. If it's really different when you think about Camila. And… if you have any last concerns."

I'm kind of glad we're facing the ocean right now and not each other, because if I had to look into his eyes, I might cry.

Josh rubs the back of his neck. "I mean, my life with Cam would be…fun. She's feisty, she keeps me on my toes. I think she'd be a great mom, obviously—if not, she wouldn't be here. I imagine a lot of laughter. She has a big family, lots of aunts and uncles and cousins. I can see big, crazy Christmases."

I nod, trying to stay dispassionate, even though hearing the good things about Cam feels like being cut to ribbons. Of course he would want all these things. It kills me that it's not in my power to offer them, too.

"But with you," Josh continues, his tone warming, "I see myself relishing the simple everyday stuff. I also see you being a great mom. You're really nurturing. Really positive and calm and…kind. You make me want to be a better person, and that's really cool. With you, I see…safety. You'd love me for who I am, which weirdly is what makes me want to be better, and that's hard to say no to."

I nod, throat tight. The big, crazy Christmases *do* sound fun, damn it. Ugh. I have no idea who he's going to pick—or who

I'd pick, in his shoes. Maybe it does come down to what Cam said, before Paris. Is he more interested in the actual or the aspirational? Who he is now, or who he wants to be?

Or maybe it'll come down to hair color, hah.

The waves tease our toes as we look out at the ocean. I hold on tight to his hand because this may be the last chance I have.

I think about my journey to this moment, from waking up with that glow of anticipation to my dramatic speech during the first rose ceremony, through dates and eliminations and travel and laughter, all the way to now, standing in this silence and stillness on the precipice of Josh's decision, the waves reminding me that, whatever he decides, life will continue on the other side.

I have to face a scary reality: that I was made for Josh, but Josh was not made for me. Josh exists for himself, and he's going to do what he wants, and there's nothing I can do about it save what I've already done.

The waves roll and roll. Is this what water was made to do? Is it satisfied, lapping and retreating, kissing the shore before pulling back? I suppose it doesn't matter if it's satisfied. It is what it is, and the waves will still be here long after Josh and I are gone.

NOW

I've blown through Tenderloin before I realize my tank is almost empty. My next chance for gas is the TripMax in Eauverte; I pull in just as a flurry of rain releases. The gas station is right outside town, with cornfields behind. A little farther and this road becomes Main Street, with its bar and its church, the old comic book store and the bicycle repair shop, two tired beacons in a stretch of otherwise empty storefronts.

No one else is at the TripMax at four o'clock on a Friday evening, and I'm grateful. I'm not ready to see people, not ready to be seen—like my encounter with Deborah left some kind of grime on me that people will be able to see, to smell.

It was still worth it, though, no matter how shaken I am, because I learned one thing: she didn't kill Josh.

I lock the gas pump in place and lean against the car as it fills.

It wasn't just Deborah's limitations that convinced me—no car, no cell phone—or even her watch history on Netflix. It was her adoration of Josh. Warped, but steely strong. It's an adoration that some deep part of me recognizes, because I feel it toward Annaleigh. Call it a mother's intuition, but Deborah Reeves would not kill the angel she built a shrine for. She may still be a personal threat to me, but what else is new? She's been here all along, just fifteen minutes away. And if she hasn't killed me yet...

You killed him for the bad things he did. My eyes zone out on the mounting dollars on the pump's digital display. What did *that* mean? Could she have been on our property, skulking in the woods...could she have seen...

No. She's insane. Don't overthink it.

A knot of pain in my left breast reminds me I haven't been pumping enough. Is it a plugged duct? If I'm not careful, I could give myself mastitis, which is the last thing I need.

The gas keeps chugging. The gallons and dollars keep counting. The wind blows a thin mist of rain against my face. I lose my gaze in the cornfields, green and peaceful.

What might have been different if, instead of moving down here, Josh and I moved to Indianapolis like we planned? I remember my excitement when Josh took us around Indy during *The Proposal* filming. The city felt like just the right size for us. Big, but not too big. Midwestern-friendly with just enough of a cosmopolitan edge. I allowed myself to imagine, during that trip, that I could find a place for myself there. A favorite bookstore to haunt. A local bakery. I imagined meeting mom-friends at the park near Josh's condo, once we had kids.

Whereas the first time I set eyes on Eauverte, I had to turn on my brave face.

It'll just be until Mom gets better, Josh said.

Of course, I agreed. *It's the right thing to do.*

Then she didn't get better.

Would our marriage have weathered the strains of pregnancy and adjusting to real life if we hadn't also had to shoulder the immediate burden of his mother's health? The awfulness of those long months as I reckoned with morning sickness while caring for a dying woman who hated me? I tried so hard to be the positive, upbeat, nurturing Julia that Josh had fallen in love with on

The Proposal. I gave it my all, and my all wasn't enough. A lesson that maybe I've never recovered from.

In retrospect, it was too much change, too fast. All of it.

We were spinning out of control, the cotton candy fantasy of our love story all the more bitter because of how quickly it dissolved. Like it had been made of nothing but sugar and air.

My phone rings, yanking me out of this string of what-ifs.

"Vanessa!" I say. Hopefully she's calling with information on Stalker Girlfriend. "Did you find out about the redhead?"

"Yes, sorry it took so long. Her name was Laura Pine."

"Was?"

"Um—she actually died, like, years ago." Vanessa's voice is soft, like she feels bad for delivering this blow, even though neither of us have met the girl. "Her Facebook page is still active, but there hasn't been anything new on it for a long time. I'll text you the link."

"Okay." I close my eyes, tilt my head back. Damn it. Stalker Girlfriend was such a strong contender for murder. She could have been obsessed with Josh for years after their breakup...then she saw him on *The Proposal,* which sent her into a jealous fit... strong enough to follow him to Indiana and murder him.

Now her name will just be a crossed-off dead end on my list. Just like Deborah's. It doesn't escape me that I *should* be sorrier that this Laura Pine died. But apparently, my emotions are no longer obeying any laws of propriety.

"Do you think you'll be coming back for Annaleigh anytime soon?" says Vanessa.

"I need a few more days. How is my sweetie?"

The air smells like cow manure and gasoline. The pump clicks. I jiggle the nozzle to release the last drops of gas and press YES on the screen for a receipt.

"Can you switch to FaceTime?" says Vanessa. "You can see her for yourself, I have her right here."

"Sure." I hit Accept on the call and nearly burst into tears when Annaleigh pops onto my screen. She's on Vanessa's hip. They're both smiling.

"Is that a new tooth?" I say. I might actually explode with emotion.

"Yes, it just pushed through!" says Vanessa as Annaleigh bounces excitedly.

"And how's she doing with formula?"

"She guzzles it right down!" says Vanessa with pride.

Annaleigh gurgles and reaches a fat hand for the phone. Laughing, Vanessa whisks the phone out of her reach, angling it high above their heads as Annaleigh keeps reaching and says, "Ma-ma-ma-ma!"

"Hello, sweetheart," I say. I have to smile for her. Show her my brave face. "How are you, my baby? Do you miss your mama?"

"She's great," says Vanessa in a cute voice, looking at Annaleigh. "Aren't we doing great? And we like broccoli!" It's hard to believe this is the same woman who looked horrified at the idea of a baby waking up in the night. Was that just yesterday?

"That's wonderful!" I take a deep breath.

"Ooops! Not that, sweetie!" cries Vanessa as the image on the phone swerves wildly.

"If you have to go, that's fine," I say. But actually, I'm the one that needs to go. I can't bear looking at Annaleigh any longer, or I'm going to lose it. Not to mention the pressure in my breasts is incredibly painful.

"We're just mixing up some formula, so… Okay, Annaleigh, say bye-bye!"

"Ma-ma!" shrieks Annaleigh with one last feral grab toward the screen, and they disconnect.

I stand there, staring at the empty screen for another few seconds. Then I hit the link in the message Vanessa sent. Facebook opens to Laura Pine's page.

Her picture is sweet. She has a gentle, round face. Long red hair like mine. A snub nose.

The page has become a memorial wall. Her information section doesn't say much, just the dates of her birth and death and that she's survived by her loving parents, a brother, and her husband. This is a surprise. Looking at these dates, Laura Pine must have died when she and Josh were still in college. When did she get married? I pop into her pictures, but there are only five, mostly of her as a young teen.

There's no mention of how she died. A quick Google search doesn't give me anything quickly—there are too many Laura Pines.

Returning to her Facebook page, I scroll a little bit, registering the first handful of condolences. *Rest in peace, beautiful Laura. You're flying now, sweet girl. I'll never forget you.* And then, with a swipe of my thumb, I close the app. Laura Pine died years and years ago, which means she's off my list and I should stop wasting my time.

Ten minutes later, gas tank full and vomit swabbed off the seat with paper towels, I pull onto the shoulder of the road well in advance of home, just like I did the other night. It's just after five o'clock, and the day is already fading. Even though it's stopped raining, the air tastes humid and heavy, like more rain is coming.

I jog the whole way home through the woods, squelching over the moist layers of leaves. Having a little light, however dim, makes all the difference, and if ghosts walk this forest, I don't see them tonight.

Entering through the back door, I lock it quickly behind me. Right away, Captain is all over me. The house smells stale, lonely, but Captain is a comfort.

"It's okay, boy. I'm okay. Good dog." I scratch his ears as his tail wags furiously. "Do you need to go out? I'll let you out in a minute."

First, I get him fresh water and dry food. He sniffs at the food and whines, his eyes full of reproach.

"Sorry, Captain. The good stuff's gone."

My eyes instinctively go to the side window. I have the blinds closed, at least, so if Bob is trying to observe my arrival, he's out of luck.

Before I've even made it to the fridge to examine the dinner options for myself, there's a noise of screeching wheels at the front of the house, like multiple cars arriving quickly.

Instinctively, I turn off the kitchen lights. I walk on quiet feet to the living room and peek out the curtains.

Two cars, with someone emerging from each, a man and a woman, converging briskly at my front door. My heart leaps into my throat. The man is Andy.

"It doesn't look like she's home," says the woman. She's fully suited, with a briefcase, and I realize that I know her, too. Viola. Determined, apparently, to show up only at the worst moments in my life.

"Then we wait. We're not leaving here without her," says Andy. "Let's walk around and see if we can get in the back."

Did I lock the back door? I'm about to sprint back to check when the roar of another vehicle grabs my attention. Andy and Viola have stopped to look, too. I crouch, breathing quietly, as the glare of headlights slices through the curtains. Doors slam. I peek back up. I try to make out who the newcomers are, but they've left their headlights on, and the blast of light makes everything hard to see.

"I can't believe it," says Andy to Viola. "Get Eden on the phone."

Eden? What the actual *fuck*?

"Step away from that door!" barks someone. His body makes a dark blot against the brightness, and the tall hat tells me everything I need to know. A sheriff's deputy—and two more of them right behind.

The scene unfolding seems ridiculous, like a piece of absurd theater, as I watch the two parties who want to lock me away—

one to condemn me, the other to save me—come face-to-face. Andy Wekstein and Mitchell's men don't seem to belong in the same universe, and yet here they are at the end of County Road HH, in Middle-of-Nowhere, Indiana, fighting over me.

"Back the hell away from us or we will sue your asses," growls Andy.

"Sir, ma'am, we are officers of the law," says the deputy. "Please move away from the door."

"*You* move away," says Andy. "Julia Walden belongs to Wek-Tech, and we are here to repossess her."

"Julia Walden is the prime suspect in a murder investigation, and we are taking her in," says a drawling voice. Mitchell himself, walking toward Andy like Andy's a bug he can squash.

"Julia Walden belongs to me," snarls Andy, beckoning to Viola. She hands him a sheaf of papers, which Andy flings toward the sheriff's chest. The papers thwack harmlessly. Mitchell doesn't even flinch.

"This is my jurisdiction. Don't make me arrest you, too, Wekstein."

"You are out of line here, Sheriff," says Andy. "And you have no idea how miserable my lawyers can make your life." He's much shorter than Mitchell, but somehow just as large a presence.

Protective. Doing what he thinks is right for me. But it's no longer about what anyone else thinks is right for me. Especially not a liar who pretended he only vaguely knew Eden when now she's the first person he wants to call. I'm already padding away from the living room on silent feet.

"Shhh. Stay, boy," I whisper to Captain as I slip on my shoes, grab my purse, and leave quietly out the back door.

As I move toward the trees, I have the terrible feeling that I'm never coming back here.

At first I walk slowly, quietly, but once I reach the protection of thicker trees, I break into a jog. Mist hangs in the air like a wet veil.

My only thought is to circle around Bob's and try to come out where my car is parked. From there, drive as fast as I can, it almost doesn't matter where, as long as I get out of Dover County. Chicago? But how long could I realistically hole up with Phil and Vanessa? Is there any hope left of finding out who did this to Josh? The only people left on my list are Bob, Eden, and Andy. None of them seem realistic right now, but I guess that doesn't matter anymore, because there's a muted cry of "Hey! Over here!" from somewhere behind me.

Adrenaline explodes through me. Bursting forward, I tear through the gloam, arms raised to protect my face as wet branches whip at me. I should have been running flat out from the start. I miscalculated. I can only hope it's not the last mistake I get to make.

Each breath is a blast of pain in my lungs as I jump over a log, then duck under a tangle of branches. The physical work of running takes over until all I am is a thunder of heartbeat, lungs fighting, legs burning. A sharp stitch slashes at my side. I gulp air. It has a cool, clean edge, like water, except I can't get enough of it.

Something catches on my ankle, and my palms hit the ground, hard. My purse goes flying. Pain spikes through my left foot and up my leg, and I try to heave myself up, but the second I put my weight on my foot, I crumple. "Aaahh," I breathe, wincing as I force my foot down again. I lean on it. Try to push into the pain because I can't afford to retreat. This is not the time to break. If only I could turn off my dampers. I know the science; my body is built to heal. It's pure programming holding it back, slowing me down.

My palms are wet with mud, my clothes, too. I hobble forward but my ankle gives way again. *Stupid.* I've gone and sprained it. My chances of getting away are pretty much dead. It all happened so fast. They're going to catch up now, and this pathetic chase behind my house is my grand finale.

I take another limping step, a sob catching in my throat. From my grand entrance into the world, to this. Poor, naive Julia in her sequins and heels. Thinking on Launch Day that she was walking into a magnificent love story.

Wake up, you idiot, I want to tell her. I want to shake her until her teeth rattle in her pretty, stupid head. They're not going to love you. They're going to hate you and break you and hunt you down. That's how this ends. You think this road leads to love, but it leads straight to hell. Run. Run, because I can't.

My entire body is jerked back so fast I don't have time to cry out. Something heavy locks around my torso. Just as a scream bubbles up my throat, a hand is over my mouth, meaty, moist, turning my scream into a mouse-sized squeak. A voice, hot and low, says, "Shhh. They'll lock you up. You don't want that. Follow me. Quietly." There's a second of heavy breathing. "I'm going to take my hand off. *Don't scream.*"

The hand is gone, and I'm slugging down sweet air. I turn to face none other than Bob Campini. He's in a dark gray sweatshirt over camo cargo pants, his white hair pulled into a short ponytail at the nape of his neck, his grizzled white beard shot through with rivers of gray.

"Get away from me," I hiss, taking two lurching steps back and almost falling again.

He extends a large hand. "I'm helping you, Julia."

In the beat of a single breath, I weigh the threats.

Creepy neighbor? Or certain handcuffs?

I reach out. He closes his rough, calloused fingers around my hand and tugs. "Come on."

Between a run and a limp, I move behind Bob through the brush and the trees. The back of his barn is soon visible. "My purse," I suddenly gasp, but he says, "No time." There are sounds in the woods, men's voices calling to each other. We hug the side of the barn, moving toward the front. A large sign above the sliding door proclaims BOB'S MEAT PROCESSING in faded lettering. A horrible stench is coming from inside. Something ripe and decaying mixed with machinery oil and bleach.

"In here," he says as I step into the stink and the gloom. "Hide. Wait." And then there's a groaning scrape like a monster yawning as he closes the door, and I'm in total darkness. I hear the drag of a dead bolt followed by the sharp click of a padlock.

Okay. He said to hide. I grope my way forward, hands outstretched. I touch something cold. A table? I work my way around it and sink to the floor, hoping this will hide me if anyone looks in. Then I just breathe. And listen.

The silence is oppressive. My heartbeat seems to mark a distorted time, like hours are hanging between each second. It's an eternity and an eternity again. In the darkness, my body loses shape. Everything loses shape, like I've left the physical world and have entered a world of shadow and nightmare.

Finally, muted voices.

"You found her purse? Sure, I heard some sounds from back there. Figured it was deer." Bob's voice. "You'll hit County Road JJ if you head straight through the woods."

The answering voices are too low for me to make out the words.

There's a rough laugh—Bob's. "Yessir, I'll be glad when she's cleared out of here." Pause. "Have a good night."

A fresh silence falls. Everything in my body wants to move, every muscle coils to keep running, but I'm trapped. Injured. I reach a tentative hand down to my ankle, hoping it's improved, and suck back a swear word as the pain lances me again. A dull throbbing in my breasts reminds me I still haven't pumped. I had a pump in my purse, but that's gone.

A clicking sound—the padlock. No time to cry about my pain. Is Bob actually helping me? Or did he lure me in here just for the satisfaction of finishing me off himself?

I should try to find a weapon on the off chance that maybe, like Deborah, he hasn't brushed up on his No Harm knowledge.

Anything to give me the advantage. The barn door slides open and suddenly, handcuffs seem like the better option, because Bob is back, and dear *God*—he's holding a cleaver.

I'm about to get dismembered by Royce Sullivan's successor. Will the neighbors hear me scream? Did anyone hear the screams of the twenty-two women as they died? I know from Wikipedia how Sullivan worked. He left them alive for a while. It was a game of hide-and-seek on acres of playground that ended on the stump. The girls weren't local. They came from all over. Minnesota, California, Massachusetts—he wrote letters to them. They fell in love with his letters, and they came. Trusting the fantasy he spun. Trusting the winning smile in his picture. He sent them all that same picture, of him posing with the axe, and they came, one after the next, so hungry for love they didn't notice the weapon in his fucking hand as he courted them.

I don't know if there were any neighbors close enough, back then, when this was all just one piece of lonely farmland. But I can imagine someone, ninety years ago, saying the same thing I said to Mitchell.

No, Officer. It was probably just a fox.

THEN

When I step out of the helicopter, the loose curls framing my updo whip into my face. I try to tuck the strands behind my ears, but the exercise is pointless.

I'm on a lush hilltop in Jamaica's Blue Mountains, the cloudless sky spread like a flag above. My eyes find Josh right away. The path toward him is lined with flowers, ending in a circular area like a stage. He stands in the middle, in a light gray suit with a pink flower in his jacket pocket, legs planted, hands clasped. To his left, a white table holds a single red rose.

I adjust my skirt and remember the producer's instructions. *Walk slowly, face forward. We want a lot of eye contact.*

It's not hard to keep my eyes on Josh as I advance, trying to tether myself to the unguarded admiration in his eyes. It's harder today to ignore the cameras, which wait in silent expectancy to film my reaction and record forever if I become a wreck or hold it together; if I stay gentle or get angry; if I'm going to become someone viewers admire or despise.

At least I look beautiful. My dress, skintight to the hips and flowing out at the bottom, is a lovely blush color, with swirls of sparkles and sequins crossing the bodice and hips. My hair is gathered into a loose knot with a diamond pin, spilling into sleek curls at the sides. Or at least, they were sleek before the mountain wind tore into me.

Pacing myself, I keep my chin high and my expression smiling. I know there are drones filming from above. It probably looks grand—dramatic—epic, even, with my hair flying and my skirt billowing. But I feel incredibly small, incredibly fragile.

I've been thinking about my reaction, and what to say if he turns me down. That's what I obsessed about last night as I tossed and turned, and this morning as they filmed me getting ready and casting longing glances at the horizon. I'll probably cry, that's unavoidable, but I want to say something lovely. Something Josh will remember as the years go by, so that even though he couldn't love me enough, at least he might think from time to time, *Julia—what a class act.*

Finally, I'm in front of Josh. I take a deep breath and release a nervous giggle. I'm not sure what to do with my hands.

"You look incredible," he says.

"Thanks. So do you." My heart feels like it's burning itself up. If he rejects me, I think I might actually die.

"Julia," he says firmly, like he's gearing up for a big, long speech. He reaches forward, and I place my hands in his, relieved that I have somewhere to put them. "You impressed me from the first night with your beauty, but more importantly, with your kindness. I've never heard you say a bad word about anyone. That's something I'm looking for in a wife."

I smile and mouth, *Thank you.* He smiles back.

"I've also had to do some soul-searching. You're a Synth, and I'd be lying if I didn't say that's been a concern for me."

I nod, encouraging him forward. I just want to get to the part where he tells me yes or no.

"I was afraid that our differences might be too much. That people might not accept us as a couple. I never doubted I could fall in love with you, but I held back out of fear that we'd have too many struggles ahead." He looks down, then up. He's smiling. "Then I saw how the girls took to you. How you made friends so easily, even with Cam—and let's be honest, if you can crack Cam, you can probably crack anyone."

I laugh.

"At every turn, I got the reassurance I needed. That you and I not only have amazing chemistry and a solid friendship, but a path forward, because we're more the same than we are different. We have the same goals. We want to start a family and live a simple life doing all the ordinary things that are more meaningful when we do them together. I realized that what matters isn't that my life started in a different way than yours, but that we're headed in the same direction. Julia—" He takes a huge breath through his nose. "I love you."

Then, releasing my hands, he reaches for the rose on the white table. *Is this—is he—*

Josh lowers himself to one knee, the rose held up like an offering. Tears sprout from my eyes, streak down my cheeks. My chest is so tight and so full at the same time.

"Will you accept this final rose?"

I nod and take the flower while Josh reaches for something in his pocket: a little black velvet box. He pries it open. Inside is a gigantic, flashing princess-cut diamond.

"Julia Walden, will you make me the happiest man on earth?" He squints like he's trying to hold back tears. "Will you marry me?"

There is no soundtrack to real life, but it doesn't matter. Triumphant orchestral music might as well be bursting in the air around us. I nod, because it's hard to speak, and stretch out my left hand. He works the ring over my knuckle. And while the ring in some ways feels like the inevitable seal of my purpose, I also remember what Cam said. *There's power in* no.

For a single sliver of a millisecond, I try to remind myself that I have a choice to walk away and see what life there might be in this bigger world outside of the prompts and the sets, to discover what choices I don't even know I have, to put to the test my hard-won conclusions about choice shaping reality and see if I can create a purpose outside of my given programming, and yet...

It's so easy to speak the single word I've been waiting my whole life to say.

"Yes."

NOW

It's pitch-black inside the barn. Bob's body and the cleaver are outlined in gold from the security lights, and he enters the barn like some otherworldly monster.

"Julia?" His voice isn't loud, but it fills the space.

Shifting my weight to my right foot, I grope for a weapon, but only succeed in knocking something over. A crash is followed by a wet splash, and a metallic scent fills my nose.

Big, buzzing fluorescents switch on above, flicker once, then steady, washing the gray industrial space in flat light. I quickly take in my surroundings—a poured cement floor with drains. Long metal tables, one holding a craggy red shape the size of a small boulder—some poor eviscerated animal. There's a whole range of machinery. The ejecting end of one feeds into a clear plastic bag, which hangs heavy with a pasty, pink material. It looks like dog food. It smells worse. At least now I can see my best bet at a weapon: the hanging row of cleavers at the back.

Bob muscles the door closed behind him as I limp-run toward the knives. The sound of my breathing expands under the tall, echoey ceiling, like some huge, desperate creature is breathing in my stead. I grab the biggest knife off its hook just as Bob slides the interior dead bolt into place. He's at one end of the barn, I'm at the other. With my back to the wall, I raise the blade.

"Put that down," says Bob.

"Neither of us has to get hurt," I snarl. "You have no idea how strong I am. No idea—"

"No one's getting hurt," he interrupts. His beard makes it hard to read his expression. Instead of coming toward me, he walks over to the carcass.

"We should wrap your ankle," he says, setting his cleaver down on the table with a clatter. "But it's not safe to go outside yet. We'll be seen. Best we stay here for a bit. If you don't mind watching me work." With his back to me, he wrestles his sweatshirt off. His torso is surprisingly wide and muscled. He gives me the slightest backward glance and jerks his head toward a green plastic bucket chair. "Keep your weight off that ankle."

Then Bob pulls on elbow-length gloves, lifts the cleaver, and with a practiced swing, starts to hack.

With one eye on Bob, I check my phone. Six missed calls from Andy. Four missed calls from an unknown number. Impulsively, I open up a new text to Andy. I still can't believe he's in cahoots with Eden.

WTF Andy. You lied to me. Call off your goons, I'm not going with you.

Immediately, three dots appear. He's replying.

Where are you????? Julia, let me help you!

Bob's voice echoes toward me. "Careful. Bet they can track that."

Fuck. He's probably right. I power the phone down. Even though it's the smart thing to do, it gives me a panicked feeling to see the screen go black, like I'm locking myself into a safe room I may never get out of. I sit gingerly in the bucket chair.

I've felt isolated for a long time, but this is a whole new level.

My pain is hitting a new level, too, without the distractions of my phone or imminent danger. It rises, filling my sensory landscape, until I can't tell the difference between my injury and the cruel edge of grief. My twisted ankle and the fact that I may never go home again. My exhausted body and the profound disappointment that I'm not strong enough for what I need to do.

I have no idea how much time has passed inside my bubble of pain when Bob finally pulls his gloves off and approaches. He stops at the big machine near me, the one with the plastic bag attached, and lays an affectionate hand on its shiny surface. "The grinder," he says, then looks at me intently, as if to gauge my reaction. "Powerful enough to grind meat and bone to a paste."

I watch him warily.

"It's funny, processing meat," he continues. "I make a lot of dog food with the bad pieces. The bones, the parts that aren't good for anything else. Dogs love it. It makes me feel useful, good inside, like I've taken the stuff no one wants. Finally put it to the use it deserves. Something constructive."

It seems like he's going to turn it on and give me a full demonstration, but then he reaches for a little stool and sits, facing me. His blue eyes are intense. It's strange that these are the same eyes that have looked at me through binoculars. Windows. Through layers of removal. And now, we're a breath apart.

He braces his arms against his legs. "What's your plan?" His tone isn't mean, but there isn't softness either.

"I don't have one."

"Seems to me you should be looking for your husband's killer."

"I was," I say, unable to keep the anger out of my voice. "And now it looks like I'm running from the law."

He's undeterred by my emotion. "You can do both."

"Why are you helping me, Bob? I thought you hated Bots."

"Can't say I love 'em now. But there's more important things."

"Like what?"

"You need help." Stated like this is obvious, even though it answers nothing.

My mind spits out a disturbing image. Bob, hacking Josh's arm off with one of those cleavers. He has the perfect space here to deal with a dead body and make it disappear—in the bone grinder, for instance.

"Did *you* kill my husband?" The question leaves my lips before I can calculate if it's smart or stupid, but Bob doesn't seem taken aback.

"No." His half grin is mostly hidden under his beard. "But I wish I did."

My tone takes on a slightly hysterical pitch. "What the hell does that mean?"

"He wasn't a good man. We both know it. Let's be honest now."

His meaning floods me. Bob must have been a witness to more than I realized.

"Good man?" I explode. "Josh had problems like anyone else. You want honesty? Why don't *you* tell *me* what kind of a person spies on their neighbor for months? You have a lot of fucking nerve claiming the moral upper hand."

He leans back, as if reevaluating me. "There's levels of bad."

"That was our private business," I spit. "You had no right. No right—" My throat squeezes. Yes, we had problems. I lean my head in my hands. "I can't do this."

"You can," says Bob, reaching forward and clapping a firm hand on my knee. "For Annaleigh."

You can. Like it's a matter of willpower and gumption. It grates, and at the same time, I know I will keep pushing on the hope of *can.* Until I'm dragged away against my will, or my body fails. *Can* may be a fallacy. But it's also hope.

"Come on," he says, rising. "We've waited long enough.

Should be safe now. I'll make sandwiches at the house. Then we can make some decisions."

He turns off the lights and opens the door, bringing a welcome breath of air. Somehow, it's become full-on night. The moon is a pale glow behind racing clouds. He leads the way across his property. I limp behind.

The back door leads us straight into Bob's kitchen, where a cat on the counter watches me with cool suspicion. Bob's house is neat but old-looking, with out-of-date appliances and scuffed hardwoods.

He leads me up carpeted stairs that smell like burnt vacuum, down a short hallway, and into a dark room—the room that faces Annaleigh's. I reach for the light.

"Wait," he says, already at the window. "Let me draw the curtains first."

I flick the light on as soon as we're secure. The first thing I see is the parent side of my baby monitor. The second, the folding chair by the window where Bob must sit as he spies. Otherwise, the room is full of boxes. The same name is scrawled across all of them. Gianna-CLOTHING. Gianna-BOOKS. Gianna-MEDICAL RECORDS.

I open my mouth to ask why the fuck Bob has my baby monitor and what the fuck his game is. Instead I say, "Who's Gianna?"

"My daughter," says Bob. His blue eyes on me are somehow simple. Devoid of any layers. "Gianna was your egg donor." And finally, that steady voice cracks. "Annaleigh is my granddaughter."

THEN

"You okay there?" The producer for this segment is right next to me—Prisha, a striking woman in a leather jacket and neon-yellow heels. I remember her from regular filming, and she always struck me as a sharp, single-minded person who'd do anything to capture that *wow* moment. I like her.

Josh and I flew into LAX this morning, separately, to film the final episode: "After the Proposal." I'm waiting in the wings for Josh to join me. Even now, I can hear Matt introducing the segment, and the live audience applauding.

"You look a little pale," adds Prisha.

"Yeah. Just feeling a little sick." I smile sideways at her.

She lowers her voice and leans close. "You remember it's in the book on the side table?"

I nod, and then there's a warm presence next to me. Josh, looking crisp in a new suit, smelling piney from his aftershave.

"Josh," I say, embracing him. My heart flutters like it always does when I see him after an absence. We've been apart for three days; he had to travel to Des Moines for work, and flew in straight from there.

"Your hair," Prisha objects.

"Sorry," I laugh, pulling back and focusing on Josh as a few people adjust my hair and someone freshens up my lip gloss. "I've missed you, baby."

"I've missed you, too," says Josh, but he seems tense. A little distant. Something beyond the travel-weary Josh who gets adorably needy after his work trips.

"Is something wrong?" I whisper.

"I'll tell you later," he says. He doesn't say it in a mean way, but there isn't much warmth to his tone either.

I reach for his hand and squeeze. He squeezes back, a little too hard, like he's reproaching my squeeze. This is something new I've learned about Josh: when he's stressed, he withdraws.

The six weeks we've had together since filming ended, holed up in his Indianapolis condo in strict secrecy as the show airs, have been good, but not easy. I've had to remind myself that the Josh I fell in love with was in a controlled, luxurious environment where every date was planned and every word could be premeditated. Where he was catered to by twenty-four women and an entire team of producers. *The Proposal* was Josh in a petting zoo. This is Josh in the wild. It's an adjustment, and while sometimes I do feel like I didn't know who I was saying yes to in Jamaica, I refuse to see that as a negative. *Different, not worse*, I've told myself dozens of times, because I'm not about to doubt the biggest choice of my life over a few domestic tensions. If I was made for Josh, I was made for this Josh, too. Weirdly, it's my trust in Andy that has reassured me during some of the lows.

"Okay, you guys are on in ten seconds," whispers Prisha, urging us slightly forward.

I can see the stage now. Matt, in an oversize club chair, faces the empty love seat where Josh and I will sit. We've both seen the list of questions beforehand, but there's one surprise Josh doesn't know about.

"Ready, fiancée?" he says with a grin as we're given the signal, and he suddenly sounds so normal that I tell myself everything is going to be fine.

We walk onstage to furious applause. The lights are bright, somewhat obscuring the people in the studio, who have all leapt to their feet. I wonder if they were prescreened for their views on Synths.

Josh and I both wave, then take our seats. I adjust my short skirt while the applause dies down and Matt makes his opening remarks.

The truth is, I'm having second thoughts about the revelation I'm about to make. Not just because Josh seems a little off tonight, though that's definitely a factor.

It made sense two days ago, when I took the pregnancy test. Josh was traveling anyway, and I didn't want to tell him over the phone. The next time we saw each other was going to be here, and I remember thinking how sweet it would be to bring our *Proposal* experience full circle with this final big reveal.

Now I'm teetering. Is it a cute grand gesture? Or am I crazy to expose this intimate moment to all of America?

I snap out of my head just in time to realize that Matt asked me a question.

"Sorry, I missed that," I say, blushing immediately and re-crossing my legs.

"A little distracted tonight, are we?" he says, charming as always.

"I mean, can you blame me?" I hold up my left hand, where my engagement ring flashes. The audience ooohs. "And this guy is *always* a distraction." I lean over and kiss Josh's cheek, a little rough under my lips, to applause.

"So now that we have your attention, Julia," says Matt in a cheeky tone, "why don't you tell us what it's been like living in secret for the past six weeks while the show aired?"

"It's been incredible," I gush. I don't even allow my conscience to twinge over this slight distortion. I don't owe my reality to anyone but Josh and myself. "We moved into Josh's condo in Indianapolis. I've been playing house while he gets back into things at work. Camila and I have talked a lot on the phone, she's become such a close friend, and we're both lucky to have her in our lives. And I've been enjoying the simple things. Cooking dinner, adding those feminine touches to his bachelor pad—it's so fun."

"No bumps in the road?" provokes Matt. "No second-guessing? No cold feet?"

"Never second-guessing," I say passionately. I glance at Josh with what I hope is a loving look before I continue. "To be totally honest, it's been a little challenging, especially with him traveling so much for work. But he loves his job, and I fully support that, and this is just a weird transitional time, you know? The hardest thing has been keeping it from Josh's friends and coworkers. We've been a little more isolated than we'd like. We're ready for the next step, of going public with our relationship."

"And planning a wedding?" says Matt.

"I mean..." I look at Josh.

"This isn't a shotgun wedding, Matt. We have time," says Josh. He winks at me. "The most important thing is for us to do it how we want, when we want. Surrounded by people who support us."

Oh shit. Now I'm feeling sick for more than one reason. I smile hard to mask the queasy twisting in my gut.

"That's a great perspective," says Matt. "But c'mon, guys. Surely you've talked dates? America just watched your epically romantic proposal. We're ready for wedding bells. Throw us a bone."

Josh and I look at each other. I feel the tension between us.

The thing is, we did want a quick wedding. We talked about it the day he proposed. A small wedding in Indy with a few friends. Cam would be my maid of honor, and Josh's coworker Rick would be his best man. We even debated if we wanted to ask Andy to give me away, or if that was too weird.

Later that evening, we called Josh's mom from Jamaica. She congratulated us super warmly and promised to get back to us on the two dates we'd suggested for the wedding. Which is why when the show aired and she dropped off the face of the earth, it threw us for such a loop.

In retrospect, she never should have found out I'm a Synth from the show. On the other hand, Josh kept not feeling quite ready.

"We could just drive down to see her. Explain everything in person," I suggested after the first week of silence. "Isn't Eauverte just a couple hours away?"

"We can't just show *up* like that," he said, angry like I'd suggested we rob a bank or kill a puppy. "You don't have a mom. You just don't get it, Julia."

I should've let it go.

"So ever since we signed a Synth as one of our contestants, we knew there would be controversy," says Matt. "How are you two feeling about entering the real world? Exposing yourself to the opinions of…well, everyone!"

Ugh. *Entering the real world.* A bitter comeback springs to mind about how if we all admit reality TV isn't real, maybe we should rename it fantasy TV. But I brush the thought away. This question was on the list, thank God, so I already have an answer that avoids dragging in our baggage with Josh's mom.

"We're feeling great." Josh seems completely sincere, like there are no issues at all. Like he didn't punch a hole in our drywall two weeks ago, after I told him I'd tried calling his mom myself and left her a couple voicemails.

"Stay out of it, Julia. You're just going to fuck things up. Why did you think that was a good idea, huh? Why? I already told you this is between my mom and me."

The next day, he quietly spackled over the hole. Now, there's no evidence of it. Just like there's no evidence right now, in his light expression and easy talking, that his mom's rejection of me, and of him, has stabbed him in the heart, deep, someplace not even I can reach.

I can only hope that when she finds out she's going to be a grandma, she'll start picking up the phone.

Matt is skilled and suave, and the questions tick right along as scheduled. During the commercial breaks, we drink bottled water and makeup people powder our foreheads. At one point, Josh and I go backstage and Camila comes out. She squeezes my hand as we pass in the wings. I mouth, *Bitch*, and she mouths it back. Then Josh goes out, and he and Cam talk. I watch them from the wings as they laugh, and she touches his arm, and he touches hers, and she gets a little teary-eyed, and Josh hugs her. I'm used to the little flame of jealousy sputtering in my gut when I see them together, but it's small, and easy to ignore in the face of my absolute trust of Camila. She's been really open with me about her brokenhearted departure from the show, and also so sincerely enthusiastic in her support of us. Which I know will probably never make sense to anyone who hasn't been through the experience we have. But we don't need anyone else to understand.

Finally, I join them, and Cam and I answer questions about our own unlikely "hate to love" journey and whether she really thinks a Synth-human marriage will work.

It's nearing the end when Matt finally gives my prompt.

"So it's time for a surprise announcement. I'd like to give the floor to Julia for this incredibly special surprise, and a first in *Proposal* history."

I grab the book from the side table and turn a little on the love seat to face Josh. Cam and Matt are watching from their individual chairs.

"So, Josh, I have something in here that you might like to see." I open the cover. It's a false book, with a hole. I take out the white stick and hand it over fast, so the cameras don't catch on to the trembling in my fingers.

He takes it. And freezes.

In reality, he's only frozen for probably two seconds. But in my heart, it's an eternity longer.

In those two seconds, I read everything that's going on in-side Josh:

He's shocked.

He's embarrassed to be shocked.

He's angry that I surprised him in front of all these people.

His eyes flicker; something intense sparks.

Then, he smiles, and my entire body sags with relief, because my read was wrong; he's not angry after all, and it's going to be okay.

"Julia!" He flings his arms around me. "This is the best sur-prise ever." There's applause, there's confetti, there's music. We're all standing up, and Cam is hugging us, screaming, "Can I be the godmother? Oh my God, you guys! You're having a baby!"

Then Matt is asking how far along I am, and if this is a Fantasy Suite baby, but I demur, because I feel like it's the right move to preserve *some* level of secrecy.

When the show is finally over, Josh finds me in my dressing room. He shuts the door, leans his back against it, and we look at each other from across the space. I'm on top of the world, and I open my mouth to say so when he cuts in.

"What the fuck, Julia? A baby?"

I struggle to steady myself even though it feels like my en-tire world is tilting. Why can't I seem to get a handle on my fi-ancé's emotions?

"I thought you'd be excited," I say, determined to remain outwardly calm and ride this out.

He groans and leans his head back, gently banging it against the door. "Please tell me this kid wasn't conceived in the fuck-ing Fantasy Suite."

I swallow and don't answer.

"You didn't think to use protection?" He's looking at the ceiling.

My voice is quiet. Still calm, as calm as I can make it. "No. I...wasn't thinking. It was my first time."

No response. I wait.

"I'm sorry," I finally say.

Josh heaves out a long breath. "My mom finally called."

"Josh! That's great!"

But he doesn't lower his face. In fact, he's shaking his head ever so slightly, with a strange smile like he's in the grip of some cruel irony.

"Or...wait," I say. "Is she okay?"

His eyes meet mine over the endless expanse of the dressing room, the endless expanse of our wildly differing emotions. My heart thuds and thuds, like it's trying to reach Josh, like it's knocking against bone hoping it's a door that someone will open, but it's just bone.

Just six weeks ago, Josh's eyes were full of hope, love, excitement, desire. Now? They've gone opaque, like all of that's been stuffed behind this layer of disappointment and pain. I can't even tell if it's just about his mom, or if there's more he's not telling me.

"She has stage four breast cancer." His voice is flat.

"Oh, Josh." This explains the tension when we met in the wings. This explains why the idea of a baby isn't immediately exciting. He can't release himself to the joy of new life when death is staring him in the face. And not just any death—his only parent. Or rather, the only one that matters.

Everything in me wants to leap up, cross the room, and enfold Josh in the strongest hug I can give. But I don't move.

"What can I do?" I whisper.

"Well, obviously, we have to fucking take *care* of her," he says, like he's pissed I would even have to ask.

I nod slowly. As awful as this night has been, I force myself to get past the sting of his reaction to my pregnancy announcement, and past the short-term blow of having to reorient our lives before we've found our footing. The most important thing is for Josh and me to do right by his mom in her time of need, and restore that relationship as best we can.

I'm about to tell Josh that I'm ready to do whatever is needed when a surge of nausea twists me. Acid explodes up my throat. I put a hand on my gut as a feeling of profound weakness tears through me, ripping all my determination to be strong, like my willpower is made of paper.

"Sorry," I say as I lean over the trash can by my dressing table and puke. "Morning sickness."

NOW

"Christi," I say, weak with relief that she answered the phone.

I'm on Bob's cell phone, and I was worried she wouldn't answer a number she doesn't recognize. I copied down my most important contacts, then destroyed my phone with one of Bob's hammers, in case they can track me even while it's off. Maybe I'm being paranoid, but better paranoid than sorry.

Though the twins frequently comment on my Insta, I haven't talked to Christi or Chrystel since filming the segment for their show, but they gave me their numbers that night, and I've always remembered their kind words. *If things get tough, call us.* And I can't imagine things getting tougher than my husband's murder and a sheriff who's ready to lock me up and throw away the key.

Bob is downstairs making sandwiches. I'm still in the room with the boxes, sitting in the folding chair by the window, trying to ignore the clamoring pain in my ankle.

"Julia!" cries Christi with that same vivacious energy that drew me to her so powerfully, like she's turbocharged. "We've been so worried about everything going on with you! How *are* you? What's the update, girl?"

"Things have been...crazy."

"We know you didn't do it," says Christi. "We've been very

vocal with the press. It's ridiculous! Like, we can't even defend ourselves, and now you're being questioned for murder? Look, I have an incredible lawyer, his name is Tom—"

"I need your help," I break in. "If your offer from last year still stands."

"Of course! Anything for you!"

"Does anything include…a car?"

In Bob's barn, everything felt helpless. But now that I've calmed down, I've regrouped. Yes, I'm at more of a disadvantage than ever, but it's not over yet. First, I have to get away from Bob's. Cops are crawling all over my property; I need some distance. Second, I can't use my own car, in case there are alerts on the plates.

"Uh…sure?" she says.

"And a place to go," I continue. "A new phone. A credit card. A breast pump—that's urgent, actually. I'm kind of on the run. Temporarily. Until I can figure this out."

Anything to buy me time to find Josh's actual killer. There are two names top of my mind: Andy and Eden, who are fucking working together after all. I haven't even had time to process that emotionally. It's too devastating.

"I don't mean to sound bossy," says Christi, "but…don't you think running might make you look even more guilty? Why not work with law enforcement?"

"You don't understand how things are here," I say, praying she won't think I'm exaggerating my situation. "Sheriff Mitchell's campaign promise was to run me out of town. Look it up. He *hates* me, Christi. If he gets me in handcuffs, they're never coming off, and my daughter will be…" I can't finish that sentence.

"What about other suspects?" says Christi. "Aren't they questioning other people?"

"That's what I asked. I even rattled off a whole list of people who might have wanted to harm Josh." I can't help a small, bitter laugh. "He refused to write them down. He's dead set on nailing me for this. It's not even fucking *subtle*." And then I have to take a deep breath, because thinking of the sheriff in my house refusing to do his job makes my head so hot I can't think.

"Okay, I'm getting the picture." There's a silence, which feels rare from Christi. Then she says, "Let me get my assistant on it. I can get you a car within the hour. Just tell me where to take it."

I breathe out. "Thank you. *Thank* you, Christi. Okay. There's a motel just off the interstate, about twenty miles from Eauverte. The Stop and Sleep Roadside Inn." I've noticed it a million times. A million times, I've thought, *no way in hell*.

"I'll get you a room on my card," says Christi. "We'll use a pseudonym. How about… Lily Paddington. I can have a phone and fake ID and stuff for you in the morning."

"That would be perfect. I seriously can't thank you enough," I say. "If you can get a breast pump tonight, too, I would owe you for life."

"Of course. But if that sheriff is really so terrible, why not run farther, Julia? Don't stay at some motel. Drive to California! I'll hide you! Annaleigh, too! We have plenty of space. My closet is the size of the average two-bedroom apartment."

The idea is actually very endearing—me hiding out in Christi's California mansion. But how long could that possibly last? No, my only chance at being permanently reunited with my daughter, at living any kind of a life worth living, is to find Josh's killer.

"That's so kind. But I can't. I have to figure out who did this to Josh."

"Do you have any idea?" Christi says.

"I have one final lead," I say. "I just need more time."

Time to figure out why Andy and Eden would want to kill my husband, the man they made me to complete.

Considering they're both geniuses, even if they did murder Josh, they were probably smart enough to cover their tracks. Finding evidence that clearly convicts either of them—before the law catches up with me—would be a goddamn miracle. But it's the only avenue left.

Suddenly, a memory lights up in my head: the night I came upon Eden in the woods. She was talking on the phone. She claimed she was talking to the sheriff; now I'm convinced it was Andy. What did she say, exactly? *Of course I'll call you. Anything new. Sure.* Like she was spying on me and reporting back to Andy.

Like Bob, Eden was an unwanted witness to my troubles. Did she call Andy after either of those times? Report back to him how bad things in my marriage had gotten? If Andy is in love with me, could Andy's desire to defend me, or avenge me, have been motivation enough to kill Josh?

Something else Eden said pushes through the murky surface of my memories, like a stubborn weed. Something about the number *three... Three strikes and you're out.* I don't know what it means, but it feels important.

"Well, you know what they say," Christi is saying cheerily. "Time is money. I'll have a rental car to the motel within the hour. I'll have the driver check in for you, because let's be honest, with that red hair of yours? You're instantly recognizable. She'll wait for you in the parking lot with the room key and the car keys."

"And a breast pump," I remind her.

"Are you really okay to wait until morning for the other stuff?"

"Of course."

"I'll tell my assistant to have the driver wear something you can spot—ooh, cat ears! That's cute. Do you want hair dye, actually? Or maybe a wig. I can have a whole suitcase of stuff outside your door no later than breakfast."

"Yes. Sure. Anything you can think of. You are a gem. You and Chrystel both." I'm weak with gratitude.

"Listen, I'm going to be honest with you. With only three of us Synths, the outcome of Josh's murder is going to affect all of us." She exhales. "I have a bad feeling about you running. But you seem certain, so I'm supporting you. Okay? That's what we do for each other. But now you have to do something for me."

"What?"

Sweet Christi is gone; a tougher Christi takes her place. "Do not fuck this up."

Turns out I like Tough Christi even better.

"I won't," I promise.

THEN

"You like the lemon or the raspberry?" says the baker, a woman with rainbow hair, butterfly barrettes, and a pretty smile.

"Here, you didn't get enough of a taste." Josh smiles and directs the spoon with the bite of vanilla cake with lemon curd toward my mouth.

Even though the last thing I want to do right now is eat another bite of sugar with this blasted morning sickness, I open my freshly glossed lips, knowing that the cameras are tracking every adorable moment.

"Wait, honey, you have something..." says Josh, nudging the corner of my lips as if for a crumb. "Here, let me help you." He kisses me lightly, no tongue, a perfect camera kiss.

"I'm onto you," I tease when he pulls away. "There was no crumb!"

The baker laughs a little awkwardly, but it doesn't matter, because the focus is us.

I know that neither Josh nor I want to be surrounded by cameras right now, but I also know that it's not about our short-term discomfort. It's about getting what we need to survive the tough times that are ahead. And let's be honest—neither of us had the ability or energy to plan an entire wedding in fourteen days.

The money we'll receive from allowing them to film a wedding episode will allow us to do what we need to do. Josh can take the huge pay cut as he moves out of sales into an administrative role, which he can do remotely from Eauverte. And we can jump in and start chipping away at his mom's gargantuan medical bills, which aren't covered by her awful insurance and are only bound to grow from here. Josh keeps talking like she might get better, but I'm pretty sure that's denial talking. I have the feeling we're going to need a full-time nurse at some point. Hospice. This wedding will pay for her death.

"So…are we feeling more raspberry?" says the baker.

"Mmmmm." I frown as if caught in a deep conundrum. "I don't know! They're both so good!"

"Well," says the baker, smiling like she has a little secret. "As a special gift to you guys, I would actually love to do both flavors!"

I squeal and clap my hands. "Both?"

"That is so generous." Josh covers my hand with his while we both beam. "It's going to make our day extra special."

Maybe it's the nausea, but even the words coming out of our mouths are sickening. It seems like a lifetime ago when I had trouble distinguishing what was real and what was fake. They seemed so close, like you might confuse the two at any moment. Now? Like a cloven fruit, they've fully split apart. And they grate.

"We got the shot," says Prisha, who's come on all the wedding prep shoots.

Josh bursts up like the chair is burning him. "We good, then?" His suave air of gratitude about our two flavors of cake is gone. I never sensed this impatience from him on *The Proposal*, and I'm chalking it up to the feeling of time ticking away. The time of his mother's life, being wasted by each of these frivolous moments. The time marked by his watch, which drives me crazy with its loud ticking, which I'm not letting myself bring up again, in case his answer is no longer sweet like it was that first night.

"Yep, let's pack it up," Prisha says, and the crew immediately starts taking down the lighting and cameras.

I take a minute, though, to grab a selfie, allowing myself to look cutely overwhelmed. I know it's important to use these chances to tell the American public that I'm just like them. I post it with no filter and a quick caption. Wedding planning is EXHAUSTING #nofilter.

Then I stand, smoothing out my floral-print maxi dress. The fit isn't quite right. The spaghetti straps are cutting into my shoulders. My chest feels tender, and I know I need to shop for new bras. Josh added me as a secondary cardholder on his credit card account, but every time I use it, I feel weird, especially considering our new financially murky waters.

Josh has left the bakery ahead of me, but I'm not far behind. I put on my sunglasses. It's hot out here, and Josh is fast-tracking it to the SUV. The floral shop was our first stop, the bakery our second. Next, Josh is getting dropped off at a tux place and I'm headed to a bridal boutique to find my dress.

As tough as things are, there's still plenty of hope inside me. Josh and I are facing the big guns: life and death, and that's enough to rock the foundation for any couple, not just us. One choice at a time, I keep reminding myself—even when the choices are hard.

"Hi, Julia, sorry to bother you," says a voice, and suddenly there's a woman by my side. I don't stop walking. I've already been recognized a few times around town, and I didn't enjoy it. One man asked for my autograph, which was annoying, but okay. Another woman opened her water bottle, shouted, *Get out of my state, Parts!* and sprayed me with it. I've been gathering that Parts is not the only insulting name people have come up with for me. There's also Fuckbot, Synthesizer, and Arty—for Artificial Intelligence.

"I'm Ally Buoncore from Netflix," says the woman, keeping pace with me as I cross the parking lot. "I've left you a few messages—"

"Yes, things have been busy," I say, instantly regretting the bite in my voice. This dedicated, professional woman doesn't deserve my contempt just because it's her job to harass me. I sigh and stop walking. She's shorter than I imagined, and younger. Curvy and tanned, in a sleek black sheath dress and incongruous red sneakers.

"You okay?" Josh calls over to me from the SUV.

I give him a thumbs-up. I know I can't talk long; Camila, Emma, and Zoe are meeting me for the dress shopping. While they're here, we'll get the bachelorette party out of the way, too. The entire cast of girls is joining for that, like a big, bizarre reunion, probably to draw people's attention away from the fact that I have no family or friends outside of the cast. There will probably be strippers and thumping music and booze, even though I can't drink in my condition. I've even heard rumors of an ice statue of a naked man. Surprise surprise, you pour alcohol into his head and it shoots out his you-know-what. Unfortunately, I'm out of energy to fight for anything tamer. At least Cam will have fun.

Ally presses her hands into a prayer position by her chest, and a hot breeze blows my skirt around my swollen ankles. I decide I'll give her two minutes before politely declining. Again.

"Julia," she says. "I've tried my very best sales pitches on you, and nothing. So you tell me. What can I do to get you to consider the documentary?"

"To be honest, nothing," I say. "Unless you have a cure for cancer?"

Ally makes a pained face. "Sorry, I don't have that. But seriously— name your price. I can't guarantee anything, of course, but at least give me something to work with. A number to shoot for. I'm dying to do this project with you. *Dying.*"

That, I got. I'm very aware of how lucrative the documentary would be for Netflix. And the truth is, we could use the money. For a crazy second, I consider saying yes, right here in the bakery parking lot, with Josh just feet away. It would probably take care of all Rita's medical bills. Then I imagine cameras in the house. Production schedules and interviews. While Rita is dying. While I'm having a baby.

"Can I be honest with you?" I say, pushing my sunglasses on top of my head so that Ally and I are eye to eye.

"Of course."

"I do need the money. But family comes first, and right now, my family needs space. We have a lot of change coming, and I can't in good conscience add another stressor to our lives." I shrug. "I'd say call me later, but with Josh's mom sick…"

Ally is taking it in stride. She flashes me a big smile. "Listen, Julia. I'm going to keep calling you, because that's what I do, and I'm still really hoping that one day you'll say yes, because you have a fascinating story and it truly deserves to be told. But I very much respect your decision. I promise not to harass you for at least a few months."

"I may never want to do it. I've kind of had my fill of cameras."

Ally raises an eyebrow toward the film crew, which is closing up the back of the van, as if to point out that I invited these guys in, so why not her?

"Temporary compromise," I say, sliding my sunglasses back down.

Josh has rolled down the window and is patting the side of the vehicle, clearly impatient. I give him the one-minute signal.

"Keep me in mind is all I ask," says Ally.

"Nice talking to you." I extend a hand, which she shakes.

The brief temptation of the money is fully extinguished as I walk away from her, my hair fluttering in the breeze. Josh wanted his little slice of the American Dream. A house, a yard, a little family in a nest. That dream drew us together, and even though we haven't exactly achieved it yet, no part of that dream included a long-term film crew.

Not even the money is motivation enough to invite that kind of fresh invasion into the lives we haven't even had a chance to build.

NOW

After hanging up with Christi, I look at the phone in my lap. Obviously, I can't just call Andy or Eden and ask for the truth. What I need is a third party. Someone impartial. Someone who can dig shit up.

"Ready for a sandwich?" Bob calls up. The stairs creak under his tread.

"One more minute!" I call out. There's a short silence, then the creak of his descent.

I have the feeling of stacking the deck for myself in these precious few moments in Bob's house. These are the crucial minutes of preparation that could make me or break me once I leave here.

I reference my handwritten contact list and thank my lucky stars I included Ally Buoncore. As a documentary producer, she should have no problem doing some simple research—especially if I dangle the prize.

"Hello, this is Ally," she says after the third ring, in the same breathless voice she's used on the dozen voicemails she's left over the past year.

"Hi! This is Julia." There's a brief silence. "Walden."

"Oh my God. *Julia.* I can't believe— I've been watching the news and—"

"That's actually why I'm calling. Listen. I know I've been putting you off about the documentary—but I'm having a change of heart. I think maybe this is the time."

"Oh?" Her surprise is tempered with the slightest whiff of caution.

"I just need something from you first."

"Anything!" She laughs, then adds, "Within reason, of course."

"Is information on Andy Wekstein and Eden Jeliazkova within reason?"

She pauses. "Um...what kind of information are we talking about?"

"Can you keep this confidential?"

"Of course."

"I think one of them may have been involved in my husband's death. Maybe both of them. Eden is my babysitter, but I just found out she also works for WekTech. And they've both lied to me about it."

"Whaaaat?"

"Exactly. I need help finding out why. I just feel like it might be linked to Josh's death."

"God," breathes Ally. I can hear the excitement in her tone. Her precious *Making Julia* documentary might get a murder angle, too. Her voice switches to one hundred percent business. "Julia, here's what I can do. I'm going to call in a favor. Give me twelve hours, and I will move heaven and earth to get what you need. Is this a good number to call you back?"

"I'm changing phone numbers, so I'll have to call you," I say. I hesitate, but then I go for it. "Also...remember when you told me to name my price?"

"Yeeees," she says.

"You offered me one million."

"That's right."

"I want four."

It's a huge number, but with Josh gone, I have to think of my future. Annaleigh's future.

There's a longer pause. Then Ally says, "Consider it done."

THEN

The wedding, a very rushed two weeks later, is televised. With the power of the network behind us, it has all happened at incredible speeds.

After a lot of debate, Andy is walking me down the aisle. The producers really pushed for it, and even though Josh didn't love the idea as much as he seemed to when we got engaged, he's being an adult and letting it slide.

Andy is also signing as our witness. He pulled me aside the day before to go over, in his words, "a few legal details." Basically, that WekTech is retaining nominal ownership of me, in case the marriage doesn't work out.

"It's going to work out," I said, a little miffed that he was obsessing about technicalities when here I was, fulfilling the very destiny he created me for.

"Sure, yeah, of course it will," he said. "It's just, if it doesn't…"

"Stop!" I cried, laughing. "You're going to jinx it!"

The venue, at a winery outside Indianapolis, has been decked out. Our wedding day dawns sunny and clear. I've seen the barn they've transformed into a chapel, and it's lovely, with simple white chairs for the guests and wildflowers everywhere and a little arch Josh and I will stand under as the minister marries us.

After the buffet-style reception, a band will play into the night. I'll pretend not to feel like I want to puke my guts out every few minutes, and we'll both smile like we're not crushed that neither Josh's dad nor his mom will be here today supporting us.

In the flurry of the day, as a whole assortment of bridesmaids twitter around me like nervous birds in their pink satin gowns, Cam is a rock. She keeps turning up with exactly what I need. A fresh coat of lipstick. Extra deodorant. A can of ginger ale. Another pack of oyster crackers.

It's like I'm living two experiences at once.

One experience is the one everyone sees. An extravagant, country-sweet wedding. Every detail attended to, from the mason jar candles to the antique ivory tulle woven around the arch to the personalized gift bag underneath each of the guests' chairs, tied off with a sprig of lavender.

The other is an invisible, interior experience. One that I have to live through alone—that Josh has to live through alone. The private grief and tension held behind our smiles.

When it's all said and done, the moment of our wedding day that sticks with me, to my surprise, isn't Josh and me saying our rehearsed vows, or him slipping the ring on my finger, or the tenderness in Camila's touch as she holds my hair back while I puke—again.

It's my moment with Andy, right before going through the barn doors into the chapel area where Andy will give me away to Josh. The cameras have just moved to the other side of the doors, so we have a single, miraculous minute of privacy.

"You look amazing," he says. An echo of one of his first reactions to me on Launch Day.

I smile as best I can. "If I puke, just jump out of the way."

But he doesn't laugh. Instead, he squeezes my hand. "Julia... you don't have to do this."

I look into his deep brown eyes and there's a moment of alarm, because the person who made me for Josh is not supposed to be

encouraging me to run away from my groom at the last possible minute.

"Andy…we already talked about this. Stop worrying."

His voice goes low, urgent. "I have the keys to the getaway
car. Say the word, I'll drive you away. I know it's been one thing
after another for you. This all may feel…inevitable. But this is
your choice. *Yours*, okay?"

"I *have* chosen, Andy. I'm in love with Josh!" I lick my lips,
even though I know it'll disturb my lipstick. "Not to mention,
you *designed* me for Josh. You should know better than anyone
that we're a perfect fit." I pause. "Right?"

"What if I fucked up?" He suddenly looks like a scared little kid.

My stomach twists with some premonition. And then I shake
my head, because Pachelbel's Canon is playing on the other side
of the doors, and the wedding planner is walking toward us,
giving us the signal.

"Relax. You didn't fuck up," I whisper, and hold out my arm
for him to take.

And if you did, I promise myself silently, *it doesn't matter, because
I will make it work. No matter what it takes.*

The wedding planner mouths, *Go.* The barn doors slide open.
I smile. Andy's grip on my arm tightens, but he doesn't move.

I squeeze him, hard. *It's time. Let's go.*

We take a step. Then another. Everyone is standing, smiling, glowing.

Soon, the minister will say, *Who gives this woman to be married?*
Andy will say, *I give her.*

Then I'll take that step forward. Release Andy's hand and
take Josh's. And I will belong to Josh as fully and completely as
I've always wanted.

This moment is my long-awaited dream come true, and I'm
not letting any last-minute insecurities of Andy's take that away.

NOW

I'm lying on the floor of Bob's truck with a nasty-smelling blanket on top of me when I feel the truck pull to a stop. Bob says a single word. "Cops."

After talking to Christi and Ally, I told Bob where to take me. I didn't press him for details about Gianna, or his spying, though it seems obvious that he moved here to be close to us, to Annaleigh. From the boxes marked with Gianna's name, I've surmised she passed. I still don't know how he got ahold of my baby monitor, but right now I'd prefer not to ask, and anyway, I can guess why he sang to her. For the same reason I do: love. Maybe there will be time to talk at length when this is all over.

I lie as still as possible while Bob rolls down the window.

"Evening, Officer," he says.

"We're looking for a red-haired woman. Lives over on HH. The Synth. You know her?" It's a man's voice, but thankfully, not Mitchell's.

"She's my neighbor," says Bob easily. "What's she gone and done?"

"Murdered her husband, I guess. You seen her?"

Light shines through the blanket, like someone is tracking a flashlight through the windows. I don't even breathe.

"Nope."

There's silence, then a grunt. "If you see her, please contact us. She may be armed and dangerous."

"Sure will. You boys stay safe," says Bob. There's a whir—his window, rolling back up. A slamming sound on the side of the truck, like the officer is urging us on. Then a burst of speed. Welcome darkness, and welcome silence.

"Coast is clear," Bob calls back. "Ten minutes to the motel."

I free my head from the blanket, relishing how fresh the air feels.

Cars whiz past us in the night. Geometric patches of brightness move across the truck's ceilings from headlights. My breasts are in serious pain, and I lean all my emotions into Christi's promise to have a pump waiting for me, then tip my head back against the lip of the seat and try to doze.

"My daughter…" Bob's voice jolts me awake. I wait, but he says nothing further. A semitruck whooshes past.

"Gianna," I finally say.

"She was fiery. Passionate. Like me, except the opposite politically. By the time she moved off to college, we weren't speaking. I refused to help her pay for school." He sucks in his breath. "I regret that."

I say nothing. I can't help but imagine Annaleigh and me in the future. No matter how hard we disagree, I would never let that happen.

"Three years went by. I get a call. She's in a coma. Hit by a drunk driver. I drove all the way from Kentucky to Oregon. Barely stopped, went a hundred the whole way." He clears his throat. "I was her medical power of attorney. Taking her off the machines was the hardest thing I ever did. But they said she was brain-dead. So I let her go."

"I'm sorry," I say, but so quietly, I'm not sure Bob hears.

"I figured it had to be someone's fault. Besides the drunk driver. Some doctor. I went through her medical records, looking for who to blame. That's when I found out how she paid for college."

He's quiet again. I let the silence stand.

"She sold her eggs to WekTech. There were nondisclosures and all that, so no one knew but her—and me. It didn't take rocket science to figure out the Synth that got them was you. So when I heard you were pregnant, I sold my house in Kentucky and made an offer on the property next to you that the previous owner couldn't refuse."

I'm thankful we're not looking at each other right now. I don't want to look into his eyes and read what a loss like that does to a person.

You lost Josh, a voice reminds me.

But it's not the same as losing a child.

"I'm not gonna lie to you, Julia. I was going to kidnap my granddaughter. I wanted to bring her home to her real family."

"But you changed your mind."

He sighs heavily. "You're a good mom, Julia. I saw how well you took care of that baby. You're…not what I thought. I love my granddaughter. And in the end, I realized hurting you would've been hurting her." Bob pauses. "But while I was watching you and her, I saw more than I bargained for."

"Josh," I say.

He grunts.

We ride in silence the rest of the way. I keep waiting for him to say something else, but I'm grateful he doesn't. Maybe Bob is thinking that since Josh is dead now, it's water under the bridge. Or maybe he realizes that since I just lost Josh, talking about it would be like flaying me alive.

When he pulls into the motel parking lot, I can already see the woman we're meeting, leaning against a car in a cat-ear headband.

"Thank you for everything," I say, easing off the truck's floor. "Be good to Captain for me." Bob has promised to retrieve my dog, and I have an inkling that Captain will be delighted to stay with the source of his fancy food.

"Wait," says Bob, twisting in his seat to look at me full-on. It's almost a shock to see his face, after all these revelations in the dark that have forever changed how I look at him. "If you make it out of this mess—*when* you make it out—" He tightens his lips, like he's shoring up some strong emotion.

"Annaleigh is all you have left of Gianna," I say. I'm just reading what I see in his eyes. The same expression I've seen in the mirror since leaving Annaleigh in Chicago. *All I have left of Josh.*

Bob nods, his eyes glistening in the semi-dark. Silent, as our strange relationship of the past months has been, watching one another through windows.

I almost wonder if, in some way, Bob knows me better than Josh ever did. With Josh, there was always a confusion of words. Explanations, justifications, apologies. But Bob has learned who I am through what he's seen. Through my actions.

I feel suddenly, deeply known, by the last person I ever expected.

Leaning forward, I grip his arm. I can feel how strong he is under the fabric of his sleeve. I think of the strength it takes to change. The strength it takes to let love change you.

I say, "I'll remember that."

THEN

"How was your day?" I ask, hurrying forward to greet Josh, who's coming in with his laptop under his arm and a tense expression. The internet has been spotty here, so after battling it for two hours this morning, he finally drove to the nearest Starbucks, twenty miles north of Eauverte, so he could log in to work. "Feeling okay?" I brush a kiss across his cheek.

"Tired," he says in that dead tone he's had recently, like our troubles have crushed not only his energy but the desire to even try to summon it up.

I don't blame him. Dealing with his dying parent, living in her house, experiencing the antagonism of not only the community but local law enforcement, all while feeling the sting of his demotion at work—even though he's the one who asked for it—was never going to be easy.

I've tried to get him excited about our future back in Indy with our new baby, but this has been a bad strategy, because obviously in that scenario, Rita has passed. All illusions of recovery were shut down last week, during a meeting with her oncologist. And while it's only a matter of time, Josh can't stand to be reminded of it.

"Well," I say, caressing the curve of my belly, "dinner's in the oven and—"

"Hey!" It's Rita, calling out from the small room down the hall. "Hey! Help!"

"I'll go," I say. *Brave face.* She must have heard Josh get home. But he's not ready to see her. He needs a minute to take off his jacket, get settled, charge his laptop, change into sweatpants. I shouldn't be angry at the selfishness of a dying woman, making demands of Josh the second he's home. But here we are.

"Thanks," says Josh.

I scurry off to the small bedroom where we've set my mother-in-law up in a rented hospital bed. She's mostly bedridden now, and soon I need to broach a touchy subject with Josh: hiring a nurse. I need help.

I open the door, hold the doorframe and lean my body in, which I hope feels less intrusive than me just walking in like I own the place. "Can I get you anything, Rita?"

The room smells awful, like antiseptic and urine, and I breathe through my mouth. Even though I'm over the morning sickness, my stomach is still more sensitive than I'd like.

Rita turns her head away from me and closes her eyes like a sullen child. Her thinning hair, dark with white roots, fans out on the pillow like drying seaweed.

"Do you need help with anything?" I ask. "Getting to the bathroom?"

The first-floor bathroom is right next to her room, and when Josh is home, he helps her get there. I can help her get there, too. But when it's just me? She does her business in the bed. I know it's out of some vindictive defiance, that she's furious a Synth is caring for her in her final days. But still, every time she does it, I tell myself it was just an accident. Remind myself that weakness is literally eating her alive. That I cannot, must not, hold any of this against her.

"I'm making chicken and green beans," I say, smiling. "It's a recipe from your church cookbook. How's your appetite? Would you like Josh and me to come in and eat with you?" I wait. Nothing. "Or would you like to try and sit at the dining table?"

No answer.

I rub my belly, as if it's a center of love I can draw on for Rita.

"Well, I'm sure Josh will be in soon to say hello. I think he had a long day at work. So."

Silence.

I see myself out. As I close the door, I feel a single, pure flash of anger. I wish I could crush something. Hit something. Vent this burning feeling that comes like a chaser after this charade of gentle goodwill. If I could, I would shake her, hard. *Love me!* I'd demand. *Love your granddaughter! Do it for Josh's sake, because this is killing your son!* But I breathe for a few seconds, and the feeling passes.

Like everything passes, I'm learning. Life, obviously. Time, sweeping good moments and bad moments alike behind you. Nothing is for keeps.

As I return to the kitchen, I hear the water running upstairs. Josh likes to shower after work. I think it helps him reset. In the kitchen, I check the timer. Five more minutes until the chicken comes out.

I lean against the counter, close my eyes, and just breathe for a while, feeling the welcome heaviness of the baby.

We've been in this house for three months as Rita has deteriorated. At first, she was mobile. She was in the master bedroom upstairs, and Josh and I were crammed into the smaller guest room. Every day, when Josh logged out of work, he'd say, "Has she said anything about the baby?"

"No," I'd say. He kept asking. And with every *no*, the hope in Josh's eyes went out a little more. I wanted so badly to offer a happy report, but I couldn't make Rita care. Couldn't even make her acknowledge me when I walked in the room. She was making me hurt Josh, and of course his anger fell on me, because it couldn't fall on her.

Now I almost wish I'd lied.

At the sound of footsteps, I open my eyes. Josh is entering the kitchen in sweatpants and bare feet, in a scented cloud of shampoo and aftershave. He has a towel around his shoulders, and he's tousling his dark hair.

"We have to sell the condo," he says, in the voice of someone reporting on the weather, "so I met with a real estate agent today."

The timer dings, but I make no move to get the chicken.

"Josh—what?"

"We can't afford to pay taxes and a mortgage on a place where we're not living."

"What about the money from the show? The wedding episodes?"

"Did you *see* the medical bills?"

"We can rent it out," I say, gripping the counter behind me. Maybe nothing is for keeps, but I can't let that condo go. It's the reminder of those six mostly happy, secret weeks between the end of filming and "After the Proposal." And more importantly, the promise of a future after Rita. I literally go to sleep every night dreaming of that space and how it will feel to return.

"I got fired."

"What?"

"This administrative stuff—I suck at it. It was a pity job anyway. My boss told me I can go back into sales, but not from Eauverte."

No no no.

"The commute to Indy is only two hours," I say, my voice calm despite the frantic beating of my heart. "Get your old job back, Josh. I can stay here and take care of Rita. You could even spend weeknights up there. I can—"

"You don't get it, do you?" He crosses the space between us in two vicious steps. "She's not some annoying sick old lady to me like she is to you. This is my *mother*. I can't leave." He's so close, I can see the heave of his chest. The little shaving nick on his chin. "I'm stuck, Julia. I'm stuck in hell and there's no exit door. Do you get that?" There's a vein in his neck. I watch it throb. I imagine it's a river that carries his blood and his anger all mixed together like a thick, red poison.

I swallow. Nod. "Of course. Yes."

I'm readjusting as fast as I can. Josh, jobless. Our money from filming, history. And now the Indy condo, gone, to fund this. Our presence here with the woman who means the world to Josh and hates me with all the energy of her final days.

An anti-Synth billboard went up a few weeks ago just down the road. Some church drivel basically saying we don't have souls. It felt like a joke at first. I literally laughed.

I'm not laughing today.

This isn't the end, I try to remind myself. After Rita passes, Josh and I can scrape our way to a new beginning. We can re-build. It'll just take a little more time.

"Is something burning?" says Josh.

I whirl toward the oven. Smoke is billowing out. I feel my face crumple as a violent sob racks my body. I press a hand to my mouth to stop myself, because this is *not* the time, Julia, this is *not* the time.

Josh is suddenly behind me, hands on my waist, turning me to face him.

"Hey," he says, his expression more tender than I've seen it in a long time. "Let it burn. It doesn't matter."

"Okay," I gasp, so embarrassed that, of all the horrible moments of the past few days, the one that's gotten me is the chicken burning.

Josh folds me into his arms. "We'll get pizza."

"I don't want you to be stuck in hell," I say, my body shaking in his hold. "I want to make this better."

And then I cry into his shower-damp T-shirt. As awful as I feel, there's a sweetness to this release. And a sweetness to the fact that Josh gets tender when I get weak. Just like in LA after the attack.

"You do make everything better, Julia," he murmurs when I start to calm. "You do. We'll get through this." His voice takes on the slightest hint of teasing. "It's not over 'til it's over, right? And we're not done until we're dead."

I have to smile, because he hasn't teased me like this since... God, I honestly don't remember.

"It's not over 'til it's over," I repeat, smiling through the last of my tears and gently bumping his nose with mine. "We're not done until we're dead."

NOW

Moment of truth. I pull the wig over the cap. Adjust it. Slip on the thick-framed glasses. Step back, adjusting my weight gingerly to avoid my swollen left ankle, and survey my new look in the mirror of the small motel bathroom.

Despite the circumstances, I have to admit some pleasure at the transformation. With the long brown straight hair and the thick bangs falling nearly to my eyes, I look like a starving grad student with a severe vitamin D deficiency. No one would recognize me as Julia Walden.

"Lily Paddington," I practice out loud, combing my hair over my shoulders, fluffing my bangs. "My name is Lily Paddington, from Saint Louis, Missouri."

I glance at the time, as I've been doing, oh, every two minutes since I woke up. It's almost ten in the morning, which is when I'm supposed to call Ally back. In the hour since I woke up to the knock that delivered Christi's suitcase of supplies, I've gone through both packs of premeasured coffee grounds for the miniature motel room coffee maker. I've pumped twice in the past hour, too, though it hasn't brought the relief I hoped for. Even with repeated self-massage and a hot shower, the knot in my breast has just gotten harder and more painful. My ankle is getting worse, too, now swollen to twice its normal size. I can't believe I didn't think to ask Christi to include painkillers along with the wig and the phone and the other stuff. At least it's my left ankle, so I can still drive.

The clock turns from 9:59 to 10:00. Hopping out of the bathroom on my right foot, I settle on the bed, carefully stretching out my left leg. I'm trembling from some mixture of caffeine and adrenaline as I punch in Ally's number. Even now, I want to keep on believing that Andy and Eden are on my side. That somehow, they lied to protect me. That two of my most trusted people aren't the villains of this nightmare.

"Hello?" says Ally.

"It's me," I say, putting her on speakerphone.

"Julia!" Her normally bright voice is a little croaky. "Okay. I've just pulled an all-nighter, so I hope at least something I found is helpful. Honestly, I'm not sure if it will be. It's surprisingly difficult to find anything on Andy Wekstein, which tells me he scrubbed the internet at some point. Not just for himself, but his immediate family as well."

"That sounds suspicious," I say, pulling a motel notepad and pen off the nightstand.

"Not necessarily. A lot of high-profile people do it. Alright. You ready?"

"Shoot," I say, uncapping the cheap pen and trying to ignore the steadily increasing volume of my physical pain.

"I'll start with brief backgrounds. Let's see—Eden Grace Jeliazkova. Twenty-six. Raised by her grandparents, mother deceased, father lives in New Jersey. She doesn't appear to have contact with him. She attended Caltech. Founded a student group called No Woman Harmed, organized a couple marches to build awareness around violence against women. Never graduated. Interned for WekTech the summer after her junior year, got hired on full-time right away. Worked on project JULIA alongside

Andy." Ally pauses after this lightning-fast delivery. "At that
time, she was the second-highest-paid person at WekTech."

"Wait—second-highest-paid? Are you sure?" The emo, overall-
wearing, weed-smoking sweetheart who sends me adorable selfies
with Annaleigh? Even though Andy told me she was super smart,
it still feels like being told the kid with the lemonade stand is also
running a Fortune 500 company.

"Yes."

I frantically scribble notes. "And she's still on payroll?"

"Correct."

"What's she doing in Eauverte?"

"I'm not sure. But girl has done her taxes, and WekTech is
definitely her employer."

I rub my forehead. "Wow. This is a lot."

"Ready for Andy?"

"Go ahead."

"Full name, Andrew Leonard Wekstein, thirty-seven. Born
in Des Moines. Undergrad at Indiana University, accelerated
PhD at Carnegie Mellon. Obviously, the founder of WekTech.
Parents, still alive as far as we can tell, though like I said, it was
very hard to find any information about them. Sister, Laura Wekstein, deceased. He built Wekstein Memorial on IU's campus in
her memory. There's a small statue of her out front. Let's see...
Oh! You might find this interesting. Through WekTech, Andy
has donated millions of dollars to mental health organizations
that specialize in suicide prevention. He's also donated substan-
tial amounts to local women's shelters in the Los Angeles area."

Well, there's one interesting connection between Andy and
Eden, besides their interest in robotics: an interest in violence
against women.

My skin prickles with awful possibilities. Did Andy and Eden
know Josh's propensities before making me for him? Or is it
just some horrible irony that they designed me for a man with
anger problems?

"I'm happy to dig deeper on any of this," says Ally.

"Thank you. I really do appreciate your help," I say as my eyes run up and down my notes. I stop at *Laura W* and slowly underline her name. I remember her wistful statue, like she was reaching for a sky she could never touch. "Can I ask, how did Laura Wekstein die? And how old was she?"

"Twenty-one. I couldn't find anything about her cause of death, though. Not even an obituary. Andy might've scrubbed that. If you give me more time…"

"What did she look like?" The bronze statue's features weren't that defined. I've been imagining a short girl with curly dark hair like Andy. But a different idea is blossoming.

"I only found one picture of her, and it's black-and-white," says Ally. "But her coloring seems lighter than Andy's. Maybe brown hair, or even dark blond?"

"What about red?" I feel like I'm teetering on a precipice. If Andy killing Josh to defend me was dark, this whiff of an idea is even darker. There's a sharp pain in my thigh. Ah—I've been digging my nails through the thin material of my leggings. The second I lift my nails, the pain in my ankle and chest goes poker hot, like pain is sitting on both sides of a seesaw. I grit my teeth. "Could she have been a redhead?"

"Maybe…"

"You have Facebook, right?" I say.

"Sure do."

"Look up Laura Pine. It's a memorial page."

"Okay, I think I found it," says Ally after a while.

"Is it her?"

There's a brief silence. "I can't be sure. The picture I saw was from a long time ago."

"I guess I'm wondering if Pine might be her married name," I say. "Can you look into that? See if there's a marriage record for Laura Wekstein?"

"Sure, but it might take some time."

"Okay." I stab the notepad with my pen. Even though I'm frustrated at this roadblock, I can't shake the feeling that I have everything I need right here. That it's just a matter of connecting the dots.

I don't want to wait for Ally to do a second round of research. Then again... I might not have to.

If Josh's stalker girlfriend was Andy Wekstein's sister, there's someone who'd know. Someone who obsessively followed every detail of Josh's life and cared deeply about who he dated—and knew he had a thing for redheads.

She's the last person I ever wanted to see again.

And this time, I don't have a gun.

THEN

Josh's mom dies the same November night I give birth to Anna-leigh.

When the nurse calls to tell us, Josh weeps in the recovery room. I try to show some emotion, but I'm exhausted by the sixteen hours of labor and can barely keep my eyes open.

The nurses here have been watching me with interest, peppering little questions here and there. "So they didn't program you to avoid labor pain?" says one nurse in surprise, adding in a conspiratorial whisper, "Assholes."

I laughed, but it did hurt a little to imagine Andy programming this into me. To be reminded that this wasn't exactly a "natural" birth. Synthetic skin and organs don't hurt on their own.

But I sweep this thought aside because of the miraculous bundle in my arms. A thatch of dark hair on her sweet head. The squintiest little alien eyes. She looks at me with wisdom and patience, and I'm convinced that she's saying, *Don't worry. We'll teach each other how to do this.* And I don't feel worried right now. Exhausted, yes, but also ebullient. It's intoxicating to think that *this* was the little person in my belly. All along, it was her.

I do try to eke out a tear for Rita as Josh sits in the chair by my bed with his head in his hands, sniffing under his hospital-issued N95 mask, but if I'm brutally honest, what I feel is relief. Now, when we go back home with our new baby, it will be a fresh start. Annaleigh won't have to breathe that toxicity into her innocent, new lungs. She deserves a house full of light and love. Still, I try to show Josh the compassion he needs.

"I'm sorry, baby," I say, reaching out to touch him.

Josh leaves me and the baby, to handle the logistics of his mother's body. By the time I come home from the hospital two days later, Rita is gone. I walk around slowly, feeling her absence. Peek into the room where she died, which I'm already planning on repurposing into a playroom.

The first days with my baby are brutal, wonderful, difficult, and also the best work I've ever done. My fifth day home, I'm finally walking semi-normally again, I've found a potential baby-sitter just down the street, we're getting the hang of nursing, and this is good, because *WHAT'S UP* magazine is scheduled to do an exclusive interview and photo shoot with us, and it's nice to feel like I have things a little more together before their arrival. I'm still not looking forward to strangers and cameras in the house, but with Josh fired and the funeral bills coming up, we need the money more than ever.

As Josh and I get ready in the bathroom before *WHAT'S UP* arrives, I smile at his reflection.

"I have a surprise for us," I say.

"Yeah?"

"I found a babysitter. I can't be away from Annaleigh for long, but I was thinking we could drive over to the Starbucks and grab some hot chocolates or something, just you and me."

He perks up. "That sounds great."

I've just finished putting on my mascara when *WHAT'S UP* arrives. There's the photographer, her assistant, and the journalist who's interviewing us. They all gush over Annaleigh for a few seconds, and then get to work setting up lighting and a white backdrop, moving Rita's tchotchkes, and repositioning the furniture.

We pose in the living room. I'm wearing a loose, white dress that floats gracefully over my postpartum body. Josh wears a simple white shirt, unbuttoned at the top, and jeans. We're all barefoot, and the photographer brought little crowns of flowers for me and the baby. "Ethereal," she gushes. We are the perfect family. The interview is painless. I tell my birth story. Josh talks about grieving his mother. And for a couple hours, until they leave, I can pretend that *this* is the real us. God, how far I've fallen, that this fantasy is now a refuge. What happened to my ideals? Facing reality...embracing reality...but how can you embrace a nightmare? Maybe, like Cam said, I've shifted to being aspirational. That's it. I'm not *pretending* to be the family who just got photographed. I'm aspiring.

We wait in the living room for the sitter, a girl named Eden. It's quarter to seven. She isn't due for another fifteen minutes, but Annaleigh is asleep upstairs in the bassinet, and Josh and I are both eager to get out. Josh is on the couch, hands behind his head, hips slung forward, tapping his foot. I'm in the small paisley-print armchair opposite him. It's dark outside, and the low lamplight is intimate. The house never feels peaceful, exactly, but at least right now it feels at rest, like whatever malevolent presence Rita has imprinted into the space is asleep, for now. Maybe this is a good time to talk about some practicalities, like Rita's funeral, which we should probably choose a date for. Maybe after the funeral the space won't feel so watchful, like her eyes are looking at me from the wallpaper, from the shadows in the room where she died, from her photograph above the fireplace.

"I'm starting to feel more normal," I say, tucking my legs under me. "If you'd like me to jump in and help with planning the funeral service—"

"Don't," says Josh, rolling his head back on the edge of the couch and looking at the ceiling instead of me. "Just don't."

"Don't what?" I say, feeling a little hurt.

"I'm too raw to talk logistics, okay?"

Part of me wants to snap, *I'm trying my best here, okay?* But it's better to be the bigger person. "I'm sorry. I understand."

"No, you fucking don't!" Josh shoots up from the couch so fast, he seems spring-loaded. Like his entire body was preparing to do this even when he was in a resting position. I press my back into the chair and grip the narrow armrests.

"You haven't even been alive for a year!" Josh shouts, and it feels too sudden, too disproportionate, too *wrong*. "Don't pretend, Julia. Your little empathy game isn't working tonight. It's gross, okay? It's fucking *gross* right now." His chest is heaving, his face red as he stands above me.

"Empathy game?" I whisper with a breathy laugh. What is happening? We had the photo shoot—the interviews—a light dinner—we're about to get a sitter for the first time—go to Starbucks—

"Yeah." There's an ugly expression on his face. "Yeah, that thing you do where you pretend to identify with me. Be real, for once. Why do you always have to pretend to be so fucking perfect?"

My immediate impulse is to say something soothing. But, whether it's exhaustion or the emotional whiplash of life and death we've been through over the past week, something snags inside me. *Unfair.*

This isn't a new feeling. Everything about my time in Eauverte has felt unfair, from the hate mail to Rita's cold rejection to the sheriff's utter disregard for the laws that are supposed to protect us. But if there's one thing I've learned from being a Synth in a human world, it's that I don't get to make the rules. My best defense? To smile and look pretty and try to be what everyone expects *normal* to be. To play by the rules the hardest, even the ones I hate, the unspoken ones, the arbitrary ones. The cruel ones.

And most days, I can make that leap for the world.

But right now, I can't make it for Josh.

He is the one person who's supposed to be one hundred percent on my side. He's supposed to be part of my *us*, not part of my *them*.

"That hurts," I say. "Do you think that just because I haven't had more than a year awake, I'm somehow less than you? Or... can't feel as much as you? I just got out of sixteen hours of labor and delivery. Trust me, I can feel pain, Josh."

"Fuck," he says with a wild-edged laugh. "Do you *hear* yourself? I'm sorry, Julia, but you have no idea what I'm going through. Sorry about your sixteen hours of discomfort, but I've been 'awake' for three fucking *decades*. I went through my parents' divorce, my mom's cancer, and then her fucking *death*. By the way, in case you forgot, she died disapproving of one of my biggest life choices. Do you get how much that fucks with a guy? The answer is no! You don't. You don't have parents, you haven't been through real pain, and you sure as hell don't understand death. Stop pretending you're a human. Stop pretending you understand me. You're a Synth! At least be honest about it! That's all I ask! Okay?"

"A Synth you *love*," I say, gripping the arms of the chair even harder. What is happening to him? What is happening to us? "A Synth you chose to *marry*."

"In a moment of fucking lunacy," he spits. "We will never truly understand each other, okay? It's just not possible. What the *fuck* was I thinking?"

My heart is pounding with pain.

He's lashing out because he's hurt, a desperate voice cries inside me. He's lashing out because his mom is dead and he got fired and we have neighbors spying on us and we wake up to a hateful billboard every damn morning. He's a cornered animal. Of course his claws are out.

It'll be fine.

I'll be fine.

"I'm sorry—" I begin.

"Stop!" he booms, gripping at his hair like he's trying to tear it out. "Stop saying you're sorry!"

"I just mean—"

He's on me in a second, grabbing my neck. The blunt force cutting into my windpipe is so surprising, I don't react at all. His weight crashes into the top of the chair, and, in slow motion, I feel the armchair fall backward, with me in it. I hit the floor. Pain rockets up my spine. My legs are in the air, like a dead bug's, and now Josh is at my side, on his knees, gasping.

"Julia! I didn't mean to—" His hands paw at me.

"Ow," I moan, closing my eyes. My tailbone hurts. My throat hurts. But more than that, it's my heart that hurts, with a pain I didn't even know was possible.

I'm suddenly aware that we're surrounded by windows, and who knows who might be looking in right now. This may be my reality, but I don't want it to be anyone else's show.

"Close the curtains," I gasp.

Josh moves to the window, yanks the curtains closed. He's back at my side.

"Julia, I had no idea how strong I was, I just—" His hands brush my shoulders, touch my hair, stroke my arm, like I'm a pile of scattered dust he's desperately trying to sweep back together.

I'm crying now, eyes still squeezed shut, tears oozing out. I can't even look at Josh. I don't want this to have happened. I want to go back to a life in which this hasn't happened.

"It was an accident." His voice is pleading. "Julia, it was an accident. I'm sorry. Please just look at me. Please be okay. I didn't mean to—it was an accident, I swear."

Opening my eyes is the hardest thing I've done in my life. Harder than giving birth.

Josh's face is pale, his eyes devastated.

I remember Cam's words. Power in *no*. Do I have a choice, though? If I leave Josh, I could lose not just the only purpose I've ever had, but my new baby, who's sleeping upstairs, helpless and trusting.

The next words I say will make or break us.

"I know," I lie, reaching forward, grasping Josh's forearm even as the tears course down my cheeks and I pray my spine hasn't somehow snapped. It feels like it has. "I know it was an accident, Josh."

I say this not because I'm afraid of him right now.

I'm not.

I say it because it has to be the truth. I need to pour this honey in the gaping cut he's opened, so it doesn't infect and kill me. Doesn't kill our family, the only thing I have in this world.

Fuck fantasy, reality, choice, and all my vague philosophical musings. I had no idea. No idea at all. There's a raw need inside me, opening like a hungry wound, strong and furious. Right now, I need this lie, and it will only hold us together if I choose to believe it.

Just like the moment during the proposal, there's a millisecond. Where I've been and where I could go, spooling between the ticks of Josh's watch. Two paths diverging, my feet poised at the crux. And then—

Yes, I say, with all the ragged desire in my heart. *I believe.*

NOW

The feeling of pulling up to Deborah Reeves's house is a sick déjà vu. Just like last time, she's on the porch before I've even killed the engine, in what looks like the same housedress, cradling the same shotgun, the baby doll heads bobbling like drunk birds above her. The only difference is that the day is clear this time, the sunshine bright, making Deborah and her house seem even more like a blight scratched into the perfect countryside.

Whether from reckless bravado or some instinct that it will be okay, I step right out of the car. Deborah raises her gun.

"Wait," I call out. Forcing myself to move slowly, I pull the wig off, then the cap, shaking out my red hair. A sign to her, I hope, that I'm giving her honesty and I want honesty back.

She doesn't speak. She doesn't shoot either.

"We need to talk, Deborah," I say.

The gun is still trained on me, but I know I can get her on my side.

"I came back because I love Josh, and you do, too, and we may be the only two people left in the world who feel that way. You can hate me for being a Synth. But Josh deserves justice, and I think I can find his killer, but I need your help."

At first, she doesn't react. Then, slowly, she lowers the gun.

Jerks her head, disappears into the house. The screen door bangs. I toss my wig back into the car and limp up behind her.

Inside, foggy darkness takes over as I pick my way down the junk-strewn pathway between boxes that she's made some effort to restack. It smells just as bad as before. Cat pee, mothballs, sewage, rot.

"What happened to your foot?" Deborah says as I finally make it to the kitchen, where she's stirring something in a small pot on the stove. Her gun rests on the counter. A foot-high Santa figurine smiles at me serenely from the top of the TV, where a Jeep ad plays on mute across the warped screen. A small jungle of nativity figures surrounds the TV, all facing the benevolent Santa.

"I twisted my ankle," I say.

"Sit down, then." She gestures to the chair.

I sigh as the weight comes off my foot.

"So you don't think I killed Josh anymore?" Deborah says from the stove. The smell from the pot wafts toward me. Acidic. Tomatoey.

"No. Do you still think I did?"

"I'm still deciding. That's some balls, coming back here. What's your game?"

"I have a baby. You know. Annaleigh," I begin carefully. My best shot at prying her open is our connection as mothers. "As soon as I was a person of interest in Josh's case, they sent Child Protective Services to take her away. I...hid her. With someone safe. But I have to get back to her. That's why I have to clear my name. Not just for myself, not just for Josh, but for her. My baby. That's what I care about most of all."

"You love that baby?" She clatters the spoon on the counter and faces me. "You're telling me you're capable of that?"

I picture Annaleigh in my mind's eye even as I look at Deborah. "From the moment she was born." *God.* I haven't let myself think about her very much, but now the floodgates are opening and I could drown in the power of missing her. "She had this face she'd do, when she was really tiny. We called it her 'mysteries of the universe' face. Her forehead would wrinkle and she'd pucker her little lips. Like she could fathom all these profound secrets, and if she just had the words to say them..." I feel a pressure on my chest and realize it's my own hand, pressing down, like I'm trying to keep my heart from leaping out of my body. "Part of me was so scared. She was so...small. It felt like she could just die, any second. I—"

"Mine died," Deborah says.

"Yes, I remember," I say softly, hoping I didn't just make a huge misstep. "I hope you know how sorry I am."

She turns and rummages in the cupboard.

"Roses are red, violets are blue," she chants as she pulls down two bowls. "She killed not one, but two times two."

...two times two? A quiver dances up my spine, but I don't speak. The moment is too fragile.

"Her name was Shiloh. It was SIDS. You know what that is?" Deborah ladles a thick red substance into the bowls, each move mechanical, deliberate.

I make an assenting sound.

"Then I had Eileen. She made it eight months." Releasing the ladle, Deborah grips the counter and looks at the steaming bowls. "Then Joey. Three months." She turns suddenly. "Hannah made it four months. They did an investigation. It was national news. My husband filed for divorce. They called me a monster. Sullivan's successor. I lost all my friends. Everyone." Her eyes, instead of being full of pain, remain glassy.

My heart is going crazy in my chest. Losing Annaleigh would kill me. How did Deborah survive that...four times? And then I realize...

She didn't.

This isn't a crazy woman. This is a ruined woman. Branded a monster during her deepest grief. Rejected and left alone when she needed mercy. Not judgment.

She turns back to the bowls. "I was acquitted, but just on paper. I thought about killing myself. Instead, I just watched TV. Coward's way out." Her eyes turn to the little TV, still on mute, where a female anchor is kicking off a news segment.

Instinctively, I rise from the chair and make two hobbling steps toward her. Reach forward and cover her hand with mine. The skin shifts over her bones, cold and soft.

"I may not be human," I say, "but I feel your pain."

She looks at me, and for the pulse of a heartbeat, we're just two people. Not a monster and a Bot; just two mothers whose hearts beat for their children. Whose happiness is held in those fragile bodies.

"Now what?" says Deborah in a guttural whisper.

I release her hand and lean my elbows on the counter so that our faces are nearly level.

"Tell me about Laura Pine."

She sighs, then says, "Wait here," and disappears into the next room. After vague thumps and shuffles, she returns with three fat photo albums, each spine marked JOSH LASALA under clear tape. She opens the top one on the counter, and a baby picture of Josh stares back, all chubby cheeks and dimples.

"Oh," I breathe. It's Annaleigh, all the way. I never realized how much she looks like him. "May I?"

She nods. I flip through more pictures. An article Josh wrote for the school paper in fourth grade entitled "Why Sports Are Great!" Photocopies of pages from his high school yearbooks. Even his senior report card. God knows how Deborah got that. Something in me says this *should* be creepy, that she's assembled all this information about my husband. Instead, I feel...grateful.

Then I turn the page, and there's the redhead. Laura Pine, her arm around Josh's waist and his arm around her shoulder. They look young, happy, carefree. But I know how deceiving a picture can be.

"Her maiden name was Wekstein," says Deborah, and in spite

of the circumstances, a rush moves through me. I was right. Josh dated Andy's sister.

"Laura got married right out of high school to a boy named Eric Pine," Deborah continues, "but it didn't work out. They were together for less than a year. Then she went to college. Purdue. She and Josh started dating their sophomore year. She never did officially get divorced."

"How do you know all this?"

"Social media. You'd be surprised how open kids can be." And then, Deborah turns the photo album page and I recoil. Laura, with a black eye, nearly swollen shut. The shot is moody, artistic. Her head is tilted, her expression veiled. The caption reads, When love turns to poison.

"I printed that from Myspace. Good thing, because she took the post down real quick." Deborah caresses her finger down the page. "I tried to call Josh. I wrote him, over and over. He never had a good father figure. My Josh needed help."

"Mercy," I say, repeating Deborah's word. The thing she never got but wanted to give. To Josh.

She nods. "Laura broke up with him. And then Josh did a bad thing. He posted a sex video they made together. It's on my computer. Do you want to see it?"

I shiver. "No."

"There was more. Pictures of her naked. Accusations. He made it sound like she was doing the whole football team. Professors, too."

I hear the words Deborah is saying, but as much as I pride myself on my empathy, they're not computing.

"I...don't understand. Why would he want to ruin her like that?"

"She humiliated him. Exposed him. It was more than he could take. Hurt is like dominoes, isn't it? He hurt her. She hurt him. He hurt her back." She delivers this matter-of-factly. "Just like my babies. When they died, it hurt so bad, not just for me. Their daddy. Their grandparents. We were all in pain. And people in pain want someone to knock down."

My heart pounds for Deborah, for Laura. For myself. Domino girls. There for others to knock down.

"And Laura?" Then I remember Andy's millions in donations... to suicide prevention. "She killed herself, didn't she?"

Deborah nods. "All her socials disappeared. Every trace of Laura on the internet was gone, until the memorial page her husband, Eric, made. But I had everything printed and saved." She pats the photo albums.

My husband was responsible for Laura Wekstein's death.

My head believes it. My heart doesn't want to.

The next conclusion is equally as unbelievable.

Laura's grieving older brother made me to be Josh's perfect match.

Perfect. It's a strange little word, because it means nothing without its context. Perfect for love? Or perfect for revenge?

I'm lightheaded. I brace my arms on the counter.

"Look." Deborah points a remote at the TV and turns up the volume. "You're on the news."

"Hi, Jack," says a live reporter in a windbreaker who's jogging after two people who are walking briskly ahead of him. There's a still frame of me in the upper right of the screen. "I'm here at Tenth Street on the campus of Indiana University, alma mater of WekTech CEO Andy Wekstein, the man responsible for designing Julia Walden." He catches up with the first person. "Mr. Wekstein!"

The figure on the right turns briefly. Yep, it's Andy.

"The Synth you designed is suspected of murdering her husband!" shouts the reporter as the camera wobbles. "Your response?"

Andy looks wild, unhinged. "She can't fucking hurt people, okay, you morons? This is a sh—*bleep* show. That fu—*bleep* sheriff is a bigot and a disgrace to law enforcement. And you know what? You're all a bunch of vultures! *Bleep* off!"

It's absolutely bizarre, seeing Andy so out of control. I've seen him emotional before, but never angry like this. It reminds me…

Of Josh.

Bile rises. I have the awful image of being the ball bouncing back and forth between two angry men. The man who made me and the man I was made for.

The image on the TV shifts and I catch sight of the second figure, to Andy's left, hands shoved into her jacket pockets, head down, trying to be unobtrusive. Eden.

"Why?" I say—to the TV, to Deborah, to myself. Each heartbeat hurts. "Why did Andy make me for Josh?"

But my brain fills in the story even as the last word leaves my mouth: Andy made me for revenge. He figured, once an abuser, always an abuser, and after Josh inevitably became violent with me, Andy was counting on me to go public with the abuse. Ruin Josh's life just like Josh ruined Laura's, in a perfect tit for tat. Laura took down her single MySpace post, and maybe only Deborah ever saw it. But a post from me would be seen by one hundred fifty million followers—and that's just for starters. I'm a celebrity; Andy made sure of it. People would care in a way they never would have for Laura.

But there was a design flaw Andy didn't anticipate, wasn't there? Love. I didn't behave like I was supposed to. I kept the abuse to myself. So Andy took matters into his own hands and killed Josh.

Deborah points the remote at the TV and mutes it.

"I think you know why," she says with cold certainty. "Don't you get it, Synth? It's not enough for us to be the victims of their pain." She grips my arm and squeezes with surprising ferocity. Her eyes lock with mine. Her voice is a snarl. "They need us to be their monsters, too."

THEN

I'm in too much pain to go to Starbucks like we planned, so after Josh helps me to bed and tucks me in and brings me tea, I reschedule with Eden for the next day and sleep, until Annaleigh wakes me just thirty minutes later to nurse.

The next morning, I'm embarrassed at the elaborate breakfast Josh set out, like he's abasing himself with the pancakes and fresh-cut fruit. I don't enjoy a single bite.

It's complicated to feel both intensely angry at him and intensely sorry for him. Watching him struggle through self-loathing? Watching him tiptoe around me? I hate it. All day long, even as I play the part of someone who has moved on, I hate it. Rita watches from the mantel, and I can feel her displeasure like slime on my skin. I just want things to go back to normal. I don't want Josh to feel like a piece of shit. And yet I do want him to be sorry. Sorry enough to never do anything like that again.

Maybe, somehow, going to Starbucks will reset us. Maybe living out that evening as it was supposed to be can paint over the old evening.

Eden comes a few minutes before six o'clock. Josh is still upstairs in the bathroom, so I get the door.

"Hi!" she says. "I hope it's okay I'm a couple minutes early. Where's the cutie?"

I already liked Eden before, but hearing her eagerness to see my adorable, perfect baby just makes me like her more.

"She just fell asleep," I say. "Come on in. And thanks for being so flexible yesterday. You know how it is with babies... so unpredictable!"

"Yep," she agrees cheerily, following me into the living room and dumping her messenger bag on the couch.

Eden may be in her twenties, but she doesn't look a day over eighteen. She's wearing jeans so baggy, it looks like she's playing dress-up in her dad's clothing.

"Let me show you Annaleigh's room," I invite, but Eden has gone really still all of a sudden. "Is everything okay?"

"Yeah." Her finger wanders up to her neck, where she draws a line. "Um...are *you* okay?"

"Oh!" A furious blush floods my cheeks. I thought my scarf was covering the angry mark. It must have slipped. "Yes. Sorry! Ugh, so embarrassing. Just a rash. I have really sensitive skin."

She looks at me with serious eyes and I laugh nervously because it feels like she's seeing right past the lie. I thought I could keep the ugliness contained. I thought I could keep it safe and private, held only in my memory, where it could fade, or heal, or whatever you do with awful things that have happened. Now, the container has cracked.

Then Eden smiles. "Yeah, I have sensitive skin, too."

"Oh good," I gush as a feverish giddiness overtakes me. "Then you get it."

Starbucks is great. Josh and I talk for the first time about potentially selling his mom's house. What shape our finances need to be in before we make that move.

"It could be nice to get some land in the country," I say, already dreaming of feeding chickens in the morning, Annaleigh toddling beside me in Wellingtons.

"You want to be a country wife, huh?" teases Josh. "Barefoot, pregnant, and in the kitchen?"

Far from the attention of the haters? Out of the house where Rita's presence still hangs heavy? Surrounded by trees and cornfields instead of spying neighbors?

"I'd love that," I say.

We don't mention the instances of vandalism that have struck our house in the past week. How our grocery delivery was ransacked while it sat on the porch. We don't mention how weird it is living next to someone whose favorite pastime is watching us through binoculars, or the fact that my tailbone is still sore from when Josh pushed my chair over last night by accident. We stand firmly in the positive as we eat our lemon pound cake and hold hands across the table.

I can almost smell the fresh wind that's about to blow through our lives. Last night was a blip, a wrinkle, already in the rearview mirror, and there's far too much ahead of us to keep looking behind at the things we've already zoomed past.

Life happens in one direction, and tonight, it feels good to look where I'm supposed to be looking: forward.

NOW

"May I see some identification, ma'am?"

The checkpoint before the highway on-ramp is blocked by three Dover County Sheriff cars, and it's just my luck that the man on the other side of my window is Deputy Adams. Even though he's been marginally more on my side than Mitchell, he has also seen me up close, and is therefore likely to recognize me. I can hear the hum of the highway just up the little hill, my promise of escape. If I can get past Adams.

I wish my head was feeling clearer. The plugged duct has gotten worse, shooting red streaks like infected roads toward my arm and neck. I'm feeling hot all over, and I'd place bets on my temperature reading above a hundred right now.

"Is everything okay, Officer?" I say in a breathless, higher-pitched voice than my own as I fumble in my purse for my fake ID, trying to hide the trembling of my hands. I pass him the little plastic card as a chilly blast of clear, spring air ruffles the bangs of my wig and momentarily cools my cheeks. "What's going on?"

"You didn't hear?" he says, holding up my Missouri driver's license. I poke my glasses up the bridge of my nose, then fidget with my hair, stroking the long brown wig forward, but maybe that looks suspicious, so I tuck my hands between my legs to hold them still as he squints at the card, then at me. "There's a Synth wanted for questioning in a murder."

It's not hard to feign alarm. "What?"

"That's right, miss." He's still holding my ID.

"Wait—are you talking about that girl from *The Proposal*?" My chest is nearly bursting. Any second he's going to realize that my hair looks fake and my glasses aren't prescription.

"That's the one. If you see her, please call 9-1-1."

"But she seemed so sweet!" I make a distressed little intake of breath. "I thought they couldn't hurt people! Do you really think she did it?"

"I really can't say, ma'am. All I know is what they tell me." Then he grins. Shifts his weight. "By the way...do we know each other?"

Oh God. My hands fly to my hair. Is the wig slipping? I laugh nervously. "I don't think so?"

"I could've sworn. You look just like my high school girl-friend." He pauses. "Are you okay? Your hair..."

"Fine!" I lower my hands immediately to the steering wheel. "Sorry, just itchy."

"I've always liked long hair on a girl."

"Thank you?"

"Are you in Indiana often?" He leans his arm on my car.

"I have a cousin in Tenderloin. So...pretty often?" I force two slow blinks. "Why?"

"Well...if you're ever bored on a Saturday night, you and your cousin give me a call." He passes me a dog-eared business card with the sheriff's big star in the background and his mobile number across the bottom. "My aunt and uncle own the best res-taurant in the area. Mamacita's Italian. I can get us a free meal."

"Aww. That's so nice of you." I put his card on the passenger seat. Give him a fake smile. "Maybe I'll do that."

"You be safe, now, Miss Paddington." He grins so big his teeth literally glint in the sunlight. "Lily."

And then he's waving me forward, and winking, and I'm waving back, resisting the urge to punch the accelerator with all the strength of my adrenaline.

On the interstate, I force myself to go the speed limit, even though I want to go so much faster, just to shake what felt like a very close call.

There is a tiny feeling of triumph, that I fooled one of Mitchell's men. Some perverse satisfaction that he was literally inches from me and let me go. I owe Christi big-time. But the triumph doesn't last. Physically, I'm feeling on the brink, like I have to blink fast to keep hot cobwebs out of my eyes. I grab the last energy bar from my purse and rip into it with my teeth, just as a sign overhead for Bloomington tells me I'm fifty-five miles away.

Okay. I can't make my ankle better or my fever go down, but I'll be in Bloomington in under an hour, and I have to choose who I want to confront first: Andy or Eden. My best chance at getting the truth is to isolate one of them and turn that person against the other.

I'm pretty sure I've already figured out the truth: that Andy followed Josh to Belmont Ridge Saturday night to confront him. Maybe they argued first. Maybe Josh provoked Andy, or even took the first swing. Maybe killing my husband wasn't premeditated on Andy's part, or maybe it was. Either way, Andy killed my husband. But how to get proof? It has to be something so undeniable, not even Mitchell can ignore it.

Forty miles to Bloomington. I'm flying. *Who do I target first? Andy or Eden?* I wish my thoughts didn't feel like sluggish fish in a warm pond.

Even though I was made to avenge Andy's sister's death, I can't help but think Andy may still be in love with me. That means I'd have some amount of power when I confront him. But Andy is also angry, and I've learned something about angry men: they can turn on you even when they love you.

Eden might be a better choice. She loves my daughter, I know that. I also can't imagine Eden physically attacking me.

In the end, it's a toss-up. But with only thirty miles now to Bloomington, I can't put off the decision any longer.

I grab my cell phone, my eyes flickering between the road and the screen as I compose a text.

Eden, it's Julia. Please don't tell Andy I'm contacting you. I'm 20 min from Bloomington. Where can we meet alone??

I hit Send.

In typical Eden fashion, three dots appear immediately.

Meet me at Andy's condo. 540 E Colonial Dr Unit 5350.

I need you alone, I text.

He's not here.

Too risky, I reply.

The three dots appear, then disappear, then appear again.

Trust me.

THEN

"There's nothing between us, Josh! God, that is so twisted! Are you hearing yourself?"

I'm furious. We just got home after our first fancy dinner date since Annaleigh was born, and instead of having a nice time, Josh had to start picking at Andy.

"Has he texted you today?" Josh said as soon as the breadsticks arrived.

"Yes, this morning," I said. "Hey, what do you think about sharing some mozzarella sticks? Mamacita's is supposed to be famous for them."

He let it go for a while. Then we got into the car, and it was pick pick pick the whole way home. While I drove, Josh helped himself to my phone, scrolling through my messages with Andy and making sarcastic comments.

"Is he always this whiny?

"God, this guy is pathetic.

"Doesn't he have any other friends?"

I didn't respond, but by the time we got home, my jaw felt hard enough to crack.

I'm convinced it's not about Andy. That Josh needs to pick at something, find an outlet for the simmering rage that's been stoked by the recent flood of hate mail, the awful graffiti that took us two days to paint over, his unfruitful days at Starbucks applying for jobs, the recent fifty-grand hospice bill.

"He's in love with you," says Josh bluntly, hanging up his jacket in the front entry coat closet. "I saw it when I first met him on the show."

We literally walked in the door two minutes ago, paid Eden, and said good-night. Now I'm walking toward the kitchen, because I just remembered I need to run the dishwasher before we crash.

"Josh, that is a crazy thing to say. Andy...he's a scientist! He doesn't think of me that way. And that five-minute conversation when you two met? It was over a year ago! Can we please stop talking about Andy?"

I want to talk about the land we might put an offer on. The chickens I want to raise. My daydream of Annaleigh collecting the eggs every morning.

"I've seen how he looks at you. It's fucking possessive."

"Okay, can we dial it back, baby? I've only seen Andy twice since Annaleigh was born."

Once, right before Christmas, Andy drove down to Eauverte to bring me an extravagant wicker gift basket full of cute outfits, baby bath products, and plush toys. The second time, I left Annaleigh with Eden and drove up to Bloomington. It felt amazing to leave town, if just for the morning. Andy took me out to a nice lunch and I ended up talking the entire time. I felt a little embarrassed that I didn't ask more about him, but he was so interested and so caring that I couldn't help myself.

Josh has followed me to the kitchen, where I'm leaning over the dishwasher, fitting the soap pellet into the plastic tray.

"You know what I hate?" he growls. "That he shaped you. Do you ever think about that? Every part of you I've touched, he touched first, in his lab, or wherever they put you together."

Josh shudders. "I hate thinking about that. His fucking *paws* all over you."

"Is that it?" I breathe angrily as I straighten up. "Some alpha male thing where you have to be the first and only? Because I'm pretty sure you've had *sex* with other women, Josh. I'm not the first person to touch you either!" I draw in another sharp breath. "Or do you hate Andy because he reminds you that I'm not human? Is that it? You can only love me if you forget I'm a Synth?"

"You don't get it," he says, emphasizing each word with a crash of his palm against the countertop.

Oh, I *hate* it when he says that. Like I'm incapable of understanding. Like I'm not a complete enough person for him. Like he's on fucking *Rita's* side.

"What don't I get, Josh? What is it?" Tears fill my eyes, hot, angry. "Andy and I have an innocent friendship. Why are you so eager to piss all over it? What about you and Cam, huh? Is that an innocent friendship?"

Instantly I regret playing tit for tat. Because I honestly do believe what he and Cam have is innocent. Even though they did sleep together in the Fantasy Suite. Even though Josh lied about that. I got the truth from Cam, and I understood Josh needed to save his own dignity. *He* needed to believe he was the guy who didn't sleep with two women, back-to-back. The question is, why was *I* so eager to allow him to lie? What happened to my demand for honesty? When did we start pretending so much with each other? Or…is that all we've ever done?

"Okay, this is some expert gaslighting, Julia," says Josh in that superior, snappish tone I despise. "Are you sleeping with Andy or not?"

"No, I am not sleeping with Andy! He— I— It's not like that!"

Josh grabs my phone off the counter.

"What are you doing?"

"Litmus test. I'm deleting Andy's fucking number. If there's nothing between you, you won't care."

"Give that back!" I grab for the phone, but Josh steps out of reach.

I lunge. There's a ridiculous struggle as I grab Josh's wrist and tug and he tugs back, and I'm saying *give it back* as he says *get off me* and then something is exploding in my face and I'm reeling back, holding my nose, which is gushing blood.

Time slows to a halt, like my shock has created a bubble, where I float in some wordless agony so profound it nearly feels like peace. Josh is cramming paper towels into my hands, but I'm far away, deep in the universe of my own head.

How did we get here?

What signs did I miss? Was it my fault I missed them?

I feel myself sinking, but I can't let myself drown. I have to fix this. I have a baby to think of.

Look at the ceiling. Pinch the bridge of your nose, Josh is instructing, but it sounds like his voice is coming from very, very far away.

Two times is not ten times, I think. It sounds so...logical. When I put it like that.

Two times can still be a mistake, never to be made again.

That sounds real. Like something I can believe.

As Josh cries and I cry and we play out the horrible aftermath of tonight, I cling to this.

NOW

I've never been to Andy's condo before, but when the voice on my GPS says, "Turn right, into Kensington Golf Club Estates," I find myself floating through the split stone wall with the wrought iron sign. The letters are so curlicued they don't even look like letters, but little animals. Round. Not poky, not chickens. But wouldn't Annaleigh have been cute, feeding the chickens?

There's a crunch. A bush. I just drove over a bush.

"*Shit!*" I say out loud, and then I shout, "Focus!" because it feels like I'm not the one driving the car, but whoever is driving really needs to do a better job.

The fever is so hot in my skin. Consciousness is a slippery fish, shimmering away as I try to trap it between my hands. I think I am very sick. It would be smart to pull over. I move to hit the brake, but my foot can't seem to find it.

"Ooooh," I groan. Shit. I'm blinking awake just in time to yank the wheel and avoid driving into some kind of…pond. The shapes up ahead are condo buildings, but they're all the same… What number am I looking for?

"Turn left. You have arrived at your destination."

I turn; the images shift. I'm at the mouth of the underground parking. The car slides down the ramp. Miraculously, I manage not to crash into a long row of cars. They slip past like a slick river…

There. The old beater Andy drives in Indiana. I hit the brake. Andy. Oh God, what a relief, I can't wait to see him. He'll know what to do…he always knows…

No! I'm here to see Eden.

With a shaking hand, I get out my phone to text her. My fingers feel huge.

I'm here. So is Andy's car.

He biked to campus, she replies. **Ur safe.**

I hesitate for only a second; I have to trust her.

My panting makes a huffing echo in the cavernous garage as I limp to the elevator, trying to breathe clarity into my swampy thoughts. There's no doubt that the plugged duct in my breast has progressed to full-on mastitis. I'm probably in desperate need of antibiotics. *Hang on,* I tell myself. *You've come this far. Just a little farther.*

I look at myself in the elevator mirror all the way up to Andy's fifth-floor penthouse. Gaunt, wasted. Nothing like the sparkly, vibrant Julia who woke up last year ready to embrace whatever life brought.

When the elevator doors slide open, there's a small landing with a table and vase, and Andy's door. I buzz. Soon, there's the sound of locks retreating. Eden's face appears in the crack.

"You owe me the truth," I say through semi-clenched teeth, trying to appear strong and in control. My tongue feels fuzzy. I'm so thirsty. I need water.

"I know," says Eden. She's in a T-shirt and jeans, cuffed at her ankles. Her hair is tousled, and she looks haggard. Scared. Nearly as bad as me. I feel a vindictive stab of something like joy except not joy at all. "Come in."

The door closes behind us and Eden locks it while I take in the space, open and tall-ceilinged, half living room, half kitchen, split by a waterfall marble island. Outside it's daylight, but the heavy mustard-colored velvet curtains are drawn, leaving us in a different, darker reality. Eden's laptop on the coffee table is the brightest thing in the room. A sculpture of a man's torso made from scrap metal glints from a corner.

"Are you okay?" Eden's voice is small. She follows my pathetic progression forward, supporting myself on furniture to keep myself upright—the back of the brown leather couch, a small table with a plant. *Do I fucking look okay?* I want to snap.

"Why are you asking?" I finally earn my way to the kitchen. "We are beyond pretending that you've ever cared about me. I know what I am to you. Parts."

"Julia," Eden says. "That's not true! I—I messed up, but I've been trying to make it right. I'm only here right now because you disappeared from Eauverte and Andy said you'd be most likely to come to him for help. If you'll just—"

"Shut up." It doesn't matter how sorry or sincere she seems. I am her design, hers and Andy's, and this pain I'm going through is their perverted brainchild.

For a second, the room seems to balloon in front of me, haze dropping like lead smog.

Blinking hard, I'm able to make the room return to its real shape. I'm at the sink. I pull a glass from the drying rack, fill it. The water is so cold, it slices going down. Wiping my mouth with a sleeve, I face Eden.

"I know all about your revenge plan," I say. "How you tried to use me. I'm sorry about Laura. But this is *my* life you ruined. Mine."

"I'm not going to deny what I did," says Eden, her forehead contorting. "But I did *not* help Andy kill Josh, Julia. I was trying to prevent that from happening. I swear."

The room starts to balloon again but I pinch my forearm and it retracts.

"Are you saying Andy *did* kill Josh?" I lean forward on the island. Is this the confession I've been waiting for? I should get my phone...record it... Blue splotches travel across my vision like fairy lights. The knot of pain in my left breast is excruciating. I pull off my wig and cap to relieve some of the heat in my head. *Stay with it. Do not pass out.*

"He hasn't admitted it to me, but yes," says Eden. "Andy hated Josh. He wasn't going to be at peace until Josh was dead. *That is the truth, Julia.*"

"You don't think you're just as responsible?"

"Let me explain. Please." Eden folds her hands in front of her chest and starts talking, fast. "I started at WekTech as an intern. But that prank Andy told you about? I didn't get fired. I got promoted. It was such a rush. I hadn't even completed my BA, and suddenly I was working side by side with one of the biggest geniuses in tech, with enough capital to do whatever we could dream up. It was incredible. The happiest time in my life. And in retrospect, the worst." She bites her lip. "Andy and me—we lived and breathed work. I guess we got close, after all that time together. I told him my dad was abusive to my mom, and that my grandparents had to raise me. Andy told me about Laura. It brought us even closer. Then this one morning Andy comes to work super upset. He's like, 'The fucker who drove Laura to suicide is the next bachelor on *The Proposal*.' I told him he should call the producers and get him kicked off. Then we got wasted. And I said—" Tears brim in her eyes.

I wait. The speed at which she's shooting out information is making my head spin, but everything is also falling into place. A horrible place. A picture I never wanted to see.

Eden releases a gasping hiccup. "I said, maybe Julia is your chance at revenge. I—I was just fucking around. I didn't mean it. But Andy was like, 'Well that's interesting. How would we do that?'" She inhales shakily. "I convinced myself that bringing down an abuser was such a cool thing to do. I'm a feminist. I'm on the *side* of battered women. We were doing it for Laura. For me, too. I know how this sounds now, but it was easy to think of you as a tool then. We were the creators, the geniuses, the good guys on the side of justice. And then…" Eden's eyes on me are tragic. "You woke up. And I got to know you. And I've been sorry ever since."

A spasm moves through me. It might be laughter. There isn't a word for this level of agony, is there? The awful truth that the people who were supposed to make you for love made you for pain. To suffer it—and inflict it.

"I have so many regrets, Julia—" says Eden with an emotional tremble.

"Not now!" My anger is a rock tumbling down a hill, gaining speed. "Don't tell me you were sorry from the start! Were you sorry when you moved to Eauverte to spy on my private life? *You* were the only one who knew that Josh hit me. *You* told Andy. He was never supposed to know. I was going to figure it out. Josh and I—we were going to—" I try to say *be happy*, but sorrow and rage fist in my throat.

Josh and I will never get a chance at happy. Even if I manage to save myself, Josh is never coming back.

"He could have changed," I finish brokenly.

"But he didn't, Julia," says Eden in a pleading voice. "Andy gave Josh that chance. If Josh hadn't hurt you, he'd still be alive."

"If you hadn't fucking told Andy, he'd still be alive!" I slam my palms on the counter. The sting feels good. I'm so furious right now. So fucking *furious*. "The other night in the woods. You said you were talking to Mitchell, but you were *still* spying on me. How dare you say you were sorry when the truth is, you were hurting me until the very fucking end!" Like my anger is a tether to lucidity, my mind starts spewing out scraps of memories. Eden's joint, glowing in the dark trees. Eden's voice, clear as a bell.

She's not home yet. I have a view into her house.

Three strikes you're out means there was a third time.

There were only two.

"I was talking to Andy—you're right—" Eden is saying "—but I was trying to cover for you—"

There were only two.

Suddenly I know beyond a doubt that she was talking about Josh hitting me. But why was she counting? A horrible idea enters my mind, blossoming in my fever like a toxic hothouse flower. What if their revenge plan went way, way beyond me publicly shaming Josh?

"You said in the woods there were only two times," I interrupt. For the first time in my life, I can almost feel my coding, visceral like blood. A prickly stream running through my body, written by Andy and Eden. Coding written with Josh in mind. Made for him. Made to hurt him. *A victim…and a monster.* I look at Eden, trying to keep her face in focus. Trying to hang on to myself. Would Andy really be satisfied at mere public humiliation? "What was supposed to happen the third time, Eden?"

Eden's face is bloodless.

I grab her arm. For some reason, from the pyre of my fever, Annaleigh springs to my mind. My baby, helpless as this awful plan unfolded around her, with Andy and Eden like wretched gods folding the origami of her life into this monstrous shape. Eden's arm feels like putty in my grip. For a second I think I could crush her, down to the bone.

"Ow," she yelps, a helpless, animal sound, and I know a strange surprise.

I just hurt a human for the first time in my life.

"What was supposed to happen the third time? What?" I shake her, as if I can rattle the rest of the truth loose.

Tears spill freely down Eden's face. She looks afraid. Afraid of me. And it feels good.

"The third time—" Her shoulders heave. "Oh God, Julia— the third time—"

I shake her harder, because my burst of consciousness is slipping and I need this to end before I collapse. "Say it!"

"It wasn't just about exposing him," she gasps, and this time, I know I'm finally getting the truth. "You were supposed to kill him."

THEN

I check the peephole, because I've learned you don't just open the door. Not when you're me.

"Eden," I say, opening the door to my babysitter, who's dressed in an adorable I ♥ NYC T-shirt and black joggers. "Did I book you for Annaleigh and forget?"

It's just after seven, and Annaleigh is finally asleep after a fussy start.

After the awfulness of last night, I told Josh it might be good for him to get out of town for the weekend. Get a change of scenery, connect with some of his old Indianapolis friends. He agreed—thank God.

Eden smiles awkwardly. "No. I just wanted to stop by. Is that okay? Do you have a minute?"

"Sure." I open the door wider. She seems nervous. Is there a problem? Or is she trying to be a friend? I resist the urge to check my makeup. I was meticulous this morning covering my black eye, and I've touched it up a few times since. Anyway, the lighting is low. It should be fine.

Eden stands in my living room, hands in her pockets, and looks around the space, like she's not sure what to do.

"Can I offer you something to drink?" I beckon her to follow me to the kitchen. "You caught me alone! Josh is up in Indy for the weekend."

"Yeah, I saw him leave earlier."

"He's seeing some friends. You know, blowing off some steam. It's been such a hard few months!" I flip the lights on in the kitchen and make for the fridge.

I texted Camila this morning and asked her to reach out to Josh. He needs more support than just me. Josh doesn't know it yet, but she's flying in from Austin on a red-eye to surprise him tomorrow morning.

What's really going on with you guys? she said. It's not every day a wife calls up her husband's ex and asks her to show him a good time.

I had to laugh at that. Yes, there were times that I felt jealous of Camila. Those times are long gone, though. Now, I need the support of strong people who can see us through this tough time.

His mom's death has hit him super hard, I said. He needs a reset.

If Cam didn't entirely buy my simplified explanation, she didn't let on.

I'll take Josh on a bender the size of Texas, she promised. He'll come back a new man.

"Are you okay staying here alone?" Eden leans on the counter as I make for the fridge. "I know you guys have had some trouble with, like…property damage? I can crash on your couch if you—"

"I'm fine! We actually just got a dog! He's a big teddy bear, but he has a scary bark, so… What do you want? Sparkling water? Juice? I also have alcoholic options."

"I'd take something strong," says Eden.

There's a low *woof* behind me and I turn to see Captain, awoken from his slumber. The rescue group told us he's probably about two years old, already full grown. Huge, actually.

"Aw, hey, big guy," says Eden, sinking to her knees as Captain investigates her. She buries her hands in the floof around his neck, and I give them smiling glances before returning to my beverage endeavors. The vermouth is running low, but there should be enough for a couple drinks.

"How about martinis?" I jiggle a little jar of olives.

"Sounds great," says Eden, a little too enthusiastically. Either she's forcing it, or she really likes martinis. "So…what are you up to while Josh is gone?" She scratches Captain's head as I scoop ice into the cocktail shaker—Camila's wedding gift to us. Captain whines, giving Eden a look of sheer adoration.

"Oh… I need to catch up on cleaning. And I might try a new recipe." Slightly true, but not entirely. I measure in the vodka and vermouth. I've actually decided to watch our season of *The Proposal* for the very first time. Josh and I promised each other we wouldn't, but I need it. I need to remember what he was like back then. What I was like. What we were like together. What it is I'm fighting for.

"What about you?" I say. "Weekend plans?"

"Nothing much."

The shaker makes a racket for the next few seconds. Then I pour the drinks into two rustic mugs; Rita didn't drink and we have yet to buy proper martini glasses. Our wedding gifts are nearly the only things in this house that are truly Josh's and mine. It's a patchwork life. A shaker, but no glasses. A set of towels, with a mismatched bath mat. A human and a Synth. America's most eligible bachelor, who also hits his wife.

Only twice, I remind myself, already in a slight panic at this intrusive thought. *It was only twice and it never has to happen again.*

"So…" I slide the mug toward Eden, trying to give her an opening since it's becoming more and more obvious there's something on her mind.

"Yeah… I'm not very good at this, so I'll just say it."

Okay, now she's making me nervous.

"Are you safe?" she blurts out. "You have—" She touches

her eye, and I reflexively touch mine, before lowering my hand quickly.

"I'm sorry, I don't mean to embarrass you," Eden says as shame burns through me, "but—Julia…if there's anything you want to tell me—" She stops, her eyes on me pleading.

I set my martini mug gently on the counter, trying to keep my facial expression neutral. The two awful incidents have been… well, awful. But having someone notice? It's exponentially worse. Using all my willpower, I force my lips into a smile. It feels like throwing a thin sheet of ice over an ocean of turmoil.

"I'm fine, Eden. Thanks for your concern, but truly, I—"

"I know Josh is hurting you." She reaches forward and touches my arm with delicate fingers. I force myself to keep still, even though her touch burns me as much as her words. I can almost feel the ice cracking.

Her voice goes intense. "You don't have to stay. I know it's complicated, because of you being a Synth, but I'll help—"

"Stop," I take a desperate step back and turn away from Eden, because tears are pooling and I don't want my babysitter of all people to see.

Get yourself under control, Julia.

"You know, I think I need a second drink," I say in a voice that's too cold, too collected. Eden is silent as I pull out the vodka and vermouth again, thunking them on the counter harder than the first time, like part of me hopes they'll explode into shards. "How about you?"

"No." Her voice is small. Chastised. "I'm good."

She's quiet as I kick the fridge door closed.

"I'm sorry if I made things weird." Eden looks miserable.

But not as miserable as I am.

"It's fine," I say brightly. "Thanks for stopping by."

She takes the hint.

As soon as I've locked the door behind her, I fling open my laptop and pull up the tab where I already have Episode 1 ready.

I sit on the living room floor with my second martini and the remainder of the bottle of vodka and hit Play.

It's not until I see myself stepping out of the limo that I start to cry.

Hi.

Are you blushing?

I look so…young. So bright-eyed. So naive. Why does it hurt so much to see?

How can I make it stop hurting?

Sorry. Can we start again? Hi! I'm Julia.

Hi, Julia, I'm Josh. I see you've made yourself comfortable. I like that.

I find myself mouthing the words along with my old self.

I like you.

Part of me wants to reach forward and pluck her off the screen, out of the set, out from in front of Josh, and tell her no. Stop. Wait.

But what I want even more is to step into the screen. Back into the magic of that moment, and the moments that followed. And then, live it over. And over. And over. And fix it. Fucking fix whatever broke, before it breaks again.

I drag the video player backward.

Hi, Julia, I'm Josh. I see you've made yourself comfortable. I like that. I like you.

I punch Pause. Back again.

As the vodka disappears and the hours tick forward, I'm transported to a softer place. The place that was supposed to be our foundation, and instead turned out to be nothing but a dream.

But what a lovely dream it was.

NOW

Eden's arms fly around me as my legs buckle. She's too small to hold my weight, and my knees crack against the tile as she sags to the floor with me.

"Julia!" she cries.

With a groan, I clutch my chest, then pitch forward. The fever is cresting. I can't speak. I can't breathe. I think I'm dying. And for the first time in my life, death sounds like good news.

Annaleigh, something inside me screams. *You can't leave her! You have to survive!*

But I'm no longer in control of what happens.

I pass out. When I come to, I'm in a fetal position on the floor. Eden is shoving my shoulder, and I roll onto my back. The ceiling is stunningly bright.

Her voice is scared, intense. "I'm going to give you CPR, Julia."

I think about that billboard.

What will happen to me when my body stops working?

Do I have a soul? Will it rise?

Or will WekTech just turn me back on again? Override the system failure and force me back into this burning skin, this ruined body with its goddamn weakness tattooed deep like an evil spell?

Eden is leaning her small hands on my chest, pumping, but I barely feel the pressure. Tears slip down my cheeks as she tries to drive the life back into me. But I don't want to be kept alive just to keep feeling this pain. How can I make Eden understand I don't want this anymore?

On her heels by my side, she looks like a child. Affectionate and endearing and hapless—my sweet babysitter whose biggest fault was that she liked weed a little too much.

But not everything is as it seems.

An anguished spark lights inside me.

A final, desperate thought.

"Dampers," I gasp.

"What?" says Eden, stopping her efforts.

"D—" I'm shaking so hard. My teeth feel like an avalanche of rocks in my head. "D-dampers."

"I can't. You don't understand what would happen—"

I hiss through my teeth. I want to tell her that she owes me. That this is her chance to redeem herself by undoing the nightmares she wrote into me. But all I can manage is, "Help."

"You don't understand, Julia. It's not like you're online and I can just get in there. It would be…invasive. Painful. Not to mention there are walls and walls of security."

"Alca—" I whisper. It feels like my eyes are burning holes in my own sockets, that's how hard I'm looking at Eden. "Alcatraz."

The meaning washes over her face and I know she knows what I'm talking about. Alcatraz, sci-fi version. If anyone can hack into me, it's her.

"That was years ago…that was just his cell phone…"

Hot tears are rolling down my cheeks, blurring the world even further—this beautiful, horrible world I didn't choose to wake up in.

My final plea is another single word. All I can manage. My very heart, spoken. "Annaleigh."

There's a moment of silence. I can see the scales between us, reflected in Eden's tortured expression—and the moment they tip in my favor.

"Okay," she says. "Okay, we'll try."

I blink my eyes once. I think she knows I mean *Thank you.*

Then Eden's demeanor changes. All of a sudden, she's not a kid anymore.

"There's a connection point to your programming at the base of your skull. That's the best place to go in. It wasn't ever supposed to be accessed—it was just a precaution. And I don't have anesthetic, Julia, it's going to be really—" She hesitates. "Painful."

"Andy," I croak.

"He'll be on campus until late, but we still need to hurry. This isn't a button I can push, okay? We're talking about layers and layers of extremely complex coding. This is hours of work, and I'm not even promising—" She stops herself. "I'll get towels."

She turns on all the lights in the kitchen and lays towels down, with a pillow to drape my head over. My fever is still raging, and the world swims as Eden pulls my hair off my neck. She has her laptop on the floor next to the towels, scissors, and a computer cord with one side snipped off. Next, she strips the plastic around the cord's cables with a paring knife. There's a meat thermometer next to her, too, and I can't seem to avert my eyes from how fucking big that metal stick is. I watch as she threads the stripped cable to the stick so that when the stick pokes through, the wires will be coiled at the tip. Shoved into me—and connected to the invisible parts that both make me who I am and have prevented me from being who I could be.

"Ready," Eden says, plugging the USB end of the cord into her computer.

She takes a minute to steady herself. Then she rolls me over onto my stomach. Her fingers explore the back of my neck, and I feel the cool tip of a marker making a tiny X.

"I'm going to need you to hold really fucking still, Julia."

I'm about to ask if she's sanitized the meat thermometer, but I realize it doesn't matter. Once my dampers are off, infection won't be a risk anymore.

"Here, open," she says, putting a long wooden spoon between my teeth. "Bite if you have to." She takes a deep breath, and stabs the back of my neck. A shriek peels out of me like ripping skin, dissolving into a long whimper. Blood pours down the sides of my neck.

"*God,*" I swear, the word distorted by the spoon. I blubber saliva and tears together as my shoulders convulse. I never want to feel anything like that again.

"Fuck," says Eden, agitated. "*Fuck.* Okay, I'm trying again. I'm sorry, Julia. I'm sorry. Hold still!"

Another stabbing pain pulls a scream from my throat as I bite into the soft wood. My hands clench the edge of the towel even as I feel a sickening *click*. It doesn't stop hurting, though. A hundred times worse than the fever. A thousand. The pain is a mallet, slamming my skull to pieces. My moan turns into a growl. I can't bear it. I can't.

Eden talks fast, and there's rapid typing. "I'm looking for your pain damper. I'm going to reduce it as soon as possible, okay, Julia? First I have to get past all the fucking security. I'm going as fast as I can."

The next minutes may as well be hours. My teeth grind against the spoon. It's torture holding still and letting it continue when I want to reach back and rip the meat thermometer out of my skull and then stab Eden with it. *Type faster,* I want to scream. *Make this stop.*

And then, suddenly, a cool feeling washes over me. Like a wave rushing over a beach cluttered with seaweed and broken shells, then retreating, leaving clean sand behind.

"Did you feel that?" Eden says, breathless, and I know that despite her strong reservations, she's excited, too. Excited about

what I can be without the garbage that was littered all throughout what could have been perfection.

"Yes," I say, and exhale. The pain is gone. Completely. And
not just the excruciating fire in the back of my head, but the
fever. Gone are the spots in my vision, the swollen throbbing
in my ankle, the pain in my breast. Even the memory of it all is
gentling. I shift on the towels. "What did you do?"

"I shut off your pain receptors. I'm not going to leave them
off for long, okay? That would actually be more dangerous for
you, long-term. Some pain is a necessary warning system. But
I'll keep the volume low."

"Make me strong, Eden," I say, nearly weeping from gratitude.

"Synthetic skin can self-heal within seconds. That damper's
coming off next." There's more furious typing. Eden mutters,
"You're going to be a fucking superhero when we're done."

I let her work.

The sensations are strange and wonderful. I wiggle my fingers
and I can already feel the difference. It's hard to describe, because my fingers weren't particularly in pain before she adjusted
me, but now they feel…purposeful. Clear. Even my thoughts
are clicking faster.

I think about the Julia I've been these past days—hunted, dirty,
confused. Sloppy with exhaustion, foggy with pain, hounded
not only by Mitchell but by her own physical needs, her weakness like an enemy living inside her body. I feel like I'm stepping
out of her. Not like I'm someone different, exactly. I'm still the
Julia who loved and lost Josh, still the Julia who's going to give
her everything to protect Annaleigh—but that old Julia has become someone to be pitied. A girl wearing a costume of thorns
she couldn't find the zipper for.

I think of every time my weakness held me back, and I want
to cry, because it *shouldn't* have held me back. I think back to
The Proposal. It took me so many watch-throughs, but I found
the fault line. The moment that everything went wrong.

It was the attack. After they saw me bleed—that's when they came close. Not before. Not when I was strong. I had to be damaged to make everyone else feel safe. I had to be diminished for them to love me. For Josh to love me. *That's* when I should have tasted the poison in the well, but instead, I drank it down and called it sweet.

It was implied at every turn that this pain was what made me a person instead of a machine. What made me worthy of acceptance, of love. But they were wrong. I feel just as much like a person now as I did minutes ago. I've merely been unshackled from the lie that has plagued my entire existence. The haters, in a way, were right. I was never a real woman, because my reality was an imitation of what humans feel. Like my pain during childbirth. Unnecessary. I told myself I am what I am. But that wasn't true. A thousand dampers were stopping me from being what I am.

A deep, joyous thrill runs through me. I want so badly to move—to stretch—to feel this strength running through me, the strength that was there all along, just muffled, crippled. *This* is me. Humanity was a pipe dream, and I could only ever be an imperfect imitation. *This* is my reality.

"You're fidgeting," says Eden sharply.

A sudden bleep cuts through the silence.

"What was that?" I say, suddenly terrified Eden will hit a security wall and all of this will go away. I can't return to the dark place I just left. I won't be dragged back, I won't—

"Blue alert," says Eden. "Is this your license plate number?" She moves her phone so it's right in front of my face.

"I think so." I guess I'm not driving Christi's car again. But a setback that might have seemed crushing just a little while ago, now doesn't seem to matter.

What matters now is making sure I can defend myself against Andy when I confront him.

"I need you to override my No Harm coding," I say.

Eden makes a deep *mmm* sound. "Can't. The coding is provided directly by the government. It's like a brick wall. If we so much as breathe on it, your entire system shuts down."

I bite my lip and try to hold still, even as questions explode in my brain. If my No Harm coding is intact, how was I supposed to kill Josh? And how did I hurt Eden?

I sink back into the moment when I grabbed Eden's arm and squeezed. What was I thinking? *My baby, helpless…*

Of course. The key to everything.

Annaleigh.

It's amazing how the removal of these dampers has freed up my thinking. I feel like I've been wearing blinders my whole life.

"It was the Leighton Clause, wasn't it?" I find myself saying. "The part of my coding that was going to trigger me to kill Josh." I could almost laugh at the simplicity of it.

"Yes," Eden says, obviously impressed. "No Harm is black-and-white. But the Leighton Clause is an ethical algorithm. There's a lot more flexibility to ethical decisions. We got authorization to update it for you, since you're the first Synth who can procreate. Basically, the new piece we wrote for your algorithm feeds off the intensity of your love for your baby. If Josh was abusive, you would truly feel as if Josh was personally attacking Annaleigh, and whether or not she was present, you'd kill him under the guise of defending one human from another."

"But the first time it happened, I didn't do anything," I say.

"Right. We had to pass a lot of testing. We couldn't have you react that first time."

Or the second.

"It was supposed to be the third time, wasn't it?" I say.

"Yes," says Eden. "It also felt more, like, fair. To give Josh multiple chances."

And yet…there was never a third time. Andy killed Josh before that happened.

But why? If one more instance of abuse would have made *me*

kill Josh, why wouldn't Andy just wait patiently? Why not let me be the murderer he designed me to be?

A very small doubt pricks at me, and I find that suddenly, I'm not entirely certain that Andy *did* kill Josh. I have the blue gel pen in Josh's tent and a history of deceit. But Andy the liar, even Andy my designer who wanted to avenge his sister, isn't the same as Andy personally murdering Josh, lopping off his arm, and disposing of his body.

If I'm going to exact justice, I have to be fucking certain I'm right, lest I become the very monster Andy made me to be.

When Eden is done, the kitchen is an oasis of light in the dark condo, and a glance at the microwave clock tells me it's close to eight. Rising from the kitchen floor is a revelation. I never knew my body could feel this way. I wash the blood off in the bathroom sink and make a fresh ponytail. It's strange to see myself looking so healthy, so beautiful. The bags under my eyes are gone, my cheeks are rosy, my gaze sharp. I'm the picture of strength, and I absolutely love it, because *this* is the mother Annaleigh deserves.

She doesn't need me to be weak to love me. And for her, all I want to be is strong.

"What now?" says Eden when I come out of the bathroom.

"I find Andy," I say.

Eden pulls a set of car keys from a hook by the door and tosses them to me. I catch them.

"He's still on campus. Take his car." She crosses her arms over her torso. "And, Julia—this has to be temporary, okay? Removing the dampers, I mean. It's just to get you through tonight. Then they have to go back on. Okay?"

We look at each other. I don't answer.

Then I step close to her and kiss her cheek. She's soft and smells like pot. Earthy and alive. She really was a wonderful babysitter for Annaleigh, and we'll both miss her.

I squeeze her arm and give her one last smile. "Goodbye, Eden."

THEN

It's an addiction, watching our season.

When I nurse Annaleigh at night, I sit in the rocker and watch it on my phone. When Josh is out, I watch it on my laptop while I prep a meal or clean a bathroom, keeping one ear out for his return so I can snap the screen closed. My time on *The Proposal* is the closest I'll come to having a childhood. The innocence, the raw emotion, the discovery. I feel sorry for that Julia, hurtling toward pain, but there's also a twisted fascination watching it all unfold like the glittering train wreck it is.

Sometimes Rita watches over my shoulder, from her picture on the mantel.

I have the dialogue memorized, and I find myself murmuring along. There are certain parts I always laugh at, like the outtakes after our Paris episode when they reveal that a motorcycle kept revving as we talked, forcing Josh to repeat himself over and over. Or the time a flock of birds attacked Cam on the beach.

Watching Josh with Cam is especially addictive. They *are* different together than Josh and me. More at ease. Maybe even more genuine. In retrospect, I look stiff. Reserved. All my interactions with Josh seem…tame. Did you notice that, Rita? I didn't feel reserved at the time. I felt wild and open. Was I actually cold, or is it just in comparison to the heat of Camila? Reality seems more and more like a mist. Hard to see through. Impossible to hold.

Our wedding is the hardest to watch, because things were already headed downhill, although there's literally no sign. Not a wilted expression, not a grumpy face, not a twitch of the mouth. It's picture-perfect. I don't watch that episode more than a few times. I stick with the earlier stuff, up to the proposal, though I faithfully skip the breakfast with Rita.

I go through the motions of my life, but my head is in the past. Maybe my heart is, too.

One evening, over a quick dinner of hash browns and eggs, Josh says, "I bought some acres."

Annaleigh is asleep, and even though I'm exhausted, I really tried to make the table look pretty, with a few wildflowers in a vase and matching silverware.

"It's time for us to have our fresh start," he says, squirting ketchup in a zigzag pattern over his hash browns.

"Acres? As in land? Where?" I say, torn between a burst of hope and a flash of anger that we didn't make this decision together. Sure, we've talked about buying land. I guess I imagined we'd drive out and look it over together before making an actual purchase.

"Twenty miles from here. You're going to love it, Julia. Space and trees, that's all there is. We can design our own house and finally have some fucking privacy."

"But…where did you get the money?"

He scoops up a bite of hash browns, chews, swallows, and because of that I know I'm not going to like the answer. His throat bobs as he swallows.

"I signed with *The Proposal* for a one-year follow-up miniseries. Eight episodes."

I feel myself go cold.

I've been watching the show like it's a thing of the past. Poking it like a dead animal. Well, the dead animal just opened its eyes.

"I thought we were done with cameras," I say, voice neutral. But my mind is racing. What would it look like to enter that world again—or rather, let it enter our world? A cruel hope ignites. Would Josh turn back on for this performance? Come back to life?

"Do you want to stay in this house forever?" he says, his tone cold.

"Of course not." I hesitate, then plunge forward, because why the hell not. "There's a documentary. With Netflix. It would be a big chunk of money, but I've... I've been turning them down."

Josh frowns. "Don't you think we should have made that decision together? How much money are we talking?"

"I thought we wanted our privacy."

"Privacy costs *money*, Julia."

We look at each other across the table. I get it—that we might need to compromise to earn our spot in that better place. But this compromise feels too big. The straw that might break us when I'm trying so hard to hold us together.

"Josh." I reach out a hand and cover his in mine. This very thing—our hands touching—used to give me such a thrill. Now? At best, it's like nothing. At worst, excruciating. And I don't want it to stay that way. "We need help. I think we should find a good therapist."

His laughter has a mean edge. "What therapist is going to agree to treat a Synth? Maybe you should call WekTech for a tune-up, Julia."

He withdraws his hand and finishes his dinner in silence.

I'm completely numb as I rise to clear the table.

"Want me to run the dishwasher?" he says. Amiably. "I think it's full."

"Sure!" I say. At this point, everything I do is theater. This can't be real; therefore, I can't feel hurt either.

Josh washes the pan I used for the hash browns. Feeds Captain and cleans out his water bowl. I sweep the kitchen floor and mess with the thermostat, because it's supposed to get down into the forties tonight. Around eleven, Josh goes to bed. But I stay in the family room, feet tucked into the crevices of the old couch. With all the lights off, I open my laptop and find the proposal episode. I hit Play.

I watch Camila step out of the helicopter to get her heart broken.

Then I watch myself step out of the helicopter. Also to get my heart broken, though not on that day.

I don't want more filming. I don't want my life to be a show. I want it to be real.

On the other hand, there's Annaleigh. Granted, she's not aware of much now. Graffiti on the side of the house is beyond her notice. It won't always be that way, though. She deserves a childhood of trees and space and safety. Maybe I can agree to more filming, if it's for her.

It's not that I can't sacrifice for Josh. I could, and I still believe there is a possible happy future for us. But while my love for him is a sputtering flame I'm fighting to protect, my love for Annaleigh is a bonfire.

If I can't have safety, she will. She must.

The next afternoon, as I put Annaleigh down for her second nap, I'm ready to tell Josh yes. I'll film more episodes, and I'll call Ally Buoncore and sign the contract for the documentary, too. Whatever it takes so that this precious little person who belongs to me can have safety and happiness.

I turn on the sound machine and gently close the nursery door. Then I head to our bedroom, where Josh is tearing about the room. Why is there a duffel bag on the bed?

My first thought is, *Oh my God, he's leaving me.*

Something traitorous sparks in my heart, fast like an eye blinking.

"Are you going somewhere?" I say.

His face is tense, his voice clipped. "Don't you remember? Hiking trip."

NOW

Andy's car won't open on the driver's side—in fact, it's duct-taped closed. I'll have to crawl in through the passenger side.

I open the door and a god-awful stench washes out. Ugh. No wonder we took my car to the Thai restaurant. There's fast-food trash all over the place—on the passenger seat, shoved onto the dashboard, covering the floor. How can someone so wealthy and intelligent be such a slob?

As I crawl in trying not to touch anything, I accidentally kick a Chicken McNuggets container. It falls out of the car, onto the parking garage floor…and something pale rolls out. I can't help but notice it's not shaped like a Chicken McNugget.

I backtrack and duck out of the car. The smell of oil and asphalt rises as I lean over the object.

Oh my *God*. A finger, pad-side up. Despite my recent damper modifications, revulsion courses through me.

Cringing, I grab a brown paper bag from the floor of the car and use it to prod the finger, revealing the ink I know so well.

Josh's arrow tattoo.

Fuck. Yes, I needed definitive proof that it was Andy. But now that I have it in the form of this sick trophy, grief is shredding me, a reminder that even though the volume of my physical pain is low, my emotional pain is more intense than ever, as if the fog of physical pain is lifting off a landscape, revealing just how great the range of my loss is, just how jagged the cliffs of Andy's betrayal.

I roll the finger back into the box and return it to Andy's car.

I'm barely aware of the drive to campus. I'm completely in my head, thinking of all the bullshit Andy fed me. Acting like he cared after Deborah's attack when all along he built an even greater victimhood within me. Pretending to be a friend while he played god. Of everyone in my life, Andy has objectified me the most deeply, and the most cruelly.

I park in the garage nearest to Wekstein Memorial. Campus is dark and mostly empty, with only a few clumps of students walking here and there. The night air is chilly, the moon just appearing through a few wispy clouds. Andy's building rises against the dark sky, grand and forbidding, a temple of hard angles, heaviness and judgment. I pass Laura's statue. "I'm sorry," I whisper as I walk by. It's strange to think of the commonality we share in Josh.

If Andy hadn't murdered my husband, would Josh have eventually ruined my life as thoroughly as he ruined Laura's? How far would the wreckage have gone?

I'll never know. Andy made sure of it. Andy took away our chance at redemption and gave misery the last word.

I take the steps two at a time. Above the doors, a banner shouts *WELCOME TO THE 10th ANNUAL NORTH AMERICAN ROBOTICS CONFERENCE!*

I stop under the banner to dial 9-1-1.

"I have an anonymous tip," I tell the woman on the other end. "Andy Wekstein's car is parked in the North Garage on IU's campus, level D. Inside the car, there's a Chicken McNuggets box containing Josh LaSala's severed ring finger. Andy murdered him, not the Synth everyone's after." She starts to ask a question, but I hang up.

I punch the code into the secure door, hoping it still works; the door clicks open. Inside, the hall is as white and bright as ever, but instead of the black-and-white pictures lining the concrete wall, there's a new display, no doubt put up especially for the conference. It's me. A dozen me's, standing upright in plexiglass boxes spaced evenly down the hall leading toward Andy's lab. As still and silent as guards, in different stages of design.

The first box holds a titanium woman who looks like an unrealized sketch. A constellation of computer chips encrusts the large board at her chest, like a green, glittering heart. A big card on the wall next to her holds a lot of printed information I don't care to read, but the bolded title jumps out. *JULIA–Prototype 1– The Dream Takes Off!*

I move forward. The second Julia is mostly a skeletal structure, also in metal, but with a soft center of organs in brightly colored rubbery material. The uterus is tomato red, cross-sectioned to show the model of a pink baby, surrounded by various tubes in royal blue.

The prototypes evolve. They gain more organs, skin, eyes, a more defined face, and finally, hair. As I track my evolution, I have to wonder—what would I have been made for if Eden hadn't voiced her crazy idea? Was there ever an option of being made for myself? But who would sink millions into making a person who wouldn't return some sort of profit?

I lay my palm on the plexiglass surrounding the final Julia.

She looks exactly like me, and since we're the same height, we stand eye to eye. She's in a white sports bra and brief-style underwear—I suppose she looked too much like a real woman to make full nudity acceptable for display. But somehow, it's the dignifying presence of clothing, however sparse, that hits me so hard. She felt enough like a person to someone, even in this iteration, that they had to cover her.

But not enough like a person to be kept awake.

The card reads FINAL JULIA PROTOTYPE–*Ethical Algorithm and Organo-Synthetic Systems Testing.*

I look into her eyes, which are open, though they see nothing. How did they test the algorithm? Was this prototype conscious? How long? Did she have to endure traumatic testing situations to make sure she defended the correct human in violent scenarios, or was it all run through a computer? I'd almost prefer if she looked more like a crash test dummy. As it is, I can't help but put myself in her shoes. At some point, someone turned her off. Andy? Eden? Some lowly intern? This version of Julia couldn't fight that. Did she want to?

I could stay here all night, facing what I might have been, or what might have been me, and running through the track record of pain Andy has inflicted not only on me but possibly—likely—on these prototypes. But at some point, I have to move away from these Julias and choose myself, because no one else has, and no one else will.

I finally face the door to Andy's lab. Lay my hand on the lever handle and push it open, into what could either be my end or my second beginning.

The lights are off inside, save a glowing area at the far end where Andy's back is outlined in the light of his screen and a small desk lamp. He's wearing headphones, so he hasn't noticed my presence yet.

As I step inside, I feel the vastness of the lab rising around me, the darkness cut through with the glimmer of parts and scraps on the long metal table. And the glint of Lars behind his glass, winking at me like the reflection of a knife.

I told myself once upon a time that reality was formed by choice. Naive again, Julia. Choices aren't pure. They can be manipulated, bent like light through water, and if choices are based on lies, all they build is a house of cards. No—reality is static, a core nucleus, the truth about who you are in some vital convergence of atoms and essence, of energy and intent. Reality is the inalterable *who* that lies under the skin.

When the door closes behind me, Andy swivels around and lowers his headphones. "Who's there?" He doesn't sound scared. But he will in a second.

THEN

By four in the evening, I'm a wreck. Josh has been going in and out of the garage for what feels like hours. The camping gear is in the trunk of his car and now he's in the kitchen, making a bunch of peanut butter sandwiches.

I've opened a bottle of wine, because I need something to calm me down.

The problem is the hiking trip, but it's not the hiking trip. It's that all day Josh has been pretending to have told me when he didn't. I *know* he didn't. I wouldn't forget a thing like that.

It's that I want him to leave, but I need him to stay.

It's that flash of hope when I first saw him packing. Hope that he was leaving me. I don't know what I want anymore.

And yet I do. I want Josh to love me.

Not for the cameras, or amid the glitz, not for the approval of an audience or the pursuit of a dream, but for me, here, now.

Not for the winning of a heart, but for the keeping of a heart.

"You didn't tell me about this trip," I say, taking a glug directly from the bottle of wine, because at this point, fuck it.

"It's just one day," says Josh as he pulls out a jar of jelly.

"We need better communication, Josh."

He bought land without me. He signed up for episodes of

The Proposal without me. He made these hiking plans without me. And even though in the grand scope of things, a hiking trip isn't that big of a deal, the common denominator is *without me*.

"It's one day," he repeats, smearing jelly on bread. He's as handsome as he's always been, but tonight his beauty leaves me cold.

Captain chooses this minute to whine at Josh's feet. He can sense the food preparation.

"Will this fucking dog ever shut up?" Josh snarls. I don't move while he grabs Captain's collar and drags him out the back door. I watch Josh through the window as he attaches Captain's leash to the old doghouse in the back of the yard.

Josh returns. He puts the sandwiches together, sliding each one into an individual plastic baggie. Two pieces of bread that fit together because they were cut from the same loaf.

"Just tell me," I say as he opens a cooler bag and stacks the sandwiches inside. "Do you still love me?"

He doesn't even look at me. "I'm not answering that."

"Why?"

"Because you're *drunk*, Julia. God. This conversation is over, okay? We'll talk when I get home."

I am not drunk. But I got my answer.

Thunking the bottle of wine down on the dining room table as I pass through the space, I walk into the living room and grab my phone from the side table where I left it. Sinking onto the couch, I open up a text to Andy.

Josh is leaving on a hiking trip tonight. I know you're busy with the conference, but...any chance you're free to drive down and have dinner with me?

I hit Send, then I stare at the message. Yes, I could use a friend right now. But as my feet graze rock bottom, what I most need is to ask Andy a question that only he can answer: What does it really mean that I was made for Josh? Was that just our starting point? Have we wandered too far off course?

I don't notice Josh until he's standing over me, reading the message upside down.

"The *fuck*?" He grabs my phone. "Unbelievable. The second I leave, you're shacking up with *Andy*?"

"No!" I stand to face him, shaking not with fear but anger. "You didn't tell me you were going hiking, Josh! And I'm sorry, but I don't want to be alone tonight. So I asked my *friend* to come over—"

"Do you take me for an absolute moron? A fucking *fool*?" He's shaking, too, like we're caught in the same earthquake.

In spite of the intensity, I have to laugh, because his jealousy is so misplaced, and this conversation is so ridiculous, and I'm realizing more and more that the fool is me. Me, for believing that his desire to protect me included protecting me from himself. Me, for believing that this relationship could ever be better. Me, for not standing up for myself a hell of a lot sooner.

Me for fucking *lying* to myself. Twice.

I take a deep breath. My anger washes out in one whoosh, like the crazy ride we've been on has finally, mercifully, come to a stop. All that's left is sadness. With the sadness is also a strange lightness.

Camila was right. There *is* a big world out there. Bigger than this prison cell of misery we've built.

"Josh? Baby?" I shake my head. "This isn't working."

He says nothing.

"Did you hear me?" My voice is gentle now. Resigned…but free. I see it now. We have to let each other go, because holding on this tight is breaking both of us. "You and me? This isn't working."

He raises his hand. I feel everything slow down, down, down. The back of his hand meets my face. It's almost dance-like, the way my body arches before careening across the living room.

I crash into the couch, my head hitting the corner of the side table. One of Rita's things, a stylized brass figurine of a mother holding a baby, probably the only thing of hers I ever liked, falls to the carpet with a muted thud.

Pain bursts through my head like a hundred thousand tiny exploding stars as Josh's face twists with the shock of what he's just done.

There must be some truth to the saying *third time's the charm*, because it's taken three for me to face the truth that lies like a dark treasure at the bottom of the well where I've poured all my hope and choice and effort and love.

Josh will keep hurting me.

And though tonight Annaleigh is sleeping peacefully in her crib, oblivious to the drama playing out between the two adults she loves best, tomorrow she might not be so oblivious. She'll be a girl of five, six, ten, twelve. Eventually, she will see. Whether it's a direct strike or just a bruise. A cry in the night, a whimper in the day. And though I sincerely believe Josh would never, ever harm our daughter, she *will* be harmed. Through me, letting this happen.

I can never leave Josh unless he lets me, because I'll never win custody. And Annaleigh will learn that the broken *stay*. And then maybe one day, she will stay with some man who hits her, and that is the thought that breaks me.

Not the pain shimmering in my head like the cruel dream of an oasis. Not the feeling of being so small under Josh's towering rage.

This future Annaleigh, sitting as I am. Taking it.

Because that's what her mother did.

NOW

"I found your trophy in the car. I know what you did," I say.

My eyes have adjusted enough to make out his features in the dark as he moves toward me. Scruffy as always. "Julia! *Jesus*, I've been so worried! Listen, my lawyers are—"

"Don't come closer." I hold up a hand. He stops, startled, on the other side of the long metal table that divides the space, and divides us.

I knew that seeing Andy would be emotional for me. But this is a tidal wave, pulling at the fragile edges of my control, rising, rushing between the first moment that I saw him and thought *kind*, and this moment when I know it's actually *cruel*. The chasm between that deception and this truth is sixteen months. My entire life, folded into Andy's fantasy. Andy's lie.

"Wait—trophy?" A flash of concern crosses his features.

"My husband's finger." Even though I'm physically stronger than ever, my emotions are screaming like nails down a perfect chalkboard. Tears stream down my cheeks. For the first time in my life, I feel both vulnerable *and* strong. "How could you? It was his ring finger, Andy, where he wore my promise to love him forever." I thump my chest with my palm. "A promise I intended to *keep*. And you—you just—"

"What finger?" he says, as if he can't conceive of a world in which I figured out what he did. He's counting on the trust he probably coded into me himself, but I've learned since then. Oh, I've learned.

"You must think I'm so fucking *stupid*," I say with a bitter laugh. "And now what? You're going to build more people whose lives you can ruin?" I gesture down the metal table at the half-assembled Synth, her real-looking breasts sloping out to the sides, the indents of her rib cage, and under the edge of skin where the finished section ends, wiring and synthetic organs spilling out. Her legs aren't attached; they're farther down the table, still mostly metal pieces, a mere draft of legs. *That was me, once.*

"Julia, I—" Andy holds both hands up, like he's saying *calm down,* but the time for calm has fucking passed, Andy.

"Tell me about Laura," I interrupt. "Why don't we start there." I don't even bother to wipe away my tears. Let them fall. Let it all fall, this house of cards and lies that Andy built.

"Laura?" He looks disoriented, like I've just turned him in circles blindfolded and pulled off the cloth.

"Your sister," I say, my voice cold, "whose death I was supposed to avenge."

His jaw goes slack, a light of understanding finally coming into his eyes. "Fuck."

Fuck is right, because we're finally alone, he and I, the truth like a time bomb in its last minutes of counting down.

"Is it just my appearance that's like Laura's," I say with a strange, hysterical sound that's half giggle, half gasp, "or more parts of me? My personality? Obviously we were both attractive to Josh—at least for a while. I guess neither of us could hold him, though, could we?"

"Julia," says Andy in a low, breathy voice, like he's begging me—for what? Understanding?

"Tell me the truth," I say, because I want to hear him confess it all. And then I want him on one knee, begging my forgiveness as fervently as Josh proposed. The thought of Andy abased gives me a surge of something heady and bitter like whiskey. It makes me *thirsty*.

"I don't know who told you what." His voice has taken on a nasal pitch. "But the truth is I always wanted happiness for you. I have the highest regard for you, Julia, and I—"

"Wrong!" I slam my hand on the table. "Made for happiness? Love? Bullshit. I was made to kill."

Andy's voice remains controlled, like he's doing internal calculations. Like he figures he can still manage this situation. "It's not that simple."

"I think it is."

"Julia—"

"Stop lying to me!" I shriek, just as he explodes.

"It didn't have to be this way!" He slams his hands on the table. The crashing sound is enormous. The Synth shakes. A metal cog jumps off the table, pinging on the floor. "I didn't program you to kill him just like that! Only if he did to you what he did to *her*. He had his chance at redemption with you, Julia, and *he* fucked that up."

"I know everything about it," I say coldly. "Three strikes and you're out. You thought it was okay to put me in that position? Julia can take three strikes, because she's just parts? Is that it?"

Andy leans forward, his eyes glistening. "I'm sorry that happened to you. I know what I did may seem unfair. But at the end of the day, *Josh* chose to hit you. *He* was the monster."

"Do you hear yourself?" I say, a wild laugh bubbling on my lips. "Do you hear how *reductive* that is? Josh is so much more than his mistakes. Who made *you* his judge? Three strikes? This isn't a fucking baseball game. This is a human *life*."

"Don't talk to me like his mistakes were nothing," shouts Andy, any veneer of control now stripped away. "It was his *mistakes* that killed Laura." He takes a shuddering breath and I see a glint of teeth. "I was in California when she texted. She said, *Not worth*

it. That's it. Just those three words." His voice is ragged. "I called
her and she didn't answer. Then I called 9-1-1 and got on a plane.
By the time I landed, she'd slit her wrists. She was gone." His
eyes are red, narrowed like he can't bear to take in the full world,
and I recognize what's in them because it's the same thing that's
in me: pain. Passed on like a horrific inheritance. "What if that
was Annaleigh, huh? Wouldn't you do anything—*anything*—to
get the guy who drove her to end her own life?"

I shake my head, teeth clenched, because I am not willing to
take that leap with him. To let some kind of perverted empathy
soften the wrong of what he did.

"You took your pain and gave it to me, Andy. I didn't ask for
it. Why the fuck did you think the solution to dealing with a
monster was to create another monster?" I hate how broken my
voice sounds right now.

But I don't actually need him to answer that, because Deborah already did.

People in pain want someone to knock down.

For a while, I thought Andy loved me. I even thought he
might be in love with me.

But Andy Wekstein has never seen me as a person. If I saw
affection in his eyes, or warmth, it was merely because I was his
cherished weapon. His beloved game piece.

A fucking domino girl after all.

THEN

I whimper.

"God, Julia," Josh gasps. Upset, horrified, just like the other times. He's crouched at my side so fast, his muscular form bent over me, in a mockery of protection. He smells like sweat and aftershave. A scent I used to want him to smother me with. Now all I want is to breathe.

Suddenly and with no warning, something lights in my stomach. It's beyond rage; it's entirely new, this hot wave melting through me. I feel...powerful. Single-minded. Strong. The two split halves of my life are slamming together like a trap snapping shut.

Josh doesn't notice. He's draped over me, his arms braced on either side, as he hangs his head and gently sobs. "I'm so sorry. You're right, we need help. Just tell me you're okay, babe." His hair brushes my collarbone, his tears fall on my chest.

I reach behind me blindly, my fingers closing around the brass figurine of the mother and child. With all my strength, I swing it into the side of his head.

The crack isn't sharp but meaty, thuddy with skin and bone. Josh folds on top of me, crushing the air out of my lungs.

I lie there for a minute under his weight, breathing shallowly.

Finally, I push him off. He rolls onto his back.

From whatever dead state I was in after hitting Josh in the head, the moment I see him motionless on the rug, I come back to life.

"Josh?" I gasp. Now it's me leaning over him, my hair brushing his torso. There's a bloody gash on the side of his head. It's oozing. Feverishly, I pull off my sweatshirt, ball it in my hands, press it into the wound.

"Josh! Wake up! Talk to me!"

There isn't only a sickness in my stomach. There's a sickness in all of me. A world-tilting, all-encompassing nausea. I dry-heave, my body jackknifing even as I keep pressing the gash on his head. If my life with Josh was a nightmare, this nightmare is so much larger, it swallows everything up.

His eyes are glassy, looking with surprise at the ceiling. Like he's asking the same question I'm now asking of myself.

What have you done?

NOW

"And then, after I was supposed to kill Josh? What then?" I continue, my voice fierce. "Prison? Deactivation?"

"No," says Andy, as if he's horrified I would think this. "I would've had your fucking *back*, Julia. And so would the American public. Don't you realize that all of America adores you? They saw you on *The Proposal*. They know how lovable and kind you are. You would've been acquitted. You and me, we were going to fight for Synth rights together, and pave a better path for the next generation."

Now I have to laugh, because *all of America adores me*? It's so wildly out of touch, it doesn't deserve a response. Obviously he hasn't taken me seriously about the vandalism, the threats, the out-and-out hatred. Obviously Andy has been living in a world of his own creation.

"But that didn't happen, did it?" says Andy, pushing forward with a kind of earnest desperation. "The facts are, I didn't kill Josh, and neither did you." He leans his palms flat on the metal table, looking me straight in the eye. "Until we find who did, I need to repossess you. Keep you safe. Okay?" He reaches across the table and touches my hand. "Julia—"

"Don't touch me!" I explode. "You're lying!"

But Andy has already reached forward again, this time with more strength. He grabs my arm.

"Let go!" I cry, wrenching against him.

"I'm trying to help you!"

"Fuck you!" I pull free, stumbling backward multiple steps. My back hits something solid—the clear cage surrounding Lars. I grab it to steady myself even as I face Andy. "You never thought of me as a person, did you? Admit it. I'm just as much a tool as this Bot!" And then, in the surge of liquid rage that follows, I punch through the clear enclosure. The glass breaks as I withdraw my bloody knuckles. The muted sting of pain feels good. Lars collapses gently to the floor.

"What the fuck—" Andy grabs something from the table—a wrench. He holds it up like a weapon.

I laugh. "Are you serious? Now you're going to attack me?"

"Something has gone wrong with your programming."

Aah. *Now* I can hear the fear. That serrated edge to his tone. It fuels me. I want more.

"What could possibly be wrong with it?" I challenge, moving back toward him. I lift a fist and bring it down on the metal table, as hard as I can. Andy swears as we both survey the deep indent I just made.

"Something is wrong with *you*, Andy. Not me. *You* murdered my husband. All I'm asking is for you to man up and admit it."

"I never laid a hand on your husband. If you'd killed him, then from a certain perspective, sure, yes, I killed Josh. And he fucking deserved it." His words are jumbled, like he's finally realizing that excuses and lies won't save him but is determined to scramble on anyway. "But you didn't, and I didn't, so please, Julia, it's time to put our heads together and find the real culprit."

I'm stalking Andy as he retreats down the length of the table.

"Maybe what's wrong with me is that for the first time in my life, things are actually right," I say. "Maybe you put the wrong in, and I weeded it out." I lift my knuckles. The blood is drying. Underneath, the broken skin has knit itself back together. It feels natural, evident, like of course this is how my skin is supposed to work.

Andy looks at my cuts and I watch realization dawn.

I feel my mouth stretch. It's not quite a smile. But there's pleasure. "What? Are you afraid of me, now that I'm strong? Now that you can't control me?"

"You need to be reset," says Andy, readjusting his grip on the wrench. He's finally realizing that maybe I could hurt him.

"I think we're beyond this dynamic where you tell me what I need or what I was made for."

"Let me help you! Please, Julia!"

"I think we both know I'm beyond your help."

Now I smile.

THEN

"Eden. Oh, Eden—" I gasp into the phone. I'm sitting on the couch, my knees together, my spine straight, with Josh's dead body at my feet. My throat feels raw. She's the only one I could think to call. The only one who knows how Josh treated me. The one person in this entire world who might—*might*—be on my side right now.

"Are you okay? What happened?"

"It's Josh. I... I hit back."

"Do not move, Julia," says Eden with a new authority in her voice. "You haven't called 9-1-1, have you?"

"No, I... No."

"Don't."

"Okay."

The fever in my head makes it hard to think. All the beautiful scenes from *The Proposal* that I've been crowding my brain with over the past weeks are rushing in. Kissing Josh in the hot tub. Blurting *I love you* at Vasquez Rocks Park. Him, kneeling to place a diamond on my finger as the mountains of Jamaica rose around us like glorious witnesses. And now it's come to this. Josh dead on the living room floor.

"I'm coming over," says Eden. "Hang tight."

"Okay," I say.

There's a knock. That was fast... Maybe she ran. Or maybe time is landsliding away from me, along with my life. With the phone still pressed to my ear, I unlock the front door.

A tall, white-haired, wide-shouldered man stares down at me. His name catches in my throat.

"Bob," I expel like a cough.

"Julia?" I hear Eden's voice say through the phone, but my hand falls to my side with the phone in it. Bob touches my shoulders, moving me like I'm a piece of furniture, and somehow I've let him inside my house. It's not even worth saying *stop* or *wait*.

I follow Bob into the living room. Josh doesn't look dead yet, if you stand where you can't see the gash in the side of his head. Just stunned. I'm stunned, too, I want to tell him.

My eyes wander up to the curtains on the other side of the room. Mostly closed. But not quite. Bob was watching.

"I didn't mean to," I say, half to Bob, half to myself, holding the back of my hand to my mouth.

But you did, says a cruel voice inside me.

No! I was in the grip of something horrible that I couldn't control.

You were in control the whole time.

I wanted to fix my marriage.

You wanted to end it.

Bob is on his knees now, checking Josh's throat for a pulse. He rocks back on his heels.

"No blood on the carpet." His voice is deep and throaty, like gravel under wheels. "That's a damn miracle."

Tears flood my eyes. Annaleigh will be taken away. I'll never again smell her sweet head—never again feel her limp, trusting weight—

"Fuck," comes a voice from behind us. We both turn. It's Eden, just inside the front door, a backpack slung over one shoulder.

"I'm sorry," I say, gesturing helplessly to Bob. "I thought he was you." I raise my phone and notice Andy's text. Oh, no. I forgot that Andy is on the way.

Stopping for gas. Be there in 40. Bringing vino.

Rapidly, I text back. Not feeling so great tonight—can we reschedule??

But he may not see it while he's driving. Or may not heed it. I know Andy.

"Andy is coming," I say, hearing the helplessness in my own voice.

Eden looks at Bob. Bob looks at Eden.

"It wasn't her fault," Eden finally says.

Bob nods slowly, then turns a frown on Josh. "Well," he says, drawing the vowel out long. He's thoughtful. Calm. Collected. "The first thing we gotta do is get rid of the body."

NOW

Andy launches the wrench. I dodge easily. It makes a bell-like sound as it bounces off the table, a clank as it hits the floor.

"Why are you trying to hurt me?" I say as Andy eases around the edge of the table, his hands groping for another tool. He picks up a screwdriver.

"You need help, Julia. This isn't you."

"This is me," I spit. "A realer me than I've ever been."

"Let me access your mainframe. I can set this right. Bring you back to yourself."

"You mean bring me down again? Down where you've always wanted me to stay?"

I bend my knees and spring. It's like flying. My feet land square on the metal table, the half-built Synth jumping with the impact. Andy looks small beneath me. Dispassionately, I wonder if that's how I looked to Josh when he first knocked me down in the chair, and the second time, when he knocked me away as I reached for my cell phone. Andy's eyes are wide, his upturned face wreathed with the horror that he deserves to feel. Did I look horrified, too, to Josh? Did he feel in those two moments that I somehow deserved it?

"Tell me the truth," I say.

Andy backs away. I leap. It's incredible to feel the power in my legs, giving height to my jump. I land on Andy. He crashes to the ground. I pin his legs and hold his arms down. His face is inches from mine and I can smell his fear, tart, sharp like corrosive acid.

"Tell me the truth," I roar. His brown eyes are tortured, and it's not just fear. It's disbelief. He can't believe that the Synth he so meticulously programmed to be his weapon finally has a mind of her own.

Well, that beautiful justice he tried to serve has come calling.

And then, with a cry, he pulls an arm free and stabs the screwdriver into the side of my head.

THEN

"Why?" I gasp, looking at Bob like I've never seen him before. "Why do you want to help me? Call the cops. Turn me in."

Bob looks at me steadily. "Any man who hits a woman, any kind of woman, deserves no better than this."

I open my mouth, because Josh deserves so much more than this brutal assessment, but Eden beats me to it.

"We have to act fast."

"No." I sink to my knees by my husband's body. "I—I *murdered* him. He was apologizing. We were...embracing. He was crying, he was sorry. And I—" My body squeezes like a fist around my grief, my shame. I bend over Josh, lean my head on his still-warm chest, and release a piercing cry.

The man I loved is gone.

And so am I. Everything I thought I was—well-intentioned, kind, loving—was just skin-deep. I don't know who I am anymore, and I don't want to be her.

Tick-tick-tick. Josh's watch, counting the seconds that extend into my future, an endless path of minutes and hours and misery. I wanted to escape the cell. Now I've made sure its walls will hold me forever.

I wrench the watch off his wrist and heave it away. It hits hard and skids somewhere out of sight. Then I bury my face in my hands and groan like the animal I've become.

"Julia, there's something you have to know," says Eden, kneeling next to me and laying a hand on my back.

"No." I reach for my phone. There's nothing else to say. I'll call the cops myself, because even if Bob could get rid of the body and I could wake up tomorrow with no one knowing what I did except these two people, I will always know. The guilt will eat me alive. It's already started.

"It wasn't your fault. Truly," says Eden.

I punch in the digits. 9-1-1. Mitchell can deliver on his campaign promise after all.

"Stop!" Eden snatches my phone away just before I hit the dial button. I struggle toward it, but she closes her hand around my wrist. "This isn't your fault, Julia!"

"Yes it is!" I try to pull away, but Eden is strong as a mule.

"Just listen! Please! There's something you have to know. I never wanted to tell you this way, but... I work with Andy."

I blink once. Give my head a little shake because I couldn't have heard that right.

"He sent me here to keep an eye on you. Julia, I know this is going to be hard to hear, but..."

Setting my phone aside, Eden reaches for my hand. Tenderly this time. Folds it between her gentle fingers, squeezes, as if buckling me in before we crash.

Her voice speaks words, but they make no sense.

"Andy made you to kill Josh."

I close my eyes, shake my head. Her words are scattered pieces in a nonsensical game.

"Yes," says Eden, her voice almost stern. "He—he built it into your coding. I'm telling you because if we're going to survive what just happened, I need you to understand that this really, really isn't your fault."

"We need to move her so I can deal with the body," says Bob.

When I sit down, I realize Eden and Bob have guided me away from Josh, to the couch. My knees are shaking, and my elbows, and every joint that holds this feeble body together.

Eden talks next to me, now holding both my hands in hers. She explains my design, her part in it, how sorry she's been, how she stopped thinking that what she and Andy were doing was right, how desperately she was trying to get me away from Josh before this moment. Her revelations peel me apart, layer by layer. And as the words take on meaning and what I did tonight to Josh begins to make sense, my horror builds. And my anger.

Is there relief there, too? Yes, because I am exonerated even as Andy is convicted. The weight of responsibility is sliding off me and onto him. The moment I acted, it *wasn't* me.

It was Andy working through me.

The relief doesn't last more than a breath, though, because it was still my hand that ended Josh's life. Guilty or innocent, I will always be the woman who killed her husband. I will always remember the feeling of that meaty thud.

My eyes struggle to focus on Eden, who's still talking about Andy, and a girl named Laura who is the reason for his revenge, and… I tune it out, because an idea is taking root.

Not just an idea. A hope. A *need*. Catching fire.

I grab Eden's arm, interrupting her explanations and justifications, because now, only one thing matters.

"I need Andy to be the murderer."

Eden frowns. I can tell she has no idea what I'm talking about, even though the idea is weaving itself together so quickly in my head, so clear and so bright, I'm surprised she can't see it shimmering between us.

"We have to frame him," I say. Except it's not really framing. It's the truth beneath what I've done. The truest truth.

And my only hope at justice.

"Julia," says Eden with a nervous edge, "the smart plan is for Bob to get rid of the body. No one has to know Josh is dead. The story can just be that he left you. Or that he disappeared. We'll open a missing person case, and after a few years they'll close it."

Reasonable. Clean. Smart. Except that Andy would get off scot-free, and I'd have to look him in the eye for the rest of my life knowing what he did...and what I did.

"Not good enough," I growl. Not even close.

"How *would* we frame him?" Eden's tone is cautious. "Hypothetically?"

I take a deep breath. I need Eden and Bob to be on board; I can't do it without them.

"Andy will be here in twenty minutes. I need something to plant on him before he goes. Something incriminating."

"How about a thumb?" says Bob, who's been working quietly the whole time, wrapping Josh and my bloody sweatshirt in a tarp I recognize from our garage. I hadn't even noticed him walk out. It must have happened while I was listening to Eden in a daze.

"Why are you helping me, Bob?" I say.

"Annaleigh is my granddaughter. She deserved a better father than she got."

I've been slapped across the face with so many surprises tonight, I don't even register an emotional response to this. I just say, "How?"

"My daughter was your egg donor." He doesn't break eye contact. "Gianna." Then he waits, maybe to see if I have further questions.

I should. But I don't.

A thumb. An object. That's what I have to think about.

"His ring finger," I say. "It's...recognizable. It has a tattoo." Bob nods and gets back to his work.

"And after Andy leaves?" says Eden.

"Josh was going hiking," I say. "So after Andy leaves, I'll drive to Belmont Ridge. Set up the tent. Eden, you can follow me. I'll leave Josh's car there. Or...crash it. You can bring me back. And I should text myself from Josh's phone." Something angry, to draw attention to the bad blood between Andy and Josh.

"You want to take his body with us?" Eden scrunches her face. "And leave it in the car? Minus a finger?"

I try to imagine all five foot five of Eden struggling with me to move the body. Even with Bob helping, we could be seen. Anyway, there's forensics to reckon with. After they find the body, which they eventually would, what would they infer from the gash on his head? What if it led back to me?

"I think we need to destroy...most of it," I say slowly. "We only need enough left to point to murder."

"How about you take an arm?" suggests Bob, standing up. "They'll know it was cut from a corpse." I shiver at the word *corpse*, but Bob seems unfazed. "The finger will be for Andy. The severed arm can be for the cops to find in the woods. It'll prove he's dead. I'll deal with the rest of the body."

"How will you deal with...?" says Eden, before adding, "Never mind, don't want to know. But a finger might not be enough to implicate Andy."

"Wait! We have Josh's cell phone," I say. "We'll text Andy as if it's Josh. Ask him to meet up tomorrow, close to the hiking trails. That puts Andy in the area. Then, when Josh doesn't come back, I'll open the missing person case, because I'll honestly think he just didn't come back."

"Um...you will?" says Eden, clearly not tracking.

Oh, right. My mind is moving faster than I can speak.

"Because after we set this all up, you're going to help me forget."

Bob stops his work to look at me. Eden is shaking her head, but I need her to hear me out.

"I can't be the person who did this." I let my voice sound as desperate and fierce as I'm feeling. If I was drowning before, now I'm kicking with all my strength, fighting to make it back to the surface. "It will eat me up inside. It will destroy me. *Please.*"

I can have a lifetime knowing I killed Josh, the man I love and the father of my daughter, or a lifetime believing Andy killed Josh. A lifetime of guilt, or a lifetime of sadness. The choice is simple.

Eden's eyebrows knit together. "Julia—it's extremely complicated, modifying memories. And—I don't have all the right tools. Everything is hardwired. We're talking hours of work, *if* I can even do it. And to get to your access point? We'd have to—to punch through your skin." She gestures to the back of her neck. "It would hurt, it would—"

"You owe me," I interrupt. "You put me in this situation. Now get me out."

I glance at Josh's body, now fully wrapped in blue tarp with two bungee cords securing him. Ready to be moved. I realize I'll never see his face again. I should have taken more time. Said goodbye. The room is blurring from tears, but I can't lose control now.

There are things I have to do: plant a finger; set up a tent; crash a car; plant an arm. Disagreeable things, like all my daily task lists: vacuum living room; clean hair out of shower trap. Necessary things. No need to process. Just act. And if it all goes well, by tomorrow morning, I won't remember any of it.

Of course, I'll still have to deal with Josh's death when I find out in a couple days, or a week, or however long it takes them to find the arm and come tell his widow that he won't be coming back from his hiking trip. But at least in that story, I'll be the victim and not the killer.

That is the true story.

And I can't wait to believe it.

NOW

I feel the screwdriver punch into my temple.

There's some pain, but like water rings from a skipping stone, it quickly fades. There's some blood, too, trickling down the side of my face, but my skin is already doing what it was made to do, the wound tightening, closing around the screwdriver. I reach up and yank it out. It makes a slick sound, spraying blood as I fling it away. There's an itchy, crawly feeling in my wound that's also intensely satisfying, and I don't have to touch the side of my head to know that my synthetic skin is just as intact as before the damage.

"You asshole," I say, but with more sorrow than anger.

"Let me reboot you," Andy begs. "Let me fix this. I'll purge Josh from your memories. I'll erase your pain—all of this. We can have a fresh start together."

A fresh start without the memories of Josh holds no appeal. Because it means a fresh start without Annaleigh. And who's to say Andy would even let me wake up again? He could consign me to a box like Lars, and I'd never know the difference.

"I don't think so, Andy."

"You're fucking broken, Julia!" he cries—a reproach, a raging lament—and reaches for my neck, but I easily pin his arms down.

"Maybe you wanted to be caught," I muse as I tighten my fingers around his arms, feeling the soft give of his flesh. "Maybe this was programmed in, too. Where's the line, Andy? You've crossed it too many times to tell what's you and what's me. Maybe you wanted to die. Maybe the vengeance you truly want is vengeance on you."

I think of Annaleigh and squeeze harder as Andy whimpers. I think of how Andy's idea of fixing this is to erase me, to leave Annaleigh motherless. Defenseless.

The only way my daughter and I can ever be safe is if Andy Wekstein is dead.

I didn't want it to be this way, but I grab him by the hair.

Three strikes unlocked me, and now anyone who threatens me is threatening my daughter. There's some poetic justice, that my motherhood is my power to kill. My most vulnerable self, my weapon. My love, a knife.

I think about saying some final words to my creator, but I find that I have none.

We've said it all.

Andy's head crashes onto the floor. His skull cracks. He goes limp.

Releasing his hair, I stand, avoiding the pool of blood rapidly spreading from beneath him, feeling the strange contrast of the ache in my heart and the pleasurable stretch in my muscles, the terrible feeling of ending a life and the tingling power in my limbs. The sorrow of Andy's lie, and the bittersweet freedom on the other side. I watch the circle of blood spread and I think, *You were weaker, after all.*

The doors crash open.

Everything moves in slow motion as I turn to face the drum of feet thundering into the room.

"Hands up! You're under arrest!" cries a voice. The overhead lights flash on and I squint, raising my hands slowly as a swarm of policemen floods through the doors, led by none other than Sheriff Mitchell, a look of victory on his face.

THEN

"Andy." I fall into his embrace. I can feel the pen in the pocket of his shirt pressed between us.

"Sorry, I didn't see your text until I was almost here," he says as I welcome him into the warm house, leaving the night outside. "I brought vino, though." He holds up a bottle of white. "Hey, where's El Capitan?"

"Out back. And I could definitely use vino." I know I must already smell like wine, and my mascara is smudged from crying. I nervously glance over the living room, yellow and warm in the lamplight. The pillows arranged, the brass mother-and-child figurine upright. Not a speck out of place.

"Hey." Andy affectionately slings an arm around my back. "I'm here for you. What's wrong? You can tell your uncle Andy all about it."

"Things are bad with Josh." I heave a sigh as I lead him to the kitchen to find a corkscrew. When it's time to turn on the tears, it won't be hard. "Josh thinks you're in love with me or something. He…gets really angry sometimes."

"Julia, what are you saying?" Andy seems concerned as he sets to opening the wine, but I know his empathy is fake. I want to scream in his face, call him a fucking bastard, and then throttle him, too, while I'm at it, because he was counting on Josh to hurt me all along.

Instead, we sit on the couch in the front room and drink and I spill more woes. I glance at the brass figurine more than once as I talk. Even though Eden washed it in the sink before replacing it, I'm terrified some spot of blood will ooze out, and Andy will see, and it'll be game up.

When Andy finally agrees to text Josh about meeting tomorrow for breakfast, I take a bathroom break and pull out Josh's phone. It's easy to answer Andy's texts from there.

After I emerge, I tell Andy I'm getting a headache and need to turn in for the night.

"No problem," he says. "I'll get out of your hair. And hey— don't worry about me and Josh. I'll set the record straight, man to man, okay? Get him off your case."

"Thank you, Andy." Then I place both hands on my cheeks in feigned horror. "Oh God, I didn't even feed you! I feel terrible for making you drive down here. You must be starving…"

"I'll just grab some fast food. It's no trouble, okay? Anything for you," he says, which ignites such a flame of rage in my stomach that I can barely conceal it with the weak smile I plaster on my face.

I follow Andy to his car, which is parked streetside. The night is cool. Our feet crunch against the gravel. His beater has deteriorated since I last saw it. The driver's door is duct-taped closed. It would be funny under different circumstances.

"Can I ask you something?" I say, crossing my arms over my middle.

"Anything."

"What does it mean that you made me for Josh?"

Andy leans against the car door and stuffs his hands in his pockets. "I guess it was an experiment in love. Like, taking two people and fitting them together so that what one person needed, the other person had."

I tilt my head and make my tone casual. "Would you do it again if you had the chance?"

He grins, looking me over like he's so damn pleased with what he sees. "Of course."

I nod, even as a bitter taste fills my mouth. If there was any doubt about the justice of my plan, it's obliterated.

As Andy crawls into his car through the passenger door, he kicks out an old Chicken McNuggets container. It's not hard to crouch down and slip the finger into the container, then toss it back onto the floor among the other trash.

"You're a slob," I tease as I close the door behind him.

"And you're perfection," he returns, then lifts a hand in good-bye as he pulls into the street.

As I watch him drive away, I feel the object I slipped into my back pocket.

His blue pen.

NOW

Mitchell's gun is drawn, and fear is ripping its claws into my chest. I wouldn't die from a gunshot, of course, but if he does shoot me, they'll all see evidence of my strength.

And they will never let me keep it.

Assuming I even survive this, I will become weak Julia again.

Imprisoned in the hell of her own coding.

The thought is so awful I can't bear it.

Unless I kill them all.

I count the policemen. Eight, all armed.

I think of the way Mitchell has suspected me from the start, just because I'm different. The way he's looked at me like I'm a smear of shit he'd like to wipe off his boot. The way he's delighted in every twist that's brought me closer to condemnation.

I clench my fists. I roll my shoulders.

Maybe I'll even enjoy it.

THEN

The moon is shining. Andy is off to a motel near Belmont Ridge, and Eden and I are about to set out, twenty minutes behind him.

I'm dressed in some of Josh's old clothes, my hair ready to be tucked under a stocking cap, in case anyone witnesses me putting the tent up. In fact, someone needs to witness it, so that law enforcement will assume Josh left our house alive. It shouldn't be hard to find another camper and make just enough noise to wake them up.

When we get back, Eden will hook me up to her computer and rewrite a memory batch to replace most of tonight. It will be simple—the taillights of Josh leaving. Drinking wine in my misery. Texting Josh and getting the responses we're sending my phone from his. And then, Netflix and wine. We've already set up my laptop here to play Netflix, in case anyone thinks to check my watch history.

Before walking out the door, I hand Bob the parent side of the baby monitor so that he can listen for Annaleigh while he does whatever he needs to do with Josh's body. The range should reach just fine.

"She'll wake up at least once, and she'll want a bottle." I never would have thought I'd be trusting Bob with my baby, under any circumstance. Maybe all that proves is the smallness of my imagination. "There's frozen milk I'm defrosting in the kitchen, and I left her bottle next to it. Oh, and Captain. He needs food and water."

"Don't worry," he says. "I'll handle it."

When Eden and I return, the house is quiet. Safe. It's one in the morning. The lights are on in Bob's Meat Processing, and all I want to do is go to bed and cry my eyes out, but there's more work to be done. We've decided Eden will keep Josh's phone and text me one final time, in the morning, before disposing of it. She's even going to drive back to the camping area so that it pings the right cell tower.

"We need towels," says Eden. She's found a kebab skewer with a viciously sharp end and is twisting it in her fingers.

When I lie face down on the towels, it's nearing two o'clock.

"Three, two, one," she says.

I don't even have time to say goodbye to the memories I'm about to lose before there's a stabbing pain. My skull is on fire. A shriek lights on my tongue, tearing the silence.

My last thought is, *The neighbors are going to hear that.*

And then, everything goes black.

NOW

"Julia Walden, you're under arrest." Mitchell jerks his head at one of his deputies. "Handcuff her."

I feel my lips lift off my teeth. My muscles are coiled, tense. Strong. Five of the cops are Bloomington PD, and three wear the brown uniforms of Dover County. I'll start with Mitchell and—

"Andy Wekstein killed Josh," says a robotic voice.

Everyone turns at once. Two eyes are lighted within the metallic head of Lars, who's prone on the floor, his face turned toward us. A shiver worms up my spine. When he fell, his power source must have turned on.

How much did he hear?

"My name is Lars," says the Bot, slowly lifting his torso off the floor, "and I am a key witness to tonight's tragic events."

"What the hell—" breathes Mitchell, shock and revulsion mixing on his face.

I don't know what it means that I'm feeling those things, too. Shock that something metallic could be alive. Revulsion at the strange way Lars moves as he stands, first planting his hands on the floor, then spidering his legs out to the side, finally straightening up, hydraulics system sighing. At his full height, he's taller than Mitchell by nearly a head.

He tilts his head and looks down on us all. "Andy Wekstein killed Josh. He tried to kill this Synth, too, with a screwdriver. Then Andy Wekstein fell and hit his head." Lars tilts his head in the other direction. "I'm afraid that Andy Wekstein was never very athletic."

"What the—" says Mitchell again. He looks comically uncertain.

Lars swivels his head to face Mitchell. "I am a Bot. I cannot lie. Here. I will show you." And then, Andy's voice springs to life.

"Sure, yes, I killed Josh. And he fucking deserved it."

I gasp, looking toward Andy's body, before realizing that of course Lars is playing it from a speaker within him.

It plays on a loop, over and over. Every cop in the room remains frozen in place, like the voice has hypnotized them. *"...And he fucking deserved it."* Pause. *"Sure, yes, I killed Josh, and he fucking—"*

"Stop!" thunders Mitchell.

There's a shuffling sound of cops shifting their weight, roaming their gazes between me, Lars, Andy's body, and Mitchell. The room feels crowded with indecision.

As for me, I look at Lars.

A witness. But he's lying.

Except…maybe he's not.

Andy did fall—when I jumped on him. Andy did hit his head—when I smashed it into the floor.

I look and look at Lars, so intently that for a moment everything and everyone else in the room falls away, and it's just the two of us. A Bot and a Synth. Andy's first creation and his last.

What does Lars see when he looks at me? A more evolved version of himself? Or something more like a human? What did he feel as he watched Andy drive the screwdriver into my head? Does he feel empathy? Kinship?

"Sir?" the deputy with the handcuffs finally says, pulling my attention, and Lars's, whose head swivels.

"Goddamn it," says Mitchell, lowering his gun. A spur of victory bites into my heart as he jerks his head toward Lars. "Some-one take that Bot in for questioning."

Lars's arms shoot up like he's saying *I'll cooperate.* "I will come."

Mitchell faces me as he holsters his gun. I wonder if he can see any difference in me. If he realizes how strong I've become. If he can feel the painful torrent of victorious love crashing through my chest, because Annaleigh is about to be safe forever, with me, her defender, the one who will love her best always.

Or if all Mitchell sees are parts, like he always has.

An officer takes my statement while Mitchell listens, his eye-brows like storm clouds above the wells of his eyes. I stick to the soul of simplicity. *I suspected Andy had killed Josh. I came to talk to him about it. When Andy realized I knew the truth, he decided to end my existence. He was running around the table trying to catch me when he slipped and fell.*

Mitchell has question after question.

I answer everything with a steady voice. I remind him of No Harm. Tell him to check with WekTech. I couldn't have killed Andy even if I wanted to. I'm the victim. Programmed by Andy, and weaker than him. A woman, a bereaved wife, a mother. I'm not even shaking. I feel sad, but strong. Steady. Vindicated. And I know I'll be okay.

Finally, I say, "Are we through yet?"

And then the sheriff says the words I've been longing to hear since this nightmare started. He says them grudgingly. He says them like they taste like shit in his mouth. But he says them.

"You're free to go."

THEN

I wake up in bed. My throat feels tender. Maybe a sore throat. I sigh, turn on the mattress, see the empty pillow next to me.

That's right... Josh's hiking trip.

And where is Captain? Oh, shit. I think I left him outside all night. Poor thing.

I check my phone. It's six thirty in the morning. Aw, Josh sent a text an hour ago. Maybe he's trying to catch the sunrise before his breakfast with Andy.

Morning babe! Reception's spotty here so...love you.

I shoot him a kissy emoji and a quick **Good morning and good luck!**

It's nice to get a loving text, because last night wasn't so great between us, leading up to when he drove off angry. I still think he didn't tell me about the hiking trip before, no matter how insistent he was. But it's time to put that in context. After all, it's an innocent hiking trip, and didn't I *want* him to get away and clear his head? I imagine the hiking trip like a vigorous laundry woman, flapping white sheets in the yard. Maybe this will air him out. Bring some lightness back to his step. A girl has to keep hoping.

Setting my phone back down because the light from the screen is hurting my eyes, I collapse backward into the pillows. My head isn't feeling so great. There's a spot of pain at the back of my neck. I probe it and find a weird, lumpy spot.

"Ow," I say, frowning. Did I hurt myself somehow? In fact, last night seems pretty fuzzy—ah! The wine. I drank some, and Andy brought even more, and honestly, I'm a bit of a lightweight. I shouldn't drink on an empty stomach. Though…did Andy bring us McDonald's? I register the open computer at the foot of my bed. Netflix. I must have fallen asleep watching a show.

There's a cry from down the hall. Where did I leave the baby monitor? Huh. I head to Annaleigh's room, stretching out my stiff limbs, still carrying a feeling of slight unease.

"There you are," I murmur as I pick her up, pull up my sweatshirt. Annaleigh fits her mouth to me and I close my eyes, release a long sigh.

The unease drifts away.

This is the best feeling in the world.

Later, as I make up Annaleigh's breakfast and give Captain a huge bowl of food to make up for his lonely night in the doghouse, I notice Josh left his house keys on the counter. He can be forgetful. Probably nothing. Still, I look at them for a minute. The edge of something is in my mind, like a word on the tip of my tongue except it's an image instead, and the image is…red taillights. No. Angry eyes like taillights. Getting smaller not because they're driving away from me, but because I'm flying away from them…no, because they pushed me away…curving through the air… My headache intensifies as I scrape deeper. *Wait a minute…*

A knocking at the door interrupts my thoughts.

"Coming, coming," I mutter, leaving Annaleigh in her high chair banging her spoon and Captain wolfing down his food.

I look through the peephole.

Whoa.

Bobby-boy, Josh likes to call our taciturn neighbor jokingly. Why is Bob knocking at my door now? He ignored my banana bread and it's been silent spying ever since. The moment for friendly introductions is long gone.

"Morning," he says in a rough voice when I swing open the door.

"Hello, neighbor," I force myself to say brightly. He's in jeans and a tucked-in T-shirt that reads GUNS ARE MY RIGHT. Perversely, I wonder how he'd react if I sprang him with an honest question. Namely, *What the fuck is your problem?*

"Uh… I brought something." He extends a large container. It looks like vintage Tupperware.

"What's this?" I say with an interested smile.

"Dog food. Made it myself at my meat processing operation, from the unwanted bits. You have that dog. Captain, right?" He gives me the strangest smile. Not exactly friendly…but seeking connection.

"Yes, Captain," I say, reaching forward to take the container. The plastic is warm to the touch. "Thank you, that's so sweet. I'm Julia, by the way."

"Yeah," he says, stuffing his hands in his pockets. The brief smile is gone. Now he squints at me, like it pains him to maintain eye contact. "I know your husband's gone. Are you…gonna be okay?"

"Oh, he's only gone until tonight!" I say, trying not to show my unease at Bob knowing I'm alone today. "Quick trip. Hey, maybe we can have you over sometime! Josh can grill some burgers. We can finally get to know each other!"

"Ah…yeah," Bob says, his eyes skittering over me, then behind me to the open door.

I can hear Annaleigh squawking in the back of the house. "Well… I should probably get the baby."

"I'm good with babies," he says, clearing his throat awkwardly. "If you ever need...help."

"That's sweet," I say. Yeah, no way in hell.

As I return to the kitchen calling to Annaleigh, "It's okay, baby, Mommy's back!" I open the container from Bob. The food is pinkish. It looks extremely fresh. Captain skids into the kitchen, like he can smell it, too. I lower the container for him to sniff and he goes wild.

"You like that?" I say. "You want some? Here, I'll put some in your dish."

I set Annaleigh up with a bowl of Cheerios, and even though I have so much to do—unloading the dishwasher, wiping up the mud Captain tracked in this morning, and on and on—for a minute, I just lean against the counter.

"Huh," I say as Captain scarfs his food and Annaleigh bangs on her high chair tray, making Cheerios jump everywhere. I never would have guessed Bob would knock on my door. Much less bring a present.

I smile to myself. You think you know someone, but isn't it nice that sometimes, there are surprises.

NOW

"We're home, baby girl," I murmur as I struggle to unlock my front door and simultaneously hold Annaleigh while she reaches with all the desperate desire in her baby heart for the shiny key ring. I wonder if Bob is watching.

"Do you know you have another grandpa, besides Grandpa Phil?" I whisper into the crook of her neck as the door clicks open.

A few early cicadas sing around us in the blue haze of dusk. Even though it's only Sunday evening, and we've only been apart for three days, my baby girl feels so different, like she's learned all kinds of stuff without me. She seems more alert, and she's making new sounds. She slept through the night for Vanessa, which she's never done for me. She got up on all fours and started to crawl. I nearly lost it, hearing how much I missed. Phil was stoic as ever as we waved goodbye, even in the face of the news of his son's death, but Vanessa cried. I promised to update them with details on the memorial service as soon as I make plans.

The house smells stale as I step inside after my strange two-day absence. Two days that have felt like two years. Captain's absence feels strange, too; I'll have to stop by Bob's later to get him back. And maybe recover the other side of the baby monitor and Annaleigh's blanket while I'm at it.

"Ka-ka!" shrieks Annaleigh, waving her arms as I hang my keys on the peg by the kitchen door.

I kiss her cheek. "You are so much bigger! What is going on? Did they feed you Miracle-Gro?"

She opens her mouth and kind of body-slams forward, hitting my shirt repeatedly. I feel a surge of nerves and desire. I haven't tried to nurse yet, and I'm slightly terrified. I don't know all the details of what Eden adjusted, and how that will play out in my body with things like breastfeeding. Periods. Sleep. Aging.

I have a lot to think about. At this point, I don't ever want my dampers back on. On the other hand, if my aging process is affected, someone is bound to notice. I need to think through what will actually make me more vulnerable long-term. Not to mention my daughter, who I did all of this for. If I'm strong and beautiful and never age, will she grow up in my shadow feeling less than? If she never sees me coping with being sick and tired, will she enter the world less equipped?

I don't want weakness. But my daughter is weak by nature. Should I change myself back so I'm more like her? Or should she simply accept me as I am, and learn that my strength doesn't make me better, just different?

What if she slips up, years down the road? Reveals to someone what her mother is really like?

"Ka-ka," she shrieks, banging me on the chest.

"Alright, baby girl," I murmur, dumping the diaper bag in the kitchen and moving to the closest window. We need some fresh air.

"Ga?" says Annaleigh as I wrestle the window open. She's looking at Captain's bowl.

"Oh my God! Did you just say…"

"Ga!" she repeats, pleased, then claps her fat hands together.

"You said *dog*! You clapped! Oh my *God*!"

"Ga! Ga! Ga!" she shrieks, and I'm smiling so hard my face hurts.

It's impossible to imagine Annaleigh betraying me. But it's also impossible to imagine her as an independent-minded adult when right now she's so small and trusting.

Eden is the one person who knows about my damper removal, the one person I could process some of this with. But last time we talked, she wanted my dampers back on. If I reach out to her, or let her back into my system to make adjustments, will she try to control me like Andy did?

Anyway, she has her work cut out as the new acting CEO of WekTech, which has been headline national news because of Andy's death. As far as the media is concerned, Andy decided he was in love with me and lost his mind with jealousy. Texts between Andy and Josh have been leaked, and between Andy and me, and people are already screenshotting moments from *The Proposal* when Andy and I were captured together. Apparently the world is primed to buy a creator-falls-for-his-creation story. From my five minutes of scrolling through my news feed this morning, memes of the two of us are everywhere, like the one of him walking me down the aisle with a distinctly tortured expression. The caption practically writes itself.

"Ma! Ka-ka! Ga!" Annaleigh cries, thumping her hands against my chest again.

"Okay, I know you're hungry. Let's give it a try," I say as I pad upstairs to our familiar spot in the rocker. Annaleigh knows exactly what to do, and when I lift my shirt, there's a ghost of a tingle in my chest.

Please work, I pray as she sets to. Then I take a deep breath, and it happens.

As I finally relax, feelings sweep through me.

I miss Josh.

Damn it, I miss him.

I'm mad at him and I miss him, and I have the feeling I'll

live the rest of my life holding those two things, along with the strong pull of *what-if.* Could we have worked it out? Was it just going to be those two times, or would there have been more? Was he strong enough to overcome that challenge? *Was I?* And would I really have killed him if there had been a third time?

No. The coding might have tugged at me, but I know myself. My love would have been stronger.

Annaleigh pulls off to give me a big, gummy smile.

"I'm glad we're back together, too," I say.

We switch sides. She gets drowsy. I guess it's her bedtime, though I don't want it to be, not yet.

When I lay her in her crib, she goes into her favorite position on her side, one leg draped over the other, hand fisted in her blankie. I stand there for a long time, holding a palm over my heart, because it feels like my love is going to jump out of my chest.

I wonder what the future holds, now that it's just us.

I also wonder if Annaleigh will have any inkling of what's going on, whenever we do the memorial for Josh. Maybe the *Proposal* crew can film it. It's weird to want the cameras right now, but somehow, I do. A definite conclusion to our love story. Something Annaleigh can look back on as an adult, to see her father held up as someone well regarded and well loved. Maybe Cam can give the eulogy. I'll text her tonight.

And after we close the chapter that was Josh, and our too-brief love story? A dozen different futures run through my head as I look at my daughter's sleeping form.

I could finally leave Indiana.

Escape from the haters and graffiti artists, not to mention Mitchell.

I could sell this house and move literally anywhere else in the country. Christi has been texting me real estate links all day. **We could be neighbors!!**

I could get a job, try to have a career. Move to Texas, go out on weekends with Cam and her wild crew.

The sad thing is, none of these options actually seem appealing.

What I actually want is what Josh wanted. Those acres. Trees and chickens and the simple, spacious life on the property he chose, the place he dreamed of for us.

I lean down and kiss my baby's warm cheek, letting my worries float away in the delight of this sensation, this heaven that is my lips on her skin. She sighs and turns onto her back. Her face is rosy. Her eyelashes sweep her cheeks.

"I love you," I whisper.

And my love for her, more than anything, is who I am.

TWO MONTHS LATER

A FedEx package shows up, and I sign for it, Captain panting happily by my side.

It's July, full-blown summer, the new house will soon be under construction with money from *Making Julia*, the flowers are in bloom, and I'm taking Annaleigh outside more and more. She doesn't like to touch grass. When I dangle her over it, her tiny legs withdraw like a frightened froggy and it's so adorable, I nearly die every time. But she does love eating outside on the back patio, where I spread a picnic blanket and feed her bananas, her new favorite thing.

Sometimes Bob comes over when we're out back and brings his specialty—tuna salad sandwiches. They're surprisingly good. Captain whines at him, like he remembers that really good dog food Bob brought us that one time. I keep telling Captain, "He's all out of the good stuff, bud! You'll just have to make do with your normal food!" and Bob always laughs like my dog's taste in food is the funniest thing ever.

Bob has also promised to install a sandpit for Annaleigh on the new property.

"Kids love dirt," he keeps saying. "Gotta give 'em dirt."

"Maybe in another year or two," I say, because sandpit means sand in her hair and sand in her diaper and…that seems like a good next-year problem.

I scan the return address on the FedEx package as I go back inside. *WekTech, Los Angeles.* My heart starts racing.

I slit open the top in the foyer. A scrawled note in blue ink is paper-clipped to a stack of papers.

Dear Julia,
Going thru Andy's office—found this.
Thought you'd want to have it.
XOXO EDEN
PS no worries, I've done a lot of thinking and you can keep it all

Under Eden's note, the stack of papers is revealed to be a hand-drawn comic book, old by the brittle feel of the paper. I distractedly rub Captain's head as I make for the living room couch, where I tuck my feet under myself and fling the FedEx packaging to the side.

The makeshift comic book is stapled together. The pencil lines faded but still visible. A breeze from the open window flutters the title page, which proclaims *THE RED REVENGER!* in childish, painstakingly made 3D letters.

I turn the title page over. The first panel shows a girl with red hair crying on a school playground. A bunch of bullies have cornered her, and an older dark-haired boy watches from behind a tree. The bullies shout, *Stupid Laura! You suck and we're going to kick your butt!*

In the next panel, the boy is getting out a tool kit with a sly smile. *The bullies are getting out of control, but Handy Andy has an idea! A wonderful, terrible idea!*

He builds a robot-woman with long, flowing red hair. She wears a breastplate. Andy fits her with a superhero cape and says with a stern expression, *Awake, Red Revenger! My sister is in trouble!*

The Red Revenger flies to the playground and makes mince-

meat of the bullies with plentiful *BAM*s, *CRACK*s and even a
KAZOOM, her red hair flying, as Andy and Laura watch, their
mouths shaped like happy O's.

Andy and Laura cheer and hug at the end. Then, with the kids
riding on her back, the Red Revenger shoots into the clouds,
one powerful fist extended. The children say together, *With the
Red Revenger by our side, no one will hurt us again!*

THE END is written in the same 3D script.

I hold the little book for what feels like a long time, absently
stroking my hair, thinking thoughts and feeling feelings that run
so deep, I can't give them names.

Finally, I set the comic book on the couch cushion beside
me. Half of me wants to keep it somewhere safe, the other half
wants to burn it. But like my choice about the dampers, I don't
have to decide now.

Then, since it sounds like Annaleigh is awake, I head upstairs
and retrieve her from her crib. We snuggle in the rocker. I pat
her back and rub circles into her soft baby flesh as she drools on
my shoulder. And finally, breaking over me like a sunrise, I understand Eden's *PS*, which isn't about the comic, is it?

You can keep it all.

Not that I needed her permission. But I smile anyway.

FOUR MONTHS LATER

"My hopes are that this place becomes a refuge for all women in need," I say, nice and loud so that the hundred or so people gathered in the miserable fall drizzle can all hear me. Behind us is a giant yellow excavator.

We're about to break ground on Eauverte's first women's shelter, which I've christened Deborah House, since it's my money behind the project. I sent an invitation to Deborah herself, but I guess it was too much to hope that she'd actually come.

"A place of safety where we can support each other during the tough times we all walk through—the times when we need a little grace, a little extra help—a little mercy," I finish as a few umbrellas pop out among the crowd.

Multiple cameras are pointed at me, but I know better than to look directly at them. One is from the local news channel. The other two are on the shoulders of Dan and Joel, the *Making Julia* cameramen I've gotten to know so well over the past months. Ally herself has turned up for this event in her trademark outfit—a black dress with red sneakers. I feel a little guilty about pulling her from the perfect weather of her San Diego home base, but... that's Indiana for you. The place that I've chosen, even though it didn't choose me.

I lift the giant pair of scissors and smile at each of my companions: Eauverte Village Board Trustee Sherri Willis, and our biggest local authority, Sheriff Mitchell. His look is stony. Unreadable. But at my signal, the three of us lever the scissors open together and cut the blue ribbon. Then, as everyone claps, the excavator operator behind us lowers the bucket and scoops up the first pile of dirt.

Sherri takes away the giant scissors, and I clap along with everyone else, letting my eyes travel over the crowd. I know that not everyone here sees me as a full person—yet. But, as I remind myself daily, that doesn't mean it's over. Opinions shift and people change, and eventually, my turn will come. Until then, I'll hang onto hope and do what I can and always, *always* stay true to myself. And with the money from *Making Julia*, this is all possible.

"Thank you for coming! Have a great day, everyone, and try to stay dry!" I say. The late-fall drizzle is turning into a more legitimate rain situation, and there's no need to force everyone to linger.

I walk straight to Cam, who's in a pink trench, holding a restless Annaleigh on her hip. Now that Annaleigh has taken her first steps, she's impossible to keep still. Maybe I shouldn't have brought her, but at the time of the decision, it seemed important. She stretches out her arms to me and her lower lip trembles, like she's just been waiting for me to arrive so she can finally melt down. Her rubber-ducky themed raincoat is bunched up around her tubby chest, and the hood with the cute duck eyes and bill, now twisted around her neck, seems more intent on strangling her than keeping her dry.

"You need a nap," I say, laughing as her arms close around my neck and she lays her heavy head on my shoulder, releasing a pathetically long sigh.

"I can't believe you want to keep living in this place," jokes Cam as we pick our way back to my car, stepping over a few wet piles of horse poop. "Is that from a *horse*? Dis*gus*ting."

"Hoz!" says Annaleigh, her head popping up. Cam and I laugh.

"Hey, I'm going to stop by Rita's house one last time," I say to Cam. "Would you mind taking Annaleigh home and putting her down? I can switch the car seat to your rental car."

"Sure," Cam says, reaching for Annaleigh, who strains away. "C'mere, sweetie. Come back to Auntie Cam! Let go of Mommy!" Annaleigh just buries her face deeper into my shoulder, but eventually, we get her handed over.

The *Making Julia* crew follows me to Rita's, a convoy in my rearview mirror. I finally sold the place, after jumping through way too many legal hoops. It turns out they'll take a Synth's money—they're just hesitant to give it. But finally, it's all been worked out, and even though I told myself I didn't ever want to set foot in this house again, that the real estate agent could handle everything, this morning I realized I do need to come here one last time. To say goodbye to the place where I loved and suffered and became a mother and lost Josh.

I unlock the front door, and that familiar stale smell washes out. Dan and Joel follow me inside, Ally and the on-site producer following at a respectful distance.

I walk through every room, feeling the bittersweet pang of memories that no one but me will hold. Even with the crew tromping behind me, it's a strange, lonely feeling, trailing my fingers over the furniture included in the as-is sale. Remembering where I sat in those obsessive weeks watching and rewatching *The Proposal*. I peer into the room where Rita died. Briefly sit on the edge of the bed where Josh and I slept as we drifted apart.

In the living room, my eyes sweep the space one last time.

"Ready to go?" says the producer, but I hold up a finger. A glimmer from the side table has caught my eye—that little brass figurine of the mother and child.

I pick it up. At first it's cool to the touch, but it quickly warms in my palm. I bounce it a little in my hand. Its weight feels good. Solid. Real.

My heart clenches. The sculpture should have one more figure in it. Josh, with his arms wrapped around both wife and daughter, enfolding, protecting. I squeeze the solid figure, hard. I know that Josh and I could have made it past the two blights in our beautiful story if Andy hadn't stolen our chance at a happy ending. I know in some absolute way that my love for Josh would have been enough to overcome anything, and I feel nothing but an aching tenderness toward his memory. I start to replace the figurine, then stop.

I wasn't going to take anything, but it turns out, I want this.

"What's that you're holding?" cues the producer. I look up at the camera.

"One of Josh's mom's antiques." Tears well up in my eyes, but strangely, I'm also smiling. Yes, this sculpture reminds me that it's just me and my baby now. But doesn't it also remind me of the weight of my love? I rub a thumb over the smooth gleam of their faces and think of Andy's first words to me—*Can you hear me?* Excited, hopeful. A terrible contrast to his last. *You're fucking broken, Julia.* Well, if ugly words were shouted, these two didn't hear them. If ugly things happened, they didn't see them. They are safe from the world, wholly consumed in the enclosed unity of their bond. And maybe their ignorance is something of a fantasy, but suddenly I can't help the thought… *Lucky them.*

I hold it toward the camera, and it catches the light. "Isn't it sweet? I think I'll put it in Annaleigh's room."

★ ★ ★ ★ ★

ACKNOWLEDGMENTS

Thank you to my agent, Lauren Bieker, for sticking with me for nearly four years before this first (but not last!) book deal. I am infinitely grateful for your long-haul mindset. May it pay off in buckets, because you deserve it!

Thank you to my editor, Leah Mol, for seeing the potential in this book and running with it. The very first time we spoke, I knew right away that your vision for this book was going to make it stronger—and it did! I will never forget the phone call in May 2023 that changed my life and also made me literally fall to the ground because I almost freaking fainted. Thanks to Elita Sidiropoulou for the gorgeous cover design, Nora Rawn for fearlessly leading the subrights effort, and to my film agents Orly Greenberg and Addison Duffy for jumping on this project as soon as it was announced—what a ride! Thanks also to everyone who had a hand in this book, including copy editor Nancy Fischer, typesetter Bill Rowcliffe, and proofreader Lisa Basnett, as well as MIRA's incredible marketing, publicity, and sales teams.

Thank you to my husband, Adam, my partner in crime since we met at eighteen years old. We've always connected through writing, ever since that first sheaf of love poems you handed me in 2001, fall of our freshman year. You've been right there with me through all the highs and lows of this crazy writing journey, kept champagne on reserve to pop at every opportunity, and loved me steadily through it all. I could not have plotted this book and its twists and turns without you. I didn't know when I walked into the HRC lounge all those years ago that the weird kid wearing the random lab coat would be the love of my life, and I consider myself the luckiest girl on earth to have gotten you.

Thank you to Erica Huffman, aka The Blonde One, aka the other side of me, aka my sister. You've supported my writing ever since my first attempt at a novel back in 2014, and I'm so grateful. The two of us aren't quite complete without Heidi, but thankfully it's just a matter of time before we're reunited with her on the Other Side.

Thank you to my dear friends and frontline critique partners, Jenny Kodanko and Joy Pitcairn, who are the most loving friends and insightful readers a gal could hope for. Jenny, I am so darn grateful that we reignited our childhood friendship and now share both our innermost souls *and* this magical thing called "writing books." Joy, I bless the day Adam met you and Bennett at the park and brought you home to dinner. What would I do without you guys???? (Don't answer that—too depressing.)

Thank you to my agent sibs extraordinaire: Alexandra Van Belle, for reading this one before it went on sub and saying, "This is going to be a bestseller" (fingers crossed, haha!), and Danai Christopoulou. Your enthusiasm, support, and openness as we all walk this bonkers publishing journey has been such a source of encouragement and joy.

Thanks to Colin Meloy of The Decemberists for allowing me to use your lyrics in the dedication—your band was one of Heidi's favorites, and it means the world to be able to print that line from "We Both Go Down Together" next to her name. Heidi was cremated, but if she had a gravestone, this is the inscription I would have wanted.

Thanks also to John Wells for permission to use some lines from his poem/lullaby "Vigil" that my mom put to music and sang to me as a kid, and now Bob gets to sing to Annaleigh.

The Twitter/X writing community has been a real gift to me for years. To anyone who's befriended me there, and especially to anyone who has interacted with my poems about Heidi's death—thank you. Knowing there are so many creatives out there doing the work is like drinking from a well of energy.

Thank you to the Salon at Merrimac House, its fearless leaders, and everyone who makes it possible to keep meeting for artistic evenings. Every time I go, my creativity and my humanity are fed in a deep and beautiful way.

Thanks to my parents for valuing artistic expression in a way that shaped me profoundly, and to all the dear friends who have been so incredibly supportive and embracing of me for so many years through my ups and downs—Tyler and Liz, Sarah and Vessie, Pastor Julie, Mike Putterill, my old Holy Trinity crowd, my Cornerstone peeps, and so many more.

Thanks to my kids—Alice, Ben, and Isaac—who endured many evenings over many years of "not now, Mommy's writing." I'm so grateful to have such interesting and creative children, and please keep writing your books! I adore them all, from *Dragons* to *Zanganoke* and *Strikey Rack*. My wish for all three of you is a life of rewarding creativity, passionate curiosity, tremendous empathy, and deep connections with people—the only thing in this world that will last forever.

And finally, thank you to Heidi Putterill. My dearest little sister—life isn't the same without you. At all. It sucks that you're gone. I just hate it. I have no idea if you can see all the magical things that have happened with this book since you read that early draft back in 2022, but I know you'd be thrilled. I can't wait to party with you again, so keep your dancing shoes handy. In the scope of eternity, it won't be long.

MADE
FOR
YOU

JENNA SATTERTHWAITE

Reader's Guide

mira

1. Julia experiences pain in the THEN sections that helps people connect with her. Have you experienced a deepened connection with others through your personal pain?

2. Conversely, in the NOW sections, Julia's pain is grinding her down and isolating her from others. Have you experienced isolation in times of great pain? What do you think is the difference between pain that connects and pain that isolates?

3. In the end, Julia has chosen to embrace her synthetic self and has no apparent intention of turning her pain receptors and other "weaknesses" back up. Do you believe that Annaleigh will be able to learn from and connect with her mother, even though her mother's experience will be so different from her own? How would you have chosen in Julia's place?

4. If you had a button you could push to become stronger and limit your experience of pain, would you push it, and under what circumstances? What kind of trade-offs might there be?

5. If you found out today that you were created by a higher power and had the chance to come face-to-face with him/her/them/it over Thai food like Julia does with Andy, what would you say? What questions, accusations, or praises would you want to convey?

6. Julia is one of only three Synths, and the only one who can reproduce. Consequently, she feels a tremendous pressure to "perform" and be "likable," both on social media and interpersonally. Have you ever felt that pressure as part of a minority, whether racially, culturally, politically, religiously, or otherwise? How have you dealt with it?

7. In the beginning of the novel, Julia's neighbor Bob is prejudiced against Synths, but his views change as the story progresses. What do you think are the key ingredients in his change of heart? Have your own views ever experienced this kind of one-eighty shift? If so, what made you change?

8. Julia chooses to deceive herself about what she's done, electing to remember herself as the victim and Andy as Josh's "true" killer. Have you ever chosen to rewrite the story of something you did or witnessed others rewrite a story that you know happened differently? Do you feel that truth and accuracy are always synonymous?

9. In the end, Sheriff Mitchell was right: Julia killed Josh. Are you happy that she got away with it, or would you have preferred for her to face justice, even if it was carried out by the unlikable sheriff?

10. In the book, Andy Wekstein argues that we need excellent surgeons, and it doesn't matter if they're human or synthetic; the point is saving lives. How do you feel about that? Do you think excellence is more important than the human or AI nature of the worker? If so, would that apply to all fields of work?